CHILDREN OF SOLRA

The Dark Underbelly of a Golden Theocracy

SAM WOODGARTH

Children of Solra

The Dark Underbelly of a Golden Theocracy

Sam Woodgarth
Pagan Cat Publishing
PO Box 507
Trinity Beach
Cairns
Queensland, 4879

sam@pagancatpublishing.com

ISBN PAPERBACK: 978-0-6457168-9-4
ISBN EBOOK: 978-0-6457168-8-7

COVER DESIGN: GETCOVERS
CHAPTER HEADING ILLUSTRATION: @ @drawgoness

CHILDREN OF SOLRA

THE DARK UNDERBELLY OF A GOLDEN THEOCRACY

is dedicated to the unclassifiable,
the weirdos, the outsiders,
those who don't fit
and harbour no desire to sacrifice their individuality
on the altar of conformity.

WELCOME TO MY WORLDS.

Contents

Seeds of Rebellion

The disobedient soul is a blight upon the faithful; only through punishment can it be brought to heel and the secret kept pure.
The Blessed Prophet Serenus

A dark red hue momentarily shimmered over High Shepherd Stark's usually pale blue face as he secreted the birth record crystal in its new home. He closed his eyes as he composed himself before turning to face the empty library.

He would deal with the overly zealous Acolyte once he'd established whether the foolish youngster had shared news of his unfortunate find with other followers.

One missing youngster could be explained. Juveniles lacking a sense of their own mortality did sometimes venture into the wilderness, never to return, but two or more would set alarm bells ringing.

Stark exited the crystal roofed library into the temple gardens, where lush green lawns and orderly flowering shrubs soothed his agitation. The tranquillity of the temple complex reflected his absolute control over the colony. Solra's rays caressed his shoulders, confirming his righteous authority.

He followed the raked gravel path to the cluster of egg-shaped Acolytes' dens and entered without announcing his presence. His authority granted him unrestricted access.

The High Shepherd interrupted Castian's enforced meditation on a line from the Solran Creed: Unity with Solra requires perfect submission.

Castian scrambled from the floor where he lay prone in humility, to kneel before his Shepherd with head bowed in deference. A faint hue of rosy resentment flashed over the Acolyte, there and gone in a single heartbeat. Stark returned an equally quick flash of orange, a vivid display of his superior status.

"You exceeded the bounds of your task, Castian. Did my instructions lack clarity?" Stark's cold eyes riveted Castian, like a cunning snake hunting an unwary rabbit.

"No, My Shepherd. The fault is entirely mine. I presumed to anticipate your next instructions." Castian kept his eyes on the floor, but involuntary flashes of bewilderment and chagrin betrayed him.

"You speak rehearsed words of obedience, but you signal rebellion within your soul. Perfect submission to the Holy Will of Solra is always the hardest lesson, because it requires practical demonstrations." A compassionate, deep blue washed over Stark's entire body. "To help you learn submission, you will perform a penance. You will deny yourself Solra's glorious presence and life-giving sustenance for three days. During that time, you will meditate on the meanings of obedience and submission."

Castian blanched. "Three days in darkness, My Shepherd?"

Stark shook his head. "You question my decision, thus proving your need for chastisement. Four days. Come." He gestured for the trembling Acolyte to follow.

The underground Discipline Chamber stood in an isolated dark coniferous glade, far from the other temple complex buildings. Fallen black pine needles deadened Castian's reluctant footsteps, while releasing a heavy resinous odour, the scent unpleasantly familiar from the mummified remains of The Blessed Prophet Serenus.

Stark unlocked the heavy outer door and stood aside for Castian to negotiate the steep steps and unbolt the inner door. Castian sidled into the rough-hewn cell, containing only a stylised image of Solra etched deep into the stone wall. Wordlessly, Stark pulled shut the cell door and slammed the outer bolt. Darkness fell with the finality of a guillotine. Without sustenance from Solra, Castian's internal light would gradually dim and induce torpor within a day and a half. Four days' confinement would adjust the Acolyte's presumptuous attitude. Four days during which Stark would lurk, peeking and prying for any scrap of evidence Castian had discussed his find with the other Acolytes.

Castian blinked, resisting the urge to put forth more light, thus depleting his energy faster than normal. He inhaled for a count of three, held for five heartbeats, then exhaled for eight. The Acolyte repeated the exercise until he achieved composure. He felt his way to a corner and slid into a sitting position. No point wasting valuable energy standing.

Stark's extreme response made clear his displeasure, but his reason puzzled Castian. Faster and more thorough than the other Acolytes, he'd flown through cleaning and cataloguing the story crystals and, unbidden, moved onto the birth records section. Castian had suppressed a satisfied smile when he saw High Shepherd Stark bearing down on him, resplendent in his shimmering lapis lazuli robes trimmed with glittering gold, certain the Priest would laud him for his initiative, but Stark labelled his actions as disobedience and hubris. Had Stark reprimanded or redirected him, he wouldn't have thought twice, but The High Shepherd's drastic response triggered Castian's curiosity.

Stark had snatched the irregular crystal, wrapped it in a silk handkerchief, and replaced it, his pulsing colours a confusing mixture of fury and terror. His lack of examination suggested he knew the crystal's contents.

Contents too dangerous or too valuable to reveal? What could one as exalted as the High Shepherd fear?

Castian shivered and drew his limbs close, curling his body to conserve energy. The absolute darkness pressed down on him, its crushing weight stealing his breath. The cell's dank chill seeped into his bones, slowing his ability to move and to think. With glacial deliverance, time passed, and the Acolyte slipped from consciousness into a realm of frigid night, a place the Sui most feared.

High Shepherd Stark prowled the library on silent slippered feet, alert for signs of gossip or subtle insubordination. Acolytes bowed their heads in automatic deference to his exalted status as he passed. Satisfied circumstances remained unchanged, Stark withdrew to his private courtyard and raised his arms to receive the midday Benediction of Solra. The white marble space amplified the heat, and the heft of the sun's rays reassured and comforted High Shepherd Stark as he offered prayers, not only for his salvation, but that of the Acolytes and lambs in his care.

Invigorated by the infusion of Solra's divine energy, he returned his attention to the problem at hand. Keeping the crystal hidden amongst the other Sui birth history records was no longer an option. The risk of discovery menaced his future. Stark stalked through the empty library to the deliberately misfiled crystal. Glancing over his shoulder, he tucked the package into his belt before rearranging the remaining records to ensure no telltale gap betrayed him.

The forthcoming election represented Stark's last chance. If he failed this time, he'd be dead before another opportunity arose. Grand Master High Shepherd. He couldn't remember a time he hadn't lusted for the prime position. He had devoted his entire life to achieving the ultimate distinction, and he refused to be derailed by an overly enthusiastic Acolyte. His supporters assured him the election was a mere formality. No other candidate demonstrated such zeal, knowledge, and modesty. Stark sighed. No other candidate lived in terror of having a shameful secret revealed. A secret which would end not only his career, but his life. He shook himself, dispersing the pale green flush of shame, and forced his usual arctic hue before stepping out of the alcove.

Beatrice's Bulletins

The camera pans across the imposing façade of the building housing High Shepherd Stark's offices and zooms in on the glossy media darling, Beatrice Max.

"Three, two …" A raised finger and a wrist flick.

With immaculately applied makeup and perfectly coiffed auburn hair glowing in the sunlight, she smiles to the camera and offers a well-rehearsed wink. "Welcome, and thank you for allowing me to invade the privacy of your dens. Excitement is mounting here in the capital Luxton, as all three Domains prepare to elect the next Most High Grand Shepherd, the spiritual leader who will guide all deserving Sui into perpetual Light."

Beatrice leans towards the camera, as if confiding to a close friend.

"Sources close to High Shepherd Stark have informed me the vote is a foregone conclusion, and our beloved High Shepherd Stark is guaranteed to assume the Holy throne. His supporters are already planning the most spectacular parties to celebrate his inevitable success."

The camera pulls back to get a head and torso image. Beatrice wags a finger in mock admonishment.

"Don't be complacent. You have a vital role to play in High Shepherd Stark's success. Remember, your vote counts."

"That's a wrap," the weary cameraman says. "You were fabulous, sweetie."

Beatrice glances behind her. The windows of Stark's office reflect the sun, but she is certain the High Shepherd is staring, devouring her with his cold, hungry eyes. She feels his gaze roaming over her and suppresses a shudder. *For a holy man, he has oddly secular appetites.*

Before releasing Castian from the Discipline Chamber, Stark engaged each Acolyte in casual conversation. Acutely conscious of each youngster's blemish-free perfection, Stark kept his unprecedented chats to the minimum, long enough only to ascertain every Acolyte's continued unquestioned respect and unwavering loyalty. He ordered two youngsters to prepare a warm nutrient dense bath in Castian's den, and he selected two of the brawniest Acolytes to accompany him to the Discipline Chamber.

As they approached the outer door, Stark noted both Acolytes flushed yellow with fear, but the shorter of the two displayed irregular dark blue splotches of calm assurance. Interesting that a youngster could demonstrate such control, albeit patchy. One worth watching.

Castian lay curled in the corner, torpid and unresponsive. Stark gestured for the Acolytes to carry him up the stairs, where they laid him in the midday sun. Like a flower, he turned his face to the light, and he uncurled, exposing as much of himself as possible to the life-giving Light and warmth of Solra. His skin darkened to absorb more energy, while his eyes fluttered but remained closed.

Stark's assistants flushed pink, and their shoulders relaxed as Castian mumbled to himself. The High Shepherd leaned close to listen, relieved to hear only babbling praise of Solra. At a nod from Stark, the Acolytes carried Castian to his den and immersed him in the waiting nutrient bath. Stark dismissed his assistants, preferring to hear the prattle without witnesses.

"Solra came to me, My Shepherd. They wrapped me in Their unconditional love and warmth. Solra saved me." Castian beamed beatifically at Stark.

"Solra loves perfection," Stark said. "Solra demands that we strive for improvement, to prove ourselves worthy of Their love."

Castian flushed a deep pink, with dark blue speckles. "No, My Shepherd. Solra loves all Their children, every single one, praise Solra." His delirium made him careless. His eyes fluttered closed, and he sank into unconsciousness.

Stark placed his hand firmly atop the Acolyte's head. A drowned youngster could not foment unrest, but questions would be raised. Why had a weak and unconscious Acolyte been left unattended in a bath? Why had he received discipline? The priest removed his hand. There must be a more effective way to silence a potential threat. Stark snapped his fingers.

Excommunication.

High Shepherd Stark lifted Castian from his bath and dried him in the warm air alcove. The youngster drifted in and out of consciousness, blissfully unaware of who was tending to him. Stark drained the water; no need to create an accidental martyr; and laid the youngster in his sleeping pod to continue his physical recovery. He left the den, locking the door from the outside.

Castian woke slowly. He blushed pale lilac with relief to discover he was back in his den with blessed sunlight pouring through the windows. He eased himself into a sitting position, surprised at his strength after his ordeal. "Hello? Is anyone there?" Surprised to find himself alone, he padded to the door, and was more surprised to find himself locked in. He rattled and shook the door, testing his regained vigour to no avail, then shrugged. The High Shepherd must be protecting him, not wanting him rambling around in a weakened state. Thankful for the care of such a selfless and loving Shepherd, Castian ambled back to the comfort of his pod and curled up to sleep.

The Heretic

> *A heretic cast adrift is no longer of the flock; their sin spreads like a plague upon the waters, unfit to set foot upon sacred ground.*
>
> The Blessed Prophet Serenus

Still in his official robes, Stark worked through the pitiless night, building a flimsy case which nobody would dare examine or contest. Hatched in the Domain of Animo, and fostered to a family in the Domain of Honoris, Castian came to study at the temple in Viribis. At least he possessed no surviving relatives to question his fall from grace or to lament his passing.

High Shepherd Stark scoured the computer records for an image of Castian, which portrayed him as less than wholesome. The lad had spoken heresy. Of course Solra didn't love unconditionally. Solra loved and protected only the worthy. Why couldn't the lad have the good grace to look like a wild-eyed heretic? Very well, Stark would use an image of the wholesome youngster in all his physical perfection; an image all the more shocking because of its insidious nature. He would use the picture to encourage people to greater vigilance, a warning against complacency.

The High Shepherd trembled as he descended to the storeroom, and his head felt unpleasantly light. Unused to stimtabs, Stark's heart raced, and he sweated a chilly veneer of exhaustion. No matter, he would indulge in a luxurious nutrient bath after setting his plan in motion.

The fine mesh hood lay exactly where the computer predicted. Stark held the ancient object to the artificial light, admiring the exquisite workmanship and high tensile strength. The chain mail pooled in his open hand like water, folding into a packet no larger than his thumb. Stark placed the hood back into its box, next to the shackles, and trudged back up the stairs, leaning on the wall for support as he battled the night stupor.

The small box sat on his desk, oozing malignancy. The Solran Church had not used such devices for generations. Stark flicked on his computer and reread the pronouncement of heresy before sending it to the populations of the three Domains. The innocent eyes of Castian gazed back from the screen and the priest's heart clenched as he pressed the send button.

An irrevocable decision.

Castian startled awake as a heavily robed figure unlocked his door, and a team of temple guards rushed into his den. Before he could call for help, or offer any protest, gloved hands seized him and clamped shut his jaws. The robed figure revealed itself as High Shepherd Stark. The priest slipped the mesh hood over Castian's head and activated the tiny button at the back. With a soft whirr, the mesh formed itself to the Acolyte's skull, tightening to prevent speech, while allowing shallow breathing.

"It is my sad duty to pronounce you guilty of heresy, Acolyte Castian. The only punishment for such a heinous sin is excommunication. That I harboured a heretic at my breast overwhelms me with distress. Because

I am a compassionate Shepherd, I give you a day to meditate on your sins, and make reparation to Solra. At dawn tomorrow, as Solra rises to witness your shame, you will be expelled from the community. You may wander in the wilderness until the beasts tear you to pieces, or you may choose to be set adrift on the Central Sea."

Guards slipped smooth cold shackles on his wrists and ankles as Stark spoke. Castian pulsed a vivid yellow terror, his eyes wide behind the mask. He shook his head violently to rid himself of the hood, while knowing the futility of his actions.

Stark and the temple guards left as swiftly as they had arrived. The click of the lock their final insult.

Castian collapsed onto his rumpled pod. This must be a test. A bizarre trial of his obedience. How, in the blessed name of Solra, was he meant to pass this trial? Obedience to The High Shepherd's will? Acceptance without question? He glanced into the corners of his den, searching for sensors. Stark must have surveillance. Castian shuffled to his knees, then stretched out on the pre-dawn cool floor and prayed silently.

Stark rubbed his hands and pressed the record button, just in time to witness the Acolyte's wordless abjection. Orange fluttered briefly up Stark's neck, but he suppressed the flash of victory, replacing it with the deep blue appropriate for a compassionate High Shepherd. He frowned, trawling his long memory. Had he ever been this gullible? Of course not. Since a hatchling, he had schooled himself in discretion and austerity, every word and gesture considered before expressed. His survival depended on his perpetual prudence.

An image of the grinning Heretic Castian flashed to every inhabitant of the Domains of Animo, Honoris, and Viribis via their identity and communication implants. To spare the sensibilities of the population, Stark offered no details of the Acolyte's heresy, only the punishment.

Castian lay on the cold floor, eyes squeezed shut, but unable to block the smiling image Stark had selected for the news report. Was this part of his penance? Surely Stark was targeting only him with this ludicrous, false message? But why?

The crashing open of his door and the heavy tramp of guards warned Castian his ordeal was not yet over. He offered no resistance when they hauled him to his feet and dragged him outside, as Solra, shrouded by a bank of dark clouds, made Their reluctant appearance.

"Wilderness or water?" Stark asked. "Nod your head for wilderness, or shake for the Central Sea."

Castian shook his head, not to indicate his choice, but to deny his guilt.

Emboldened by his passivity, the silent guards made no pretence of respect when they shoved him into the rear of the levi-car. Stark sat upfront, a victorious general displaying his captive to the empty streets. Castian sat with head bowed, consciously adopting the posture of an obedient and docile hatchling, but he couldn't control the vivid yellow flashes of abject terror flushing over his skin in wave after wave.

The colony gates opened as the hover car approached, then ominously slid shut behind them, like a deliberately blind eye refusing to witness injustice. In the untamed wilderness, only the sonic pulses emitted by the car, and the guards' laser weapons, protected the occupants from the marauding wild beasts.

The vehicle zoomed smoothly over broad grasslands, skirting massive herds of glossily plump grazing beasts, who did not deign to raise their heads to acknowledge the passing vehicle. By midmorning, the thunderous clouds had dispersed, and Solra proudly displayed the Central Sea, a sapphire jewel of unsurpassed beauty, set in a broken ring of platinum sands.

A gently sloping sandy beach ran to the sea, foam-laced waves frolicked back and forth, teasing the white sand with frivolous kisses. Sea and sky melded seamlessly. Castian risked a glance; this idyllic scene could not be the setting for his death-sentence. Nothing brutal could happen in so delightful a location.

Stark dismounted and stretched his limbs while the guards dragged Castian onto the sand. The High Shepherd gestured for him to turn, and Castian almost fainted with relief when Stark's cold fingers brushed his nape. The ordeal was over. Stark was removing the hood.

A slight buzz and jolt of pain, but the hood remained.

"There, I've disengaged your chip from the community. Excommunication means you will have no links whatsoever with the faithful. Officially, you no longer exist. You are a stranger to me. You are dead."

Castian heard Stark crunch over the sand, back to the car, but shock kept him immobile. The guards pulled a moulded raft with a small crystal powered engine from the car's storage area and dragged it into the shallows. The Acolyte turned, searching for an escape, but knowing he could not outrun the guards. They lifted him from his feet and carried him to the raft, locking his shackles to rings fixed to the floor. One guard fiddled with the engine, setting it to a quiet rumble, while the other pressed a short knife into his hands.

"Could be hours or days before the shroaks find you. Might be easier to do it yourself rather than be eaten alive or dragged to the depths." The guard patted his shoulder and muttered the first line from the Solran Creed as he pushed the frail raft out onto the vast sea. "All life derives from Solra, all life returns to Solra."

Beatrice's Bulletins

Beatrice fluffs her hair and checks her lip-gloss one last time. "Are you certain this is my colour?" she asks her hovering makeup girl, who nods and smiles as she pushes the half-asleep journalist towards the camera.

Beatrice slips a stimtab under her tongue and smooths her form fitting dress over her rounded hips. She turns to face the studio camera, a professional smile on high beam.

"Three, two …" A raised finger and a wrist flick.

"Thank you for allowing me into your dens." Beatrice assumes an unusually serious demeanour. "A shocking revelation has rocked the Domains. The exposure of a heretic in our midst comes as a complete surprise, but High Shepherd Stark acted swiftly to excise this cancer."

A smiling image of Castian fills the background. His wide eyes shine with hope.

"Naturally, the High Shepherd is devastated to discover one so young and innocent looking could harbour such evil within his soul. In a private interview earlier this morning, High Shepherd Stark expressed great sorrow and reminded us that evil can hide in the most unexpected places. He urges us all to greater vigilance, while assuring his flock of his continued care and humble love."

A solemn image of High Shepherd Stark in full ceremonial regalia replaces the image of the heretic.

"Rest assured, High Shepherd Stark is praying for the salvation of all his flock. May Solra's blessings be upon us all."

The Isle of Nefas

To save the wayward is to risk corruption, for the infected may yet poison the hands that would lift them.

The Blessed Prophet Serenus

Prudence replayed the bulletin from the mainland. The fuzzy reception forced her to concentrate. She blanched as she listened, a constellation of freckles across her nose marking her unmistakably as Nefan; an abomination, one unworthy of living under the loving rule of Solra.

Her fingertips danced over the keyboard of her home communication centre, searching the records for the heretical Acolyte. She could have used voice commands, but they drained the batteries. Prudence skimmed Castian's records, finding a perfect foster child and a keen student, but no mention of heretical tendencies. She hacked into the identification chip program. The flashing cursor showed him travelling quickly, so not on foot, towards the coast.

With luck, the Nefans could intercept him before the shroaks scented his fear and dragged him into the depths.

Prudence downloaded the relevant information on a crystal data cube and dashed from her den to Callida's spacious office. As always, the door stood ajar, and Prudence saw an image of the smiling heretic projected onto the back wall, above the circular conference table.

"You've already heard." Prudence nodded at the picture. "I've tracked his progress. He's in a vehicle heading for the coast." She nudged away the news bulletin, replacing it with a map from her crystal data cube. "Accounting for the weather and tides, I estimate we can intercept him around here. He'll be out of sight from the mainland, but not yet in shroak territory."

"Good work," Callida said. "What do we know about him?"

Prudence shook her head. "Not much; standard upbringing, no trouble to his fosters or the temple until this. Seems out of character. Then again, I only skimmed the surface of the records. The authorities may have already tampered with them. I can interrogate the records later for signs of interference."

"Don't bother for now. I'd prefer to discover his character for myself."

In the boatyard adjacent to his workshop, Felix hunched over an old engine, humming to himself as he coaxed more power from the reluctant machine. Prudence tiptoed up and tapped him on the shoulder.

"By the Light! You nearly gave me a heart attack, Prue." Felix cocked his head. "You've not come to listen to me expound the theories to increase the life of our crystal batteries. What do you need?"

"Fancy a fishing trip? There's an interesting catch coming our way."

"Another hatchling?"

Prudence shook her head. "An Acolyte, condemned for heresy. He could be useful." She circled her finger at the marine chart on the wall. "I reckon he'll be in the danger zone by midday."

Felix patted the machine beside him. "Perfect opportunity to test this little beauty."

Prudence gave him a blank look.

"Highly focused pulses of sonar, to repel the shroaks."

"And if your test fails?"

"Good old-fashioned harpoons, with explosive tips. And a fast boat." Felix grinned and punched her shoulder. "Not nervous, are you, Sis?"

"Nervous? Why would I be nervous? Venturing into shroak territory during mating season, with untested technology? No, I'm not nervous; I'm terrified."

"Good. You won't be complacent."

With practiced ease, Felix and Prudence loaded the tools and weapons into their allotted compartments and manoeuvred the many times repaired anti-gravity vessel to the shoreline. Felix winked when the engine started on the second attempt and the craft wobbled above the damp sand and onto the shallows.

Felix pushed the craft to greater speed, smoothly skimming the choppy waves, whisking them closer to deadly shroak territory.

Prudence scanned the horizon while Felix studied the instrument panel and patted his beloved gadgets. He adjusted the steering a few degrees when a faint blip appeared on the scanner.

"The target's stopped moving," Felix said. "Looks like the Lightless bastards gave him just enough juice to plant him right in the middle of shroak territory."

"Can we go any faster?" Prudence leaned forward, willing the vessel to greater speed.

"Hold tight." Felix eased the throttle forward, and the craft smoothly accelerated. He activated the sonic shroak repellent and cast a glance at the harpoons.

"How does that thing work?" Prudence asked.

"Overloads their senses, disorients them. Equivalent to you spinning on the spot while someone screams in your ears." Felix tapped a screen.

"Two of them are circling below. I'm guessing a mated pair; the female is significantly larger than the male."

"Can you tell if they've noticed him, or if they're simply courting?"

Felix kept his eyes fixed on the flickering screen. "I'd say they were hunting, looking for meat to lay their eggs in. But they're still wary, keeping their distance for now. Get the harpoons ready, just in case. Their urgent desire to provide for their offspring might outweigh their more cautious desire to avoid the sonic repellent mushing their tiny brains."

Prudence prepped the harpoons and stashed them upright in the holders. She hunkered down in the prow, scanning the horizon for the heretic's boat, an impossible task on a choppy sea. Salty spray stung her eyes, forcing her to retreat and follow their progress on the array of colourful monitors.

"The shroaks are moving." Felix pointed to the screen. Two blurred shapes swam in ragged circles, spiralling incrementally closer to the surface with each revolution.

Prudence blanched a sickly yellow, her freckles standing out in stark relief. "Don't tell me, just get me next to the raft." The low-lying craft bobbed aimlessly, and she struggled to see a passenger. "He's either dead or unconscious."

Felix steered their vessel alongside the boat. Castian lay unmoving in a puddle of blood, his shackles glinting in the sunlight. "Be quick." Felix handed Prudence a laser cutter.

The craft rocked as Prudence clambered aboard, but Castian remained still. She checked his heartbeat; no point risking their lives for a corpse. The heretic's pulse beat slowly, but steadily. Prudence plucked the blood-sticky knife from the youngster's fingers and tucked it in her belt. She focused the laser on the thin shackles, burning through the bands while muttering colourful imprecations; cursing Solra, the Mainlanders, the shroaks, and the unresponsive heretic for making her task harder.

The male shroak's shriek drowned Prudence's scream. The giant sea worm thrashed on the surface; a circular mouth, filled with endless rows of jagged teeth, and surrounded by a fringe of poisonous barbed tentacles howled the creature's unholy anguish. Five times the length of the anti-gravity vessel, the monster sent wave after erratic wave scudding across the surface, tossing the boat like a hatchling's bath toy. The enormous female breached the surface, crashing back into the waves, screaming her fury and fear. The pair writhed together in confusion, biting each other in an orgy of agony, too disoriented by the repellent to flee.

Felix threw a line and harness to Prudence. "Strap yourself in and grab hold of your catch. I'll winch you both aboard."

Prudence nodded and shrugged into the harness, clipping it tight around her torso. She hugged the deadweight of the heretic to her chest, and her brother activated the winch, pulling the raft and its occupants close.

The shroaks beat the sea to a foam, threatening to spill Prudence and Castian into the depths. Prudence tightened her grip and yelled at Felix, "Pull!"

Felix stretched over the side and grabbed Prudence by the harness, yanking her and her prize aboard in an ungainly tangle of limbs. Without waiting to check on either of them, Felix turned to the console. "Hold on." He slammed the throttle, and the vessel leapt forward.

Slick with sweat, Prudence wriggled into a sitting position, propping her back against the side of the vessel. She wrangled the boy onto his side, making sure he still breathed.

"Are they chasing us?"

"No. But they found the raft. You were just in time."

Prudence clawed her way upright and swayed towards the console. She leaned her head on Felix's shoulder. "Thanks. I couldn't have done this without you."

A Second Chance

To question the truth is to invite the rot of doubt, and doubt is the fertile soil in which heresy takes root. Better a life of blind obedience than an eternity of damnation.

The Blessed Prophet Serenus

A sense of ineffable wellbeing flooded Castian. Although every cell of his body burgeoned with health, he could neither open his eyes nor move his limbs. *I must be in The House of Solra, awaiting rebirth.* He basked in the warmth, relieved his ordeal was over, and pleased to have another opportunity to praise Solra and prove his unwavering loyalty.

A whispered conversation played out, just beyond his hearing range. Soft feminine voices. The tone identified the speakers as benign. Light but steady footsteps drew closer and stopped beside his pod.

"Hello? Castian? Can you hear me? I'm Prudence. How are you feeling?"

"I feel well, thank you. But I can't move my limbs or open my eyes." Castian hesitated, unsure how to address a celestial being. "Where am I? Is this The House of Solra?"

"You're in our medical centre, being treated for severe dehydration and sunburn, not to mention the nasty hole you poked in your abdomen."

"This isn't the afterlife?"

Prudence snorted. "Not quite, but you came close to dying. My brother and I rescued you from a pair of sex-crazed shroaks wanting to lay their eggs in you. Think of this as a second chance."

"The current must have washed me back to shore, praise Solra," Castian said.

"No, your battery ran flat, leaving you plumb in the middle of shroak territory. You're safe on the Isle of Nefas."

This must be a continuation of the test. "There is no Isle of Nefas, only a myth."

Prudence huffed. "I'm sure the High Shepherds would like you to believe that." She patted the side of his pod. "The physician will remove the bandages covering your eyes later this afternoon. I'll come back and see you then. In the meantime, rest."

Castian listened to her retreating footsteps as he pondered her words. *She didn't try to convince me, nor attempt to trick me into committing heresy. What's she up to? They wouldn't have gone to all this trouble if they didn't want something.* He drifted into a troubled sleep; dreaming monsters had rescued him and planned to use him for nefarious purposes.

Callida raised an eyebrow when Prudence dropped into the chair opposite her desk.

"He's awake, and Doctor Bonna says he's recovering well." Prudence chewed a tail of hair. "He's no heretic. He's too … naïve. I doubt he's ever broken a rule or entertained an original thought in his life."

"You can tell this how?"

Prudence shrugged. "Instinct." She grinned at her friend and widened her eyes. "Depraved animal instincts."

"Idiot. Seriously, could he be a spy?" Callida leaned forward. "I must consider the worst and most ludicrous options, Prue."

"If I was sending a spy disguised as a heretic," Prudence said, "I'd make certain he had a believable backstory. Nothing too outrageous, but someone with a record for asking awkward questions, or a few blank spaces in his record that could be explained away as discipline while he really undertook training."

"How thoroughly did you search?" Callida asked.

"I can show you my report," Prudence said, "but I came up blank. Nothing. Not a single question or demerit on record. His files haven't been tampered with, either. Castian appears to be the most perfect rule following Sui ever hatched. A model citizen, from the capital colony of Compliance."

Callida leaned back in her chair. "Why would Stark expel such an impeccable youngster as a heretic? If he's neither done nor said anything to draw the wrath of High Shepherd Stark, then he must have seen or heard something."

Prudence nodded. "Setting him on a direct course for shroak territory with a limited charge ..." she shuddered. "That's the action of a cruel and desperate man."

"The election is coming," Callida said. "It's no secret Stark expects to be voted Grand Master High Shepherd." She laced her fingers together. "See what you can excavate from the records; Stark himself, but also his supporters. Anyone with the slightest connection. Be discreet, no need to alert the Domains we're meddling in their business."

Beatrice's Bulletins

Beatrice adjusts the neckline of her shimmering cobalt blue dress and waits for her cue.

"Three, two …" A raised finger and a wrist flick.

"Good morning, and thank you for allowing me to visit you in your dens." She flashes a dazzling smile and her trademark wink.

An image of Castian pops up behind her, and she adopts a mask of indignation.

"I know you are still reeling from the revelation of a heretic conducting his vile business within our community. But I can assure you, the wicked young man acted alone. Only the utmost vigilance of our esteemed High Shepherd Stark saved us, especially the emotionally vulnerable young adults, from exposure to the heretic's disturbing and warped ideologies."

A solemn image of Stark replaces the image of the unrepentant heretic.

"I want to impress upon you, my friends, how fortunate we are to be governed by an individual as selfless as High Shepherd Stark, and to remind you to cast your votes wisely in the upcoming elections."

Beatrice swivels on her chair to face another camera.

"On a brighter note, I am delighted to introduce to you a singing sensation. An extraordinarily talented performer who I know you'll love as much as I do …"

Back in her den, Prudence assumed her online identity as a librarian researcher in a far-flung colony. The digital disguise served her well; nobody tracked the queries and traces of a dusty curator of antiquated crystals. She slipped unnoticed down the pathways of vast data banks, peeking into files and alcoves forgotten by the real world.

Stark's well-documented life revealed itself to her searches almost too easily. He and his sibling were nest mates, hatched a day apart. Unusual, but not unprecedented. The midwife discovered the brother was an abomination and summoned an official to dispose of the hatchling. Before the official arrived, the abomination died, and the doula handed the swathed package over for disposal.

In early infancy, the surviving hatchling developed strict religious beliefs. Soon after being fostered, Stark announced his intention to devote his life to the worship of Solra, to atone for his nest mate's sin. He studied every waking hour, and chose a life of deliberate austerity, long before they ordained him as a lowly Herdsman.

Unlike other fosters, Stark chose not to return to his nest of origin on holidays, but spent the time in temple libraries, studying ancient laws and impressing the Shepherds with his precocious erudition.

Despite deep searches, the parent simply faded from existence, appearing on no records of any kind, after Stark moved to his foster family. Death seemed unlikely, since no record of a tomb for the parent's mummified remains existed. The other option, based on Stark's strict religious ideas, was that the parent had walked into the night; sacrificed themselves in the wilderness to avoid the possibility of committing further sin. The practice was rare, but fanatics existed.

Prudence sighed. Stark had not enjoyed the most joyous childhood, but the historic records contained nothing to arouse suspicion.

A tiny flashing light in the corner of her screen warned her she was late for Castian's unveiling. Taking as much care about leaving as she had on entering, Prudence withdrew, taking a circuitous route out of the system. Satisfied she had left no tracks or unusual prints, she filed her information crystal in a hidden compartment of her desk and locked the door behind her.

The sun beat down on her uncovered head as she sped over the mossy grass to the medical centre. She welcomed the energy boost; sitting at a desk wearied her, although she enjoyed the thrill of the digital chase.

Castian turned his bandaged head to greet her as she burst through the door. "You make a dramatic entrance," he said.

"Not much fun going unnoticed," she said, smiling to herself.

Doctor Bonna nodded to the nurse, who took firm hold of the patient's head. "Remain still," she said, scissors in hand. "I prefer not to create work for myself. I expect most of the swelling to have gone, but don't expect to look pretty immediately."

Castian held his breath as the surgeon snipped his bandages.

"Keep your eyes closed," Doctor Bonna said as she unwound layers of dressing, allowing light to filter gradually through. "Give your eyes time to adjust."

"Can I take him outside?" Prudence asked. "An orientation tour?"

Doctor Bonna surveyed Prudence from head to toe. "That depends, young lady. Can I trust you not to do anything foolish?"

"I will be a model of circumspection, an exemplar of caution."

"Indeed? Why do I doubt you know the meaning of those words?" Doctor Bonna folded her arms. "You may take our guest on a brief tour in a canopied chair. You will remain in the shade at all times to protect his eyes. At the first symptom of fatigue, you will return him here to rest and recover."

Prudence grinned her agreement and Doctor Bonna left, followed by the nurse, who carried away the dressings.

"May I open my eyes?" Castian asked.

"I guess so. Won't be much of a tour if you keep them closed." Prudence crouched next to Castian and tapped his knee. "I'm right here. Try not to scream at your first blood-curdling sight of a Nefan."

Castian gulped. "Are you truly hideous?"

"Terrifying." Prudence sniggered. "Hatchlings run away screaming at the mere sight of me. Then again, you're not too pretty yourself, right now."

Castian took a deep breath and reminded himself he still didn't understand the situation, or why Stark had selected him for such arduous testing. He tentatively opened his eyes, and they immediately flooded with tears, shattering the light into a blurred kaleidoscope of colour. Prudence dabbed away the dampness with a soft cloth. "Try again," she said, pressing the cloth into his hand.

Castian tilted his face down, away from the light, and tried again. He wiped a single tear, grateful the torrent had passed, and squinted. The tunic covering his knees resembled those he always wore, although as his focus improved, he noted the superior fabric quality. He gritted his teeth and gathered his courage. Determined to hide his revulsion, Castian raised his eyes to his rescuer.

He gaped at the bare-armed female hunkered beside him. Her symmetrical features were perfection, marred only by the sprinkle of coppery freckles across her nose.

She smiled at his surprise. "Boo!"

"Ephelides." Intrigued, Castian reached out to touch Prudence's face. "Do they cause you pain?"

Prudence jerked away, wide-eyed with shock at the unexpected familiarity.

Castian pulled back his hand. "I'm sorry. I meant no offence, but I've never seen freckles before."

"Of course you haven't. You cull freckled hatchlings. You can't go around touching things, just because you haven't seen them before. Not unless you plan on spending a lot more time in here." Prudence waved her arm, encompassing his recovery room and the medical centre as a whole.

"I most humbly apologise. You are not what I expected."

"Shut up." Prudence handed Castian a mirror. "Telling me I'm not what you expected is ridiculously offensive. Neither I, nor any other Nefans, are asking for your approval. I'll be back with a chair." She strode out of the room, scarlet flashes cascading over her body.

Castian listened to her retreating footsteps. *That didn't go well, but I'm not entirely sure why she's offended.*

He held up the mirror, horrified fingers traced the swellings on his face. Hatchlings would certainly run screaming if they saw him. He pulled at the neck of his tunic and poked at the unusual wrapping encasing his torso. The film moved with him like a second skin, defying his attempts to peel it away.

Prudence returned, guiding a moulded egg-shaped chair which hovered silently a handspan above the ground. "Hop aboard."

Castian shook his head. "I can't do that. Our cultural differences are too wide, and I fear causing more offence through misinterpretation. I should remain in seclusion until I can be repatriated, praise Solra."

Prudence plopped into the chair, which dipped and rose automatically adjusting to her mass. She leaned forward, elbows propped on her thighs. "You don't mix much with females, do you?"

"Orthodox Solran principles discourage socialising with the opposite sex. Fraternising can lead to … well, it's just not done." Castian flushed a rosy hue and lowered his eyes. "As an Acolyte, I am pledged to avoid contact with females. Secular behaviours and interactions are … more relaxed."

"Humph!" Prudence snorted. "Well, telling a female she isn't as hideous as you expected is not a compliment. I'd go so far as to say it's close to an insult."

Castian frowned. "But—"

Prudence raised her hand. "I know. I misled you. The fault is mine for teasing you. If I am being completely honest, I freaked out when you tried to touch my face. Your action was unexpected. Can we start over?"

"That seems like the sensible diplomatic course, praise Solra," Castian said. "Am I meant to offer a compliment to your beauty?"

"No, please don't." Prudence rocked back in the chair, smothering her giggles. "Complimenting a person on their physical appearance makes you sound creepy, unless you're nest mates, or you know them exceptionally well. We reserve our admiration for a person's achievements, for those things they can genuinely claim responsibility."

"I will rely on you to guide me, if that is permissible?"

Prudence clambered out of the chair and offered her hand to help Castian stand. "Get yourself comfortable, and strap in. Doctor Bonna would never forgive me if you tumbled out."

Castian slowly eased himself into the chair. "This is an unfamiliar experience. We don't have floating chairs in the Domains."

"That must make rehabilitation harder for the sick or injured."

"Rehabilitation?"

"You know, helping people get back to their normal lives after sickness or injury. Exercises and coping techniques for the permanently disabled."

Castian shuddered. "The Sui have the decency to treat themselves in the privacy of their homes if they develop an infection or sustain injuries. Medical centres only provide pharmaceutical goods and short-term care. Those who fail to fully recover arrange for their removal into the wilderness. They walk into the night. They do not burden the healthy with their misfortune, praise Solra."

Prudence guided the chair down a glass walled corridor, bright with sunlight. "You don't have real medical centres? Or physicians?"

"Of course we have physicians," Castian said. "We have skilled healers, experts in their fields, but we don't parade the marred or mangled. Imagine the shame of being imperfect. We allow them the dignity to re-join Solra."

Prudence blew out a long breath. Her freckles stood out against her blanched skin. She steered the chair through the open doors and onto a tree shaded pathway.

"Stop!" Castian squinted at the sunny sky. "More proof of your lies. Everyone knows Nefas is shrouded by heavy cloud and Solra refuses to shine Their Holy Light upon the monster inhabitants."

"You've already admitted I'm not a monster."

Castian folded his arms and mustered as much dignity as his mangled state allowed. "Please take me to the Temple? I should very much like to meet the local Shepherd."

"There is no temple; we have no Shepherd. We don't subscribe to a religion which has abandoned us."

"Then who is in charge of this colony?"

"That would be Callida, but she isn't in charge. Not in the way you mean."

"A woman? A female leads the community? Does that not cause discord?"

Prudence snorted and shoved the chair. "Callida is best suited for the work. Are you suggesting a less qualified male should lead the community?"

Castian shook his head. He had inadvertently offended Prudence once again.

Prudence pointed out landmarks and places of interest, but Castian listened only to her tone. Although her words were neutral, her clipped voice and staccato sentences indicated her displeasure. As an actress playing a part, surely she should attempt to befriend him? Or would a sophisticated player pretend indifference?

"Are you an actress?"

Prudence paused her tour-guide spiel and smiled. "Not my area of expertise. I could never master flashing colours on cue to emulate emotions. I'm a musician. Not very good, but I perform with friends whenever I can. What about you?"

"An excruciatingly inept poet," Castian said. "The nuances of language, and the weight and texture of words enthral me. I recognise talent, but regardless of how hard I study, I will never achieve greatness."

"Is that your goal? To be recognised?"

Castian recited a line from the Solran Creed. "Solra is the source of all talent and wisdom, praise Solra." He shrugged. "Solra does not require my meagre contribution, but I confess my weakness; I desire to write the perfect line. A sentence which sings and pierces the hearts of listeners, and remains in their souls for eternity."

Prudence laughed. "I'm content if my audience don't cover their ears, or run away screaming. I'm not sure if my friends are exceptionally tolerant, or tone deaf."

"I lack the courage to be authentically original," Castian said. "Tutors and peers labelled my work derivative and I cannot disagree. I take my inspiration from the works of Holy Serenus."

"We learn through mimesis," Prudence said. "We all begin by imitating those we admire. Developing a voice or recognisable style takes time. The important thing is never conceding defeat."

"Being realistic, mediocrity is the most to which I can aspire, praise Solra."

"Better than no goal at all," Prudence said. "Who knows, being in an unfamiliar environment might be exactly the spur you need to flourish."

Castian glanced sideways at his guide, confused by her apparent concern and misplaced enthusiasm. She guided him towards a low building of no particular style or architectural merit, surrounded by colourful variegated shrubs and elegant fountains. The designers had paid more attention to creating the magnificent gardens than constructing an impressive public office. He swallowed back an uncomplimentary comparison with the magnificent temple complex of Luxton.

"Slow down." Castian flapped an arm. "I can't see any plaques or signs."

"That's because there are none." Prudence shook her head. "Why would we spoil the gardens with signage? We know where we are and who works here."

Castian opened his mouth to protest, then snapped it shut to avoid offending her. Prudence guided them through open-plan offices, with wide windows and as many tall leafy plants as desks. His shame pulsed deep red as she guided him past Nefans, engaged in their official daily activities. They greeted Prudence by name and smiled at him, showing no fear or revulsion at his disfigured face. His chair didn't merit a second glance. Their regular features and well-formed bodies confused his expectations. Yet another puzzle.

As always, Callida's door stood open, and Prudence barged in without knocking. Callida stood and glided around her desk to greet him.

Prudence waved her hand between them. "Callida, Castian. Castian, meet Callida."

Castian choked back his shock at the informality and tried to stand, forgetting he had strapped himself into the chair.

Callida patted the air. "Please, remain seated. Welcome to Nefas. Prudence tells me you nearly didn't make it. How are you recovering?"

"I was unconscious when Prudence and her brother found me. There is nothing I can add to her story." Castian looked to Prudence for guidance, then back to Callida. "I beg your pardon, but I don't know the correct way to address you."

Callida bit her inner lip. "Callida is sufficient."

"Addressing you without an honorific feels deeply disrespectful," Castian said.

Callida perched on the front of her desk. "We Nefans tend to informality. You'll get used to us, given time." She locked her eyes on him; one blue, one brown; holding him helpless with her gaze. "They say you're a heretic, young Castian. Why?"

Castian shrank back into his chair. "I'm not. I'm a true believer, an ardent worshipper of Solra. High Shepherd Stark is testing my obedience." He glanced around at the foreign surroundings and lowered his voice. "I know this is all part of an elaborate evaluation, but I assure you, I will not fail, praise Solra."

Callida raised her eyebrows at Prudence, who shrugged in return.

"Castian? Are you afraid?" Callida laced together her fingers on her knee.

"No." Castian blanched a sickly yellow, giving lie to his answer. "Not afraid, only confused."

"I cannot remove your fear," Callida said, "but maybe we can alleviate your confusion. This is not a test, and we are not here to trick you into committing any heresy. Prue? Show our guest around the village, answer his every question."

Castian kept his head bowed as Prudence guided him outside.

"Contact lenses," he said with a sagacious nod. "I've seen actors getting into costume, praise Solra. A subtle but disconcerting disguise. You've gone to a lot of trouble setting this up." He gestured to the gardens.

"You must be awfully important to warrant this much effort," Prudence said, halting the chair.

"I'm not. I'm nobody." Castian shuffled back in the chair. "I don't know why you're testing me … unless you've mistaken me for another?" A tint of green suspicion flickered on his brow.

"What makes you so certain this is a setup?"

"Assume High Shepherd Stark made a mistake. I know, it's unthinkable, but less unthinkable than accepting this is real." Castian waved his arm to encompass the colony. "I've been unconscious, so I only have your word I was rescued from marauding shroaks, or even injured. You claim we're on the fabled Isle of Nefas, but really you brought me back to the Domains. I haven't figured out where exactly, or why, but I will, praise Solra."

"Fine." Prudence pushed the chair into motion. "I can prove we're on an island."

"Are we venturing beyond the walls? Without protection?"

Prudence snorted. "Of course not." She slapped the side of the chair, her mirth bubbling over. "There are no walls."

The Travel Portal

The sinner clings to comfortable delusion when holy truth is too terrible to face; faith tests, but doubt damns.

The Blessed Prophet Serenus

An expanding balloon of resentment filled Felix's chest as he leaned against the doorjamb of his workshop. He angled his wristcomm to re-read the message from his sister and sighed like an ancient overworked steam engine. In his opinion, if the ungrateful boy was intent on repatriation, they should let him return. As Felix blinked away the too vivid images of the shroaks, a pale green hue washed over him. He didn't consider himself a coward, but he didn't share the same sense of responsibility which plagued Prue.

He ambled through his old-style workshop and pushed through the double doors into his high tech inner sanctum, where bright sunlight streamed through floor to ceiling windows. A row of four transport cubicles hunkered at the far side of the room, their smooth egg-shaped sides softly reflecting the light.

Felix ran his fingers over the control podium, checking and double checking the settings, before sending and retrieving test flowers. The barely audible hum of the machines soothed him, and he inspected the returned blossoms. Perfect, as always.

He heard Prue and her refugee arrive but allowed his sister to sneak up and surprise him with her non-existent stealth, a routine of which she never wearied.

"Castian doesn't believe we're Nefans, or on an island. He's convinced himself we're all actors in an elaborate conspiracy, so I'm taking him to the lookout. Thanks for agreeing to help."

Felix grunted at his sister and forced himself to nod at the gangly youth for whom he and his sister had risked their lives. "You've a high opinion of yourself, if you think the Solran authorities would go to this much trouble."

"Not at all." Castian flushed pink as he struggled to unfasten the chair's restraints. "High Shepherd Stark must have me confused with another, far more important person, praise Solra."

Felix leaned in and flicked open the fastenings. "Wouldn't have thought there'd be two such incompetents in close proximity." He pulled Castian from the chair and pushed him towards a cubicle. "Just stand still. Can you manage that?"

"Leave him alone," Prudence said. "He's still recovering from his ordeal."

"He's not the only one."

Prudence ushered Castian into the cubicle. "Like my brother said, stand still. You'll feel a tingle. It's a smidge uncomfortable the first few times, but you get used to it."

"Wait." Castian grabbed Prudence's wrist. "What is this?"

"A travel portal, to take us to the highest point on the island. We'd never make it up the mountain with your chair."

"Like an elevator? Or a tunnel?"

Prudence shrugged. "You could describe it like that." She pulled her arm free and closed the door. "I'll go first and you can follow. Close your eyes, you won't feel so dizzy when you arrive."

Castian took a deep breath and closed his eyes. An intensely bright light ran the length of his body, head to toes, then darkness.

"That was me scanning you for the records." The cubicle walls muffled Felix's voice, but Castian still heard the smirk. "Ready, now? Count backwards in your head from ten."

Ten, nine—

Castian collapsed to the floor as searing pain tore through every particle of his body. Before he could open his mouth to scream, Prudence yanked open the cubicle door and dragged him out onto brittle grass. He lay gasping, his eyes clenched against the pain.

"Sit up." Prudence helped him untangle his limbs. "Open your eyes. It helps to orient yourself in the new place."

Castian felt the brassy heat of sunlight weighing on his shoulders, and a steady breeze ruffled his hair. He squinted into the dazzling glare reflected from the ocean far below. Using both hands to shade his eyes, he surveyed the spectacular view. A rock-strewn mountain fell away at his feet, and the crinkled surface of the Central Sea spread in every direction. Above, a raptor hovered, wide wings still, taking advantage of the warm thermals spiralling up the steep mountainside.

Prudence pointed. "Over there. That's the colony."

Castian peered at a miniature model village at the foot of the mountain. At this distance he couldn't see movement, but he recognised the nondescript building in which he'd met Callida, and the medical centre. He shook his head. "How …?"

"Long version short: your atoms are ripped apart and sent to a target, then reassembled. That's why he scans you; to get a base pattern. Felix can explain in tedious detail, if you really want to know, but I always feel more confused after he's explained the scientific theory."

Castian struggled to his feet and swayed an unsteady revolution. "I don't know what to say. I hurt too much to think." He sank back onto the wind-dried grass, holding his head.

"The first time can be a touch nasty. Sorry. I should have warned you." Prudence flopped next to him. "Might as well take advantage and absorb some rays before we return. You need the energy boost."

"This can't be real. Scholars have theorised about travel portals, but the High Shepherds decreed them a physical impossibility. Solra gave us time and space because we are a physical manifestation of their perfection, praise Solra."

Prudence leaned back on her elbows; her face tipped to the sun. "You sure about that?"

"We would be gods ourselves if we gained the ability to travel instantly through time and space. Solra would strike us from existence. They would exile us into perpetual darkness for the sin of pride."

Prudence wriggled her fingers and toes. "Hmm. Either Solra doesn't exist, or They don't care about such trivial matters." She sat up. "Or maybe Solra gifted us the knowledge and They are pleased we accepted Their blessing?"

"Solra will smite you for your heresy." Castian curled into a ball and covered his head with his arms.

"Well, heresy or not, you can't deny you're on the Isle of Nefas." She nudged him with her toe. "Time to be getting back. Doctor Bonna will be looking for you, and her wrath, I won't risk. Come on."

Castian uncurled himself and looked fearfully at the skies. He shook his head. "I'm not going back into your sacrilegious device." He shuffled back on his bottom. "I was ignorant the first time, but if I return with you, I'll be deliberately challenging the supremacy of Solra."

"I can't leave you here, Castian. You're still weak. Either you get in of your own volition, or I go back alone and send Felix."

"There's nothing your brother can say to convince me."

Prudence stood and planted her fists on her hips. "Who said anything about convincing you? He'll just knock you out cold and shove you back into the cubicle."

Unable to formulate an argument, Castian allowed Prudence to manoeuvre him into the ominously bland cubicle. He glared at her as she closed the door and tapped her wristcomm, sending a message to Felix requesting their return. He braced himself against the pain, but before the discomfort developed beyond a tingle, Felix yanked open the door and Castian stumbled and crashed to his knees on the workshop floor.

"Are you convinced now?" Felix hauled him unceremoniously to his feet and dropped him into the chair.

Castian threw up his hands. "Please, don't hit me."

"Now why, for Light's sake, would I hit a cripple?" Felix loomed over Castian. "Unless you've upset Prue?"

Prudence burst out of the cubicle as Castian cringed from her brother. "Boys? What's going on?"

"Why does he think I'm going to hit him? Did he do something he shouldn't?"

"Not like you're thinking." Prudence pulled Felix away from Castian. "He believes we're committing heresy using the portal, and we're all doomed to perpetual darkness."

Felix swivelled his eyes to Castian, cowering in the chair. "I see." He gestured for Prudence to follow him to the far corner of the workshop, where he huddled over her. "I take it he doesn't know about the skin grafts yet?"

Prudence closed her eyes and took a deep breath. "I'm not telling him. I take responsibility for him, but the medical stuff? That's down to Doctor Bonna." She put a hand on Felix's arm. "He takes his religion seriously; it's his entire life. He refused to re-enter the cubicle until I threatened to get you to knock him out and shove him in."

"Say the word, Prue. I'd take a great deal of pleasure knocking sense into the ungrateful little yolk sac."

"Please, Felix. Try to see the situation from his perspective. He's terrified and confused. He's denying reality, because the truth he knew and understood turned out to be lies and manipulation."

"What can I do? Do you want me to escort him back to the centre? Give you a break?"

"Thanks, but no. Castian is my responsibility. But dealing with an adult refugee, who didn't choose to come here, is harder than I imagined."

"If he insists on repatriation, I can always send him to a portal in a Domain of his choice. Then he'll have to take his chances."

"We both know that would be suicide for him, and not safe for us. He wouldn't be able to keep his mouth shut. Sending him back isn't an option."

Felix folded his arms. "If you say so."

Prudence shrugged. "Is my colour back to normal?" She stretched out her arms and pirouetted. "I get so vexed with his sanctimony, but none of this is his fault." She glanced across the workshop at Castian leaning on the cubicle.

Felix followed her look. "Oi! What do you think you're doing?" He strode across the workshop, blotches of puce anger exploding over his face. "That's precisely calibrated equipment you're messing with."

Castian lurched backwards and retreated to the confines of his chair. "I wanted to see if I could move your ungodly contraption, praise Solra."

"Time we were going." Prudence snapped the safety buckles and set the chair in motion. "See you tomorrow, Felix." She guided Castian through the front workshop and outside into the sunshine.

"I've worked out how you did it," Castian said, pride staining his brow a vivid orange. "Holographic technology. I've seen lots of dramatic productions use holograms, but not as sophisticated as these, or on such a grand scale. Felix is highly skilled and imaginative, praise Solra."

Prudence snorted, then ground her teeth. Castian squirmed, unsure of the source of her anger, and unwilling to further inflame her mood or risk the fury of Felix. Prudence maintained a diplomatic silence until they reached Castian's room.

"You couldn't be more wrong, but this isn't the time for the necessary discussions." She unfastened his restraints and helped him into his pod. "I'll see you soon."

Prudence left him without a backward glance. Castian listened to her diminishing footsteps as he pondered the least offensive way to check whether her freckles were theatrical cosmetics or permanent tattoos.

Castian tossed and turned all night. The excursion and his brilliant deductions had exhausted his energy reserves. The darkness pressed on him, making his body sluggish, but the excitement of his discovery refused to allow sleep or to calm his thoughts. A dim glow pulsed from within, casting dancing shadows on the walls.

His thoughts spun in a wild vortex: High Shepherd Stark would eventually realise he had misidentified Castian as a heretic, and being an honourable Sui, would release him. Or, he'd been deliberately targeted by an unknown person intent on their own agenda? If Castian could identify the motives behind his bizarre situation, he'd be better able to choose an appropriate course of action. Did obedience in this circumstance mean meek acceptance, or should he fight to uncover the truth?

Trying to decide the what, proved less taxing than working out the why. Despite his best efforts, a valid reason eluded him, and his thoughts swirled faster and more chaotically than before. Tired and confused, Castian slipped into a troubled dream-filled sleep, pursued by monsters and hordes of freckled hatchlings.

Doctor Bonna wore a professional smile. "Time to remove your dressings."

Castian nodded, aware the Doctor did not require his permission, her words only a courteous formality. "I recognise this as a further test of my obedience," he said. "Receiving treatment from a female doctor is disconcerting, but I submit to the Holy Will of Solra."

Doctor Bonna poked at the site of his knife wound before glancing up, her lips pursed in a wry smile. "You noticed I'm female? Nothing gets past you, does it, youngster? Best if you close your eyes, and I promise to treat you like a lump of flesh, nothing more, nothing less."

Castian gulped and shut his eyes. He blanched to an icy blue as he concentrated on suppressing each flinch when Doctor Bonna prodded him.

"Stupidity and naïveté are inevitable accoutrements of youth," she said. "Fortunately, they're balanced by a superior ability to heal. You'll be pleased to know the grafts have all successfully taken and the nanobots have performed excellently. In a day or two, you won't even find a scar from the hole you foolishly gouged."

Castian staggered from the examination table, his eyes wide. "What grafts? And what are nanobots?" He grabbed his tunic and slipped it over his head, acutely aware of the inadequacy of his frail armour.

"When Prudence and Felix brought you in, you were almost dead." She frowned. "Indeed, losing fluids from your self-inflicted wound meant you suffered severe dehydration. Coupled with exposure and extreme sunburn, you were lucky to survive, assuming the shroaks didn't find you. Without radical treatment, you were guaranteed a painful death."

"You saved my physical life, yes, but at what cost?" Castian ran panicked fingers over his face and limbs. "What exactly have you done to me?"

Doctor Bonna reached out to guide Castian to a seat, but he flinched from her touch and retreated across the room.

"Stay away from me, woman. Just speak the truth, if you dare." His colour shifted to a sickly green, and his legs trembled as he fought to support himself. Castian leaned back against the wall, his eyes fixed on Doctor Bonna.

"Much of your skin had peeled away, and the exposed flesh began cooking." Doctor Bonna watched for a reaction, but Castian continued to stare. "I used laboratory grown skin to replace your natural skin. Indeed, if you look, you'll see you have perfectly immaculate skin, just like a new hatchling."

"You covered me with a Nefan abomination?" Castian quivered from head to toe. "I am no longer a Sui, but an experiment to your pride. Solra will turn from me in disgust." He sobbed, terror bursting out of him.

Doctor Bonna stepped forward, but Castian shot out an arm. "Stop! Stay away." His ragged breathing filled the room, hoarse and desperate. A pulse flickered erratically in his neck.

"I am doomed to perpetual darkness because of your egregious actions," Castian moaned. "Tell me about the nanobots. What further degradations have you inflicted upon me?" He slipped to the floor and wrapped his arms around his knees.

"You should rest," Doctor Bonna said. "We can talk about the other part of your treatment another day, when you've had time to reconsider. Indeed, you'll realise—"

"No. I will not allow you to patronise me. You have condemned me in the eyes of all Sui and denied me the love of Solra. You will at least have the courtesy to tell me the extent of your unholy meddling."

"Very well, but first, I must make clear you are not an experiment. We have successfully used these technologies for many years."

"You begin with a lie, to cover your own culpability. Let me make clear, woman, you and all Nefans are already doomed to perpetual darkness, praise Solra."

"Indeed, I suppose acknowledgement we Nefans are real is progress." She held up her hand. "I apologise. That was unnecessary and unkind."

Castian glowered.

"Nanobots are too small to be seen with the naked eye, and tens of thousands fit on a pinhead. I injected them into your wounds to repair the torn and burnt flesh, to regenerate and knit it back together. The nutrient enriched dressing you wore fed you, boosting your system and increasing your sense of well-being."

"So, not only am I wrapped in a monstrous skin, but you drugged me, and unnatural creatures colonise my flesh?"

Doctor Bonna shook her head. "I programmed the bots to perform a task. Upon completion, they shut down and your body expels them, just as you normally shed skin and hair."

"I should have died."

"As you would, had not Prudence and Felix risked their lives to save you. Indeed, you are lucky to be alive, young Castian."

"Lucky?" Castian clenched his fists atop his knees. "I am an abomination. Every breath I take mocks the sovereignty of Solra." He closed his eyes, squeezing back tears.

"Do you have any questions?"

"Yes." Castian lifted his head. "When can you remove this perverted fabric of skin?"

Penance

"Good morning, Doctor. How is Castian faring?" Prudence leaned through the doctor's door. "He had a bit of a shock yesterday when I transported him to the lookout."

"Not as great a shock as he had this morning." Doctor Bonna frowned. "He came to have his dressings removed, but I hadn't accounted for his religious fervour. Indeed, the foolish boy wants me to remove his grafts, saying he prefers to die in his natural state."

"And when you refused?"

Doctor Bonna shrugged. "I couldn't get a word of sense from him. He left for his room, muttering about everlasting darkness and performing penance."

Prudence raced towards Castian's room, silently cursing Doctor Bonna's insouciant attitude to religious matters. The doctor jogged in her wake. She shouldered her way through the door into an empty room. "What exactly did he say?" Prudence asked, flickers of dark blue streaked with deep green fluttered up her neck. "His beliefs dominate every aspect of his life. Penance will mean more than skipping a sunbath."

"The last thing he said to me? Some rubbish about preferring to die without skin, rather than live as an abomination. He was muttering to himself … or praying? Indeed, I couldn't really hear and thought he needed a little time to adjust." Doctor Bonna shrugged. "Perhaps he's taken himself into the gardens to commune more directly with Solra."

"Or he's searching for a dark place, away from Solra's gaze, where he can flay himself?"

"You don't really think …? I didn't realise. I'll organise a search of the grounds and storerooms." Doctor Bonna scurried back to her office, slapping the alarm button on her way out.

Prudence perched on the edge of the pod as she considered Castian's state of mind. He lacked the traditional qualities of a hero, yet under pressure he'd ripped open his abdomen, an act requiring a certain perverse courage. From his official records, he appeared bland and unimaginative, but Prudence recognised a granite steadfastness in matters of faith. Death of his physical body posed less of a threat to him than a stain on his immortal soul. Knowledge of his treatment could easily send him on a course of self-destruction.

His modesty and aversion to scrutiny meant he would select an un-populated area for whatever act of penance he planned. Not the medical centre or its grounds. Assuming he wanted to die, he'd head for the wilderness. Prudence sighed. How far could he get afoot?

A nurse tapped on the door. "Prudence? A chair is missing. No one saw him, but we're assuming Castian borrowed it."

"Light and Dark! Tell Doctor Bonna to extend the search." Prudence tapped her wristcomm. "Felix? Are you at the workshop? Good. I need you to rustle up as many aerial cameras as you can monitor. Castian is missing."

Prudence questioned every pedestrian she met, but not one Nefan remembered seeing Castian, with or without a chair. Frustration and fear waged war within her as she made her way to the workshop. Red and green shimmered across her face in uneven splotches.

Felix met her at the door and immediately enveloped her in a hug. "We'll find him. We've snatched him from the jaws of death once, we can do it again."

"But we haven't rescued anyone who didn't want to be helped before. Forcing our way of thinking on him is just as wrongheaded as the Shepherds brainwashing their flocks."

"We don't have time for philosophy. Let's find him first, then decide what to do." He drew her to a table covered in gadgets and gizmos. A map of the island hung above, marked with irregular concentric rings spreading out from the medical centre.

"You didn't waste any time," Prudence said.

"I calculated his best distance over different terrains. That's why the circles are wonky. I've rigged the cameras with heat sensitive sensors, too. I've started cobbling together some night-vision units, if we don't find him during daylight."

"Great work, brother, but I don't have the first clue about direction."

Felix pointed to the map. "I'm assuming Castian remembers at least some of what he saw yesterday, so he'll avoid the roughest ground. If he's as smart as I think, he'll head broadly in this direction." He waved his hand over the north-east quadrant of the map, a mostly flat area populated by grazing herds of wild cattle, preyed upon by fierce sabre-toothed spotted felines.

"If we do find him," Prudence said, "he'll resist. I wouldn't put it past him to deliberately provoke a sabre cat. Yesterday, he convinced himself we tricked him with holotech, but today … I think the truth finally hit him, and he can't fit the reality into his world view."

"It may be kinder to leave him to his own devices; safer for us, too. But you'd never forgive yourself if we didn't give it our best shot. And you'd never forgive me, either." Felix gathered an armful of fragile looking mechanical devices. "Let's get these birds in the air, then collect the doctor. We're gonna need her and her darts if Castian kicks off."

Doctor Bonna perched in the back of the open-topped vehicle, clutching a field medikit. "I'm sure you could do this without me. Indeed, you're both experienced and very competent." A sickly yellow hue tinged her cheeks.

"You're probably right, Doc," Felix said, "but if I'm driving, and Prue's fending off the toothy felines, that leaves you darting our reluctant friend."

"Do you have a top for this thing? Indeed, we're rather vulnerable." The doctor looked anxiously at the dented roll bars. "Are you sure it's safe?"

Prudence swivelled around in her seat. "Neither of us described this expedition as safe, Doctor. You ought to buckle up; the ride will be rough."

Felix steered his custom-built vehicle beyond the colony's boundaries; the massive caterpillar treads gouged a path which the island would soon heal. Prudence concentrated on the monitors of the aerial cameras, while adjusting the drones' flights lower.

Herds of shaggy-haired bovines drifted across the plains, raising choking clouds of dust, and followed by hordes of insects, and flocks of tiny birds who eagerly plucked fleas and ticks from twitching ears and tails. Predators lounged under shady trees, their casual indifference fooling only the youngest and least experienced grazers.

Doctor Bonna leaned forward to nudge Prudence's shoulder and pointed to a gathering circle of cleaner birds high in the sky.

Prudence tapped one of the monitors. "I don't think it's Castian," she said, zooming in on the image. "It's too big, but we should check it out."

Felix changed direction, and headed towards the growing wake of vultures, none of whom paid attention to the approaching vehicle. More birds swooped in and crashed the party, jostling for space and stabbing their neighbours with viciously sharp beaks. Smaller, less confident birds hopped on the outskirts, darting back and forth, snatching scraps which they gulped awkwardly, and squabbling over the bigger chunks.

"Indeed, if it is Castian, we're too late." Doctor Bonna gripped the grab bars, white knuckles betraying her agitation.

Felix slammed his foot on the accelerator and drove straight at the wake, horn blaring. The birds screamed their defiance, but clattered into the air before resuming their positions when he swerved at the last moment. "Not the youngster," he said.

Prudence shrugged out of her harness and clambered to a standing position on her seat. She gripped a grab bar with one hand and shaded her eyes with another as she surveyed the savannah. "He could be anywhere. Fallen down a ravine, sheltering in a cave. He could already be in the bellies of those sabre cats we passed. They looked pleased with themselves." She slumped back into her seat and hitched her seatbelt back in place. "There're too many creatures out there to find one small Sui."

Felix slowed the vehicle to a halt. "Maybe we're looking at this wrong." He slid out and crouched, estimating Castian's height in a chair. He called up to Prudence. "You get a different perspective from this height."

Prudence joined him. "How does this help? I can't see much from down here."

"Exactly," Felix said. "People naturally gravitate towards a structure. What can you see?"

"Grasses, a few scattered shrubs." Prudence turned slowly. "If I wanted to perform some kind of ritual, I'd be looking for privacy; somewhere I'd be safe until I chose not to be."

Felix nodded encouragingly. "Go on."

"There." Prudence pointed to a modest butte. "Looks more impressive from down here," she said. "I imagine there're plenty of hiding spots there, too."

Felix grinned. "Not to mention snakes, skaxnats, and spiders as big as your fist."

Brother and sister clambered back into the car, and Felix set the aerial cameras to search the rocky formation. Thinning grass gave way to sand and gravel as they grew closer to their target, and the vehicle crushed the stones under its wide tracks, noisily announcing their presence.

Prudence toggled the camera controls. "Is that the chair? Or a smooth rock?"

Felix glanced at the monitor and adjusted course. "Only one way to be sure."

The chair lay upside down, deep gouges in its sides suggesting the machine had toppled and rolled. Felix righted the equipment and made a cursory test of the controls before loading it into the back of his vehicle. He stared at the steep track ahead, noting the dislodged pebbles, darker than those which had been sun-bleached for countless seasons.

"We're on foot from here." He pointed up the track. "You can see how far the chair fell. Castian can't be far, especially if he's injured."

Felix handed out bundles of rescue and safety equipment before leading the way up the scarred track, followed by the doctor, then his sister. They noticed the peculiar silence: no birdsong or insect calls, no rustling from the sparse vegetation. A lizard, still as stone, stared silently as they passed, jewelled eyes gleaming with curiosity.

"We'll hike as far as the chair travelled," Felix said, "then look for clues. He isn't showing up on heat sensors."

"Are you sure they're working?" Doctor Bonna asked, wiping a film of sweat soaked dust from her brow.

"We're showing as a glowing blob," Felix said. "That's good enough for me."

"Castian can't have cooled that quickly," Doctor Bonna said. "He must be undercover."

"So look for caves or fissures," Prudence said. "We don't know if he's deliberately hiding, or accidentally fallen and can't help himself. I'm betting on an accident; he's scared off the wildlife; recently, too."

A lost hospital slipper marked the site of the mishap.

The trail widened, forming a convenient lookout, then narrowed again. A single tall step led upwards. The crumbling step spoke volumes, echoed by the snapped brush and crushed grasses.

"Pretty stupid, trying to mount that step in a chair," Felix said.

"Not stupid," Prudence said. "Desperate." With her back to the rocky wall, she eased her way over the collapsed step before dropping to her hands and knees. She examined the ground for evidence of dislodged grit or footprints. "Definitely not onwards and upwards. He's somewhere between here and the chair." She accepted Felix's help to climb down.

"I didn't spot any evidence that he'd tumbled over the edge," he said.

Prudence shrugged. "If the chair bounced hard enough, could he have been thrown clear?"

Doctor Bonna shuffled to the edge of the trail and peered down the side of the rocky formation. "Not much to break his fall, if he did."

"Righto. We backtrack, calling his name," Felix said. "We know the chair slid and scraped most of the way. Look for a section of path without skid marks. The bounce will be at the lower end."

The careful search down the butte took longer than the hike up. They shouted Castian's name and every few steps they stopped to listen for a response. They followed the chair's skids and scrapes, slamming from rock to rock, careening down the path until—

"Is that a broken branch?" Prudence pointed to a precariously rooted tree with one torn limb, the wound fresh and white.

Felix and the doctor crowded behind her. Flattened grasses and dislodged scree below the tree betrayed the passage of a bulky object. The recently gouged pathway ended at a crevasse. A spew of small stones vomited past the opening, which had swallowed the track's maker.

With practiced efficiency, Felix and Prudence rigged the ropes for her to rappel down. Each landing shivered free a hail of pebbles, gleefully highlighting how high she hung. She clung to the rock face next to the mouth of the crevasse, her heartbeat loud enough to send another scattering of pebbles to the savannah floor. As she worked to calm herself, a chittering filled her ears.

A sound only produced by multitudinous creatures.

A sound designed as a warning.

Lightheaded with fear, Prudence fumbled for a flash stick and tossed it into the hole, briefly illuminating her worst nightmare.

Castian, glowing moon-pale, lay on his back with one leg twisted behind him in an impossible position. Hundreds of skaxnat babies, a handspan long, swarmed over him, looking for wounds to enlarge and chew into. The flash stick momentarily scattered them, but they increased the volume and intensity of their chittering as they fled into the shadows.

Prudence called up to her brother. "Lower more flash sticks. As many as we've got."

"Can you not see?"

"He's lying in a nest of skaxnats. No sign of the mother."

"By the Light! I'm hauling you up." Felix gathered the slack of the rope, but Prudence unclipped herself before her brother could drag her up and she slithered into the Stygian hole.

Felix threw himself to the ground, head over the edge to get a better view. "Prudence!" His bellow rolled down the butte, unanswered as he expected. He rolled to his feet and bagged the remaining flash sticks. "Get the anti-venom ready, Doctor." He tossed the lights down on a length of rope, manoeuvring the package to the entrance.

Prudence snatched the bag and clipped it to her belt. "Castian? Can you hear me?" She crept forward, flash sticks ready to scare away the ravenously aggressive arachnids.

"Leave. This is my chosen penance." The cavern swallowed Castian's thin voice. "Solra guided me here and sent the skaxnat to flay my unnatural skin, cleansing me of my sins, praise Solra."

"Can you move?"

"Go. Let me perform my penance in peace."

The skaxnats surged back, searching for meat. They scurried over floor, walls, and ceiling, their scalpel sharp pincers waving, and their venom-laden spiked tails curved over their segmented bodies.

Prudence lobbed a handful of flash sticks into their midst, scattering only a few. Quick intelligence and voracious appetites urged them to ignore the fast-fading lights. Prudence waded ankle deep through the nest, the intermittent flashes of fear exploding from within her, ignored by the nestlings.

Shuddering with terror and revulsion, she brushed the creatures away from Castian's face. Enraged by her incursion into their territory, the skaxnats stabbed their needle-sharp stingers into her, Castian, and each other.

Castian bit back a scream, and tears poured down his cheeks. "Go."

Prudence yanked him into a sitting position and looped a harness around his chest. "Help me, or we'll both die."

"All life derives from Solra, all life returns to Solra."

"Solra be damned!" Prudence swiped the stinging skaxnats from her exposed flesh and yanked Castian to his feet. "Lean on me." She threw another handful of flash sticks into the nest and lurched towards the entrance, dragging Castian with her.

Castian sagged, his smashed leg unable to support his weight. "Leave me."

"Not a chance, Heretic. Now hop, or I swear, by Light and Dark, I'll drag you out of here by your hair."

Castian wrapped an arm around her shoulders. "You called me Heretic? Did Solra send you? Praise Solra."

"Yeah, I'm Solra's glorious messenger. Now, move."

The skaxnats whirled and eddied around their ankles in a mindless orgy of stabbing and slicing. Prudence kicked a way through, creating enough confusion in the swarm to force a pathway to daylight. The sickening stench of crushed skaxnats dizzied her as she snapped Castian's harness to her own and reattached the unhitched lines.

One skaxnat, more viciously determined than the rest, dropped onto her shoulder and plunged its venomous stinger into her cheek. Her scream rang out as Castian tore the creature away and flung it down the mountainside. Blood and venom dribbled down Prudence's neck, mingling with the veneer of savannah dust. Exposed to sunlight, the few skaxnats buried in folds of clothing hurled themselves clear of their unwilling hosts, desperately seeking the deeper shadows.

Felix and Doctor Bonna hauled a delirious Prudence and an unconscious Castian to comparative safety. The doctor jabbed them both with anti-venom while Felix freed them from their harnesses.

"There's only one stretcher," Doctor Bonna said.

Felix glared at the unconscious lad and nudged him with his booted foot. "Load him on the stretcher. Make sure you fasten him in tightly." With a mother's tenderness, he picked up his sister and harnessed her to his back.

Felix gripped the front of the stretcher and led the way back to his vehicle, securing Prudence in the front seat, before tossing Castian, still bound to the stretcher, into the back next to the doctor and the mangled chair.

"I need to splint his leg before we leave," she said.

"Do whatever you like once we're in transit. I need to get my sister to the medical centre. The useless yolk-sac is your problem, Doctor."

Dark purple patches pulsing up his neck warned the doctor to remain silent as Felix rammed the vehicle across the savannah at top speed.

Clem

The background symphony of beeps and clicks played counterpoint to Felix's smouldering scarlet fury, a regular and reliable confirmation that his sister's brain and vital organs functioned within expected parameters. He padded around her room, barefoot. His hiking boots lurked under her pod like sulky pets admonished for making too much noise. Flashing lights and zigzagging graphs created a detailed report of Prudence's status for those equipped with the skills necessary to read the language. Felix satisfied himself with the regularity of the patterns.

A stream of nurses, intimidated by his vermillion and puce blotches, nodded reassurances when they tended to his sister or made minuscule adjustments to the array of technology keeping her alive. None dared suggest he go home to bathe or recharge.

Felix stretched, clenching and relaxing each muscle from head to toe, then rested a hand on his sister's pod, not daring to touch her for fear of disturbing her progress. Superstitious dread prevented him from leaving her room. He promised himself, once she spoke, he would allow himself a cleansing shower and a restorative sunbath.

Doctor Bonna knocked and sidled into the room. She nodded to Felix before checking her patient. "Prudence is making excellent progress. We've neutralised the toxins and I'm putting her on an intensive course of nutrients as a booster. More than anything, she needs rest. Once she returns to optimal health, we can rebuild the necrotised flesh."

"What can I do to help?"

Doctor Bonna looked him up and down, then dug in her pocket for a capsule of glowing liquid. "Go home and clean yourself; use this in a nutrient bath. Don't argue with me. You're a stinking mess. Not only are you frightening my staff, but seeing you like this won't help Prudence."

"What if she wakes up and I'm not here?"

Doctor Bonna folded her arms. "Prudence is sedated. She will not regain consciousness until I deem her fit. Besides, you're almost ready to collapse. How will that help your sister?"

Felix flared an embarrassed roseate hue and squared his shoulders. "Prudence needs me."

Doctor Bonna stepped close and stabbed his chest with a stubby finger. "Indeed, she does. She needs her calm and capable brother, not this shambolic putrid mess. Go, get yourself sorted."

Castian drifted on a silky-soft cloud of painkiller induced contentment. His remaining fingers fluttered like butterflies, but his arms and legs refused to move. *Am I dead? No.* He smiled as he remembered the messenger Solra had sent to rescue him.

Solra loved him, despite his unnatural Nefan skin, and his escapade in the portal. Praise Solra.

Solra gave life to all, and loved all equally and without prejudice. Solra bathed all creation in Their generous Light.

The nurse smiled when Doctor Bonna bustled into the room. "His vital signs are stable, but his brain is unusually active."

Doctor Bonna checked the readouts, and nodded her satisfaction. "Keep him comfortable and notify me when he regains consciousness. If he exhibits distress or aggression, sedate him."

Felix stripped off his sweat stained clothes and entered the cleansing cubicle. He leaned his head and hands on the walls, quivering with exhaustion, then dragged himself to the bath and dropped in Doctor Bonna's nutrient capsule. He slid into the hot water and an intense flush of well-being overwhelmed him. Every cell of his body received an energy boost, and Felix tingled from head to toe with vitality. His indiscriminate fury dissipated, and his skin regained its normal healthy blue tint.

Dressed in fresh clothes, Felix prepared to return to the medical centre. A vibration from his wristcomm snagged his attention. He hesitated, then switched off the device. The message from the mainland could wait. He would allow nothing to delay his return. He got as far as the door, before duty compelled him to open the notification from a distraught midwife.

He read the message twice and swore softly to himself. Unable to ignore the plea for help, he tapped a response and sprinted to the workshop. Despite the urgency, he forced himself to follow the safety procedures. Only when he had sent and retrieved a flower did he message the midwife to place the bundle into the capsule.

The tightly swaddled hatchling possessed more than adequate lungs, but blind eyes. According to the midwife's hasty message, after breaking free from the egg, the tiny scrap had deteriorated, growing pale and thin. The baby curled into a ball and screamed in terror when laid in the sunlight. Only when tightly wrapped did the creature relax.

Felix cradled the whimpering bundle to his chest with one hand while securing the workshop doors. The piteous mite mewled non-stop and tried to bury his head in the shelter of Felix's clothing.

Doctor Bonna greeted him with an approving smile at the medical centre entrance, then frowned when she saw his cargo. "Come." She gestured for him to follow, throwing scraps of information over her shoulder as she led him into an examination room. "I'll wake Prudence after we've settled this little fellow. Does he have a name?"

"Clem." Felix handed the infant to Doctor Bonna, and Clem immediately howled his distress. "He quiets if you hold him tightly," Felix said. "I think he feels more secure that way."

Doctor Bonna raised an eyebrow. "Indeed, I had no idea you're a qualified paediatrician or psychologist. Congratulations." As she unwrapped the bindings, Clem screamed louder; his pale face infused a furious red.

"Why don't I sit and hold him while you examine him?"

Clem's shrieks reduced to whimpers, and he snuggled into the familiarity of Felix.

"Are we against the clock?" Doctor Bonna asked as she peeled away layers of swaddling.

Felix shook his head. "The parent submitted him for wilderness culling, but the midwife took him to one of our portals. We'd have got him sooner, if we hadn't been tied up with that Lightless heretic."

"Look on the bright side," Doctor Bonna said. "You can take the time to build him up and when he reaches an acceptable weight, you can bring him in for surgery. A very simple procedure."

"What do you mean, 'you'? I've brought him here; that's my part over."

"The infant isn't sick, Felix. He's underweight and, as you suggested, anxious. Like it or not, he's formed a bond with you. I'll give you all the supplements you'll need. All you need to do is hold him and reassure him. Indeed, you're a natural. Wait here." Doctor Bonna chuckled as she left the room.

Clem whimpered and squirmed, hiccupping his distress.

Felix traced the creases in Clem's wizened face. "Don't get any ideas, little man. This is a temporary arrangement."

The doctor returned bearing a crate. "Dress him in these, they're nutrient enriched, like your capsule." She ripped open a dark-blue packet to display the tiny coveralls. "The colours fade as the infant absorbs the nutrients. He'll probably use one every few hours, at least to start." She dug in the box again and gleefully dangled a hatchling sling. "Wear this, and you can keep Clem secure and happy wherever you go."

Slack-jawed, Felix stared at the doctor.

Between them, they wrangled the wailing hatchling into his suit. His cries fizzled out, and he waved his arms to Felix.

"Looks like he wants you to pick him up," Doctor Bonna said. "He's already less tense. He'll quickly learn to associate being changed with feelings of comfort and well-being."

Felix scooped up the wriggling hatchling and held him to his chest. Clem snuggled closer, tiny fingers gripping the fabric of Felix's tunic. Felix tucked back his chin to look down at the infant. "He's gaining colour."

"Indeed," Doctor Bonna said. "This is his first feed. He'll fall asleep shortly. Shall we visit Prudence? You can show off your parenting prowess. Come."

Doctor Bonna led Felix to Prudence's room, her shoulders shaking with mirth all the way.

"I don't know what you think is so funny," Felix said, his hand cradling Clem's head. He eased through the doorway, taking care not to nudge the snoring hatchling.

"You're quite right. Indeed, there is nothing remotely amusing about your transition from ferocious cave-bear to gentle foster parent." She examined her unconscious patient's vital signs, and nodded to herself, before plunging a hypodermic needle into Prudence's arm. "You and Clem make yourselves comfortable. Prudence will wake slowly. She might be a little groggy and disoriented. I'll be back to check soon, but press the buzzer if you need me."

Felix hitched his chair closer to the pod and held his sister's hand while caressing Clem with the other. He hoped she wouldn't immediately ask for a mirror. Although Doctor Bonna had neutralised the toxins, she had not yet repaired the necrotised flesh, explaining the nanobots were most effective when all vestiges of the poisons were removed.

"Prue? Can you hear me? Take your time, there's no rush." Felix blinked, unsure if he had imagined the pressure on his fingers. He squeezed back.

Eyes still closed, Prue smiled in his direction. "Felix?"

"I'm here. You're safe in the medical centre." Felix knuckled away a tear.

Prudence sucked in a deep breath, then slowly blew it out. "Everything hurts, even my freckles." She forced a feeble laugh. "How is Castian?"

"He's recovering, as far as I know."

She glared through slitted eyes. "As far as you know? You haven't even asked, have you?" Her gaze slid down to the snuffling hatchling, and her eyes grew wide. Prudence struggled to lean up on her elbows. "Who's this?"

"Meet Clem, our most recent refugee. A midwife rescued him and sent him through the portal."

"He's a rescue? Not a repair and return? Is his condition treatable?"

"Glaucoma's in both eyes. He's anxious and refused to feed, but Doctor Bonna says once his weight is up, she'll perform a very minor surgery, and little Clem will be fine." Felix rubbed the hatchling's back. "Doctor Bonna said I must keep him close to allay his anxiety. Seems to work. He's sleeping peacefully."

Doctor Bonna poked her head around the door. "Did I hear my name?" She nodded and smiled at Felix before fixing her attention on Prudence. "Glad to see you're awake, young lady. How do you feel?"

Prudence shrugged. "Better than I have a right to. I ache all over, but I'm kinda surprised to be alive. How's Castian?"

Doctor Bonna poked and prodded at Prudence, flexed her joints, and palpated her flesh before answering the question. "Physically, the boy's doing better than I expected, but his brain activity? He doesn't stop. Indeed, he dreams and mutters to himself every moment of the day."

"Dreaming isn't a problem, is it?" Prudence asked. "We all dream."

"We all cycle through three stages of sleep, then into REM sleep. For reasons I don't yet understand, he's staying permanently in REM sleep and experiencing vividly intense dreams, so he isn't getting the rest he needs." Doctor Bonna cocked her head to one side. "Indeed, Castian seems fixated on you as a divine messenger sent by Solra. He chunters about you frequently. He's filed you into his framework of religious beliefs."

The Chosen Acolyte

Stark perused Acolyte Espio's file, intrigued by the youngster who had consciously maintained a calm demeanour. Espio consistently achieved good, but not outstanding, grades and reports in all areas. A tingle of apprehension ran the length of Stark's spine as he pulled a comparison report of all Acolytes from the previous decade.

Even in his creative endeavours, Espio's achievements were average, a flat plane on a graphed landscape of hills and valleys. The evidence might incline a suspicious mind to think the youngster maintained a deliberate mediocrity to avoid notice. Stark steepled his fingers and tapped the tips in asynchronous pairs.

The Quarter Day Festival loomed ever closer. What better opportunity to get to know Espio than to assign him a role in the celebration preparations? Stark ran a finger down the weekly work schedule. Gardening. An opportunity for immense creativity or backbreaking tedium.

Stark donned a hooded cloak and took himself to the vast ornamental gardens surrounding his offices. He wandered the meticulously raked gravel paths, enjoying the mild sunshine caressing his nape and the sharp breezes whipping his robes. The Acolytes maintained a respectful distance and ostensibly averted their eyes. The High Shepherd found Espio working with a gang, pulling weeds. Not much opportunity to wreak havoc, nor for an ambitious Acolyte to distinguish himself.

Espio worked steadily, keeping but not setting the pace. Utterly unremarkable, and in Stark's opinion, unbelievable. Stark crooked a finger at the supervising herdsman, recognisable by his shabby forest green robe.

"Yes, High Shepherd Stark? How may I be of service?"

"Tell me about Espio."

"Who?"

Stark pointed.

"Espio? Yes, a good lad. Reliable, but," the herdsman lowered his voice, "not one to use his initiative, High Shepherd. May I ask why you're asking? Only, if you're seeking an assistant of any kind, there are others I can recommend." The herdsman ducked his head and hid his wiry arms in his wide sleeves.

"Are you suggesting Espio is unworthy of patronage?"

"No, My Shepherd. But there are less dull candidates."

Stark smiled thinly. "Perhaps with a little encouragement and polishing, the lad will find his sparkle. Send him to my office when he's finished here."

With his acute hearing, Espio heard every word of the exchange between High Shepherd Stark and Herdsman Hebe, but feigned modest surprise and appropriate humility when Hebe singled him out at the end of the shift.

"Are you certain he wants me? I am surely unqualified to assist High Shepherd Stark."

"That's what I told him," Hebe said, "but he asked for you by name. Clean yourself before you go. This could be your big chance. Good luck, lad."

Espio neither dawdled nor hurried to present himself at Stark's office. He wanted to appear neither reluctant nor eager. The austerity of the outer offices testified to Stark's public reputation, but the understated opulence of the inner office didn't surprise him. While nothing screamed excess, the superior quality of the furnishings spoke with a quiet confidence that the inhabitant expected the best this world could offer.

"You sent for me, My Shepherd." Espio's voice expressed mild curiosity. He kept his eyes fixed respectfully on the gleaming floor.

As Stark clicked off the array of monitors on his wide and imposing granite topped desk, Espio listened to the High Shepherd's irregular breathing. The High Shepherd enjoyed notoriously good health; the erratic breaths must be evidence of nerves. Not a good sign.

"I summoned you for two reasons," Stark said. "You recently suffered the unexpected loss of a friend and colleague, as did we all. These things are difficult to bear. I am assigning you to my Quarter Day Celebration Team. You will be fully occupied, so will have no time to brood, and I will be able to offer you personal support and guidance."

"My Shepherd, I am unworthy of your attention." Espio risked a glance at Stark. "I doubt I possess the skills to contribute meaningfully to your team."

Stark stepped around the vast desk and clapped Espio's shoulder. "I sense hidden depths. You demonstrated unusual composure when you helped bring the heretic from the Discipline Chamber."

Espio shrugged. "I didn't know then he was a heretic, My Shepherd."

"Do we ever really know our friends?" Stark bowed his head. "True character reveals itself under pressure, don't you agree?"

"My Shepherd, if you say so. But the heretic and I were not friends. We shared some classes and work details, but he always outperformed me. He outshone us all."

"And now his light is extinguished."

As scheduled, Espio attended the recital afternoon with a loose group of acquaintances. He clapped approval just long enough, but without overt enthusiasm.

A young woman tugged his sleeve. "Your turn. You haven't performed for weeks," she said.

Espio laughed. "I haven't performed because I have nothing worthy to offer. I'm working on a praise piece, but I only have the opening lines."

"Give us your opening lines then," she said. "We'll tell you if they're worth working on, or if you should abandon them."

"I already know they're rubbish. I'll never be as good as the rest of you."

"Come on, you'll never improve unless you dare to expose yourself to critiques." She shoved him to his feet and turned to the group. "Finally, our most reluctant poet will perform his opening lines. Give it up for Espio."

Espio blushed pink. "It's not very good." He shuffled to face the audience. "O Shepherd! My Shepherd! / These fearful sheep are saved, / The flock has weathered every test, the lamb is in the fold." Espio shrugged. "That's all I've got. Sorry."

A flutter of polite applause whispered through the assembly.

"It's a start," the young woman said. "I'm sure you can make something of it, if you put in the effort."

"Yes, it's a beginning," Espio said. "Maybe this will be my magnum opus."

Espio hoped his message had been heard and understood.

Beatrice's Bulletins

The crew fluster around Beatrice, touching up hair and makeup, tweaking her clothes and assuring her she looks fabulous. The park throbs with the construction of colourful temporary booths and small stages. Equipment clutters the pathways as performers line up for rehearsals.

Beatrice checks her position and nods a curt approval. At least this time the sun isn't blinding her and making her squint, although the fitful breezes ruffle her carefully coiffed curls. She waits impatiently for her cue, her dazzling smile firmly in place.

"Three, two ..." A raised finger and a wrist flick.

"Thank you, my friends, for allowing me into your dens." Beatrice winks. "Preparations for the Quarter Day Celebrations are frenzied as artists and performers come together to entertain and delight you, the citizens of Luxton. High Shepherd Stark, a renowned patron of the arts, is generously funding this extravaganza, and invites you all to enjoy the culture and art, both traditional and experimental. I'll certainly be here, cramming in as many exhibitions and performances as I can. Believe me, the choices are mind-boggling."

The camera pans to show the chaotic activity filling the park.

"I urge those of you from the outer colonies to book your reservations, before spaces sell out."

Seeds of Doubt

The false believer wears a mask of faith, but Their gaze sees all;
no treachery can be hidden from Solra's burning eye.

The Blessed Prophet Serenus

High Shepherd Altor paced the bare floor of his office as he listened to his agent's report via a scrambled comm-link. Sunlight gleamed through the wide windows, sparkling on the rows of crystals, giving an illusion of life to texts composed by authors long dead.

"Are you confident our boy is not in danger? This is an unexpected and welcome development," High Shepherd Altor said, "but if the lad's in jeopardy, we must pull him out."

"Shepherd, there are no guarantees, but Espio knows what to do. He'll maintain his mask of mediocrity. For now, I recommend we see where this leads. We trained him for this."

"Training isn't the same as experience," Altor said.

"No, Shepherd. But unless you trust him in the field, he will never gain experience. He's a steady lad."

Altor sighed and tucked his folded arms into his sleeves. "Stay as close to him as you can. Solra be with you." Altor flicked off the link and squeezed shut his eyes to ponder his options.

He pulled Espio's file to refresh his memory. A long-term placement, with no expectations other than gathering and confirming low-level intelligence. Altor's deep-seated dislike of using junior agents invariably caused them to be placed in safe positions. His nerves jangled at the thought of Stark's personal attention focused on the lad.

Altor reached out to call High Shepherd Miles, but his link buzzed first. As usual, Miles had beaten him to it.

"I hear your lad's attracted Stark's attention," Miles said, without pre-amble.

"I was about to contact you. How did you hear?"

"You're not the only one with assets. I heard Stark went looking for him, asked for the lad by name? Assigned him duties on the Quarter Day Celebration Team?"

"I confess I'm worried," Altor said. "Stark also chose my lad to help move the Acolyte from the Discipline Chamber before declaring him a heretic."

"Were they friends? Does Stark suspect your agent of heresy?"

"No, I don't think so. Espio is careful not to get close to anyone, yet remains friendly with everyone."

"Did he overhear anything compromising?" Miles asked.

"Stark is too cunning for that. He sent the assistants on their way before the heretic boy regained consciousness. But Espio said the boy didn't have a heretical bone in his body. A lamb who desperately sought his Shepherd's approval and lacked the imagination to produce an original thought. Perfect material for a smaller colony Shepherd, when he grad-uated."

"Why would Stark turn on him? Declaring someone heretic, excom-municating them, that's almost unheard of these days," Miles said. "He must have presented an enormous threat for Stark to take such extreme measures."

"All we know for certain," Altor said, "is that Stark sent him from the library in disgrace, then confined him to the Discipline Chamber. Almost immediately after his release from the chamber, Stark declared him heretic and eliminated him. I'm worried for Acolyte Espio, he's inexperienced."

"My man will keep an eye on him. High Shepherd Stark's ruthless lack of compassion disturbs me," Miles said. "He sees no grey, only Light and Dark. I cannot help but question his zeal. Have we allowed him to lead the flock into dangerous territory?"

Espio entered the long room at the tail of a twittering group of eager assistants. Team Leader Ludion pointed to a vacant spot at the end of the row, and Espio dutifully took his seat. The other junior team members nodded a cursory welcome, their attention fixed on Ludion.

"I always think it boosts morale, and therefore productivity, to know the reason for each task." Team Leader Ludion beamed a smile at the group, who uniformly beamed back.

Espio mustered his brightest brainless smile.

"You'll see before you a list of names." Ludion gestured widely with both arms.

Espio guessed the team leader's creative outlets lay in the arenas of drama and the performing arts.

"These are High Shepherd Stark's honoured guests for the Quarter Day Celebration. Your task as scribes, and I cannot overstate the importance of your work, is checking the personal details against the files and updating them. You must record any change of circumstance, no matter how trivial." The leader's chest swelled with pride. "Our High Shepherd must be able to converse intimately with his honoured guests and show them how much their support means to his campaign."

Espio glanced at the list before him, noticing the columns dedicated to donations. He quickly masked the green flicker of distaste which flashed across his face.

As the morning wore on, junior assistants ferried trays of crystal data files back and forth, as Espio and the other scribes updated their lists. Team Leader Ludion pranced along the rows, vomiting indiscriminate praise. Espio clenched his toes when Ludion patted his shoulder and lauded his mediocre output as inspirational.

Ludion clapped his hands for attention. "I know you'd gladly go all day, my little lambs, but I insist you all break and partake in the Benediction of Solra. Come." He led the group to a private grassy courtyard. "Find a space to replenish your energy, my lovelies."

Espio hovered at the rear of the group. Some assumed a traditional praise pose, others flung themselves to the grass. As an Acolyte, Espio chose a praise pose, standing erect with arms wide and head tipped back.

Although lacking warmth, the clarity of light helped Espio clear his head of distractions and the morning's irritations. His blue tint intensified as he absorbed Solra's benediction, and his muscles relaxed. Although training for Shepherding, Espio didn't relish hunching at a desk, studying the words of dead men. The outdoor work details, even menial weeding, gave him more satisfaction, and time to ponder the big questions, the meaning-of-life issues, which the orthodox Shepherds believed already answered beyond further debate.

The afternoon passed in a miasma of self-congratulatory smugness, generated by Ludion.

"High Shepherd Stark requests you attend him before going home." Ludion arched an eyebrow. "Perhaps you'd do me a great favour and drop the updated files at the library on your way?"

"Of course, Team Leader."

Ludion closed Espio's hand over the files in a double handed grip. "I'll be sure to tell The High Shepherd what a valuable asset you are, when I next speak to him."

"Thank you, Team Leader Ludion." Espio looked directly into his eyes. "I appreciate your support."

Espio walked calmly to the library, his heart beating wildly. Why had Ludion referred to him as an asset? Why not help or assistant? Could the language be a part of his dramatic persona, or was the man giving him a message? Or making a threat? And if so, why entrust him with the files?

The flaming reflection of the dying sun on the expansive windows concealed High Shepherd Stark from casual observers as he watched Espio cross the lawns to the library. The youngster looked neither left nor right, ignoring the glorious gardens and magnificent sunset.

Perhaps Herdsman Hebe had correctly described the Acolyte as dull, but Stark's instincts buzzed like agitated skaxnats, alerting him to concealed dangers.

Stark rose to greet Espio, clasping his hand with the familiarity of an old friend. "How did you like your first day on my team? Did Team Leader Ludion treat you well?"

"Team Leader Ludion is charismatic, My Shepherd. I hope I didn't disappoint either of you."

"I'm sure you made your usual sterling effort. A solid, reliable man, that's what my team needs. Are you that man, Espio?" Stark gripped Espio's shoulder.

"My Shepherd, I hope so."

"Well, best you get yourself home before dark." Stark glanced at the blazing sunset. "Another big day tomorrow. Solra's blessing be upon you." Stark prided himself on reading people, but the Acolyte's utter blandness offered no purchase, and talking to the lad felt like scaling a glass wall.

Espio studied his fellow team members, grinning and gushing, but chose not to adopt the same attitude. Ludion showered him with the same bewildering cascade of compliments as he did the rest of the team, but hovered more frequently and attentively, unspoken questions burning behind his eyes.

The team updated details of the endless list of supporters, amending addresses or new fosterlings, creative pursuits or recent accolades. When Ludion clapped his hands and invited them to participate in Solra's Benediction, Espio confidently placed himself in the centre of the group. He claimed a sun-drenched spot and assumed the traditional position, welcoming the flood of energy.

At the end of the afternoon, Ludion effusively thanked the team for their heroic efforts, reminding them of the vital importance of their task. "A quick reminder, my lambs. This afternoon, you're all invited to a private viewing of my paintings. I hope you won't be too unkind about my poor efforts." He tittered behind his hand. "Ooh, Espio. Short notice, I realise, but I'd love you to join us. Think of it as a team building exercise."

The team giggled and smirked, writhing in pink-cheeked excitement as they echoed Ludion's invitation.

Tastefully illuminated by expensive sun-globes, the small venue thronged with guests. Canvasses of varying sizes hung from the walls; Ludion's signature discreetly etched in the corners. From behind a screen of glossy foliage, musicians played soft music.

"Not what you expected?" Ludion slipped his arm through Espio's. "Allow me to give you a tour." A ghastly combination of orange pride and green fear pulsed over the artist's features, in opposition to his exquisitely rendered watercolours and pastels.

Espio closely examined each piece, stepping up to admire the infinitesimal details. "These are very good. No, they're excellent. Sublime."

"Thank you. Exposing your soul to the public gaze is so difficult, don't you agree?"

"By the Light, if I possessed a fraction of your talent, I'd hang my work in every public space."

"Your friend had talent and passion to match," Ludion whispered.

"My friend?"

Ludion looked over his shoulder. "The heretic. He could capture the grace of a bird in flight, or the majesty of a storm and make you believe you were in the painting, not observing from the outside."

Espio raised a hand. "I didn't know him well enough to call him a friend. We're not supposed to talk about him."

"Such a waste. All that talent." Ludion flicked his fingers. "Pouf. Gone."

"Do you think he was? A heretic, I mean?"

Ludion pulled away and stood straight. "High Shepherd Stark declared him a heretic, although I never scented the slightest whiff of heresy. Most of the time, I thought he was a sanctimonious little … Enough. I must mingle with my guests."

Ludion slipped into the river of bodies. Espio, an immovable rock in a swirling tide of Ludion's closest friends, tried fitting the pieces of the puzzle together; but until he found the correct perspective, he was only guessing and unable to make sense of the entire picture.

Beatrice's Bulletins

Beatrice's crew transforms Stark's inner office, shifting furniture and laying a complicated array of cables over the floor, ready to ensnare the unwary. Camera's, lights, and sound equipment encircle a pair of upholstered chairs, poised to capture every nuance.

When the makeup girl moves away, Beatrice removes her outer wrap, revealing a daffodil yellow knit dress, which clings to every ample curve. The colour compliments her golden eyeshadow. She sits in her assigned chair, crossing her ankles, and tucking them demurely to the side.

Beatrice's smile is set to rival Solra's rays.

The manager begins the countdown, silencing the circus.

"Three, two …" Only a finger signals one, and a wrist flourish indicates they're now recording.

"Welcome, my friends, to a very special bulletin. I am honoured to invite you into the inner sanctum of High Shepherd Stark's office, to meet the great man himself."

The camera pulls out to show the artificially cosy setting.

"High Shepherd Stark needs no introduction, but I can't resist sharing a little known fact before he joins me." Beatrice glances left and right, then leans forward to share the tidbit of gossip. "I can reveal to you, my friends, that our own beloved Shepherd was the youngest ever anointed High Shepherd, and is the longest serving. Despite his youthful good looks, High Shepherd Stark is the most experienced and well-respected Shepherd in Solran history."

Beatrice stands and holds out her hands. "Welcome, High Shepherd Stark. Thank you for allowing me to steal a moment of your valuable time." A delicate shell-pink flushes her temples.

High Shepherd Stark squeezes her hands, then smiles to the camera as he sits. "May Solra's blessings be upon you and yours. Spending a moment with you gives me great pleasure, Miss Max. As you know, I'm an avid fan of your show."

Beatrice giggles and bats her eyelashes as she lowers herself into her chair. "You're too kind, My Shepherd." She tugs the hem of her skirt, smoothing the soft fabric over her knees. "Can you tell us a little about how your election campaign is progressing?"

"My supporters have been incredible. We live in troubled times and my duties are sometimes unpleasant, but the increased devotion of the pure-hearted to Solra's ways keeps me buoyant, Miss Max. Serving Solra, and guiding my lambs to salvation and everlasting Light, is my only purpose."

"I've heard you are certain to win the election, My Shepherd. You must be pleased to have your superiority recognised?"

"Miss Max, I prefer not to consider a promotion to the position of the Most High Grand Master in vulgar terms of winning or losing. Rather, I and my colleagues submit ourselves in absolute humility to Solra's divine will. We are mere servants. As for certainty?" Stark shakes his head. "The only certainty is Solra's loving mercy. All else is mere vanity and illusion."

Visions

To serve the shepherd is to strengthen the faith; those who shirk their duty shall bear the weight of divine judgment.

The Blessed Prophet Serenus

Castian floated in a liminal space between waking and dreaming, but a growing sense of urgency propelled him towards the permeable surface of consciousness. With arms and legs immobile, he experienced an unpleasant sense of déjà vu and shied away from wakefulness before gathering his courage and breaching the barrier.

Cool fingers stroked his forehead. "How are you feeling? The doctor's on her way."

Beeps and hums provided a too familiar background. *I'm not dead. Solra sent an emissary to save me.*

Footsteps, heavy with authority approached his pod.

"Castian? It's Doctor Bonna. Can you hear me?"

He turned towards her voice and nodded.

"You're lucky to be alive, young man. Twice Prudence risked her life to rescue you."

Prudence. His saviour. The divine messenger of Solra. Beautiful Prudence with the flawed face. Castian cracked open his eyes. The cool-fingered nurse hovered in the background, and Doctor Bonna loomed over him, her expression expectant.

"I can't move my limbs."

Doctor Bonna nodded to the nurse, who adjusted the pod into a sitting position. "The skaxnats pumped you full of toxins and snipped off two of your fingers," Doctor Bonna said. "I've flushed your system of poison, but the full-body nutrigel suit is restricting your mobility."

Castian flexed his remaining fingers. "A message from Solra; punishment for my pride."

"I know nothing about that," Doctor Bonna said. "You have a choice: stay as you are, or accept reconstructive surgery. If you choose to stay as you are, I will arrange an occupational therapist to work with you, and we will fit you with prosthetic fingers. If you opt for surgery, I'll have you as good as new in only a few days." She smiled. "I recommend surgery, but the choice must be yours."

"Hubris," Castian moaned.

"Indeed, I've performed similar procedures many times, with outstanding success." Her smile slipped. "I'll leave you to consider your options."

Prudence smiled into the mirror Doctor Bonna held. She fluttered her fingers over her new cheek. "I can feel everything. Thank you, Doctor." She turned from side to side. "You've performed a miracle."

"Indeed, it's a pleasure to have a patient who appreciates my skills." She placed the mirror within Prudence's reach, knowing one look would not be enough. "Castian is awake. When I told him I could reconstruct his missing fingers, he accused me of hubris."

"He often speaks without thinking, but he doesn't mean to give offence. Can I visit him?"

Doctor Bonna sniffed. "Indeed, I see no reason why not, but I must warn you, he isn't making much sense."

Prudence tapped gently on the open door. "May I come in?"

Castian beamed. "Prudence, I'm so pleased to see you. I need your advice." He patted the seat next to his pod with his ruined hand.

"We worried about you not sleeping properly. But you look well." She glanced at his hand. "Mostly."

Castian raised his hand, twisting and turning his wrist. "This is a message. Praise Solra."

Prudence snorted. "Sorry, I don't speak mangled hand. You'll have to translate."

"Solra is the source of all talent and wisdom, praise Solra." Castian nodded eagerly. "The Solran Creed. I ignored my Solra given talent and pursued another creative outlet. This is my punishment."

"Nope, you're gonna have to give me more."

"Remember when I told you I was a poet? Albeit a poor one?"

Prudence nodded.

"That wasn't quite the truth. My true Solra gifted talent is painting. Everyone at the studio marvelled at my abilities, but I failed to value them. The Blessed Prophet Serenus didn't paint or draw. He created sublime poetry." He shrugged and hung his head. "In my hubris, I attempted to emulate Holy Serenus."

"You think you lost your fingers because you angered Solra? To prevent you painting? Because you rejected Their gift?"

"Exactly. I knew you'd understand."

"I'm not sure I do. Punishing you for trying something different strikes me as peevish. Not exactly the action of a loving god." She flapped her hands. "Sorry, don't listen to me. I'm not a believer."

Castian looked sideways at her. "But Solra believes in you. That's all that matters. And They sent you to save me. Twice. They must want me to listen to you."

Prudence blew a long breath through pursed lips. "I'm not qualified to offer theological advice, but if you believe all skills and knowledge come from Solra, that means Doctor Bonna's expertise is Solra given, too."

"That is a challenging concept. Are you suggesting I accept her offer to replace my fingers?"

"I'm not suggesting anything, other than you consider all your options." Prudence touched her face. "A skaxnat stung my cheek, and the necrotising toxins ate the flesh. I looked hideous, but Doctor Bonna repaired me."

"While I slept, I experienced intense dreams." Castian wriggled up in the pod. "You might call them visions. Would I offend you if I shared them?"

"If talking helps you make sense of them, fine. But don't take offence when I remain an unbeliever."

Castian laid his mutilated hand in his lap. "I can't be sure if this is a dream, or a memory, but when Stark released me from the Discipline Chamber, he sent away his assistants and tended to me himself, praise Solra. That's when I told him Solra loves all Their children, without exception."

"A compassionate Creator? Is that why Stark cast you out?"

"No, I don't think so." Castian tapped his remaining fingers on an invisible keyboard. "He'd already reached his decision, but for a fleeting moment he looked almost victorious, as though my words vindicated him."

"What else did you dream? You haven't yet offended me. Try harder."

"Solra spoke directly to me, like they did to The Blessed Prophet Serenus."

"According to your belief system, isn't that ... a sin? Getting above yourself?"

"Do you think it is a sin?"

"You're asking the wrong person. I believe blind faith is foolish. A faith which cannot tolerate questions must be weak at its core. And a system which culls hatchlings is indisputably wicked."

Castian clutched Prudence's hands. "You are Solra's emissary. You echo what Solra said in my visions."

"No, Castian. I am no emissary or messenger. You've had a shock; two life-threatening shocks. And for the first time, you're asking questions rather than accepting the pompous controlling drivel the Shepherds tell you."

"Questioning the Shepherds is disobedience," Castian said.

Prudence shrugged. "If the rules, written by Sui, are not robust enough to withstand scrutiny, then why should you feel obliged to obey them?"

"Holy Serenus received the Solran Creed directly from the Creator."

"According to Serenus, who obviously possessed enough charisma to make people believe his every word."

"You dare challenge the veracity of The Blessed Prophet Serenus?" Castian's eyes grew wide.

"I challenge anyone and everyone. Show me incontrovertible proof."

"But we do not base faith on proof, praise Solra."

"Which is why I'm an unbeliever."

"Do you not fear being damned to perpetual darkness?"

"Ask yourself this question. If people are only virtuous because they fear punishment, how genuine is their virtue? Shouldn't a person regulate their behaviour by internal, not external, factors?"

"It's not actions, it's faith which determines salvation," Castian said.

"Solra welcomes selfish and vicious believers, but casts kind unbelievers into perpetual darkness? Is that what you're telling me? I'll take my chances in the darkness, thanks. If Felix is there, we'll find a way to make our own Light."

Castian stared through the open doorway, her words repeating inside his head. *Make our own Light. Make our own Light. Make our own Light.* So many possibilities. Prudence dismissed her role as emissary, but he recognised Solra's divine voice speaking through her. Speaking to him. Castian squeezed shut his eyes. Why would Solra choose an imperfect vessel as Their messenger, unless the medium played part of the message? "Nurse? Hello, nurse?"

The nurse appeared in the doorway. "How can I help?"

"May I have writing materials? I need to get these thoughts out of my head so I can make sense of them."

The nurse returned, pushing an art-studio cart. "I took the liberty of bringing a selection of materials."

Castian opened his mouth to send the cart away, then clamped his lips. The nurse's kindness didn't deserve a curt response. "Thank you." He raised his maimed hand. "I'm not sure I can do justice to the materials yet, but thank you. One more favour? Could you set up a writing station next to me? The nutrigel suit is restrictive."

The nurse assembled an angled desk on his pod and arranged an array of equipment. "Anything else you need, call out."

Castian selected a stylus and rolled the instrument between the fingers of his good hand. The familiarity of the action soothed him. He wrote a line from the Solran creed, then scratched it through.

~~An imperfect body signifies imperfections within and is anathema to Solra.~~

He sucked the end of the stylus. Dare he write his private opinion?

Solra loves all Their children, each one is perfect in Their eyes.

Castian glanced out of the window. Solra continued Their journey across the sky, unaffected by, and uncaring of, Castian's new heresy.

~~Unity with Solra requires perfect submission.~~

Solra delights in an enquiring mind.

Out of habit, Castian looked about, searching for hidden recording devices, before reading aloud his own lines, timidly the first time, but more confidently the second. He squared his shoulders. *Maybe it isn't the sophisticated beauty of the words that shine, but their simple truth.*

Prudence plonked herself in the chair before Callida's desk. "He insists I am a messenger from Solra. Me! Could you imagine a less likely candidate, Callie?" She snorted.

Callida leaned back in her chair. "Twice you saved his life. Are you really surprised he assigns you a semi-divine role?"

"Hatchlings are so much easier," Prudence said. "They have no ridiculous delusions or prejudices."

"You mean, hatchlings don't challenge your prejudices?"

"You think I'm prejudiced?"

"Everyone entertains prejudice," Callida said. "You nurture a prejudice against Castian's faith, calling it ridiculous."

"His faith is ridiculous, Callie. It makes no sense."

"Setting out on the Central Sea, knowing shroaks infest those waters, to rescue a stranger is crazy. Leaping into a skaxnat lair to rescue a man bent on performing terminal penance is another kind of ridiculous. Neither of those acts makes sense."

"Are you saying I should have left him to die?"

"No, not at all. I admire your crazy courage. Your deep-seated beliefs, no matter how illogical or dangerous to yourself, informed your actions." Callida leaned her elbows on her desk. "As are the actions of our guest. I think your prejudice stems from Castian's belief in the innate superiority of his society, and your need to prove him wrong."

Felix adjusted the volume on the heartbeat amplifier and backed away from Clem on his knees. The hatchling cocked his head to one side and listened intently to the steady rhythm of Felix's heart in his earpiece. Clem nodded in time to the beat, his tiny fingers tapping double-time.

"Looks like a musician," Prudence said from the workshop entrance.

"As long as he can hear me, he's fine," Felix said, rolling a jingle ball towards the youngster, who pounced with a gleeful whoop and tossed it back. "Doctor Bonna says he's gained enough weight. She'll perform the surgery tomorrow."

Rather than playing with Clem as she usually did, Prudence huddled on a stool at the workbench. "Can I ask you a question?"

Felix stood and rolled his shoulders. "You're upset."

"Do you think I'm prejudiced?"

"You have strong opinions."

"Is that a polite way of saying yes?" Prudence frowned up at him. "I need you to be honest."

"Is this about Castian? What's the ungrateful yolk-sac said now?"

"Castian has said nothing. Callida accused me, and I don't know what to think. I'm not prejudiced. I defended him when he took off into the wilderness."

Felix hoisted himself onto the neighbouring stool. "Why were you so keen to bring Castian back? Because you believe all life is sacred? Or because you wanted to prove our culture is superior to his?"

"But we are better. We welcome everyone, and we don't murder hatchlings."

"I'm not arguing." Felix held up his palms. "How can I not despise anyone who could send Clem into the wilderness? But if I'd been raised differently ... who knows? The Mainlanders must believe they're doing right. No doubt, they think we're monsters, living lives of unholy depravity."

Prudence covered her face with her hands. "Prejudice is such an ugly word."

"Think of it in terms of self-preservation. If you had a mission on any of the three Domains, you'd disguise your freckles, right? Until you knew exactly who you were dealing with, right?"

Prudence nodded behind her fingers.

"If you're worried about your biases against Castian and his religious beliefs, why don't you talk to him? And listen to what he tells you. Somehow, he's angered the hierarchy enough to be excommunicated." Felix smirked. "You've probably got more in common than you realise."

Prudence snorted. "He's convinced I'm an emissary from Solra."

"What did I tell you? He thinks you're semi-divine, and you've always had a high opinion of yourself." Felix dodged away before his sister could swat him.

Art as Heresy

Beware the whispers of heresy, even in the heart of those closest to you, for the unclean spirit is cunning beyond measure and loves to pollute the unwary.

The Blessed Prophet Serenus

Castian's fingers itched to hold the charcoal stick. The creamy paper begged for his skilful touch. As he conjured her face with delicate but sure strokes, tension slipped from his shoulders. Her image stared back at him, eyes filled with wisdom, her lips parted to speak the sacred words of Solra—

"Can I come in?" Prudence leaned in the doorway. "You looked so engrossed I didn't want to disturb you."

Castian looked from his paper to the figure in the doorway and flushed a faint pink. He flipped shut the pad and shoved it aside. "I am always pleased to see you."

Prudence grabbed the pad. "May I?" She flicked the pages without waiting for an answer, then froze, lips parted exactly as in the sketch. "This is me?"

"I'm sorry." Castian lunged for the pad, but Prudence whirled out of reach. "I should have asked your permission. Forgive me."

Prudence held the page high. "By the Light. When you said you had talent, I assumed you exaggerated your abilities. This is like looking into a mirror, only better. You've made me beautiful." She traced her fingers over her repaired cheek, then stroked the sketch.

"You're not angry? Or insulted?"

"Why would I be anything other than delighted?" Prudence kept her eyes on the sketch.

"We are forbidden to reproduce the face or form of Sui, the pinnacle of Solra's creation, praise Solra."

Prudence snapped her gaze to Castian. "What? Why?"

"Representation of the Sui form is sacrilegious. The Shepherds teach such acts are akin to challenging the sovereignty of Solra."

"Don't tell me." Prudence raised her hand. "You will be sent into perpetual darkness."

Castian hung his head and groaned. "What have I done?"

"You have created the most gorgeous art with the talent Solra gave you. May I keep this?"

"Possessing such an image is sacrilege. You risk your everlasting soul. The sketch should be burned, to prevent sinful thoughts, praise Solra."

"Is that what you truly believe?" Prudence asked.

"I no longer know what I believe. I know Solra is responsible for all creation, for our daily life … but after that? My head is a whirlpool of questions. Even thinking these thoughts damns me to darkness, yet I am compelled."

Prudence blew a long breath through pursed lips. "I came here to apologise. Felix advised me to listen carefully without discrimination."

"Your brother said that? By the Light. Have we both jumped to ill-considered opinions?"

"I have rescued countless hatchlings. The idea of culling makes my blood run cold. I cannot understand the reasoning behind the action. You're the first adult Mainlander I've met, and I expected you to be a monster. Although I saw your fear and confusion, part of me blamed you for every atrocity."

"May I ask a question?"

"Ask away, but I reserve the right not to answer." Prudence smiled, to take the sting from her reply.

"Why do you risk yourself? Why do you rescue the rejected Sui?"

"That's a difficult question to answer, without giving offence to your beliefs." She waved a hand across her face. "Obviously, I am a rejected hatchling. Many people on the island are, and who has the authority to decree worthiness? As far as I'm concerned, the person who condemns a hatchling to the wilderness is the true monster."

"Would I give offence if I said I am surprised to have received such kindness from Nefans? The whispered rumours tell of depraved beasts, wilder and crueller than the predators living beyond the colony walls. I thought you were a myth."

"Shall we agree not to take offence, but to seize every opportunity to learn? To overcome our foolish antipathies?"

The Shepherd's Gaze

*Even discord may weary and pause, yet the righteous know peace
with a heretic is but a fleeting deception to be fought.*
The Blessed Prophet Serenus

Stark's overt attention to Espio sparked jealousy coupled with clumsy attempts at friendship from the other team members, none of whom Stark had deigned to notice. Espio ignored the envy, and mildly rebuffed the gauche overtures of rapport, careful to avoid implicating the gullible innocents in whatever machinations Stark engineered.

Espio timed his arrival at Stark's office politely early, but not annoyingly so. Worded as a casual invitation to catch up before work, Espio recognised Stark's request as a command.

Stark sailed out of his inner office, arms wide, splendid robes flowing, to greet him. "May Solra's Light shine upon you, my young friend. How are you?" Stark guided him towards the expanse of windows.

"As always, My Shepherd, I am well, and hope you also are enjoying good health."

"You appear lacklustre," Stark said, his voice louder than necessary. "You mustn't allow yourself to get down." Stark wrapped an arm around the Espio's shoulders in an oddly physical display of avuncular concern.

"My Shepherd?"

"Your persistent mediocrity won't necessarily prevent a career, but prepare yourself to be restricted to the smaller outlying colonies."

"With respect," Espio said, his voice muffled by Stark's voluminous sleeves, "I am content with my moderate achievements, and I harbour no ambitions for greatness. With humility, I accept Solra's plan for me."

"Nonsense, nonsense." Stark's voice boomed throughout the office. "With my guidance and a little more application on your part, you'll be fine. But you made the right choice, coming to see me. Why don't you spend the rest of the day in the gardens? Recharge your energy? Consider that an order." Stark smiled with the sincerity of a famished sabre cat stalking a wounded deer.

Espio roamed the gardens, doubling back and making sudden irregular turns. Avoiding eye-contact, he observed four individuals, strangers, engaged on similarly random walks. He selected a bench against a wall and flopped down, spreading his arms along the backrest and turning up his face to absorb the light.

Through slitted eyes, he noted two of them saunter towards the gates. Another took up position, basking on the edge of the fountain. The fourth developed an interest in the hothouse. Espio smiled to himself. The one by the fountain would soon be drenched in spray, and the one inside the hothouse drenched in sweat. Small victories.

Herdsman Hebe chugged along the gravel walk towards him. "I thought I recognised you. Unusually busy this morning, so many tourists, come early for the Quarter Day Celebrations." The Herdsman brandished the shiny digging fork clutched in his gnarled hand. "If you've time to waste, young man, you can come and help me with my seedlings." Hebe pulled Espio to his feet and dragged him along. "You're exactly what I need. My fingers are getting too stiff for this delicate repotting business. I crush as many as I successfully transplant."

Hebe propelled Espio through a narrow door and into the private section of the gardens and locked the door against casual visitors who misread the privacy plaques.

"I've missed the gardens," Espio said. "Administration doesn't suit me."

"High Shepherd Stark selected you. He must hold a different opinion." Hebe ushered Espio into the potting shed. The scents of rich earth and richer fertiliser wrapped the Acolyte in a blanket of familiarity.

Espio nodded as he reached for a tray of exuberant seedlings. "The High Shepherd holds strong opinions on every subject. Nobody contradicts him."

"But you would like to?" Hebe teased apart the fragile rootlets of his seedlings with unerringly gentle fingers.

"Not I." Espio shrugged. "I lack relevant experience and knowledge. I am sure High Shepherd Stark is correct in his pronouncements."

"A High Shepherd may be fallible."

"You flirt with danger, old man."

"Advantages of old age." Hebe shot him a wink. "Experience and an accumulation of knowledge."

"Old age isn't infallible," Espio said.

"True. If I am wrong, then you are not in danger, and the goons loitering by the gates will not follow you home."

Espio tamped the dirt on his tray of transplanted seedlings. "What do you think you know?"

"High Shepherd Stark does not mentor lowly Acolytes. His interest in you is out of character and therefore arouses my suspicion. I also know Castian committed no heresy. Stark is frightened, and a frightened man is dangerous."

Espio nodded slowly. "I am touched by your concern, Herdsman, but you labour under a misapprehension. There are no lurking goons, and

The High Shepherd presents no threat. Thank you for allowing me to help with the seedlings."

"You might want to slip out the rear staff entrance," Herdsman Hebe said. "Few people realise it exists."

Espio hummed along to the music, his fingers conducting an imaginary orchestra. The sharp rap on his door startled him upright. A second peremptory rap accompanied by an impatient shuffle of feet prompted him to switch off the music.

"Yes?" Espio recognised the man from the fountain as soon as he opened the door.

The man shoved his way inside, pushing Espio ahead of him.

"What do you want?"

The intruder crushed the musical recording between thick fingers and replaced the crystal without activating it. "For your friends to find. You're coming with me."

Espio sprang back as the man reached out, but the goon crashed face-first to the floor, the back of his skull a bloody mess.

Herdsman Hebe brandished a heavy pair of secateurs. "You never know when you'll need to do a spot of pruning." He knelt over the twitching goon and felt for a pulse. "Good, he's still alive."

"Who is he?" Espio asked.

"One of Stark's agents, from the park. I followed him here. Pack a change of clothes."

"Where are we going? We can't leave him here. He needs help."

Hebe ignored the questions and read the crystal. "A suicide note. Say's you're walking into the night. Make sure you pack a pair of sturdy boots."

Espio blanched. "He planned to kill me? Why?"

"Boots, and a change of clothes. Go." Hebe shoved Espio towards the dressing area.

By the time Espio returned, clutching his Acolyte's duffel bag, Hebe had shifted the body. "Where …?" Espio pointed a shaking finger at a smear of blood.

Hebe chivvied Espio into a mud-spattered vehicle and handed him a capsule. "Put this under your tongue. It'll keep you awake through the night." Hebe demonstrated. "See? They're not harmful. Not in moderation."

The Herdsman steered the battered car through the colony gates and parked in a shadowy patch of undergrowth. "Wait here." He leaped out and scurried to the rear compartment. Espio heard a wet thump as Hebe dumped the unconscious thug on the road.

"What do you know about the Nefans?" Hebe asked as he clambered back into the driver's seat. "Before we move on, I gotta disable your identity chip. Dip your head." He pulled a finger length tube from his pocket and pressed Espio face down. "There, all done."

"The Nefans? Only what every hatchling knows. They're a myth, a story told to scare unruly youngsters. The Nefans are hideous monsters and live on an isle permanently swathed in darkness. According to the stories, they are jealous of Sui perfection, and steal children to torture and experiment upon. Those whisked away by the Nefans never return." Espio frowned as he rubbed his nape. "What about your chip? Won't they come looking for you?"

Hebe laughed. "Transferred mine to a rabbit years ago. Anyone looking will find me in the gardens."

"Where are we going?"

"To expand your education, lad." Hebe steered through the impenetrable darkness, relying on technology which had no place in a humble gardener's vehicle. Screens glowing an eerie green showed the surroundings in startling detail, and red and yellow shapes represented the heat signatures of night predators and their prey.

"Who do you really work for?" Espio asked.

"High Shepherd Miles of Animo. As you answer to High Shepherd Altor of Honoris. Altor wanted to pull you, but Miles convinced him to let the situation play out, on the condition I kept an eye on you."

"You can't go back. I'm sorry you had to break cover to save me."

"Don't be sorry. Waste of energy. And my instincts tell me this may be the beginning of Stark's downfall."

"His popularity stands at an all-time high. He fully expects to win the election and become Grand Master High Shepherd."

"Until recently, I agree. But circumstances have changed. He's tried to eliminate two Acolytes. What does that tell you?"

"He's not what he seems. He has a public and a private persona, like his outer and inner offices."

"Keep going. Don't worry about what you can prove, only what you can infer."

"All life is sacred, so he must be desperate to try to kill two of us." Espio twisted in his seat to watch Hebe's responses. "The most important thing to him is the election. He's utterly consumed, so the threat must be linked."

Hebe nodded. "Agents in the three Domains scoured the records for clues, but found nothing. But your apparent suicide, and Castian's excommunication, might stir up fresh evidence. At the very least, they'll bring attention and put pressure to bear on him."

A scream rent the night air, followed by a victory roar which reverberated inside the vehicle's cabin.

"What was that?" Espio huddled deep into his seat.

"Sabre cat's supper. Listen, can you hear that low chuffing? Sounds like a mother serving a feast to her cubs."

Beatrice's Bulletins

Hollow-eyed and wan with night stupor, Beatrice slips a stimtab under her tongue, while an equally exhausted makeup girl dabs powder on her face. Irritated, Beatrice pushes her away. "I'll do it myself." She peers into the mirror and expertly swipes colour onto her pale face. She drags out the hair curlers and finger combs her locks into a fetchingly tousled display.

Her manager whispers in her ear and then pushes her in the direction of an older man, distress etched deeply on his moon pale features.

"Three, two …" A raised finger and a wrist flick.

"Sir, I'm Beatrice Max. Thank you for agreeing to speak with me. Can you tell me what happened?"

The man raises blank eyes. "His door was open. He never leaves his door open. He's very private. Keeps himself to himself, if you know what I mean."

"What did you see, Sir?"

"I didn't want to be nosy, so I stood outside and called his name." The man trembled.

"Take your time. What happened next?"

"Nothing. There was no answer. I started towards the temple … I was already late … but I turned back. The lad might have had an accident … he could've been laying helpless … so I went back."

Beatrice rolls her eyes and takes a deep breath. "What did you find?"

"He'd left a crystal. A suicide note. The lad's damned himself to perpetual darkness. According to the Blessed Prophet Holy Serenus, all life derives from Solra, all life returns to Solra." The man wrings his hands. "Only Solra has the authority to end a life. Killing yourself is throwing Solra's gift in their face. There can be no salvation."

Beatrice glances at her manager, who twirls his finger to wind up the interview. She thanks the man and watches him stumble to his door.

"I wanted pathos, not pathetic. Can you salvage any of that?" She asks.

The camera man yawns and nods. "Some."

"I'm dragged out of my pod for some nobody from nowhere, who can't cope with the pressure of Acolyte life, and there isn't even a corpse to show?" Beatrice drags on a coat against the predawn chill. "What else do we know about him? Who're his friends?"

Beatrice's wristcomm buzzes, the sound unnaturally loud in the semi-darkness. Her eyes grow wide as she reads the message, and she flushes deep violet with excitement.

"Let's hustle. Stark's offering an exclusive interview."

Beatrice jogs into Stark's offices, surrounded by her pack of eager assistants, keen to hunt down the truth and present their victory findings to the public.

Stark meets her in his reception area, sternly resplendent in his lapis lazuli robes of office. "He came to me yesterday, disheartened by his lack of academic success. He'd made no friends, except the heretic. The poor boy felt betrayed and confused."

Beatrice flutters her eyelashes. "I'm sure you did all you possibly could, My Shepherd."

"Guilt and futility combined into existential despair, Miss Max. I offered my support, but he refused, saying he could cope." Stark held out a data crystal. "This is a recording of our conversation, Miss Max. I hope you can make use of it. Encourage young people to seek help if they're occasionally overwhelmed by the complexity of adult life. Nothing is so dreadful it can't be overcome with a little guidance. I fear poor Acolyte Espio has damned himself to perpetual darkness, but I will pray for his soul. Solra is merciful."

Mirror bright shards of light spiked the horizon, diffusing into a golden glow as Solra rose in solemn majesty. Long shadows stretched thin fingers across the grassland, then inexorably retreated in defeat as the sun continued to traverse the skies, blessing creation.

Espio leaned forward, squinting against the light. "Isn't that a colony? Won't they report us to the authorities?"

"They haven't in the past. Besides, I need to hear the morning news." Hebe glanced at Espio. "Don't look so shocked. Did you not realise we're following the Midwife Trail?"

The crumbling and partially collapsed walls had long abandoned any defensive role, and now hosted innumerable lizards and spiders. Mosses and creeping plants blanketed the broken masonry with a riotous display of wild beauty, covering the shame of failed ambitions.

"Why don't they repair the wall?" Espio asked.

Hebe shrugged. "Because it's unnecessary and they have better things to do, I suppose."

"But the sabre cats?"

"Like most large predators, they're crepuscular. Our friends are safely abed behind locked doors and barred windows when the sabres are hunting."

Hebe drove down a wide boulevard lined with glossy-leafed trees and massive urns of cascading flowers. Iridescent hummingbirds and fat striped bees darted from blossom to blossom. Rainbows arced across the mists of artificial irrigation, adding an ethereal layer of beauty. He parked beside a spluttering fountain.

"We'll leave the car here to recharge the solar batteries. Take the opportunity to unstiffen these old legs. The temple's dead ahead." Hebe touched Espio's elbow. "Do yourself a favour: eyes open, mouth shut."

Hebe sauntered along like a hatchling released early from classes, swinging his arms and rolling his neck.

"Hey, have you seen this?" Espio pointed at the sparkling tiled pavement. "A mosaic of the creation story." He stepped back towards the car. "Look, they've got the fishes and insects that way, and the higher animals towards the temple. We probably shouldn't walk on this."

"Keep moving, you can come back later, if there's time."

"This is magnificent," Espio said, jogging to keep pace with the old man. "Work like this should be in the capital, where it can be properly appreciated."

Hebe whirled to face him. "Stop right there, youngster. This work is exactly where it ought to be. Being enjoyed by the artists of Crearaton, who designed and crafted it. Don't assume people choosing to live in the outer colonies are any less refined or talented than those living in the capital colonies."

"I didn't mean—"

Hebe held up his hand. "Mouth. Shut. Follow me."

Espio gaped like a stranded fish, then obeyed.

Hebe strode through the temple with a confidence borne of long familiarity. Espio trailed in his wake, wide eyes drinking the astonishing array of art.

He tapped Hebe's shoulder and whispered, "This is more like a high-end gallery than a temple."

"The creed says: Solra is the source of all talent and wisdom, praise Solra. This colony chooses to worship through art. A delightfully dynamic style of worship, in my opinion."

"Hebe, Hebe, Hebe. I've been expecting you, although not so soon." The voice filled the temple, far too large for the tiny man standing with open arms to welcome them. His flamboyantly paint-stained apron indicated a profound lack of reverence for protocols.

"Shepherd Picto, I hope we find you well?" Hebe said.

Shepherd Picto appraised Espio. "Are you resurrected, or are the reports of your suicide exaggerated?" Picto threw back his head and cackled.

Espio opened his mouth to respond, but Hebe laid a hand on his arm. "The youngster has taken a solemn vow of silence. I speak on his behalf."

Picto cackled again, the sounds bouncing off the walls. "Hebe, Hebe, Hebe. You never change. Come, come, come. I've compiled the news bulletins."

Picto led the way into an inner office crowded with unfinished paintings and partially created sculptures. Tucked into a corner hunched a communication centre. Hammers, chisels, and tools Espio failed to recognise littered the desk and obscured the keyboard.

"Stark's performance brings tears to the eyes," Picto said. "Polished, polished, polished, like a jewel. No genuine warmth or compassion. All authenticity rehearsed out." He rubbed a smudge of paint from a crystal and played the recordings he'd made.

Espio bit his lip to prevent himself from laughing. Standing behind the seated Hebe, Picto mimicked each word and overwrought gesture of High Shepherd Stark.

"…persistent mediocrity …" Picto clutched his apron "… unable to cope with the rigours of the curriculum … made no friends …" Picto clasped his hands to his chest and stared into the distance "… refused my mentorship … as much support as I could … poor lamb fell victim to depression …" Picto swiped an imaginary tear. He winked at Espio. "Not amusing, no, not amusing, not at all amusing."

"I know what you're doing, Picto," Hebe said without bothering to turn around. "Stop leading my lamb astray."

"Stark led your lamb to the slaughter, even getting the recording in his outer office yesterday with dozens of loyal witnesses." Picto's switch to seriousness astounded Espio. "Of course, only Stark's voice is audible, and with his arm wrapped around the victim, there's no chance of lip-reading what the lad actually said."

Hebe leaned back and clasped his hands behind his head. "Any chatter yet on the back-channels?"

"Nothing of note," Picto said. "A couple of snide whispers, anonymous, about the inconvenience of losing two Acolytes in service to a High Shepherd hoping for the ultimate promotion."

Hebe dug into a pocket and retrieved a flat palm-sized parcel, which he handed to Picto. "Bio-samples, including a chip, from the thug sent after Espio. Can you trace them?"

"How fast do you need them?"

"I'll be in contact when I can. A few days."

"What else do you need?"

"Only your discretion."

"Where are we really going?" Espio asked as he stared out at the endless grasslands, which billowed and swayed, creating an illusion of waves in motion on the ocean.

"The Isle of the Nefas."

Espio double checked the digital displays. "But we're heading inland."

"We're taking the fastest and safest route." Hebe said.

Espio fiddled his fingers at the nape of his neck. "Until I saw the recordings, none of this seemed real. When Stark noticed me and assigned me to his team, I naively hoped to get access to files or other evidence."

"Evidence of what?"

"Proof he excommunicated Castian without reason. What did I achieve? Blowing your cover and almost getting myself killed." Espio shook his head. "I failed."

"You watched Stark's performance on the bulletins. What did you notice? Either by commission or omission?"

"Nothing. I don't know."

"You're rattled, that's to be expected. A neighbour noticed your open door and investigated, because such carelessness is out of character. They found your note and alerted the authorities." Hebe sent Espio a sideways glance. "When? What time did your neighbour raise the alarm?"

"Predawn. He was on his way to dawn service at the temple. That's why he looked groggy. He's ultra devout. The rest of my neighbours worship from the privacy of their dens."

"Keep going. Follow that train."

Espio frowned and hunched forward. "I'm sorry, but I don't know what I'm looking for. I saw and heard nothing out of the ordinary."

"Exactly. Nothing appeared out of the ordinary ... or unexpected."

"By the Light! Stark spoke from a prepared speech and had the video clips ready for the investigators. And he appeared wide-awake and wearing his official robes, not just roused from his pod and still fighting the night stupor."

"My guess? He took stimulants, as we did, and he rehearsed his speech and bulletin materials all night. But he forgot two things: old men are bleary and confused at that hour, and even the least emotional person feels shocked by a suicide, especially when the victim is a youngster and in their care."

"His audience will realise his guilt," Espio said. "His culpability is obvious."

"You're trained, and you were looking, but you didn't spot the clues. His audience, especially his ardent supporters, will accept his words without a second thought. They have no desire to challenge his authority, or reason to suspect wrongdoing. Until his malignancy touches their lives, they'll ignore all the warning signs."

Stark solemnly accepted the condolences of his staff; he gripped outstretched hands in a double handed shake, to emphasise his compassion. He begged not to be disturbed, before locking himself in his inner office, to pray for the soul of the unfortunate lamb.

He gleefully reviewed his performance in the bulletins, silently mouthing his well-rehearsed lines. Yes, he appeared dignified and in control, a man destined for greatness. A man to whom you would gladly entrust your temporal welfare and your perpetual soul.

Although his agent's lack of response gave him momentary pause, he reminded himself the man knew his job. Stark's limited experience in such matters forced him to rely on the expertise of others, a situation he tolerated, but resented. He planned to deliver a stern rebuke to the man when he made contact, possibly impose a penance for disobedience.

Investigators flooded the newsfeeds with sound bites from Espio's peers. Each tearful and shocked youngster spoke to the theme: Espio, although pleasant, didn't fit in. He lacked social skills and academic ability. With hindsight, his depression defined him.

Stark smiled grimly. The little lambs may as well have been reading a prepared script.

Beatrice's Bulletins

Beatrice taps an impatient tattoo with her feet. "Can someone please get this door open?" She sighs and refluffs her hair, while one of her crew forces Espio's door. She positions herself in front of the opened door and squares her shoulders.

The production manager signals 'action' with the wave of a hand.

Beatrice turns on a Solra challenging smile, drawing the camera like a pollen laden blossom draws bees. "Hello, my friends. Thank you for allowing me into your dens. If you're anything like me, you're still bewildered by the suicide of the enigmatic Espio."

The camera pulls wide to show the open door.

"Those who knew Espio all say the same thing. He was a struggling underachiever, clearly out of his depth in the Acolyte program. The authorities have granted me access to his grades, and the kindest description would be that he was persistently mediocre, in his academic studies, his physical skills, and his attempts to write poetry."

Beatrice clasped a hand to her bosom.

"What breaks my heart is how this poor young man isolated himself, raising barriers to keep his inadequacies secret from those who could have offered guidance to his troubled soul. He even rebuffed an offer of friendship and support from our beloved High Shepherd Stark, only hours before he took the final, irrevocable step."

Beatrice steps back and gently pushes the door.

"No friends ever crossed this threshold. He firmly shut down all avenues of support. My friends, I beg you. If you are experiencing feelings of inadequacy or loneliness, reach out. Walking into the darkness should not be your first option."

The Assassin

A loyal heart listens to command, but the faithless follow their base instincts, drawn into the snares of doubt and corruption.

The Blessed Prophet Serenus

Pain radiating from the back of his head blinded him and sapped his will to move. He reached with tentative fingers for the source of his agony and swallowed a scream of terror when he discovered the wound. Fragments of bone moved under his fingertips, and an explosion of exquisite pain detonated in his skull. A rank animal odour irritated his nostrils, and dark stains besmirched his clothing. He rubbed the greasy streaks between his fingers. Sabre musk.

The man reached for coherent thought as he fought to piece together the fragments of knowledge dancing on the periphery of consciousness.

Start with here and now, work backwards. With a movement he recognised as habitual, he reached for his missing wristcomm. The shallow indentation proved he normally wore one. He sucked in a breath and held it as long as he could.

A death-defying wound to his skull; a stolen wristcomm; and a natural predator repellent smeared liberally on his clothes. Despite the pain, he pushed himself into a sitting position to survey his location. Tall grasses surrounded him; a faint trampled track led to what he assumed must be a road. He instinctively knew the rough surface at his back was the wrong side of the colony wall.

Unknown assailants had near killed him, robbed him, dumped him outside the colony, but then protected him from marauding predators. Why?

Images skimmed the surface of his mind like dragonflies hunting on a stagnant pond. A fountain in a well-tended garden. Snatches of music from behind a closed door. Had he been attacked while calling on a friend? Who was the friend and were they harmed? He crawled on his hands and knees, shoulder to the wall, searching for another victim. The effort proved too much, and he collapsed into unconsciousness.

High Shepherd Altor stood on the open balcony of the dirigible, enchanted, as always, by the silence of the ship sailing through clear skies. He pulled his quilted robe closer and tucked his folded arms into the sleeves. The insignificant unnamed island between the two Domains hove into view, wide and flat, with high cliffs and no beach access. The perfect isolated meeting place.

High Shepherd Miles' craft raced towards the landing zone, like a newly independent hatchling nabbing the sunniest Benediction spot. The High Shepherds disembarked without ceremony and exchanged subdued greetings.

"Have you heard anything?" Altor asked as he linked arms with Miles, and the two set forth on their meandering walk across the windswept landscape.

Miles shook his head. "Hebe checked in, confirming Stark's surveillance of Espio, then nothing. But Hebe's silence offers comfort. I believe he's whisked the boy away."

"You suspect Stark sent an assassin?"

"He appeared too calm and controlled in the bulletins, especially in the clips of him offering Espio support. An obvious set-up." Miles shook his head. "Stark planned to eliminate the lad. He probably thinks he's succeeded."

"Where will Hebe take him?" Altor asked.

"Hard to say. He has contacts in countless far-flung communities, but I'm guessing he'll avoid the Domains."

"Does he have the resources?"

"Hebe is the most resourceful person I know," Miles said. "He'll keep your asset safe."

The Midwife Trail

The polluted mind forgets its crimes, but the stain of sin endures,
seen and judged by the eyes of the righteous.
                                    The Blessed Prophet Serenus

Hebe guided the car under a wide spreading tree bedecked with lacy foliage and long hanging seed pods. He shut down the engine. "Well, lad, this is as far as we can get in the car. We hoof it from here." He handed Espio a pendant hung on a synthetic thong. "Drop this round your neck; it'll help keep away the wild beasts."

"What is it?"

"A sonic predator repellent. A friend sent it to me."

"Does it work?"

Hebe shrugged. "It's experimental."

"Experimental? I see." Espio slipped the thong over his head. "Feels like I've put my neck in a noose." He peered through the windscreen at the range of steep hills growing from the savannah. "How far?"

"Two days, maybe three." Hebe beckoned Espio to the back of the car. "Take one of these backpacks. They've got everything we need."

Espio shrugged his shoulders through the straps of the backpack while Hebe dragged free a shaggy bundle and flung it over the roof of the vehicle. The camouflage fabric slithered down the sides of the car and clung to the ground with finger sized claws. "In case they send drones."

Hebe set a relentless pace, but Espio was determined to keep up with the old man without complaint. He didn't have breath to spare for idle chit-chat. The higher they climbed, the narrower the path became, forcing Espio to follow in Hebe's footsteps. They paused briefly for Benediction, but neither wanted to dally.

By late afternoon, irregular gusts of wind buffeted the path, and Solra's descent brought a chill. Scraggly thorn bushes clung to the precarious trail, the only plants hardy enough to survive.

"We'll camp overnight. This track is too dangerous in the dark, especially with the rising wind," Hebe said. "There's a cave ahead, usually unoccupied this time of year."

Fat raindrops spattered the trail, darkening the rocks and forming fast-running rivulets through the gravel. Espio sent a silent thank-you to Hebe's foresight and insistence on wearing strong hiking boots.

Hebe dropped his pack to rummage for a laser tool. "Ever use one of these?"

Espio shook his head.

"Thought as much. Wait here while I check we have undisputed occupancy." Hebe disappeared into the lashing rain, only his feet slipping on wet gravel betraying his position.

Espio stared into the gloom and shivered as icy fingers of fear and trickles of frigid rain danced down his back. A clatter of wings made him stumble backwards, and an outraged cawing set him on his rear; only the bulk of his pack stopped him from cracking his head.

Hebe reappeared and pulled him to his feet. "I won't ask," he said. "I scared off a raptor. Hard to tell which species in the dark. She might come back, but she's no threat to us."

Espio and Hebe crawled into the cave, pulling their packs behind them. The roof soared high above their heads and dipped gently towards the rear wall. Hebe's laser showed an assortment of gnawed bones and scattered claws and horns.

"I thought we were the only occupants," Espio whispered.

"We are. They're months old. Nothing to worry about."

"Are you certain?"

Hebe picked up a gnawed remnant and held it out for inspection. "There's nothing edible left; even the bugs have abandoned the scraps. I'll build a fire at the entrance to deter anything slithering in during the storm, then I'll take first watch. Get some sleep. We've a long walk tomorrow."

Espio cleared a patch of floor with his booted feet and wrapped himself in a shiny thermal blanket. When he began snoring, Hebe grinned and swallowed two more stimtabs. He wrapped a blanket around himself and squatted beside the fire. He tuned out the slashing rain and dribbling trickles, as he listened for sounds of intelligent life lurking in the darkness. Pattering of tiny feet over gravel, and stifled shrieks as owls found careless prey, punctuated the night. A distant chuffing warned of a sabre cat hunting lower down the hill.

Hebe fed judiciously small pieces of kindling to the fire, only enough to keep the flames alive through the night. The storm fled ahead of the dawn, leaving a freshly washed world to welcome the arrival of Solra. Even the unlovely thorn bushes wore a temporary glamour of glittering droplets.

"Our path beckons," Hebe said, nudging Espio awake.

"My shift," Espio mumbled.

"You needed the sleep. If we make good time, we'll reach our destination by day's end. Come and greet Solra with me." Hebe chivvied Espio outside to make the ritual morning orison.

"How long before Stark notices you're missing?" Espio asked as he shrugged his backpack in place and adjusted the straps.

"Can't say for sure. Temple maintenance staff are almost invisible, unless there's an urgent job or a complaint. The crews can work unsupervised for a while before anyone notices. There're many layers of well-padded management between us."

"But they'll notice your vehicle is missing. That's why you tried to hide it yesterday." Espio grinned. "Do you think they'll send drones?"

"Officially, my vehicle doesn't exist. There's no record whatsoever, so when they realise that I'm missing, they'll search how far I could travel on foot. But yes, I took an extra precaution because that's good fieldcraft."

"Noted," Espio said. "Stay ahead of the opposing team by being sneakier."

"That's one way of looking at things, but if you treat this as a game, you'll end up dead, real fast."

"My apologies. I meant no disrespect, Herdsman Hebe."

"I know. Working in the field is a far cry from classroom discussions, lad. For what it's worth, you've impressed me. You don't panic and you listen. And you can drop the title when we're alone."

"Will you teach me what you know?"

"No. There isn't time. But we'll see if we can sharpen your skills as we're walking. Look around and tell me what you see and hear, what you feel and smell. Employ all your senses. Take your time."

"I feel stupid. This is a hatchling game."

"Feeling stupid is an excellent start. You recognise you have work to do. So …?"

Espio turned in a slow circle, his arms crossed over his chest. He rubbed his biceps. "I feel cold. Clear skies, sparse vegetation, narrow track. There's nothing to see."

Hebe frowned. "What about the black clouds boiling low on the horizon? A potential storm heading our way. A possible threat, at best an inconvenience." He pointed to a tenacious thorn bush rooted in a barely discernible crack. "You missed the closest and most immediate threat. Look carefully. What can you see?"

Espio shuffled to the edge of the track and knelt to examine the plant. He looked up at Hebe and shrugged. "I don't know. Is this plant poisonous?"

Hebe plucked a snaggle of coarse hairs from a thorn. "A sabre cat passed this way very recently. The hairs are dry. I deduce the cat sheltered from the storm and passed our camp once the rain ceased."

Espio scrambled to his feet and backed away from the ledge. "Is it still around?"

"Listen. What do you hear?"

Espio closed his eyes and stood stone still. He tilted his head, then paused, a slow smile spreading over his face. "A pigeon is cooing in the trees below us, and I'm almost certain there's a herd of small animals grazing the hillside above us. I hear them chewing."

"Goats." Hebe pointed to the sides of the track and piles of scat. "If the goats are placid, it's a good indication the cat has moved on. Not a guarantee, mind. But give yourself permission to dial down from panic to alert."

Espio fingered the sonic repellent hanging around his neck. "How experimental is this? I mean, are we the first test?"

"I'm told it proved useful against shroaks," Hebe said, "but sabre cats possess more sophisticated brains." He led the way, again setting an unforgiving pace.

Espio hustled to keep up with the old man, who moved with the grace and energy of a mountain goat.

"Where did you learn this stuff?" Espio asked. "I can't recall anyone at the Academy offering fieldcraft courses teaching us how to avoid death by sabre cat."

"I grew up in a remote community, which gave me an advantage over my big colony peers. I learned to read my environment as easily as you read a crystal text. Luckily for me, I enjoyed exploring beyond the walls. Before you ask, yes, that could be a metaphor for my career."

"Could I learn to do that? Read the environment?"

"You have acute hearing," Hebe said. "I know you heard Stark asking for you by name because you stiffened. You can learn to pay attention to what you hear and decipher what it might mean; a technique you can use in a natural or built environment."

An uneven row of pink splotches blossomed on Espio's brow. "I'd like to do more than that, though."

"You're attracted to the glamour of what you don't understand," Hebe said, "but improving your observation skills will be useful wherever you are."

"Where do we start?"

"Tell me what you notice about the state of the trail we're following."

Espio looked down at the trail and sideways at the hillside. "The goats must come this way often; there's dried and fresh scat and their hooves keep the grass down." Espio scuffed the ground. "This is dry. Shouldn't there be puddles after last night's storm?"

"Good question. Most of the rain will have soaked into the clay soil. That's what helps keep the meagre grasses alive. If you come back later in the season, you'll find streams on this hillside, feeding into a yet to be spawned river below."

"Would I be correct in guessing that a well-frequented goat track is a magnet for the sabre cats?"

Hebe nodded. "Sabre cats, cave bears, wolves. Prime hunting territory for all of them. Are you worried?"

"They're all bigger and heavier than me, faster, too. And they all have huge fangs and claws. Any reason not to be worried?"

Hebe stopped and dropped his pack. "I'll show you how to use the dart gun. Each shot delivers enough tranquilliser to drop a cave bear within seconds, but an angry bear doesn't need that long to disembowel you."

"So, this is pointless?"

"Of course not," Hebe said with a wink. "You distract them and sacrifice yourself, while I run for my Lightless life."

"Sounds like a workable plan, but I need you to demonstrate the sacrifice part first. Wouldn't want to get that wrong."

Hebe unzipped a compartment on the side of his backpack and removed a palm sized packet. "There's one exactly the same in yours."

Espio found his new toy and gingerly unwrapped it. The white rectangular box looked utterly innocuous. Green and red buttons lay flush to the surface to prevent accidental activation.

"The red button activates a laser light. That shows where your dart will hit. Press the green button to fire. The gun holds five shots."

"Do we have refills?"

Hebe sucked his lip before answering. "There's two full cartridges in your pack, but if you need to reload in the field … you'll be dead."

"Not a game, no referees to stop play. Right." Espio pointed the tranquilliser at a rock, playing the red light over the rough surface. "Looks straightforward. Thanks."

"Just remember, lad, the darts are to tranquillise predators, not sedate your senses." Hebe nodded towards the approaching storm. "We'll skip today's Benediction. I want to get to shelter before the tempest hits."

Espio nodded his agreement and picked up the pace.

Forks of lightning stabbed the ground beneath the grumbling black clouds, sparking small fires on the savannah, which the following deluge extinguished. Rolling thunder crashed against the base of the hillside, trembling the earth with immeasurable force.

"At least the storm will delay any potential searchers," Hebe yelled over the commotion, his words whipped away by wild winds.

The two men staggered, bowed double against the wind, towards the promised shelter. Like a convocation of lost souls condemned to perpetual darkness, the storm raged in pursuit, lashing their cowering forms with vicious, stinging rain. Deafened and blinded, they stumbled into the cave. The air was thick with the rancid odour of rotting bat droppings which carpeted the cave floor, almost to the entrance.

"By the Light," Espio said, wiping his stinging eyes. "This is foul."

Hebe kicked a pile of dried guano. "Think positive: we have the place to ourselves, an endless supply of fuel, and if we stay near the entrance, the stench will be almost bearable."

Espio stared into the early darkness. "The night you rescued me? I've never experienced the fullness of the night before and I wasted the opportunity. Befuddled by what had happened, I paid no attention." He turned to Hebe. "Would you mind if I kept you company tonight? I don't want to miss the magnificence of the storm … and I've heard rumours you can see twinkling lights in the sky. I'd very much like to see for myself."

Hebe rummaged in his pockets for the stimulants. "You're welcome to storm watch with me, I won't deny you that thrill, but I can't promise to show you the stars; not with all this cloud cover. One night, when all is calm, I'll take you star gazing and teach you the names and myths associated with the constellations."

Thunder crashed, stuttering their hearts, the weight of the noise forcing them to their knees. Sheets of bright white lightning turned the world negative, burning a temporary image on their retinas. A spear of lightning shattered a nearby spindly tree, leaving it charred and smouldering.

Espio shuffled back from the entrance, his pale face floating in the shadows.

"We need a fire," Hebe said. He produced a trowel from his pack. "Your choice: dig the fire pit or collect bat droppings?"

"I'll collect the droppings, but only because you saved my life."

"A fair exchange. Look for any blown in leaf litter while you're back there." Hebe wielded the trowel with expert precision, using the excavated dirt to build a windbreak for the campfire.

Torrential rain pounded the earth with unholy fury as the storm raged over them, screaming with unabated ferocity at its unreachable victims.

"Sounds alive," Espio said. "How I imagine shroaks sound."

The tempest fought and clawed its way over the hills, screaming and bawling its impotent savagery, dragging ragged remnants of clouds in its wake.

"We might be able to see the stars now." Hebe beckoned for Espio to follow him outside.

Shredded clouds scudded across the skies, obscuring the constellations; but both Sui stood with their heads tipped back, grateful to inhale the clean ozone of the storm after being trapped in the fetid odour of guano.

A nightmare shape emerged from the wet shadows, darker than the skies and deadlier than the storm. The snarling cave bear rose onto its hind legs and towered over them, fangs glinting from a maimed muzzle, its one remaining eye searching for vengeance.

"Back behind the fire," Hebe shouted.

The bear whirled and swiped a long-clawed paw, tossing Hebe from the trail. Dropping back to all fours, the massive bear turned its attention to Espio, swinging its head as it snuffled to separate his scent from the filthy melange. The beast growled, and the rumble reverberated in Espio's chest. Campfire embers reflected red in the single ursine eye, and the bear pawed ineffectively at the raw wound on its lightning scorched muzzle.

Espio fumbled for the dart gun. The bear bellowed, and Espio dropped the gadget, his trembling fingers no longer under his control. As the beast lumbered forward, Espio kicked the embers, sending a spray of sparks into the bear's already burnt face. Startled by his own courage, Espio stumbled and landed on his back.

Still bellowing and shaking its head, the furious creature slammed a paw over Espio's leg; the razor-sharp claws gouged the meat of his thigh, the scent of fresh blood further stimulating the beast's aggression.

Espio shrank backwards as the bloody muzzle huffed closer. *All life derives from Solra, all life returns to Solra. Blessed Solra, make this quick.*

The bear raised its head, then soundlessly collapsed, trapping Espio under its gaping jaws.

"Can you wriggle free, lad?" Hebe appeared above the bear's shoulder, brandishing the dart gun.

"You were supposed to escape with your Lightless life while I selflessly sacrificed myself." Espio burst into shuddering tears.

The Cave Bear

Beyond the walls of protection, one learns the cost of ignorance,
for nature favours none, and faith alone offers shelter.

The Blessed Prophet Serenus

Hebe clambered over the comatose beast to reach Espio. "On three, shuffle back, lad." He knelt on one knee and put his shoulder against the massive drooling muzzle. "Three." Hebe forced the bear's head to loll sideways and Espio, gasping with pain, crabbed backwards.

"I'm dizzy." Hebe collapsed next to Espio and closed his eyes. "But the effects are wearing off."

"What effects?" Espio asked through clenched teeth.

"The sonic repellent. Once you're within two arms' lengths, you're in the safe zone." Hebe reached to pat the bear's flank. "That's why our friend here moved so slowly. The repellent disoriented him. Didn't do me much good either. But we can tell Felix how it worked. Maybe he can come up with a way to shield the users from the effects."

Espio pushed himself into a sitting position and gently prodded his mauled thigh. "I think I'm going to die before we get to wherever you're taking us."

Hebe hauled himself to kneel over the wound. "You're bleeding heavily, but you're not going to die." He staggered to his backpack and dragged it close to his patient, scattering the contents near the dying fire. "This field dressing works wonders," he said as he tore open a packet. He swabbed the wound with one sheet, immediately numbing the pain, and wrapped a clear membrane around the leg. "Antimicrobial, antiviral, and infused with clotting agents so you don't bleed out. Marvellous stuff. A gift from the Nefans."

Espio flexed his leg. "I'm sure I can walk. Shouldn't we get as far as we can before the beast wakes?"

"We've got hours before dawn, and I'm not risking walking this trail in the dark, especially after a violent storm. Besides, this fella won't wake for at least two days." Hebe examined the bear's muzzle and tore open a second packet.

"What are you doing?"

"Without treatment, the wound will become infected, and the poor fella will be in excruciating pain. If he can't feed, he'll die."

"You're going to treat a bear? A wild beast that attacked and would have killed us?"

Hebe tenderly swabbed the bear's wounds and draped a membrane over its muzzle, then patted it into place. "Is he not part of Solra's creation? He acted according to the nature Solra gave him."

Espio clambered to his feet and took a few tentative steps to test his leg. "I can't decide which is the most unexpected: this rapid healing, or you tending to a bear." He shivered in the predawn chill. "Shall I light another fire?"

"Not worth the effort," Hebe said, as he repacked his backpack.

Espio's jaw dropped when Hebe tossed his duffle next to the bear and leaned his back against the beast's rumbling flank.

Hebe winked. "Shame to waste a perfectly good heat source. Join me. Not only will he protect us against the cold, but his lingering scent will deter other predators when we leave."

Espio nudged his pack closer with the foot of his good leg. "He's snoring," he whispered, eyes wide in a blanched face.

"This is likely the safest spot in the three Domains right now." Hebe reached up and tugged the bear's ear. "Do you think I'm cracked enough to endanger us both?"

"No." Espio sucked in a deep breath and released it slowly. He eased himself down, then tentatively leaned back. The bear's flanks rose and fell with a steady rhythm, and an erratic snore fluttered its lips. "I can hear his heart, the valves opening and closing, and his lifeblood coursing like a storm swollen river."

"Not so different to you and I after all." Hebe pointed at the bear's twitching paws. "He dreams, exactly as we do."

The stars faded and the sun sidled over the horizon without fanfare, and dawn slunk a weak light across savannah and foothills. Pale sunlight crept into the cave entrance, like an uninvited visitor unsure of their welcome. Mist steamed from the damp ground, clinging to sparse trees and thorn bushes, decorating invisible spider webs with glittering baubles.

"We should be on our way," Espio said without stirring.

"Not easy to break the spell when you're communing with nature." Hebe stood and shrugged into his backpack. "Come. We've a ways to go over rough ground."

Espio sighed as he followed suit. "I'll never again spend a night like this. Who'd believe me if I told them?" He limped after Hebe, casting a final look over his shoulder at the slumbering beast.

"Watch your footing," Hebe said. "The rain's damaged parts of the trail and the edge is crumbling."

As the morning wore on, Espio's thigh throbbed with greater intensity. Although clear of infection, he struggled to sustain the pace with mauled muscle. "Any chance of a rest?"

Hebe stopped; his arms wrapped protectively around his chest, and nodded.

"Are you all right? You're unusually pale?" Espio peered into Hebe's eyes. "You're hurt."

"I broke a rib when our friend sent me flying. Now the adrenaline's worn off, the pain's flooding in."

"What can I do? Have you got another marvellous gadget tucked away to fix it?" Espio looked hopefully at the backpack.

"If we can get to the top of this rise, we'll send up a distress flare. If the colony sees it, they'll respond and send a rescue team."

"I can do that. You stay here."

Hebe shook his head. "Not a good idea. We're being stalked. If we split up, we present easier targets. We stay together."

Espio spun around. "What? Where?"

"Porcuxes. Juveniles. One ahead on the downside of the track, two or more behind and above us."

"We can fend them off, right?"

Hebe jerked his chin skywards. "See the cleaning birds gathering overhead? They're betting against us." Hebe pressed a hand to his chest and breathed open-mouthed. "Your dart gun is trapped under the bear, but I still have mine. The sonic repellent is keeping them at a distance, at least for now. The bear's scent is probably confusing them, too. Help me off with this pack."

Espio eased the pack from Hebe's shoulders and dumped his own.

"At the bottom, flare guns." Hebe wrapped his arms around his chest. "Get both, and all the flares. And the thermal blankets."

Espio tipped out both packs and found the items Hebe asked for.

"Leave the packs behind," Hebe said. "A distraction."

Espio ducked under Hebe's shoulder to support him, and half carried, half dragged the old man along the track. The squeals of glee as the porcuxes attacked the packs prompted him to lurch faster. Together, they slipped and skidded to the top of the rise.

"Flap the blankets," Hebe gasped as he launched a flare into the pale sky.

The juvenile porcuxes circled at a distance, snouts raised to scent the air. The young male sported a short pair of sharp tusks, and a ridge of thick black hair sprouted from his muscled back. He snorted a challenge and mock charged, but his sisters held position, their tiny black eyes alert for any sign of weakness before risking an outright attack.

"Yes!" Hebe pointed to the skies. "They've seen us."

Espio risked a skyward glance. An orange streamer hurtled towards the clouds before blossoming like a giant chrysanthemum against the steel grey skies. "How long? Before your friends arrive?"

The aerial pyrotechnics startled the porcuxes, who scampered a short way downhill before turning and snorting their belated defiance. The male trotted back and forth while the females stamped their shiny black hooves.

"They'll have noticed the cleaner birds gathering, so they'll hurry," Hebe said.

"Give me the flare gun." Espio held out one hand while flapping a thermal blanket with the other.

The porcuxes edged closer while Hebe reloaded the gun. "I've got this. I'll fire above their heads."

Espio nodded, keeping his eyes on the porcuxes. The females trotted away from the male in a flanking manoeuvre. "They've split up."

Hebe muttered something Espio suspected to be unholy as he loaded the second gun. "Aim for the larger female on your left," Hebe said, holding out a loaded flare gun. "I'll scare the male. If we can make them run, the smaller female should follow. On three. Three!"

The flares raced over the hillside, trailing red smoke. The blossoms obscured the view, but the diminishing squeals reassured Hebe and Espio that the porcuxes were in rapid and undignified retreat. Hebe reloaded both flare guns. "Just in case," he said.

A steady whomp-whomp-whomp grew louder, and Hebe smiled. "A conchatus," he said as the noise and wind of the flying machine bent them both to the ground. The draft from the conchatus fought to whisk the thermal blanket from Espio's flailing arms. As he struggled to bundle the metallic sheet to his chest, a movement from the corner of his eye snagged his attention.

The smaller female porcux darted from the swirling smoke and dashed at Hebe. Espio opened his mouth to scream a warning, but a spear smashed through the creature's torso, and pinned her to the ground. She died before she could squeal, and before Espio could utter a sound.

The conchatus thumped to an ungainly landing, its rotor blades spinning to a stop. The still silence and the dead carcass shocked Espio, who simply stared.

A man wearing a wide smile and a tattered sky-blue robe dropped to the ground and embraced Hebe with the fervour only engendered by close acquaintance and long absence.

Hebe's friend and rescuer turned his attention to Espio. "Ah, you must be the famed Espio. I am Ami. Welcome to Termitun."

Termitum

To be pursued is the fate of the unrighteous; only the faithful may walk untroubled in the shadow of judgment, protected by the shield of virtue.

The Blessed Prophet Serenus

"You caused quite a stir," Ami said as he guided the conchatus towards a clutch of plant-clad single-storey buildings. "Stark doesn't seem to do too well with his young Acolytes."

"I assure you, I did not seek the attention," Espio said. "Unfortunately, a rather forceful gentleman had other ideas."

"Has Picto been in touch?" Hebe asked.

"He warned me you were en route," Ami said. "I was looking out for your arrival. He has information you'll find interesting." Ami looked at Hebe. "But all that can wait until Doctor Bonna has fixed you up."

"Is that the hospital?" Espio nodded towards the semi-derelict building, a concerned frown creasing his brow.

"That, my friend, is a doorway to everywhere." Ami refused to explain further, and Hebe only winked.

Ami landed the conchatus on a sparsely grassed area. The craft settled and sank flat to the ground with a sigh; the rotors drooping like exhausted bird wings. Espio limped off the craft, brown and red stripes of frustration marking his neck at his elders' wilful prevarication.

Espio's scowl disappeared when Ami led them through the creaking door and into a gleaming space furnished with shining machines that Espio couldn't identify. When his eyes grew wide, Hebe gave him a gentle push. "This way." He guided Espio to a large egg-shaped structure and opened the door, revealing standing room for one. "I'll go first. Follow Ami's instructions." Hebe stepped inside the peculiar device and closed the door. Ami busied himself at a console, then nodded to Espio. "Your turn. Step in, close your eyes. Count backwards from ten."

Espio pulled open the door and looked inside. "Where's Hebe?"

"You'll be fine," Ami said. "Close the door firmly. You might experience a moment of discomfort."

Espio patted the seamless walls, looking for another exit, then shrugged and pulled the door shut. *I'll play along.* A sliver of blinding light raced up and down his body. "Ten, nine—" Reality shattered into shards of black light, which stabbed his brain and tore apart his very being. He crashed backwards onto the door, a soundless scream cascading from his nonexistent mouth. An eternity of agony compressed into a single heartbeat, where everything and nothing existed at once.

The cubicle door opened, and he collapsed onto an immaculately clean floor. Hebe beamed down at him. "Welcome to the Isle of Nefas."

Espio gawped at Hebe and the tall stranger jiggling a hatchling on his hip. "Am I dead?"

The tall man laughed. "Depends who you ask. Stark says you walked into the night. You've made a marvellous recovery. Better get you to Doctor Bonna to get that scratch fixed up, though. Can you walk?"

Espio frowned as he struggled into a sitting position and looked around. "Where's Ami?"

"Sorry, I didn't introduce myself. I'm Felix, this is my foster, Clem, and you're in my workshop on Nefas" He hauled Espio to his feet, who stood with his jaw hanging open. Felix turned to Hebe. "Is he …?" Felix rotated his index finger beside his head.

"Tired and confused? Yes." Hebe said. "Poor lad's had a traumatic few days, and he's in pain. Are you driving us?" Hebe steered Espio through the workshop and into the backseat of a battered car.

Espio blinked at the well-kept buildings and lush gardens. The place bore no resemblance to Ami's ramshackle colony. Espio craned his neck to look out the window, and even the hills looked different. Taller and drier.

A stern-faced woman waited at the medical centre entrance, her arms folded, but she burst into girlish smiles when she spotted Hebe. "What's the damage this time?"

Hebe winced. "Nice to see you, too, Doctor Bonna. A broken rib. Or two. But Espio's leg is more urgent."

Doctor Bonna snapped her fingers, and two orderlies appeared with levi- chairs. "Take them to the treatment room."

Hebe winked at Espio. "You'll be as good as new soon."

Espio risked a nod, not daring to speak and betray his confusion. The orderlies whisked them along bright corridors hung with cheerful pictures, and through double doors into a spacious room crammed with state-of-the-art equipment.

"Espio, isn't it?" Doctor Bonna glanced at his wound. "You'll keep, whereas you …" She turned to Hebe. "Hop onto the table and lie down. Arms by your sides."

Hebe closed his eyes as Doctor Bonna scanned him.

"What did you do? Fall out of a tree? Two fractured ribs, neither presenting a threat to your lungs. Indeed, you're lucky." She pulled a hood over the table and adjusted its position over Hebe's chest. "Don't move." The hood lit up and hummed like a hive of contented bees.

"Doctor?" Hebe whispered. "Be gentle with the lad. I think the events of the last few days have caught up with him all at once."

"I said don't move, that includes talking. Unless you want crooked ribs?"

"He didn't fall out of a tree." Espio clenched his fists in his lap. "Hebe saved my life when he fought off a bear. He could have just saved himself, but he didn't. He came back to save me."

"Can you stand and walk to the other table, young man? I want to see how well you can move."

Espio gritted his teeth and limped to the treatment table. "Can you fix me, like Hebe said? I know I won't really be as good as new, but …"

"Hop up." Doctor Bonna removed the dressing and examined the torn flesh. "A bear you say? Your injury is certainly consistent with a bear attack. I need to irrigate the wound, inject antibiotics and stitch together what I can, leaving you with an ugly scar." She stood up and looked him in the eye. "Or, I can have you as good as new, as Hebe promised, but I'll need to use technology unavailable on the mainland. Do you have any religious objections?"

"I'm not sure I understand the question, Doctor. Why would I object?"

"I had to ask. I'll tranquillise you, so you won't feel a thing. When you wake up, the flesh will have regenerated, but you'll have a gel dressing on the wound."

"Regenerated?"

"We've been doing it successfully for years, but the Mainlanders refused our offer to share the technology, saying such knowledge is an abomination and challenges the supremacy of Solra. Do you want time to think it over?"

"Have you used this technology on Hebe?"

Doctor Bonna smiled. "Too many times to count."

"Then I accept, with grateful thanks, Doctor."

The Nefan Way

The heretic speaks of freedom, but their words are chains, foul utterings to bind others to an eternity of icy darkness.

The Blessed Prophet Serenus

Hebe tapped Espio on the shoulder. "Are you awake, lad?"

Espio opened one bleary eye. "No."

"Doctor Bonna said you'd be waking up around now. How do you feel?"

"Under the circumstances," Espio said, "you'll need to be more specific."

"How's your leg? Are you ready to walk? We can enjoy Benediction in the gardens."

Espio pushed back the covers and swung his legs over the side of his pod. He wriggled his toes. "No pain." He ran his fingers over his thigh. "I expected the gel dressing to be bulkier." He tested his weight on each leg before venturing to the window. "Where are we?"

"I told you, this is the Isle of Nefas. We came through a portal, safer than crossing the sea."

"But the man at the workshop, Felix, and the Doctor … they look … ordinary. Aren't the Nefans misshapen monsters? I thought Nefas was shrouded in perpetual night?"

"The mainland authorities have a vested interest in making you believe the Nefans are fundamentally different to us, but it's not true."

"They must be smarter than us." Espio waved his hand. "All this advanced technology. I can't think about the portal, not yet; my brain can't process the idea of being here one minute and somewhere else the next. But this." He tapped his thigh. "This is a miracle."

Hebe perched on the windowsill. "Scientists here are encouraged to explore possibilities, whether that's a safer and more efficient mode of transport, or a method of rapid healing. There are no overzealous Shepherds to shut down research that they believe inappropriate."

"How can healing be inappropriate?"

"Making a parent give up their hatchling is the ultimate expression of power and authority," Hebe said.

"I'm looking at the thorn-bush and missing the sabre cat tufts, again," Espio said.

"Currently, the Shepherds hold all control. If they allowed certain medical advances, they'd be forced to concede some of their authority to surgeons. They would lose power."

"That's perverted."

Hebe nodded. "Walk with me? There's somebody I'd like you to meet. Come." He led the way into the corridor and paused before an arrangement of small paintings. "Remarkable, aren't they?"

Espio blanched and turned away. "Representations of the Sui form are forbidden. Verboten."

"Why do you think that is?" Hebe studied the paintings. "Whoever painted these hands is gifted. So lifelike, you expect them to move."

Espio stared resolutely out the window.

"Perhaps this is more to your taste?" Hebe wandered down the corridor and planted himself before a life-sized painting of a door opening onto a flower garden. "Look at that tiny hummingbird. Each time I pass, I have to stop and listen for the sound of those jewelled wings."

"This is the proper use of talent," Espio said. "This artist has a sense of decency. There's no need to shock or provoke an audience. Art should be a celebration of Solra and Their creation."

"Art should be comfortable and reassuring?"

Espio nodded.

"Don't ask questions, don't test the boundaries, right?" Hebe shot Espio a sideways look. "Maintain the status quo at all costs?"

"I didn't say that. But testing boundaries doesn't mean creating indecent images."

Hebe grabbed Espio's wrist and held up both their hands. "I see nothing indecent about our hands, nor those incredible studies. What worries me is unthinking acceptance of ridiculous rules designed to stifle independent thought and creativity." He released Espio's wrist. "I can show you an endless stream of tufts. Won't mean anything unless you dare risk thinking for yourself, though. Maybe you got a bit too comfortable in your role of persistent mediocrity?"

Espio rubbed his wrist. "That's unfair."

Hebe sagged against the wall. "Aye, you're right. I apologise. I'm angry with myself. My whole life I've watched and listened, passing intelligence up the line, but nothing's changed, and I fear it's too late for me. But not for you. You can change the world. If you have the courage."

"I snuggled a bear. How much more courage do I need?"

Hebe hauled himself upright. "You have a steadfast soul, lad; the fault is my lack of patience. Come, I want you to meet a friend."

Castian wandered the perimeter of the garden, too agitated to officially accept Solra's benediction, although the light and warmth still energised him. He'd reluctantly agreed to the meeting, but doubts plagued him.

Footsteps crunching on the gravel pathways alerted him to their arrival, and he flushed with relief. Hebe he recognised immediately, but Espio looked only remotely familiar. The Herdsman and the Acolyte approached with outstretched hands to greet him; no flinty reserve about socialising with a condemned heretic.

"Solra's blessings be on you both," Castian said, clasping hands first with Hebe, then Espio. "The news bulletins are proving unreliable."

"The previous few days have been … educational," Espio said. "I am learning to question and re-evaluate all I believed, including the existence of this fabled isle and the character of its inhabitants."

Castian gripped his arm. "You dare to question? You do not fear reprisals? Praise Solra."

Espio shrugged one shoulder. "What can they do to me? Officially, I'm dead."

"My mind is swirling with thoughts I had never dared previously entertain. May I share some of my ideas? Or would that be an imposition?"

Hebe pushed the two Acolytes towards a bench. "I'll leave you to get to know one another. I have urgent business with Felix."

Espio waited until Hebe left before speaking. "We've met once before, but you were unconscious. I helped carry you from the Discipline Chamber back to your den."

Castian slumped. "I still cannot understand why High Shepherd Stark punished me. I wanted to be noticed for my hard work and dedication. Instead, High Shepherd Stark accused me of disobedience, then excommunicated me for heresy."

"If it's any comfort," Espio said, "I never believed you were a heretic."

"Not then, but the thoughts currently flooding my mind are heretical. I've recorded some of my ideas. I'm inclined to think the authorities are more concerned with creating shadows than bringing Light, praise Solra."

Espio nodded. "When Hebe and I arrived, we both bore injuries. The doctor treated Hebe's broken ribs without a qualm, but hesitated to use her gifts to treat my wound. Wanted to know if I had religious reservations." He ran his hand over the gel dressing. "Why would I choose to be crippled? On the mainland, I'd be expected to remove myself beyond the walls, to walk into the night, to not become a burden on the colony, but here I am made whole again. Surely a miracle."

Castian ducked his head. "Doctor Bonna saved my life with her nanotechnology, but I reacted ungraciously. Convinced I needed to perform a penance, I fled to the wilderness." He held up his hand. "I lost two fingers in a foolish accident, but Doctor Bonna reconstructed my hand, as good as new, praise Solra. She probably expected your behaviour to be as misguided as mine."

"May I?" Espio reached to examine Castian's hand. "Which fingers? I can't see a scar."

Castian waggled his two middle fingers. "This procedure forced me to examine my beliefs. The ability to heal must be a gift from Solra; therefore, physical imperfections, either from birth or acquired, cannot be a sign of inner corruption. The Nefans have proved themselves kinder and more compassionate than the Sui, praise Solra."

"Not all Sui are bad," Espio said. "Unless tragedy impacts your life, you have no reason to question traditions. Hebe rescued me, and brought me here via the legendary Midwife Trail. I suspect more people share our opinions but lack the courage to speak out or challenge the Shepherds' authority."

"Then we must reach out, encourage people to ask questions and demand answers, praise Solra."

Espio frowned. "If you want to start a revolution, you need to provide a viable alternative. And not endanger those already doing good work. We are accused of imagined crimes – you were excommunicated and Stark sent an assassin after me. To what lengths would he go to destroy the Midwife Trail or anyone who dared question long held traditions?"

Hebe knocked on the workshop door and entered without waiting for a response. "I have a question." He waggled the sonic repellent pendant before Felix. "Can you make the device stronger? With a shield or protective bubble for the user? The device stopped an enraged bear, an impressive feat, but it also discombobulated me."

Felix tossed and caught the gadget one handed, a tiny frown creasing his forehead. "What sort of range are you thinking?"

"The width of a convention hall, or temple precinct."

Felix dropped the device on his workbench and folded his arms. "Do you want to tell me what you're planning?"

"No. At this stage, I have only the glimmer of an idea. Can you do it?"

"If you can imagine it, I can make it. What's the timeframe?"

"I need multiple units, hundreds, before Election Day."

The Amnesiac

The Blessed Prophet Serenus

High Shepherd Stark thumped his fist on the granite desk. The status and position of his asset remained unknown. A purple flush clung to his temples as he cleared the backlog of unanswered messages. He perused the morning bulletins with a jaundiced eye.

Stories featuring Espio and his sinful suicide had blossomed and died like a hothouse flower left in a draft. Still, Stark trawled the newsfeeds on the off-chance an acquaintance might make a foolish statement.

As he reached to switch off the monitor, a minor story snagged his attention. An unknown male, bearing no identification, lay in the medical centre suffering amnesia, thought to be caused by an accidental blow to the head. Stark read and reread the story, squeezing every possible nuance of information from the sparse words.

Lack of identification set alarm bells clanging. Sui received their identity chips shortly after hatching and updated them at regular intervals. Only a character engaged in nefarious activities would be blank. Sui abhorred violence, hence, the assumption of an accident.

Stark knew better.

The mysterious amnesiac's appearance fit the description of his missing asset too well.

Stark's unscheduled visit to the hospital caused a flurry of uncoordinated activity, which he dismissed with a magnanimous wave of his hand. "A High Shepherd's duties include attending to lost lambs. Has the patient recovered any memories? However insignificant?"

A flock of white-coated staff accompanied him to the unidentified man's room, each vying to provide useful information.

"No, he couldn't recall his name."

"No, he showed no interest in any of the therapeutic activities offered."

"No, he has no discernible accent."

Stark fought his growing exasperation and maintained an expression of mild concern as the flock ushered him into the man's room. "If you could give us some privacy?"

The medical attendants milled outside the door, unable to intrude, but unwilling to disperse and miss an opportunity to impress the High Shepherd.

The man sat up straighter when Stark positioned himself at the foot of the pod, but showed no flicker of recognition.

"Do you know who I am?" Stark allowed his mask of deep blue compassion to fade.

The man jutted his lower lip as he considered his answer. "You've caused an uncommon fuss, so I assume they think you're important." Orange flickered at the man's temples, there and gone in a heartbeat.

Stark flinched at the casual lack of deference. He touched a finger to his own head. "What happened? Did you have an accident?"

"I must have, but I don't remember. Why do you want to know? Are you a physician?"

"I am High Shepherd Stark." His vibrant robes identified his status, and he struggled to keep the impatience from his voice.

The man cocked his head. "Nope, can't say I recognise the name, but I do recognise their desperate eagerness to be acknowledged." He nodded towards the waiting mob. "Would I be correct in thinking you rarely visit the afflicted?"

"Your plight intrigued me. I came to offer spiritual support."

The man leaned back into his pillows. "There is one thing I remember." He closed his eyes. "I see a pod door and I hear music. Not popular music, more refined." The man snapped open his eyes. "I'm worried someone else got hurt, but the medics say I'm the only one."

"I wouldn't worry about that," Stark said. "All my flock are accounted for."

"High Shepherd Stark? You don't strike me as a man accustomed to spending time on trivial matters, or small people. Do you know who I am?"

Stark shook his head. He revived his compassionate, deep blue flush, but his eyes remained icy. "You are a stranger to me."

The man listened to the bleating flock retreat down the corridor, and he shuddered. Stark's parting words were the closing lines of a dreaded ritual. The last thing an excommunicant heard before being banished.

How do I know that? Were the words deliberate or an unhappy coincidence?

Stark returned to his office in stately silence. The man clearly didn't recognise his face or title; not a flicker, but Stark didn't trust the amnesia to last. Physically, the patient appeared in reasonable health, not hitched to any life-support, but the man's insubordinate attitude unnerved Stark. If he regained his memory, could Stark trust him, or would he present a risk? At this vital juncture, all risk ranked as unacceptable and must be eliminated.

The nurse who came to change his dressings simpered and flushed a rosy pink. "You must be important. High Shepherd Stark never visits the sick or afflicted before they're asked to take their final walk into the darkness."

"High Shepherd Stark is most kind. He suggested I spend the night in the temple to aid my mental recovery," the man said. "Could you find me a set of warm clothes? I'll be sure to tell High Shepherd Stark how you helped me."

The nurse giggled. "Because High Shepherd Stark's attention to a patient is unprecedented, we've started calling you Novus." She giggled again. "Do you like it?"

"I'm certain it's better than my previous moniker. High Shepherd Stark also recommended I look through the recent bulletins, to see if anything sparks my memory." Novus smiled at the nurse. "Would you be a darling and fetch me the news crystals?"

The nurse scurried away, and Novus seized the opportunity to snatch a handful of fresh dressings and painkillers from the cart, which he slipped under his pillows. He grabbed a handful of what he hoped were stimulants to see him through the dark hours and added them to his stash.

"I've brought the local and Domains news," the nurse said, when she returned. She proudly placed the reader and assorted crystals next to the pod. "Don't overexert yourself. And you will remember to tell High Shepherd Stark how I helped you?" She wheeled the cart halfway through the door before she turned around. "Why don't I come back at the end of my shift with a wheelchair? I can see you safely to the temple."

Local bulletins revelled in the shocking news of a mediocre Acolyte's unexpected walk into the night. His bland features filled the screens and Novus studied them carefully, searching for the faintest tingle of recognition, but nothing. Novus flicked through each story, each snippet, hoping for a revelation. Only the last piece-to-camera, recorded outside the boy's den, sent a frisson of excitement down his spine. Novus recognised the door, and when he closed his eyes, he recalled the refined music within.

Novus struggled to string together a coherent narrative from the scraps of information he knew. Although he couldn't recall the boy, he'd been at his door at least once. As a friend? Unlikely, since everyone recognised the lad, but nobody recognised Novus. Stark had taken an interest in the youngster, for no apparent reason; and had taken the trouble to visit the medical centre, an unprecedented occurrence. Stark formed a link between a dead Acolyte and an injured amnesiac. But what was the nature of the connection?

You are a stranger to me. The High Shepherd's implied threat hovered like the odour from a rotting carcass, and his lust for power shimmered in his cold eyes. Every instinct warned Novus to flee. One predator recognising another deadlier predator?

Novus ducked his head, avoiding eye contact with each staff member they passed, but the nurse cheerfully greeted them all, pleased to have witnesses to her special mission. Outside the medical centre, the colony's streets were almost empty in the pre-dusk.

"We've all speculated about your past. You don't have the soft hands of a shepherd librarian. Too many callouses for an administrator." She giggled. "Your clothes reeked of sabre cat, so I guessed you might be a hunter, someone who culls the dangerous beasts marauding outside the wall."

Novus shrugged. "Doesn't sound familiar, and I don't think I'm that brave."

The nurse stooped to retrieve a bundle from behind the chair seat. "I rescued these before the orderlies sent them to the incinerator. I thought the odour of your hunting outfit might spark a memory." She placed the tightly wrapped package on his lap.

Novus ran his hands over the bundle, masking his excitement. The contents may or may not trigger his memory, but they offered a layer of protection from what lay beyond the wall.

"You can leave me at the temple gates. I should enter alone."

"Are you planning to meditate all night?"

"Until I succumb to the darkness, yes."

"On the rare occasions we need to monitor patients through the night, we use these." She held out a tiny bottle and a shuttered lamp. "One tablet keeps you awake all night, but combined with the painkillers, you might get a little manic. I fear the dark, so I find the lamp helps. You can have the shutter wide open or showing just a sliver."

Novus tucked the unexpected gifts inside his tunic and stood, arms outstretched, to embrace her. "Thank you, you've done more than I hoped."

Eyes shining, she stepped into his embrace. "You will tell High Shepherd Stark how well I assisted you?"

His fingers found the tender spot on her neck and squeezed. "When they find you, tell them I lied." Novus maintained his grip until satisfied the nurse would not regain consciousness until morning. He wrapped her in a blanket and propped her in the chair, tilting her head to keep her airways clear.

Novus slipped his old clothes over the clean ones, not from any delicate sensibilities, but to protect himself from the chill of the night. He compared the stolen tablets with the bottled gift. The same. He swallowed swallowed one, tipped the rest into the tiny bottle, and experienced an immediate surge of energy. With the blankets rolled and strapped to his back, Novus headed for the colony walls. He allowed his feet to guide him to a small door hidden behind a spiny bush. Muscle memory guided him to the key secreted under a loose rock.

He refused to waste time wondering how he knew this, but couldn't recall his name, instead concentrating on putting as much distance as possible between him and the colony, before daring to light the lamp.

His mind travelled faster than his feet, and he reached an uncomfortable conclusion. *If I know my way in and out of this colony, am I willing to bet my life Stark doesn't know what I know? That he won't anticipate my destination?* Novus jogged to a halt. The tug of familiarity jerked him forward a few more steps, but self-preservation dragged him back. He spun on the spot. Danger lurked behind, and a spurious promise of safety danced ahead. The stimulant racing through his system made coherent thought difficult.

No matter which direction, I won't get far without transport. Don't overthink, choose a direction at random. Without giving himself a chance to second guess, Novus strode into the darkness, towards he knew not what.

The Island Meeting

A divine vision is infallible; the faithful submit, but the unbeliever challenges and earns Solra's everlasting punishment.
The Blessed Prophet Serenus

High Shepherds Altor and Miles waited for High Shepherd Stark at the agreed remote island location. They snugged their long, quilted coats tight against the brisk breeze. Their dirigibles sat side by side like sun basking sea cows while Stark sailed slowly towards them, making no effort to increase his speed.

"He enjoys making a grand entrance," High Shepherd Altor said, squinting at the approaching craft.

"Making us wait inflates his self-esteem. The idiot doesn't realise how rude he appears," High Shepherd Miles said. "The man believes his own publicity; not a sign of wisdom."

The pavilion erected by Altor's and Miles' assistants fluttered and snapped in the breeze, protecting two throne-like chairs from the elements. Only when Stark's assistants brought his seat could the meeting commence. Protocol decreed the High Shepherds must sit simultaneously. None of the trio must ever assume precedence.

Stark's dirigible settled on slightly elevated ground, a short distance from the others. Minutes passed before the waiting High Shepherds spied movement and steps slithered to the rocky ground for the occupants to disembark. Four husky assistants carried Stark's chair into the pavilion, meticulously placing it equidistant between the other two to form an equilateral triangle. Not only scrupulously fair, but a subtle reminder of Solra's rising, zenith, and setting.

While waiting for Stark to appear, Altor nudged Miles. "Is it my imagination, or has Stark got himself a new chair? Taller and fancier?"

"A Grand Master High Shepherd's throne," Miles said. A dark flicker of annoyance flashed at his throat before he suppressed the emotion.

Stark stalked towards the pavilion, gripping the edges of his shimmering robes, like an amateur actor in a travelling troupe. He sneered at his plainly attired peers and headed straight for his throne without any preamble. "May Solra bless you for waiting patiently," he said. "Official business detained me." Stark laid a hand over his heart and briefly closed his eyes.

"You might consider upgrading the engines in your dirigible," Altor said. "You looked to be having difficulty with the headwind."

"A High Shepherd is a slave to his schedule," Miles said as he rearranged his cushions. "Sometimes you must sacrifice austerity for efficiency."

"I have experienced visions," Stark said, ignoring his colleagues' facetious comments. "Solra has spoken to me about the sacrifices I must make for the sake of the flock."

Altor leaned forward. "Solra told you to abandon your ambitions?"

"Solra bathed me in Their holy Light and showed me the glorious future."

"What sacrifices does Solra demand of you?" Miles asked.

"I saw myself on the Grand Master High Shepherd's holy dirigible. Unlike previous Masters, who spent their final years in prayer and meditation, sailing the skies to remain close to Solra, They are calling upon me to bring all Their children closer, to address the moral decline of the flock. My reign shall be eternal."

"You dreamed you won the election? Hardly a surprise for a man of your aspirations," Altor said.

"I did not dream. Solra sent a holy vision. The flock has become complacent, and I am the Shepherd sent to protect them from themselves."

Miles leaned back in his chair. "You asked us here to tell us the election is a foregone conclusion?"

Stark gripped the padded arms of his new chair. "I called you here to give you the opportunity to do Solra's holy work and withdraw from the election.

"Elections are always stressful, especially for the ambitious," Altor said. "You should consider a brief holiday to recharge your batteries."

"You'd think Solra would have sent us the same vision," Miles said.

"Are you refusing to do Solra's bidding?"

"I'm suggesting you are overtired and would benefit from a short break," Altor said. "Risking your health, either physical or emotional, does not serve Solra."

"That would suit your purposes, wouldn't it? To discredit me? To tell everyone I cannot deal with pressure, that I'm weak and unfit to wield authority?" Dark red stained Stark's temples.

Miles stood. "I see no point prolonging this meeting. You will win the election to the position of Grand Master High Shepherd, if it is Solra's wish, but the flock must see due process. They will not accept an arbitrary imposition of authority."

After instructing the captain to move as slowly as possible, Stark mounted to the highest deck. Only in solitude could he allow his fury to surface. Arbitrary imposition of authority. This lack of obedience to Solra's will clearly demonstrated why Solra had chosen him, and not Altor or Miles.

He mused briefly on the fate of the previous Master, who had been incommunicado for the last four years, presumed deceased. Not that he'd offered much guidance to the flock for the first six years of his term. Previous Grand Masters boarded the dirigible, knowing they could never again set foot on land, vowing to dedicate themselves to prayer and meditation for the next decade.

Stark did not intend to die in his decade of service, or follow tradition and cast himself to the shroaks at the end of his term to make way for the next incumbent. He doubted the average Sui could name the current Master, but Stark would pass into history as a reformer, the greatest Grand Master High Shepherd ever known. He intended to strengthen the flock by whatever means necessary and to remove all temptations. His authority would be absolute. This coming election would be the last election.

Such was the Holy Will of Solra.

Altor and Miles watched without speaking until Stark's dirigible sailed out of sight, and beyond the range of listening devices.

"He's finally snapped," Altor said. "He's utterly delusional."

"He's dangerous," Miles said, side-stepping the assistants disassembling the pavilion. "Until today, I didn't care about the election, but if Stark succeeds, I doubt he'll ascend and quietly drift into temporal obscurity."

"Making an occasional pronouncement won't satisfy his lust for power," Altor said. "If he believes Solra is speaking directly to him, he'll do something ridiculous. Claim to be Solra incarnate, nothing is beyond his bloated ego."

Miles folded his arms over his chest. "Solra sustains all life, but I no longer believe They are a sentient entity."

Altor gaped like a stranded fish. "Why did you become a Shepherd?"

"I used to believe, or at least, I didn't question my beliefs as a youngster. The process from believer to doubter took time; but I still believe

Shepherds play an important role. We offer support and encouragement. Faith in Solra provides many with moral structure." Miles grinned. "And we have unlimited access to study."

Altor frowned. "If you're not spiritually committed, will you still challenge Stark for the Mastership? We both know I wouldn't last in isolation. You're our only hope."

"Stark has changed his way of thinking," Miles said. "We must change ours. There is nothing in the scriptures describing the role of Grand Master, only the weight of tradition."

Stark leaned his forehead against one of the dirigible's viewing panels and closed his eyes. Miles and Altor must not be allowed to stand in his way. Removing two Acolytes had caused no ripples, but removing High Shepherds? *Am I ready to take such decisive and irrevocable action, or should I be more cautious? Nonsense! I am the Chosen of Solra. My will is Solra's will. I am the Bringer of Light.*

He returned to his throne and snapped his fingers to summon Captain Pupa, who, along with the rest of the crew, was drawn from his private army: The Revised.

"Change course, Captain. Intercept the craft of The Grand Master High Shepherd."

Captain Pupa nodded. "Sir!"

Stark waited while the airship changed bearings and gathered speed, the slight juddering an anticlimactic indication that his life had also changed course. He smiled to himself, acknowledging Solra's subtle sign that his plans would play out painlessly.

For him.

After tedious hours, the tiny speck grew larger, and what Stark had always fantasised about as a young man now loomed close, his prize finally within his grasp.

Their hails remained unanswered, and no curious faces gazed back. The gigantic quarry sailed on, gloriously blind and deaf to their pursuit. Stark nodded, and the Captain barked the orders. Grappling hooks landed on The Grand Master's ship, clawing vicious gouges. Still, nobody came to investigate.

Stark's smaller vessel shuddered as it bumped alongside its prize, and Captain Pupa extended a covered passage onto the deck of The Grand High Master Shepherd's ship. The Revised lined the pathway, an honour guard ready to defend High Shepherd Stark with their lives.

Unlike Stark's gleaming vessel, dust and debris covered The Grand Master's airship. A dead gull mouldered on the deck and guano stained the hull. The High Shepherd stared down his nose at the unprepossessing surrounds and twitched the hem of his ceremonial robes higher. Emboldened by the lack of confrontation, he stalked down the deck, heading for the state cabin. Revised guards dashed ahead to clear his path.

Stark hesitated outside the open cabin door, giving an opportunity for two Revised to dart through, ready to assail any lurking combatants. They re-emerged stony-faced, but gestured for Stark to enter.

The master suite glowed with walls of gold and crystal windows, a cocoon of opulence. On the sumptuous pod lay The Master, clad in his golden robes of state.

Mummified.

In nearby chairs, swathed in age stiffened robes, sat his equally dead and preserved attendants.

Stark crept forward and gingerly poked the desiccated Grand Master. A cascade of dust tumbled from his garments with a soft sigh. Gritting his teeth, Stark removed the sun disk chain of office from the deceased Grand Master's neck and eased the massive Ring of Radiance from a bony finger. "Toss the corpses to the shroaks. And clean this filth. Make it fit for the new perpetual Grand Master."

Captain Pupa disengaged the sophisticated autopilot and left his lieutenant commander in charge. The two airships flew in convoy and landed outside Luxton, away from prying eyes. Stark wanted his new symbol of authority to sparkle and shine before making his public revelation at the Quarter Day Celebration.

Beatrice's Bulletins

"Three, two …" A raised finger and a wrist flick.

"My friends, thank you for allowing me into your dens." Beatrice gives her trademark wink.

On the screen behind her runs aerial footage of the ongoing transformation of Luxton's parks into temporary stages, booths, and galleries.

"I'm brimming with excitement to see so many cultural opportunities. Luxton is bursting with talent from all over Viribis, and tourists coming to explore our capital colony. Thanks to our most generous patron, High Shepherd Stark, this Quarter Day Celebration will be the largest and most spectacular ever staged. A truly once in a lifetime event."

The aerial view is replaced with a close-up image of High Shepherd Stark.

"Our forecasters assure me even the weather is cooperating, with mild sunny days. Absolutely perfect for showing off your Quarter Day Celebration outfits. I know I'm looking forward to checking out the latest fashions."

The recording light dims and the clatter of people moving around the studio grows.

"You were fabulous, Sweetie." Her manager pats her shoulder as he passes, and Beatrice rolls her eyes.

"Sunshine and hemlines," she mutters. "Not exactly award-winning investigative journalism."

Reclaimed Memories

The Blessed Prophet Serenus

Novus tracked inland, away from where he sensed settlements grew. Cloudless skies offer no refuge from Solra's omniscient gaze, and the pain in his skull flared and dimmed and flared again, a rhythm which dictated his progress. When the agony grew too debilitating, he placed a painkiller under his tongue and lay on the parched grass until he regained the strength to walk. Fine dust caked his face and arms, and rivulets of sweat painted strips of misery down his neck. Cleaner birds cruised the thermals with studied nonchalance and implacable patience.

While he waited, he waded in slick black pools of lost memories, where glittering fragments darted tantalisingly out of reach, luring him deeper. A persistent scrap flitted back and forth, out of range, nudging his memory, nibbling at the edge of recognition. Cold eyes. An opulent office.

Stark.

Novus lurched to his feet and shook his head; the newly roused pain was infinitely preferable to the tattered memories of the High Shepherd. He staggered forward as Solra burst over the horizon, scattering the memories and offering hope of absolution. Novus fell to his knees and stretched out his arms. *Burn away my sins; make me anew.*

Novus welcomed the brassy weight of the sun, heavy on his shoulders, as he trudged forward. The familiar touch warmed his night chilled limbs, and he lengthened his stride. He dragged his elongated shadow behind while contemplating his murky past. As Solra gained dominance in the sky, the shadow shrank. *Solra obliterates my past and offers me a new future.*

As Solra reached its zenith, Novus adopted the traditional pose to accept benediction, and dedicated himself to living in the Light, a prayer he'd lisped as a hatchling. A memory wriggled to the surface, bright and fully formed. Gentle hands steadied his outstretched arms as he leaned back against a parent's leg to receive benediction in an enclosed courtyard. A finger touched his lips as he struggled to articulate the prayer, and the muscles in his parent's legs tensed in fear.

Other hazier memories spun off like tendrils. Angst filled eyes and frowning brows, concerned voices shushing him whenever he spoke. Whispered conversations abruptly ended, but not before hearing of far-flung fosters in isolated colonies.

Defective.

Abominations.

Nefans.

Novus plunked to his knees. Rough hands tore him from the parent's embrace, screams shivered the air until the uniformed stranger backhanded the parent, sending them reeling into shocked silence. Darkness as strangers wrapped him in heavy cloth and tossed him into the cargo hold of a hover car. Small squirming bodies of other stolen hatchlings fighting for space before losing consciousness in the unnatural darkness.

Novus fell forward, face touching the dirt. Betrayed by a sanctimonious neighbour, a fact his soul recognised, but he couldn't prove. Dozens of hatchlings, kept in dormitories, poorly educated, harshly trained, rigorously disciplined. A loveless existence punctuated by infrequent visitations of a lofty personage: Stark.

The memories ended abruptly, and Novus scrabbled in the dirt to uncover more, fingers grasping to make sense of the revelations. Nothing. Blank. Darkness. Novus curled into a foetal ball and sobbed. *Not my fault. Not my fault. Not my fault.*

Solra poured golden grace over the weeping man, soothing the hurt and instilling a new purpose.

Sucking painkillers, Novus plodded across the semi-arid plain towards a range of low, hunkered hills, skirted with pale boulders. As the westering sun cast irregular shadows on the enormous, rounded rocks, the inner masses revealed themselves as unnaturally smooth domes: a clutch of Sui dens within a nest of rough rocks.

Novus hesitated. Arriving unannounced immediately before nightfall and the onset of night stupors could be interpreted as an act of aggression. He opened his lamp and swung the beam in a slow, wide arc to advertise his presence to any watchers, and waited patiently for a response.

Solra slipped silently below the horizon, and the early evening shadows extended their inexorable reach and blanketed the remote colony.

Resigned to another frigid night, Novus slid another stimulant tab under his tongue and scouted the outskirts. No light or sound escaped from the dens. Nonexistent colony walls suggested poverty, but the dens appeared well maintained, with sturdy window bars and reinforced doors to protect the inhabitants from predators.

Packed-dirt trails edged with smooth pebbles meandered between the buildings and converged on a sunken stage area surrounded by tier upon tier of benches. An intricately painted backdrop and side panels glowed with pseudo life in the moonlight. The amphitheatre steps dipped in the centre, worn by frequent use or many generations. Novus smiled, thin-lipped. Could he trade a song or story for transport? He stood centre-stage and struck a dramatic pose but couldn't recall a single line. *I guess I'm not a bard or singer. So much for trading.*

After the splendour of the amphitheatre, the temple's modest size and spare design surprised Novus. A ring of rough stone columns supported a pergola style roof over an altar, above which hung a stylised flaming orb of beaten brass. Dust carpeted the mosaic floor, signalling months of sustained neglect. Novus settled himself on the steps with a blanket draped around him and his back propped against a column. *I wonder if they'll let me clean the temple in exchange for transport?*

The orchestral nightlife played an exploratory riff before launching into a sophisticated symphony for their silent and solitary audience: a light breeze rustled dry leaves, tiny feet pattered, shrieks and snuffles, snaps and grunts, distant chuffs and howls added drama. Stars cartwheeled gracefully across the skies; an owl glided noiselessly under the pergola roof.

Solra burst over the hilltops with the enthusiasm of a brass band, banishing the darkness. Novus stood and stretched, grateful for the morning's munificence. He tipped back his head, washing his face in the golden glow.

"Greetings, Stranger. May Solra's blessings be upon you."

Startled, Novus whirled to locate the source. A young woman, wearing a kaleidoscope of clashing colours, stood in the middle of the path.

"You've spent an uncomfortable night, and your dressing needs changing." She tapped her head. "I am Sana, the Temple Guardian. May I assist?"

"Novus. I have dressings."

Sana smiled. "But you cannot properly apply them by yourself. Come."

Novus grabbed his bundle and followed her to a small building with a wide door. Sana pushed her way inside and led him to a room lined with haphazardly stocked floor to ceiling shelves, and a treatment bed in the centre.

"Sit." Sana prepared a tray with a bowl of sharp smelling liquid, a stack of cloths, an empty bowl, and a pair of scissors and tweezers. "Your dressing is baked on, so I'll have to soak it off. Try to relax. You'll experience a sting at first."

As quick and light as a lizard, Sana snipped the dirty bandage and swabbed the dirt-stiffened remains with the odorous liquid. The promised sting morphed into a cooling sensation, numbing the wound.

"Do you have other bruises or abrasions?"

"No. Only headaches."

Sana redressed the wound and came around to lean against the shelves before Novus. She folded her arms. "Are you experiencing any difficulties with speech or balance? Blurred vision? Any memory issues?"

"I have amnesia."

"At least you know your name."

"One of the nurses in the hospital named me." Novus clamped shut his lips, wary of betraying himself to a stranger, regardless of how harmless or kind she seemed.

"I imagine whoever walloped you is pleased. Can you remember what you did to earn such violence?"

"I had an accident, I don't know."

"Phttt! An accident? Your wound says otherwise. But it's not my business. Where are you headed? This community isn't exactly on a bustling route to anywhere?"

"How can you tell? What does the wound tell you?"

"You're lucky to be alive, and you're trouble. We don't need the danger you bring. I've fixed you up as best I can. You should leave, before the others see you."

"I'm sorry. I meant no harm. Please, what does my wound say? Knowing the cause might help me recover more memories."

Sana turned and emptied the soiled dressings into a bin and poured away the remains of the liquid. "You were hit from above by a sharp-edged object, a single blow. An unlikely position for an accident. Does that help?"

"I can't tell. Maybe pieces of the jigsaw will fall into place, but thank you." Novus took a deep breath. "One more favour? I need transport. Can I clean your temple in exchange for a vehicle of some sort? I have nothing to offer but my labour."

"We don't have spare vehicles," Sana said.

"Then I shall continue afoot. Solra's blessings be upon you." Novus slid off the treatment bed and repacked his meagre bundle of belongings.

"You were wide awake at dawn," Sana said. "Do you have stimulants?"

Novus delved into his bundle and rattled the tablets. He tipped half into his hand and offered her the bottle. "Payment for my treatment?"

Sana examined the contents before placing them on a shelf. "I can't offer you a car or truck, but if your balance is good enough, you are welcome to my hoverboard. Faster than walking, with the additional benefit of not leaving tracks."

A Masterful Performance

The hidden plans of the wicked wither before the righteous, who strike with a justice as swift as it is merciless.

The Blessed Prophet Serenus

Ludion flitted around his team, praising and preening in equal measure, as he collected the updated donor information. He pranced to the front of the room and threw wide his arms. "High Shepherd Stark is delighted with your hard work, my lambs. As a reward, he has generously granted a two-day holiday while he is in conference with the other High Shepherds. Go, recharge your batteries, create wonderful art. Solra's blessings be upon you." Ludion herded the flock from the room, anxious to complete his self-imposed task before his nerves failed. He gathered the data crystals into a basket and squared his shoulders.

Stark's office windows stared blindly as Ludion approached the building. A bored receptionist greeted him without asking for security clearance. She held out her hands for the basket, but Ludion winked.

"This is the final batch. I can file them myself. You stay here and do what you do best: providing the lovely welcoming face to the Grand Master's — whoops, silly me — the High Shepherd Stark's kingdom."

The receptionist giggled and blushed as Ludion pranced his way to the archives.

"Halloo! Anyone home?" After checking he was alone, Ludion locked the door behind him. He pulled the recorder from his voluminous sleeve and darted down the aisles to where the updated files were stored and copied the information, thankful for the speedy cutting-edge technology.

He fell to his knees and scrabbled in the dust under the shelves, before returning breathlessly to the receptionist.

"I'm so clumsy, tripping over my own feet." Ludion waggled his filthy hands. "Ruined my outfit, but that's not important, is it?" He plucked at his trouser legs, drawing the receptionist's attention to a tear on his knee. "A man of my age falling over! How embarrassing! At least I retrieved all the data crystals. No damage there. You won't tell anyone, will you? Most undignified." He made a moue and shook his head.

Ludion limped out of the door; confident his performance explained the extended time he'd spent in the archives. If anyone checked, they'd find evidence he'd rummaged under the dusty shelves to gather the supposed spilled crystals.

He locked his den door and leaned back against the reassuringly solid surface, taking a series of deep breaths to steady his jangled nerves. Ludion booted up his communication system and set his favourite music moderately loud. If anyone called, he'd claim he'd fallen asleep and hadn't heard.

Dropping his frivolous persona, he dived into Stark's accounts. The High Shepherd had collected a fortune in donations over his career. Determination to find the purpose of the immense wealth pushed Ludion past twilight. He wilted as the night stupor defeated his enthusiasm, and he crawled into his pod before he collapsed.

At dawn, Ludion returned to his investigation. At midday, while accepting the Benediction of Solra in his courtyard, he experienced an epiphany.

File name: Revised.

Hardly a file to attract the attention of a casual browser, yet the sheer volume of data demanded scrutiny. Folders within folders. Ludion skimmed through a selection, looking for names or locations, finding only numbers. He sat back and massaged his temples.

One file, devoted to scores, intrigued him. The first column of numbers ran in order; the second featured eight seemingly random digits. Subsequent columns showed scores, ratios, and percentages. Frustratingly, the columns lacked headings. The final column featured another eight-digit number or an X.

Ludion drummed his fingers. *Why X? Why not blank?* He allowed his eyes to roam the columns, seeking patterns. *Why do some eight-digit numbers repeat in small clusters? Why are these numbers returned to?*

Returned? Revisited?

Ludion copied a number at random into his favourite search engine and watched the images blossom on the screen. Each eight-digit number produced the same result.

Map coordinates for isolated colonies. Not one major or influential settlement. An itch tickled the back of his skull. Ludion selected a location and searched birth and death records, praying to the Light his intuition had malfunctioned.

Although imperfect, the birth and death records connected with the data in the stolen files in a way which made his head spin. Ludion pushed away from his desk, reeling at the implications. He held up his hands to confirm the reality of the tremors.

He returned to the computer, selected a number from the first column, and searched the other files. Hits, too numerous to read, trickled down his screen, a veritable deluge of data. He clicked in and out of indecipherable files until he found the ones he hoped were a fevered dream.

The files identified the allegedly culled hatchlings by number, no name. Photographs recorded their physical development. Graphs and charts showed their strengths and weaknesses, their aptitudes and skills.

Traditionally, High Shepherds ran intelligence networks; many assets knew and occasionally collaborated with their counterparts. But this?

Knowing High Shepherds Miles and Altor pooled much of their intelligence, Ludion prepared and sent an encrypted report to both, although technically, he reported to Altor. He begged for exfiltration, saying he would make contact from a safer location. He shut down his communication centre as Solra dipped below the horizon.

Ludion retrieved the emergency satchel from under his pod and reviewed the contents. From the medical kit, he laid out a scalpel, a surgical sewing kit, and stimtabs. His fingers quivered as he wrapped the data crystal in a thin bio-membrane and placed it next to the threaded needles.

He closed his eyes and reached behind his neck. The identity chip popped out on his second attempt. Then he removed his tunic and examined his pectoral muscles and their accompanying layer of fat. Ludion gritted his teeth and firmly inserted the scalpel, slicing a pocket between the muscle and ribs, into which he pushed the slim crystal packet.

Cursing Stark, he sutured the wound with figure-of-eight stitches to prevent a disfiguring ridge. He slid a stimtab under his tongue, and chose to forgo any painkillers, at least until he reached safety.

He slung his satchel over his right shoulder, hugging his left arm to his chest. The dark streets lay deserted, and only the shrieking bats witnessed his hurried departure.

Darkness enveloped the savannah, cloaking the mundane in mystery. Trees revealed themselves against the starry sky, limbs raised in futile attempts to reach the celestial light. Cursing the night, Ludion steered between massive boulders, until one turned baleful bovine eyes upon him, snorted its displeasure and retreated into sweaty slumber.

Ludion held his breath as he eased the car away from the sleepy herd, his nerves jangling like cheap wind-chimes in a fitful breeze. The rolling grasslands formed a silver and black patchwork, tempting him to speed while simultaneously threatening to mangle his vehicle in one of the Stygian patches. Remaining awake allowed him to travel at night, but didn't guarantee his survival. His hand crept to his chest, and as his fingers traced the row of stitches, he reminded himself of the value of his unique cargo.

Whispers of War

To deny the righteous is to invite judgment; no sanctuary shall endure that rejects the Holy Will of Solra.

The Blessed Prophet Serenus

Callida leaned back in her chair, fingers laced over her midriff, as she listened to Hebe's proposition. The audacity of his plan astounded her.

"What do you think?" Hebe stopped pacing and sank into a chair.

"No." She unlaced her fingers and laid her palms flat on the desk. "Providing the technology is one thing, but directly involving the Nefans in your rebellion could lead to outright war. I will not risk my people."

"But without your help, we cannot succeed."

"Our presence would make your success look like a coup. You need to engage Mainlanders, the people most directly affected. You cannot impose such sweeping changes; they must come from within."

"If we don't act, Stark will win the election. He'll impose his perverted will and twisted vision of Solran theocracy on everyone. Don't make the mistake of believing because you're an island, that he'll ignore you."

"You are overestimating our importance. Most Mainlanders believe we're a convenient myth. Stark has nothing to gain by attacking, or even acknowledging, us."

"You're judging High Shepherd Stark by your own standards." Hebe stretched to touch Callida's fingers. "He is driven by a desire to punish the Nefans, merely for existing. He will find a way to annihilate you, and your Mainlander supporters. You have an obvious weak spot – although the authorities pretend Nefas is a myth, you can't afford to assume they believe their own propaganda. Only one midwife has to betray the location of a single portal and Stark will send assets to destroy you."

Callida gripped his hand. "You're overprotective. Even if Stark becomes Grand Master High Shepherd, he won't be all-powerful. He can't conjure an army out of thin air, can he? Even the most gullible Sui wouldn't tolerate a return to violence. The most he can do is rant and sermonise from his fancy airship, and stir up bad feelings. We'll get a flood of hatchlings with imagined imperfections, then people will settle back to normal."

High Shepherd Miles skimmed the files, the creases of his frown deepening with his growing comprehension of the potential horror. He locked his office door before contacting High Shepherd Altor.

Altor's pale face filled the screen; the sickly hue matched his faltering voice. "Solra's blessings be upon us."

"I fear we are heading into darkness, my friend, and Solra's Light isn't strong enough to combat this evil," High Shepherd Miles said.

"I have a conchatus standing by, for when Ludion next makes contact."

Miles waved aside his friend's concern for his asset. "An operation of this magnitude needs privacy and space," he said. "Initially, I thought the base must be an offshore location, but that would present too many logistical issues. Stark must have set up in the Domain of Viribis, isolated from other colonies, and away from any trade routes."

"But what is he planning?"

"Why does anyone create an army? To impose their rule," Miles said.

"Most people already expect him to win the election; he doesn't need an army."

Miles tutted. "Look at the evidence. Stark set this plan in motion at the beginning of his career. I suspect the election is irrelevant. Stark won't be content to be a spiritual figurehead. He's planning a rule of holy tyranny, and not a single tyrant in history allowed challengers. He needs us out of the way. Dead or discredited, preferably both."

"Are you suggesting we flee? Where would we go?"

"We are Shepherds," Miles said through gritted teeth. "We fight the wolves, even when we're hopelessly outnumbered."

Delighted by the results of his piratical detour, Stark swept into his outer office and brushed aside the plethora of calls for his attention as he headed for his inner sanctum. He flapped a hand at Obduro, his personal secretary. "Summon Ludion."

"My Shepherd, that's what I'm trying to tell you." Secretary Obduro bobbed his head, refusing to meet Stark's eyes. "Ludion disappeared days ago. The Celebration Team is distraught, although as far as I can tell, their work is complete."

Stark froze mid-stride. "Have you visited his den? He may have suffered an accident and be lying helpless." He forced a deep, compassionate blue into his cheeks.

"My Shepherd, his den is vacant and his car is missing. He's taken off, telling no one of his plans. No note, nothing."

"Track him."

The secretary bobbed again. "My Shepherd, we can't. We found the smashed remains of his identity chip in his den."

"Then track his car?"

"We tried, My Shepherd. The tracker is either malfunctioning, or disabled."

Stark tucked his trembling hands into his sleeves. Streaks of furious puce marbled his face. "Do you at least know his final movements in the colony? Where he went? With whom he conversed? Are you at least that competent?"

"My Shepherd, the last person to see Ludion, was the library receptionist, when he delivered the last batch of updated crystals."

"I need those crystals," Stark said. "Bring them, and the wretched receptionist, to my office. I need a copy of every communication to or from Ludion for the last week." Stark's voice rose. "I will not tolerate dissent. Those who malign me shall feel the Holy Wrath of Solra!"

Secretary Obduro scurried away, leaving Stark to contemplate plausible reasons for the disappearance of the middle-management officer. Removing his personal and transport chips suggested dark motives and forethought, neither of which Stark had ever suspected of the flamboyant team leader.

A timid tap on his door announced the arrival of the flustered receptionist.

"Come in, my dear. Take a seat."

With eyes firmly on the highly polished floor, the receptionist laced and unlaced her fingers, while a deep pink flush rose inexorably up her neck. "My Shepherd? You wanted to see me?"

"I'm told you were the last person to see Ludion. How did he seem?"

"My Shepherd, Team Leader Ludion appeared in excellent spirits, excited about the upcoming election." She risked a quick glance at Stark. "He even referred to you as the Grand Master, before correcting himself."

"I see." Stark steepled his hands. "So, he seemed ... upbeat?"

"He asked me not to tell anyone, but I'm sure I can tell you. He fell and hurt his leg when he took the data crystals for filing. Ruined his suit, too. I watched him limp out of the door, poor man."

Stark narrowed his eyes. "How long did he spend in the archives?"

"My Shepherd, not long. Well, a bit longer than usual, because he had to scrabble on the floor collecting the spilled files, but he assured me he'd got them all, My Shepherd. Team Leader Ludion is most meticulous, My Shepherd."

Either she's extraordinarily gullible, or an astoundingly talented actress. "What do you do? As a creative outlet?"

"I'm a glass worker, My Shepherd. May I send you an example? Something inspirational to hang in your window?" She beamed with the naïveté of a new hatchling basking in sunlight.

"Thank you. You've been most helpful." Stark ushered the confused girl into the outer office, firmly closing the door on her questions about where to deliver her art.

He pressed the buzzer to summon his secretary, who wheeled in a trolley laden with trays of data crystals. Stark dismissed him and locked the interoffice door, then laid out the array of trays. Amongst the Celebration Team's updated crystals, hidden in plain sight, lay his birth record file and The Revised file.

Stark sagged against the desk; his knees too weak to support his weight.

The Coup

*The weak may tremble, but the righteous rise; those who defy the
ordained shall reap the whirlwind of their rebellion.*

The Blessed Prophet Serenus

Stark sank into his chair and rested his head in his hands. Ludion's treachery provided the impetus to set plans in motion earlier than anticipated. Solra's nudge to action reassured him. Solra had not promised being The Bringer of Light would be easy, but, They had selected Stark above all others, and he would not disappoint. Like Solra, he would rise.

The coded messages reached their targets, activating long embedded commands. Both teams assembled as night fell, after the High Shepherds and their households succumbed to the night stupor. Armed with skeleton keys and countless hours of assiduous training, the stim-fuelled squads entered the dens, shackled the helpless High Shepherds, and whisked them away.

Tossed into the rear compartments of fast levi-cars, Miles and Altor remained unconscious and vulnerable to whatever indignities the squads imposed. Both cars travelled without incident to remote locations, where Revised personnel dumped the High Shepherds into the cargo holds of midnight black conchatuses and delivered them to The Revised Training Camp.

A stony-faced man wearing an elaborately braided uniform directed the squads to carry the High Shepherds to a shared underground cell. Satisfied the prisoners were physically unharmed by their nocturnal ordeal, he sent his report to High Shepherd Stark.

News crews flocked and twittered, jostling for the most advantageous positions. Stark let them wait. Every word they uttered, every look they exchanged, he recorded and filed for future dissection.

High Shepherd Stark entered the conference room at a stately pace and gripped the sides of the podium. His gorgeous robes of state glittered under the intense media lights. He surveyed his audience, making eye-contact with each individual.

"I come to you in a state of humility," he said. "I am blessed with visions from the Mighty Solra. When I shared this revelation with my fellow High Shepherds, they fell to their knees and begged me to immediately assume the role of Grand Master High Shepherd." Stark clasped a hand over his heart, as a tide of urgent whispers swept the audience.

"Solra touched the souls of High Shepherds Miles and Altor, who have retreated into isolation to meditate and pray. They refuse to participate in the planned election, secure in their knowledge Solra has chosen Their permanent divine representative." Stark closed his eyes and bowed his head.

"Not since The Blessed Prophet Serenus has Solra communicated directly with the faithful, and the responsibility weighs heavily upon me. However, under direction from Solra, and with the support of my esteemed colleagues, I will humbly assume the Grand Mastership on the

Quarter Day." Stark allowed Secretary Obduro to escort him away as the conference exploded in a tumult of shouted questions.

Beatrice's Bulletins

Beatrice composes her face and suppresses her pulses of shocked puce. A most unbecoming colour. She fluffs her hair and fixes in place her most dazzling smile.

Three, two … a hand gesture signals she is now live.

"Thank you for allowing me into your dens on this most auspicious day. I told you Grand Master Stark was the favourite candidate, but even I, an ardent supporter, didn't dare dream he would be confirmed by Solra Themselves." She offers her trademark wink.

"The celebrations will take on even greater significance. Never before has Holy Solra directly chosen the Grand High Master Shepherd. High Shepherd Stark will not only become our new Grand High Master Shepherd, but will join ranks with the Blessed Prophet Serenus. Prepare yourselves for a once in a lifetime event."

Stark studied every bulletin and scoured every snippet of news, delighted to see the reporters compare him to the Blessed Prophet Serenus. "Blessed Prophet Stark." He rolled the phrase around in his mouth, enjoying the shape of the words and the frisson of anticipation they brought. He would outshine Serenus, and he would create a legacy such as the Sui had never seen before.

His supporters flooded his office with messages of congratulations. At his swamped secretary's suggestion, he hired a crew of Acolytes to respond to all his well-wishers.

Miles surfaced from the murky darkness and floundered, unable to reach the light. The night stupor retreated, but he felt the weight of physical shackles. Nearby, ragged breathing warned he was not alone. He pushed back the thin, scratchy blanket and swung his legs to the ground. Shackled, but with enough chain between the cuffs to allow him to walk.

Following the snores, Miles shuffled to the other pod and shook the man awake. "Altor? Is it you?"

Altor snorted and muttered, tugging at his meagre blanket. "Where …?"

"Shush, don't speak," Miles whispered in his ear. "I assume we're in Stark's custody. He hasn't killed us, which means he has a use for us. And we're underground. This must be the RTC."

Altor rattled his restraints as he struggled to sit up. "Why are we whispering? It's only the two of us."

Miles shook his head in the dark. "For security reasons, keeping us apart makes more sense. But what could be more natural than two prisoners talking? If I ran this place, I'd have microphones and infrared cameras monitoring our every word and movement."

"Very good, High Shepherd Miles. A Sui of your intelligence should join us. We would welcome your talents." The disembodied voice filled the small cell. A sun-globe slowly brightened. "We will reward your cooperation."

"And if we choose not to cooperate?" Miles asked.

The globe extinguished, and an ominous silence followed.

Hebe closed Callida's office door. "No point starting a panic," he said.

Prudence replayed the compilation of news bulletins intercepted from the mainland.

Felix shrugged. "I don't see what we can do. Stark has staged a successful coup and seized control of the three Domains." He looked around the group. "I say we hunker down and mind our own business. This is how we Nefans survive."

Hebe stood and leaned his fists on the desk. "Like it or not, this is your business. Stark will come for the Nefans. He'll wipe you out unless you disable him."

"The Grand Mastership is a matter for the Domains," Callida said, gesturing for Hebe to resume his seat. "The Grand Master has no authority over us, and we have no licence to interfere with the legal or spiritual governance of the Domains."

"Maybe it's because I'm not a believer," Prudence said, as she twisted a strand of hair, "but I'm shocked Shepherds Miles and Altor accepted Stark's word."

"Stark is lying," Hebe said. "Neither High Shepherds Miles nor Altor would step away. I suspect he's had them killed. If they genuinely supported his claim, they'd be with him on the bulletins, exhorting the faithful to rally behind the only candidate."

"You're letting your imagination run away with you," Callida said. "You have no evidence for such an inflammatory statement."

"I have all the evidence I need," Hebe said. "Experience. I know the High Shepherds, and they'd never retreat into isolation to meditate and allow that megalomaniac to seize control."

Castian held up his repaired hand to the sun and flexed each finger. "I'm ashamed of my initial response to the care I received. Make no mistake, the medical team truly cared for me, they didn't just treat my injuries, praise Solra."

Espio ran his fingers over his thigh. "I don't dispute that. Dr Bonna did an excellent job on my leg. I don't even have a scar. But, your art makes me … uncomfortable."

"Don't you see? If we don't study the Sui form, how can we learn to repair injuries? Ask yourself, is there something inherently wrong with the art, or do your uncomfortable feelings grow out of what we've all been taught? Why is a perfectly rendered image of a bird acceptable, but a charcoal study of a Sui hand anathema?"

Espio shrugged. "I'm being a hypocrite. I had no problem with the nanobot treatment because I saw the personal benefit."

"Solra didn't strike us down for breaking the rules," Castian said. "Maybe the rules are Sui-made."

Hebe plonked himself onto a sun warmed bench opposite the Acolytes. "Whether or not the rules come from Solra, I believe they're going to be more strongly enforced than ever before. Stark has seized power. The news is on every bulletin."

Espio leaned forward, elbows on his knees. "Stark was almost guaranteed to win the election. Why would he usurp authority? High Shepherds Miles and Altor will challenge him."

Hebe shook his head. "Not if they're dead."

"If?" Espio asked. "What do you know?"

"Stark is claiming Solra speaks directly to him, and the High Shepherds have gone into seclusion, to meditate."

"This a thorn bush with sabre cat fur, isn't it?" Espio asked.

Castian blinked at him.

"What am I not seeing?" Espio muttered. "Fact: Stark has taken power. Fact: the other High Shepherds are conspicuous by their absence."

Hebe nodded encouragement. "What can you deduce?"

"Stark is delusional? And dangerous," Espio said. "If the High Shepherds believed him, they'd stand beside him, offering their support. Why would they meditate? That implies there is an issue which requires great consideration."

"Solra hasn't communicated directly since the Blessed Prophet Serenus," Castian said. "This should be a time of glorious celebration. Although, as the emissary Prudence pointed out, we only have the Holy Prophet's word."

"Do you trust Stark's word? Knowing he excommunicated you and tried to assassinate Espio?" Hebe asked.

"So we are assuming Stark is lying, and has murdered the High Shepherds?" Espio asked.

"Stark wouldn't be so confident if Miles and Altor could challenge him. They must be dead."

"What can we do?" Espio asked.

"We must mount the challenge in their stead," Castian said, eyes shining. "This is why Solra twice sent Their emissary to save me, praise Solra."

Prudence joggled baby Clem on her knee while her brother tinkered with his gadgets. "Stark is as crazy as a porcux in heat, or he's a flat out liar. Either way, he's dangerous. We can't sit by and do nothing."

"What, exactly, do you think we should do? Transport ourselves to some decrepit mainland colony and hitch a lift to Luxton? Knock on Stark's door and ask him to play nicely with the other children?" Felix shook his head. "This isn't our problem, and it's not our job to fix it. For all we know, Stark as Grand Master is precisely what the Mainlanders want. Maybe they don't care how he came to power. Have you heard any rebellious chatter?"

"No. His supporters are organising celebrations," Prudence said, "but that doesn't mean everyone agrees."

"Your prejudices are working overtime," Felix said. "You don't agree, so can't imagine anyone else thinking differently."

"Stark and his supporters would eliminate us with as much remorse as you swat a stinging fly. Look at baby Clem. They sent him to be culled. Don't you care?"

Felix carefully replaced his tools in their correct places before responding. "You, and now Clem, are my world. Keeping you both safe is the only thing I care about. Mainlanders want nothing to do with us Nefans.

We should keep out of their way. Let them destroy themselves if that is their fate, but we protect ourselves, as we always have, by staying out of their business."

Flight

*A heretic caught is a mercy, for the cancer of their corruption can
be excised from the body of the community.*

The Blessed Prophet Serenus

Ludion drove slowly through the swaying grasses to avoid startling into frantic flight the grazing herbivores, and to lessen the jolting of his throbbing pectoral muscle. He shook his wristcomm, but the primitive action failed to provoke a response from the sophisticated technology. His message to High Shepherd Altor remained unanswered.

A growing agitation gnawed at his innards.

High Shepherd Altor always acknowledged messages. Altor's silence screamed a warning louder than any alarm bell. Ludion unclipped the wristcomm, lowered the car window, and flung the gadget into the sea of grass. Choosing a random direction, he increased speed, jouncing over the uneven ground, teeth gritted against the searing chest pain.

He'd committed a rookie mistake. His message to Altor gave his approximate position and his direction of travel.

Tears blurred his vision, and he didn't notice the tiny black aerial specks zooming towards him.

A susurration of worried whispers ebbed and flowed as the amphitheatre filled with solemn faced Nefans.

"You only speak if asked a direct question, and you answer with verifiable facts, not fanciful opinions. Understand?" Callida glared at the Mainlanders. "If in doubt, refer to me." She led them to a long table on the stage, where Felix and Prudence were testing the communication system. Felix nodded and handed Callida the remote control.

The audience shuffled into attentive silence.

"Some of you may have already heard High Shepherd Stark has staged a coup and declared himself Grand Master," Callida said.

A swirl of sighs rose and subsided over the audience.

"A Grand Master has no authority here and his actions should not concern us. However, there is speculation, and I must stress it is only speculation, that Stark has violent intentions towards the Nefans."

Hebe half rose, but Felix pulled him down. Callida shot the Herdsman a warning look before continuing.

"We know Stark is untrustworthy. He falsely accused Castian of heresy and cast him adrift to die. He sent an unknown assailant to murder Espio and frame the death as suicide. We have been unable to discover his reasons, but we assume such extraordinary actions are motivated by fear."

Callida stepped aside and pointed the remote. "These are recordings of the news bulletins when Stark made his announcement. Please watch carefully. I will make copies available to anyone who would like to review them later."

The Nefans watched the bulletins with the concentration of matriculating students. Flushes of anger, fear, disgust, and confusion flashed over their faces, but they maintained their calm.

"As your leader, I make decisions for which I assume full responsibility." Callida looked out over her people. "This time, I am seeking your guidance. My initial response to this news was to lie low and let the Mainlanders deal with the problem. If it is a problem. I still believe Stark offers no threat to us, but our Mainlander friends strenuously object. They believe, based on their knowledge of his character and his escalating behaviour, Stark will target us Nefans for destruction."

"… can't touch us, we're an island …"

"… protected by shroaks."

"The Sui are resolutely nonaggressive …"

"… boards his dirigible, we'll not hear from him again."

"… the support of most of the Mainlanders."

Words spouted and frothed; voices cascaded over one another in torrents of confusion.

Callida patted the air for quiet. "Herdsman Hebe and the Acolytes want to launch a rebellion from our island. I have refused. I have no desire to start a war. But—" Callida raised her hands. "But what if I am wrong? What if Stark brings conflict to us? The community must make this decision, for we are all involved."

Murmurs of apprehension rippled through the audience.

"Do we mind our own business and continue to rescue those who come our way? Or do we take a proactive approach and meddle in the business of the Domains, bringing attention to ourselves? We will reassemble in three days' time to cast our votes."

The flock of matt black conchatuses whomped closer, their thwump-thwump and swirling drafts startling the herds into graceful action. Ludion slumped over the wheel. His car couldn't outrun them. He was dizzy with pain, lost, and hopelessly outnumbered.

Helmeted figures wearing beetle black body armour swarmed out of the flying craft and surrounded his vehicle. Ludion didn't recognise the instruments they pointed at him, but he understood the threat and stepped out of the car, arms raised above his head.

The man carrying a parade stick and sporting a massively peaked hat appeared disappointed by his easy compliance, but he compromised by jabbing Ludion in the shoulder with his pompous baton. "Move!"

Ludion couldn't suppress his yelp of pain, and tried to hide it with a cough, but the officer noticed, his eyes slitting in predatory interest as Ludion lurched towards the fleet of conchatuses. Without taking his gaze off Ludion, the officer ordered the car to be loaded into the cargo bay of another craft.

"You are injured, no?" The officer leaned in, like a hound sniffing prey.

Ludion looked away, but the officer grabbed his jaw and twisted his face upwards.

"Choosing defiance over cooperation will not go well for you. Help me, and I will help you, yes?"

Ludion jerked his head away and closed his eyes. Eventually, he would submit. He couldn't withstand physical torture for long; nobody could. But right now? He turned back to his captor and looked him dead in the eye. "Your mother must have mated with a mutant skaxnat to produce a creature as putrid as you."

The vicious blow to the side of his head came so swiftly he failed to see it coming.

Ludion woke shivering in a lightless cell. His captors had deliberately dumped him on the cold floor, when they could as easily have dropped him in the pod. He rolled to a sitting position and hugged himself. His captors had stripped him of his clothes, the first stage in the ritual humiliation of torture. A naked victim is a vulnerable victim. *What's the next step? Of course, offer a small kindness or act of decency and make the victim grateful for your mercy.*

His stitches remained in place, although one of his new friends had torn away the dressing, and a lump the size of a hatchling's fist throbbed above his ear. Ludion risked putting forth a faint light to scan the featureless room. Not a speck of dust, not a scratch on the wall to indicate previous occupancy.

Ludion increased his light output, and fingertip searched his cell. He traced a door without a handle but with what felt like a window or viewing panel, a handspan wide.

Lightheaded with pain, he perched on the edge of the coverless pod. *Why keep me alive? Because I have more value alive than dead, at least for now.* Ludion laced his fingers together to stop himself from touching his chest wound. *Always assume your captor is watching and analysing your movements.*

Fierce blades of sunlight pierced the warehouse skylights, spotlighting a junior officer meticulously ripping apart the seams of the prisoner's clothes, and examining them for hidden data chips. Although he dissected the boots with surgical precision, they revealed nothing more exciting than their owner regularly oiled them, and had been light on his feet.

The officer bundled up the shreds and sent them to his superior. He sighed and turned his attention to the car and its assorted contents. Today promised to be a long day.

The braided officer poked his stick at the remnants of clothing arrayed across his desk. From the intercepted messages, they knew Ludion had stolen data and passed intelligence to High Shepherds Miles and Altor. What they didn't know was exactly which files, or if copies existed.

The officer's fist clenched around his baton, knuckles white. He would teach prisoner Ludion to show respect.

On the way, he collected a thin sheet. His boot heels clicked with a staccato authority as he marched to the cells. He flicked the exterior switch, filling the cell with a blazing white light. The officer slid open the viewing panel, subtly reminding the prisoner of his utter lack of autonomy. The prisoner's lack of response irked the braided officer, who took a deep calming breath before entering the cell. His first genuine encounter with a mere civilian.

"You must be cold, no?" The officer tossed the folded sheet onto the pod beside Ludion, who ignored the speaker and the sheet. Unclaimed, the sheet slithered to the floor.

Ludion stared at the wall and waited.

The officer smacked his baton into his cupped palm and beat a tattoo of frustration. "You may address me as Officer Auxilium, yes?" He moved directly into Ludion's line of sight.

Ludion shifted his gaze a fraction sideways.

Auxilium tapped his stick against his booted calf, then jabbed the prisoner's chest.

Ludion flushed a sickly green. He locked eyes with the twitchy officer. "I shall address you as Filius Skaxnat."

"I could beat you to a pulp."

Ludion shrugged. "But you won't. You need something from me, Filius Skaxnat, so you'll keep me alive. For now."

Officer Auxilium stabbed his cane once more into Ludion's shoulder. "But, my friend, you'll wish yourself dead." He snatched the fallen sheet and stalked out of the cell, snapping off the light as he slammed the door.

Shortly after Officer Auxilium left, the humidity rose, and the temperature plummeted. Ludion huddled into a ball as a film of ice crusted his naked skin. The frigid chill numbed his pain but made coherent thought impossible. He mumbled half-forgotten hatchling prayers and hoped not to wake.

Shock Tactics

The High Shepherd's assistants stared through the windows in silent consternation as massive tracked vehicles rumbled towards their offices, ignoring the paved pathways and carving new roads across the gardens.

Silent squads of hard-shelled Revised personnel swarmed the offices and herded the flocks of support staff outside and into the bellies of the juggernauts.

"Orders from Grand Master Stark." An unidentified officer brandished a crystal. "His Holiness is taking control. Your services are no longer required."

"There are protocols. This isn't how we do things." A middle-aged woman pushed her way forward. "We know nothing about this. I must receive clarification from High Shepherd Miles. This is most unexpected."

"I represent His Holiness. My authority is unassailable."

"But—"

The laser weapon, unseen for millennia, burned a bloodless hole in the woman's throat. She crumpled to the ground, dead before she knew she'd been shot.

"Does anyone else require clarification? No? Good. Remove your wristcomms and pass them to the nearest Revised." The anonymous officer gestured with his gun to the armoured personnel moving among the prisoners.

A similar scene played out at High Shepherd Altor's office where an elderly man protested, and the officer made an example of him. The juggernauts swallowed the prisoners and rolled unopposed out of the capitals of Animo and Honoris, leaving behind teams of armed technicians who immediately mined the computers and libraries for information.

Stark scanned the reports from his Revised Officers, dismissing the deaths of the inconsequential protesters. They had anticipated their fate by mere hours. Doubtless, their peers now rested in mass graves away from the colonies. His fingers clenched as his dream of absolute control over the three Domains became reality.

Next.

The Isle of Nefas.

An Unexpected Guest

The wayward shall return, though their minds may be shattered;
the righteous remember what sinners would forget.

The Blessed Prophet Serenus

Felix frowned and rechecked the data. Prudence leaned over his shoulder and tapped the screen.

"I thought that colony was long abandoned," she said.

"Someone, or something, has tripped the sensors. A creature with the dexterity to open doors."

"You don't think Stark could have his people checking out the portals, like Hebe suggested?"

Felix shrugged as he sent and received the test flower. "I doubt it, but I have to look, in case it's a midwife. Still works." He unlocked a drawer and removed two tasers. "You remember how to use this?"

Prudence nodded.

"Anyone who isn't me? Zap them centre mass, full power. Don't try to be clever."

Taser in hand, Felix stepped inside the portal. His world fractured into needles of light as the device tore him apart and reassembled him. He shoved open the door and stumbled into a musty cavern.

The Sui male lying on the floor moaned and twitched, but seemed unaware of Felix's presence. Felix nudged him, none too gently, with a booted foot. He loosely aimed the taser at the injured man while he searched for a hatchling. The only item of interest Felix found was a decades old classic hoverboard.

Felix grabbed the semiconscious man by his collar and hauled him into the portal. Prudence yanked open the door, and the man toppled out and lay in a crumpled heap at her feet. She slammed shut the portal door, keeping her taser aimed at the stranger. Seconds later, weapon drawn, Felix jumped from the cubicle.

"No hatchling?"

"No, just this fella. Looks like he lost a fight," Felix said, still aiming the taser. "Why didn't you zap him?"

"He doesn't look much of a threat." Prudence shrugged. "Thought I'd give him a few seconds."

Felix wrapped the stranger in a thermal blanket and hoisted him over his shoulder. "You drive. Dr Bonna can give him a once over."

Prudence snatched the keys and sent a brief message to the medical centre. She strapped Clem into his sling and bound him to her chest. Prudence drove with one eye on the road and the other on her brother in the backseat with the unconscious stranger. A nurse and two burly orderlies met the car with a stretcher and took immediate charge. The nurse shooed the siblings into a waiting room. Prudence immediately unslung Clem and handed the hatchling to her brother.

Felix paced up and down, Clem clinging to his chest. "I should have left him there. We don't need the kind of trouble he'll bring.'

"You don't know he's trouble. And we can't ignore someone, anyone, who needs our help."

"Of course he's trouble. He's filthy and wounded, and obviously on the run from something."

Before Prudence could respond, Dr Bonna bustled into the room. "We've cleaned him up and dressed his wounds."

"How is he, Doctor?" Prudence asked.

Dr Bonna tutted and frowned. "He'll be fine once we flush his system. High on a cocktail of painkillers and stimtabs."

"How soon before he can talk?" Prudence asked.

"Come back after Benediction, but I doubt you'll get any sense out of him," Doctor Bonna said. "He didn't hurt his head falling off his board; someone attacked him. His identity chip has been removed, too. Indeed, whoever he is, he's trouble."

Novus lay as still as a stone, while his mind raced to piece together fragile fragments before they fluttered away. Half buried under the debris of recent shattered memories lurked a secret, dark and threatening. Intrigued, Novus scraped away recent layers of deceptions, searching for the contours of the puzzle.

Shapes shifted and swirled, blocks and lines entangled, defying comprehension. He opened his eyes and peered around the unfamiliar room. Tubes carried fluids into and out of his body, while beeping machines measured and recorded his physical functions, finding order in chaos.

Order.

Discipline.

Classrooms and cells.

Barracks and training grounds.

The snarls and knots smoothed out into straight lines, revealing a detailed multidimensional map. Novus didn't know where, but he knew what.

Doctor Bonna remotely monitored her patient's brain activity. Like meticulously choreographed fireworks, his brain fired in rapid synchronicity. She wanted to witness first-hand his return to consciousness.

As she jogged down the corridor, she slapped the buzzer to summon assistance. Although unarmed, wounded, and barely conscious, her patient exuded danger. She intended to take no chances.

She gestured for the two orderlies to remain outside the door. No point needlessly antagonising the patient. Doctor Bonna slipped inside and automatically checked the array of monitors, nodding her head with satisfaction. "How are you feeling?"

Her patient wriggled into a sitting position. "Terrific. I don't know what you're pumping into me, but I feel great." He raised a hand to his head wound and smiled. "No pain. I thank you, Doctor …?"

She maintained a distance from the pod. "Doctor Bonna. And you are?"

A flush of confusion flashed dark on the man's brow. "Novus."

"Not the name your parent gave you?"

"No. A delightful young nurse named me."

Doctor Bonna nodded and decided not to pursue a naming timeline. "Do you know where you are, or how you got here?"

"I'd hoped you'd furnish that information, Doctor. My memories are … confused."

"Indeed? We found you in the middle of nowhere, delirious from an unwise combination of stimtabs and painkillers. Where are you from?"

"I can't say with any certainty, but I am sure I have no family or friends."

Doctor Bonna smiled. "Indeed, you have at least one enemy who administered the blow, and I'm guessing a female friend who dressed the wound recently. Will either of them be searching for you?"

"The friend was a passing acquaintance." Novus smiled. "She was eager to send me on my way."

"And your assailant? Are they looking for you?"

"Would you give me up, Doctor?"

"Indeed, I don't know enough about you or the threat you present. Convince me why you deserve protection."

"I can't, because I don't." Novus twitched the pod covers. "May I get up and move about? While we talk?"

"We can walk to the courtyard, absorb the sunlight. There'll be a few other people there, too, but not close enough to overhear us." Doctor Bonna led him down a wide corridor.

Novus gestured over his shoulder with a thumb at the orderlies. "Why don't you trust me?"

"You show up in an abandoned colony under peculiar circumstances. You are clearly comfortable with a level of violence at which most respectable citizens would balk. And you have no identity."

"That's the second time you've referred to this place as abandoned or isolated, but I'm seeing a modern, thriving community." Novus blanched. "Have you moved me back to Luxton?"

"You remember being in Luxton? Is that where you're from?" Doctor Bonna ushered Novus into the courtyard.

A blaze of blossoms and flowering trees convinced Novus he had travelled far from the cave in which he'd sheltered. Far from the egg-shaped artefact, which clearly didn't originate in the cave.

"I have been to Luxton," Novus said, "but I can't remember when or why."

An older man weeding a nearby garden bed jerked upright at the mention of the capital and stared at Novus.

"Doctor Bonna? Allow me to introduce myself to your new friend?" He ambled over and planted himself before Novus. "I'm Herdsman Hebe. I'm the one who knocked you senseless."

Torture

No torment is too great for the heretic who defies the ordained path; their suffering is justice given form.

The Blessed Prophet Serenus

Officer Auxilium tapped his baton against his uniformed thigh as he strode the bare corridors to the cells. His Holiness wanted him to encourage the High Shepherds to tell what they knew, without resorting to physical violence. But Stark had authorised the use of extreme measures against Ludion, whom he considered a traitor and therefore deserving of retribution.

High Shepherds Miles and Altor looked expectantly at Auxilium when he entered their cell, and he nodded an almost courteous greeting, and tucked his hat under his arm.

He pointed his swagger stick at the grills in the ceiling. "Fresh air, yes?" Auxilium narrowed his eyes. "They also carry sound from cell to selected cell. Currently, all ducts are closed. You are deaf to other guests, yes?"

"Guests?" Miles snorted. "Are you suggesting we're not detained against our will, and we are free to leave?"

"You are honoured guests, for your own safety, yes? Tell me, what information did Ludion share with you?"

"We don't understand the question, and we are unacquainted with anyone called Ludion," Altor said.

"Very well," Officer Auxilium said. "I will open a channel between this cell and the cell Ludion inhabits, yes? You may remember more when you hear his screams, no? If you can answer a question your friend cannot, you need only call out, to relieve his pain." Officer Auxilium offered a thin smile before he left the cell and locked the door behind him.

Miles and Altor flinched as the gears ground, shifting the squealing duct baffles into new configurations. As one, they moved to the centre of the room to be closer to the source. They cocked their heads, straining to build a picture to marry with the organic grunts and scuffles.

"You have an audience, Ludion." The accent of glee in Auxilium's voice carried clearly. "High Shepherds Miles and Altor are eagerly listening. They can intervene and stop your punishment at any time, yes?"

Boot heels clacked.

Miles and Altor exchanged glances.

"The wound on your chest is fresh and inexpertly stitched," Auxilium said. "Self-administered treatment, yes?"

A muffled grunt.

"That pain is nothing compared to what I will inflict. I know you colluded with the mediocre Espio, yes? A failed and insipid asset. Who else?"

Altor shook his head.

Miles gripped his arm. "We are under observation. Do not respond," he mimed.

"I ask myself, why would a man cut himself," Auxilium said. "Penance? No, I think not. Not your style, no?"

Metallic objects rattled.

"These scalpels are virgin blades. They haven't yet tasted blood," Auxilium said. "So sharp you'll barely feel the cut. I welcome an opportunity
to feed them. A matching slice on the other side, to maintain symmetry,
no?"

Scuffles. A bitten back sob.

"What information did you steal?"

More scuffles. A wounded animal noise, low and guttural.

"Your friends could intervene," Auxilium said. "Save you much suffering, no? Perhaps you are expendable, yes? Not worth saving?"

"Did you get this job because you're a pathetic excuse for a Sui, Filius
Skaxnat," Ludion gasped, "or did the ignominious work deform your
miserable soul?"

A wet thump followed by a choking cough.

"You will learn respect!"

"Respect is earned, Filius Skaxnat. Slither back into your Lightless
hole." Ludion's voice dripped with contempt.

"Cooperation benefits you, not childish defiance, yes? Tell me which
files you stole."

Scuffles and booted feet scraped. Another suppressed howl of agony.

"We shouldn't leave the flesh hanging. Tell me what I want to know,
and my man will stitch the flap back into place, yes?"

"Spfftt."

The High Shepherds frowned and shrugged in confusion.

"You will regret that," Auxilium said. "Gag him."

Altor leaned close to Miles and whispered, "I think Ludion spat on
him."

The High Shepherds listened as boots scuffed and metal jangled, then
a door slammed. The duct baffles squealed back into place.

"We should have called out," Altor said, moon pale.

"Nonsense. Ludion understands. He's as good as dead once Auxilium
extracts the information. Our best gift is the dignity of silence."

"Why is he deliberately provoking Auxilium?"

"Ludion knows he's going to die," Miles said. "Maybe he hopes to provoke Auxilium into making a mistake, killing him quickly, before he breaks."

"After what we heard? You think Ludion will break?"

"Everyone breaks. Ludion is counting on Auxilium's inexperience, and hopes his patience snaps first."

The High Shepherd's cell plunged into skaxnat nest darkness, and a recording of the torture session played on a loop, drowning out their ability to think, and flooding them with despair.

Ludion curled naked on the floor, too exhausted by his ordeal to clamber onto his pod. His fingers crept to the weeping wound, and he pushed the ragged flap of skin back into place. Tears stung his eyes, and he bit his lip.

The temperature plummeted once again, and Ludion slipped into a helpless torpor.

Officer Auxilium, in his braided uniform and imposing hat, and accompanied by his henchmen, returned. The steady rise in temperature, from frigid to mild, alerted Ludion of the impending visit.

The henchmen rolled in the now familiar trolley, bearing glittering instruments of torture, and assumed their positions on either side of him. Filius Skaxnat strode back and forth, clacking his booted heels and slapping his cane against his thigh, while Ludion, ostensibly staring over his head, missed not a twitch.

"I think you have nothing worthwhile to tell me," the Officer said, running his fingers over the array of shiny tools. "You are worthless, yes?

Keeping you alive is pointless, no?" He selected a cruelly slender blade and nodded for his underlings to seize Ludion. They pinned him to the wall with his arms spread wide. Ludion slumped, forcing his captors to take his weight.

The Officer smiled thinly as he approached, wielding the glittering blade at eye level.

Faster than a chameleon snatching a fly, Ludion raised his knees to his chest and kicked both feet into Auxilium's chest, smashing him into the opposite wall with a sickening snap of broken ribs. The prisoner twisted his hands and dug his fingers deep into his captors' eye-sockets and slammed their heads together. Blind and stunned, they collapsed in a shrieking tangle of twitching limbs.

Ludion whipped the laser weapons from the downed guards and tossed one onto his pod. With barely a downward glance, he zapped both guards in the head, sending them into perpetual darkness.

Auxilium moaned as he fought for breath. Ludion snatched the swagger stick and kicked aside the fallen blade.

"Strip." Ludion jabbed Auxilium with the stick. "Remember, cooperation is better than defiance, no?"

"You … killed them." Auxilium gasped, clutching his chest. "Two … of my best."

"What did you expect? They showed no respect for their opponent. Strip."

Auxilium leaned his head back against the wall and squinted up at Ludion. "I will not."

"Then you are no use to me." Ludion blasted a neat hole in Auxilium's forehead. He wrangled the uniform tunic from Auxilium, substituted a pair of trousers from the longer legged guard, and dressed himself in authority. The boots and braid helped him assume his new persona, but the swagger stick and aggressively peaked hat added an extra layer of confidence.

Slapping his thigh, he strode down the corridor. A junior officer, with a naturally beardless chin, froze to attention, eyes averted.

"I require your assistance, yes? You must escort the High Shepherds to benediction."

"Sir?" The junior officer flicked a glance at Ludion. "On my own, Sir?"

"You will accompany me." Ludion cracked the cane against his boot and the junior officer flinched. "Lead on."

The junior officer took a deep breath, turned on his heel, and marched smartly ahead of Ludion to the end of the corridor. He halted outside a locked door and keyed a code into the pad.

Ludion slapped the stick into his open palm. "Go ahead and clear each section, yes? Our guests must have no opportunity to make contacts."

"Sir! Yes, Sir!" The junior officer marched back the way they'd come and Ludion slipped inside the cell.

"My Shepherds."

Miles and Altor sprang to their feet.

"Tuck these up your sleeves." Ludion handed them each a laser. "An enthusiastic but gullible Private is clearing our way."

"What's the plan?" Miles asked.

"No idea, My Shepherd. Flying by the seat of my borrowed pants here. Seize whatever opportunity presents itself. Let's go."

Miles and Altor walked with heads bowed along the almost familiar path. Chest puffed with pride to be noticed by Officer Auxilium, the Private cleared the prisoner's way to the surface elevator.

They exited into a massive warehouse shed, with doors open to blessed sunlight. Vehicles of every description, from single person hover scooters to caterpillar tracked juggernauts, lined the floor. Camouflage suits hung from the walls, alongside hard-shelled armour.

Ludion turned to the junior officer. "You served well, Private." The perfectly centred hole which opened in his forehead lent him a surprised expression. Ludion reached forward before the body could fall and laid him across the elevator threshold. "Hold the lift, Officer."

Miles raised an eyebrow while Altor blanched and wrung his hands.

"I'd hoped for an all-terrain vehicle, but I'll settle for that." Ludion pointed to the matt black conchatus crouched near the open doors, wings drooping. He swiped an armful of suits from the wall and thrust them into Miles' arms. "Climb aboard, I'll be right behind you."

Without waiting to see what the High Shepherds did, Ludion raced across the warehouse to a pallet of drums. Grimacing with pain, he tipped them over, spilling a shallow lake of paint across the floor. Taking careful aim, he shoved more drums to roll under and beside the rows of vehicles, creating a sea of stinking solvent.

Hand over his latest wound, he dashed to the conchatus and clambered into the cockpit. "Strap in," he yelled over the rising scream of the engines. The aircraft rose, fell and rose again as Ludion familiarised himself with the controls. The craft wobbled out of the warehouse and Ludion swung it to face inwards, while searching for the icon he needed. "Bring the Light!" The burst of fire exploded the spilled paint drums. Flames swept across the warehouse floor, engulfing every shining new vehicle. Ludion yanked on the collective pitch, sending the conchatus high above the raging inferno.

"Unless I'm very much mistaken," Ludion called over his shoulder, "we've just declared war on High Shepherd Stark."

"You are mistaken," Miles said. "By taking us prisoner, Stark declared war. How far will this bird fly?"

"Can't say for sure, My Shepherd. Where do you want to go?"

"The Domains are unsafe," Miles said. "We must seek assistance from the Nefans."

Sanctuary

*The truth burns brighter than heresy; in its Light, the wicked are
exposed and the righteous vindicated.*

The Blessed Prophet Serenus

L udion sighed with relief when he found an inflight map. He needed
to make only slight course adjustments to plot a route to the Isle
of Nefas. The High Shepherds had copied his example and donned
headphones, but when they switched on the communications headsets,
Ludion suspected they had more experience aboard a conchatus than he
did.

Below, spotted and striped herds swarmed the savannah, startled into
panicky gallops by the appearance of the low-flying aircraft and rapidly
dropping back into browsing mode when the perceived danger had raced
past.

Ludion failed to notice the High Shepherds leave their seats and change
their robes for more practical camouflage suits. He flinched when High

Shepherd Miles tapped his shoulder and flicked a switch on his helmet, activating the communication system.

"Get changed," Miles said. "The suits are warm and practical. They're clean, too. Probably unused."

Ludion glanced around to find High Shepherd Altor holding up a fresh suit. "This looks your size."

"I'll take the pilot's seat," Miles said; a knowing smile crinkled his eyes.

Ludion accepted and clattered his way to the rear of the craft. The suit fitted perfectly, and the soft soled boots cradled his cramped feet.

Altor intercepted him before he reached the cockpit. "Miles and I owe you thanks. You could have escaped without us."

"You might want to reserve any thanks until after we've landed."

"I can't decide which is braver: breaking out or stealing a craft you don't know how to operate," Altor said. "High Shepherd Miles is out of practice, but he is a trained pilot. The most useful thing you can do now is rest."

In the cockpit, Miles relaxed into the pilot's seat, a subdued excitement buoying his mood. He flipped the switches on the radio and adjusted his microphone.

"This is High Shepherd Miles, seeking contact with the people of Nefas. I require your urgent assistance." He provided a heading, and an estimated time of arrival, and set the recorded request on a loop.

"Do you expect them to respond?" Altor asked.

"Not immediately," Miles said. "Shepherds don't usually travel in a craft like this military monster. We could be anyone. They'll monitor our progress, and they'll scan us."

"What if they ignore us?"

"The won't, at least, not until they have no choice but to acknowledge us. We'll land away from the main colony, be as unthreatening as possible."

Felix raced to Callida's office to replay the message. "I'm tracking their progress. The craft is unknown to me, not one designed for personal use, but capable of carrying a company of a hundred soldiers."

Callida widened her eyes.

"My scans reveal only three occupants," Felix said. "The belly of the conchatus is empty. What concerns me are the weapons bristling from the craft. Some projectile weapons I recognise from historical texts, but most appear to be recent developments."

"Can you identify the occupants?" Callida asked.

"Prudence is interrogating the scans, trying to find a match. One individual has identified himself as High Shepherd Miles, so we're assuming one other is High Shepherd Altor, but we don't have a clue about the third."

"Prepare a landing ground." Callida rose and studied the map behind her desk. "I'm thinking a valley, or a beach. A place where we can control the narrative."

Felix pointed to a narrow cliff-lined beach. "Hard to use their weapons once they land, and we'd have the upper ground. Unless they ignore our instructions, and land atop the cliffs, or fire on us without landing."

Callida frowned. "I never expected to face weapons. And they call us abominations."

"We can defend ourselves," Felix glanced sheepishly at Callida. "Hebe and I are developing a device which renders victims dizzy and incapable of coherent thought. Like the shroak repellents, but more refined. Much more powerful. And we have tranquilliser darts."

"If our guests are genuine, we must welcome them, which means I must be there to greet them. However, we must also be able to defend ourselves and neutralise any threat. Who is our best shooter?"

"Me, followed by Prue. But you don't necessarily need a sharpshooter," Felix said. "Not if we incapacitate them. Hebe knows how the devices work, and he knows the High Shepherds."

Felix and Hebe scrambled down the cliff face and marked the landing site with smoking torches; a courtesy to show the erratic updrafts to the pilot. Callida followed, one eye on the perilous path, one on the approaching black dot.

"Make sure Doctor Bonna stays hidden until I call for her," Callida said to Felix as he checked her shield. "Get yourself out of sight. No need to provide easy targets if our guests prove unfriendly." She shooed him away.

Hebe stood, arms akimbo, his back to the cliff face. "What a monster. If it's not the High Shepherds aboard, we're all as good as dead."

"What about the repellent gadgets?"

"If they're friendly, we won't need them. If they're unfriendly, it'll be too late."

Miles caressed the controls. Since attaining the rank of High Shepherd, he'd not piloted a craft, yet the muscle memory remained. A grim smile creased his face in acknowledgment of the smoking flares convulsing across the beach, throwing a challenge to his rusty skills. "Buckle in. The landing promises to be rough," he called over his shoulder.

Altor and Ludion exchanged nervous glances as they fastened their harnesses.

Miles coaxed the conchatus closer, the steady thwump of the blades keeping time with his excited heartbeat. The craft dipped and bucked, tossing the occupants with careless abandon. Miles murmured sweet nothings as he eased the massive machine towards the target, kissing the cliff side. Ludion raised an eyebrow and Altor shrugged as Miles spoke in honeyed tones, cajoling the deadly hulk into sulky cooperation.

Miles killed the engine and punched the air. The blades fluttered to a reluctant stillness like a wounded insect. The conchatus sank onto the gravelly sand, silent but bristling with terminal threats.

"I'll go first," Ludion staggered to the door and yanked it open. He blinked back his pain and cast out a ladder. He descended with as much grace as he could muster and performed a slow pirouette with raised arms when he reached the uneven beach. "My name is Ludion. I am unarmed. My companions, High Shepherds Miles and Altor, and I seek your assistance." He addressed the tall man, but the woman responded.

"I am Callida. Welcome to the Isle of Nefas."

Ludion bowed. "Thank you. May I introduce High Shepherds Miles and Altor?" He turned as they slithered down the ladder.

A cascade of soil and gravel betrayed Hebe, pelting down the steep path. "My Shepherd, My Shepherd!"

"Herdsman Hebe? What are you doing here?" Miles embraced his asset.

"That resolves any lingering questions about identity," Felix said.

"When Stark announced you'd taken yourselves on a retreat, I thought you were dead." Tears streamed down Hebe's cheeks.

"Retreat?" Miles snorted. "Is that what the Lightless wretch said? We have much to discuss, my friend, but I think Ludion needs medical attention before we do anything else." Miles caught Ludion by the elbow as he swayed.

Doctor Bonna huffed across the beach as the High Shepherds laid Ludion on the gravel. She examined him while Miles described what he knew of his wounds and his torture.

"He must be touched by Solra's grace to have lasted this long," Altor said.

"Indeed," Doctor Bonna said without conviction. "Felix? Can you carry him up the cliff? I need to get him to the clinic immediately."

Felix scooped Ludion into his arms and trudged up the path, one shoulder braced against the cliff face as he climbed.

Ludion awoke, swaddled in warm blankets. His fingers automatically reached for the rough stitches securing the data crystal, but found only a smooth gel dressing.

"Looking for this?" Doctor Bonna held the packet between forefinger and thumb. "Must be something of exceptional importance for you to take such dramatic measures." She slipped the treasure into Ludion's outstretched hand.

Ludion nodded as he searched her face.

"The High Shepherds are hovering outside," Doctor Bonna said. "Are you up to having visitors?"

"May I dress first?"

"I'll send an orderly to help you."

The orderly brought a long tunic and loose trousers. He helped Ludion pull on the soft soled boots in which he'd arrived, and brushed his hair. "Doctor Bonna said you mustn't raise your arms yet," the orderly said. "Anything you need, push the button." He nodded at a fat buzzer next to the pod before allowing the High Shepherds entry and discreetly slipping away.

"Well, you both look fabulous." Ludion beamed.

High Shepherd Miles shook his head. "Doctor Bonna insisted we immerse ourselves in her special recipe nutrient bath. I confess, I feel twenty years younger."

"An intimidating woman," High Shepherd Altor said, "but with a generous heart. Her treatments almost make the deprivations imposed by The Revised worthwhile."

"She explained the damage inflicted on your pectoral muscles, and the trauma to your system caused by keeping you torpid," Miles said. "We authorised your treatment."

"I don't understand how you summoned the energy," Altor said, dragging two stools closer to the side of the pod.

"Ancient texts, written by warrior priests," Ludion said. "I studied long forgotten arts of physical and mental control. Wonderful exercise for body and mind, but I never expected to need them."

"Can you remember what was on the data crystal you copied?" Miles asked.

"No need, My Shepherd." Ludion held out the membrane wrapped crystal.

Nenimem Rises

Even in death, the heretic's stain lingers and corrupts; the righteous must cleanse until nothing impure remains.

The Blessed Prophet Serenus

Stark stared slack-jawed at the report detailing the extensive damage to The Revised Training Centre. Recapturing Miles and Altor, before they could speak publicly, must be top priority; but without vehicles?

His mind spun, unable to fix on a solution. During decades of planning and preparation, not once had he considered the possibility of two elderly clerics and a preening administrator derailing his elaborate operation.

Stark didn't recognise the name, but in the absence of his superiors, Lieutenant Nenimem had the initiative to assume command. Stark skimmed Nenimem's file before sending him a brief command to restore order and dispose of the bodies without ceremony.

How long before the High Shepherds break cover?

Stark summoned Obduro, his personal secretary. "I'm pushing forward the schedule. Activate our media assets." He glanced outside at the mid-morning sun. "I need full control by the end of today's benediction."

"Your Holiness? I'm not sure that's possible."

Stark tucked his hands inside his sleeves. "You have your orders. Such is the Holy Will of Solra. Make it happen."

A pall of black smoke lay over the training camp like a shroud, teased by a fitful breeze too timid to expose the chaos to Solra's unforgiving gaze. Lieutenant Nenimem searched the sky for the slightest promise of rain. Disappointed, he kicked the smouldering debris; the unexpected stench clung to his charred uniform and stung his bloodshot eyes.

The emergency firefighting equipment had proven inadequate, resulting in an almost total loss of transportation. A handful of close-range scooters survived; perfect for whizzing around camp, useless for mounting a retrieval mission. Not that he knew where to look. The conchatus had a massive range, designed to transport personnel and heavy equipment between Domains.

Determined not to suffer further losses, Lieutenant Nenimem organised a construction team to build a solid room to store their remaining pitiful supply of ordinance. Not only had the blaze feasted on vehicles, but the flames had gorged on weapons and explosives, adding an extra dimension of danger.

Scorched crews shifted shattered masonry blocks and twisted steel girders, shoring up corridors and semi-collapsed rooms with heavy joists. Lieutenant Nenimem forbade non-emergency workers access to the underground levels until engineers established their safety or otherwise. Survivors erected a forest of temporary accommodation and office spaces.

Those trapped underground could die or dig themselves out. Lieutenant Nenimem considered the situation an opportunity to weed out the weak or incompetent.

The wounded treated themselves and each other as best they could. Those too damaged to respond to first-aid, either slunk away to hide themselves or were carried away by friends to be executed. Not all Sui customs had been revised.

The largest work crews organised by Lieutenant Nenimem were the grave digging teams.

Obduro locked himself in a tiny cubicle which masqueraded as his inner sanctum; a place none of the staff dared disturb him. Publicly, he welcomed a return to greater orthodoxy, but privately, he quaked at the brutal methods Stark employed. With eyes closed, he mumbled a prayer, a jumbled plea for both success and forgiveness. Then pressed the button.

Within moments, identity chips reprogrammed their hosts' minds. Experienced journalists and copywriters, editors and camera operators, all happily made room for junior colleagues, giving them preferential treatment, accepting their suggestions as though spoken by Holy Serenus himself. The newly activated assets accepted their positions as though granted by divine authority.

Secretary Obduro shivered as he whispered a line of the Solran creed. "Solra is the source of all talent and wisdom, praise Solra." *Have I sinned? Have I destroyed the talents bestowed by Solra?*

A junior assistant taps Beatrice's shoulder. "I'll take it from here," she says.

Beatrice smiles and vacates her seat for the upstart. Dazed and confused, she wanders outside to clear her head. A throbbing headache pulses at her nape, making her dizzy and lethargic. Because the parks are temporarily closed for the Quarter Day Celebration preparations, Beatrice walks home.

She wanders around her pod as though a guest in her own home. Nothing feels quite right. Dusty from her walk, she takes a shower and walks into her dressing room.

A riot of colour greets her. Violet, emerald, fuchsia, tangerine, scarlet, sapphire. Aggressively bright look-at-me colours. Immodestly cut garments revealing far more than any decent female should ever wear.

With trembling fingers, Beatrice drags the offending articles off their hangers and drops them haphazardly onto the floor. Hidden at the back of her closet, she discovers two dark-coloured dresses, one midnight blue, the other storm cloud grey. Long-sleeved, high-necked, with no pretensions to tailoring. Garments designed to allow their wearer to pass unnoticed. Attire suitable for a demure and modest Solra fearing woman.

Soothed by her discovery, her headache dissipates to a nagging background accompaniment, reminiscent of poorly chosen music at an art exhibition.

Beatrice kneels amidst the mountains of sensuously silky fabrics and weeps.

Callida leaned her elbows on the desk. "Are you certain?"

"I don't wallop that many people that I forget their faces," Hebe said. "Novus, or whatever he's calling himself, belongs to Stark. A thug for hire. I left his bio data with a contact, a man I trust implicitly. According to him, our man Novus doesn't officially exist."

"Indeed, Novus is a man of mystery," Doctor Bonna said, "even to himself. He could fake amnesia, but I can't see what he'd gain by such a ruse."

"You're both missing the point," Hebe said. "I didn't say his data had been altered or tampered with, or that there are gaps. No. I said, he doesn't officially exist."

"Go on," Callida said.

"Keeping one person's existence secret requires an array of resources, but there were four of these goons stalking Espio. What's the odds I clonked the only one without a history? We know Novus worked for Stark; we know Stark has removed High Shepherds Miles and Altor from the competition."

"Your concern for our safety is making you see dangers where none exist," Callida said. "Stark is ambitious and cunning, but you credit him too much. I will speak to this Novus character. In the meantime, I forbid you to foment unrest among my people."

Novus sprawled, arms stretched along the back of the bench, head resting against the wall, absorbing the sunlight. The tight lines around his eyes suggested his relaxed attitude masked an inner tension.

Callida slipped into the courtyard with a nod to the guards to keep their distance. She positioned herself between Novus and the sun, interrupting his basking. He squinted, then smiled broadly and shifted along the bench.

"You're the famous Callida," he said. "They're right: your mismatched eyes are mesmerising."

"You are the enigmatic Novus, but who exactly are 'they'?"

"The ubiquitous they, who spout opinions as facts, who infest every layer of society but who, in this case, are startlingly accurate."

Callida flicked a dismissive hand and perched on the arm of the bench, one foot on the ground, the other planted on the seat. "Skip the hyperbole. What I really want to know is, who are you? And why are you here?"

Novus pulled a knee to his chest and wrapped his arms around the leg. "Much as I'd like to oblige, I can't give you a satisfactory answer. Herdsman Hebe has already told you I am a paid assassin, but that's in the past."

"You're a reformed character? Or did Stark fire you because your target escaped your incompetent attempt?"

Novus flushed rosy pink. "I failed? Are you sure?"

Callida nodded.

Novus sucked in a deep breath, then slowly blew it out. "I'd love to indulge myself and spend the afternoon digging into my murky past, but I think there are some specific memories I need to share with you. Is there a place I can draw a map?"

Accompanied by the guards, Callida led Novus to her office and pointed to a huge whiteboard covering one wall.

"There is a massive training complex in the centre of Viribis … I think I lived there." Novus sketched rapidly. "Stark stole defective hatchlings … trained them as his personal army … he has a vast network of informers … when he wins the election, he plans to impose harsh orthodox rules … he has assets across the three Domains."

"Why are you sharing this information?"

"Blame the heavy-handed Herdsman." Novus added details and neatly lettered labels to his diagram.

"Are you avoiding the question, or am I particularly obtuse?"

"Herdsman Hebe knocked me unconscious, and he removed my chip." Novus shook his head. "Since then, my memories are scattered. Fragments I recover are unpleasant. Did he dislodge something in my brain? Did the chip control my thoughts and behaviour? I'd like to say yes, but I don't know for sure." He turned to face Callida. "What I am certain of, is that I possessed deep capacities for cruelty. What if they return as my memory glues itself back together? What if I revert to being a monster? That possibility terrifies me."

Beetle Men

Divine justice does not rest; what sin steals, Solra reclaims ten-fold.

The Blessed Prophet Serenus

Prudence took charge of the hastily set up computer room. "This amount of data is incredible. I need more skilled analysts."

"I know some on Viribis who might join us," Hebe said. "They're mostly along the Midwife Trail."

"Consult with Felix," Callida said. "Bring them through the portals, if they're willing. The Nefan community must vote on whether or not to get involved, but Ludion and the High Shepherds have presented us with new and disturbing evidence, which we must consider.

Hebe burst through the inner doors into Felix's high-tech workshop. "Callida said you'd help me."

"I'm fine. Thank you for asking. Baby Clem is learning to talk, he's very advanced for his age."

Hebe blinked. "Good, very good. Clem's a fine young hatchling."

Baby Clem raised his arms. "Be-be-be-be-be."

"He knows your name," Felix said with a wide smile. "He-be. Say He-be."

"Be-be-be-be-be." Clem bounced on his toes, demanding to be picked up.

Felix scooped him up and settled the hatchling on his hip. "What's so urgent, Herdsman?"

"Prudence is overwhelmed by the volume of data Ludion brought, and she needs more skilled analysts. I have someone in mind, if you will send me to Viribis."

Felix shrugged. "I can, but I don't see why it's so urgent. Didn't the High Shepherds say Ludion destroyed The Revised Training Centre? They're no longer a threat, are they?"

"Ludion damaged the Centre, but we don't know how seriously. Nor do we know if, or how many, assets are secretly awaiting orders. We've slowed them down, but don't underestimate Stark. His fury will drive him on, like a wounded sabre cat."

Felix gestured for Hebe to follow. "Where do you want to go?"

"To Ami, in Termitun, at the end of the Midwife Trail, please. I'll make my way to Shepherd Picto and hopefully convince him to return with me."

"How long will you be gone?"

"A day, maybe three. Depends on whether I can find transport and my powers of persuasion."

"Take these." Felix handed Hebe three of the improved shroak repellents and shields, and a dart gun and ammunition. "Stay out of trouble, Herdsman."

Ami greeted him with an anxious expression. "Black uniformed thugs are on the march, destroying portals. They kill anyone who resists."

"How long before they get here?" Hebe asked.

"A week if we're lucky, perhaps only days. They are not moving predictably. I'll stay as long as I can, before disabling the portals," Ami said. "Then I'll run for the hills. See if I can team up with anyone else crazy enough to resist."

"If you're serious about resisting, join me and my friends on Nefas." Hebe raised a hand and shook his head. "I can't say more, too risky."

Ami looked around at the dilapidated colony. "I'm the last, and I have nothing and no one to lose. Count me in, but you didn't come here to recruit me. What do you need?"

"Shepherd Picto. We need his expertise."

"Assuming you don't wish to renew your acquaintance with the porcuxes or the cave bear, we can take the conchatus to Crearaton." Ami led the way to a ramshackle shed and tugged open the doors, revealing the gleaming craft. He yanked the wheel of his pulley system, and the walls collapsed outwards, providing ample space for the rotors to spin.

Ami and Hebe clambered aboard and strapped themselves into the snug bucket seats. Ami grinned with unalloyed pleasure when the craft purred to life at his touch and soared above the treetops.

They skimmed the flank of the hill and headed towards the plain and the vibrant artist colony of Crearaton. Hebe spied the thin column of smoke on the horizon and nudged Ami. The pilot frowned and lifted the craft higher, hoping to stay out of weapon range.

Ami's infrared scans revealed only typical savannah prey and predators, no black clad troops. He flew closer, circling the colony, joining the growing flock of cleaner birds.

The smouldering ruins reduced both men to wide-eyed silence.

A blackened skeleton of girders stood amidst shattered shards of crystal; the demolished temple reduced to sooty rubble. The mosaic footpath celebrating creation, and so much admired by Espio, had been repurposed. Sui of every age lay maimed and twisted along its length. Dead. Burnt.

Beyond mortal help. Food for the scavengers who would soon breach the crumbling walls.

"We should leave," Ami said. "There's nothing we can do."

"No, we must search for survivors. I cannot conceive that the entire colony is wiped out."

Ami glanced sideways. "You want to search the length of the pyre?"

"Yes, and every building and potential hiding place."

"You'll have nightmares for the rest of your life if you look too closely."

"I'll have nightmares if I don't," Hebe said.

The stench of roasted flesh hit them as they clambered out of the cockpit. They squinted against the drifting greasy smoke and coughed away the taste of incinerated corpses. Only the screams of argumentative cleaner birds broke the eerie silence.

Ami lurched into a stumbling run to chase away the half-feathered scavengers.

"Stop. You're wasting your time," Hebe said, tears streaming down his cheeks. "We can't defend the dead. We're looking for the living, and time is running out."

By mutual agreement, they started their search at the beginning of creation, where the hatchlings lay, tossed haphazardly over mosaicked fish and crustaceans. Each tiny corpse sported a bloodless hole in their forehead. Although careless with the disposal of the bodies, the troops had been meticulous with the dispatch.

"Try not to look at their faces," Hebe said. "Look for the hole and keep moving."

Ami nodded, flushing vile greens and yellows. "They were utterly defenceless … such a vicious and senseless waste …"

The afternoon sun sank inexorably towards the horizon, casting long shadows which partially disguised the devastation.

The remains of the elderly cluttered the temple steps, the horror of unspeakable atrocities etched on their withered faces.

Ami sank to his haunches on the fire-cracked paving, and Hebe stared blindly towards the edge of the colony. A light breeze rustled through the scorched leaves, whispering a useless commiseration.

"Hebe, Hebe, Hebe. Is that really you?" The short, pudgy man in paint-stained clothes shouldered through the bushes, a floppy hatchling clutched to his chest.

"Picto?" Hebe dashed to greet his friend. "You survived? Are there others?"

"We hid overnight." Picto rubbed the back of the hatchling. "I heard your conchatus, but I was afraid you were the beetle men returned."

"Beetle men?" Ami scanned the bushes for an enemy.

"They wore hard black shells and fired lightning," Shepherd Picto said. "More deadly than skaxnats."

Hebe held out his arms. "Give me the little one."

"She stopped breathing last night," Picto said. "I've tried to keep her warm, but she won't wake up."

Hebe eased the dead hatchling from his friend's arms and cradled her to his chest. "Come, we're going somewhere safe." A sob caught in his throat.

"The beetle men destroyed the temple and smashed our art," Picto whispered, glancing furtively at the ruins where flashes of joyous colour, remnants of slashed art, fluttered in the breeze. "Their leader said only art clearly praising Solra is allowed under the new regime."

Ami placed himself between Picto and the pyre, while Hebe distracted his traumatised friend.

"Who is she?" Hebe asked. "A friend or a relative?"

Picto pursed his lips. "I've seen her around, sculpting models of animals from clay. She's a talented little thing, a brilliant eye for detail. I don't know her real name."

Ami helped Picto into the body of the conchatus and strapped him securely into his seat.

Hebe wrapped the deceased hatchling in a thick blanket and strapped her beside Picto.

"I called her Lady Lutum," Picto whispered, his voice thick with grief. "She won't be making any more animals, will she?"

Hebe shook his head. "No, Lady Lutum won't make any more clay animals."

The Ascension

The faithful shall ascend into glory, and the doubters will bow,
for no soul escapes the gaze of the Most Holy Solra.

The Blessed Prophet Serenus

The Quarter Day Celebration dawned with all the golden magnificence Stark desired. Thanks to Captain Pupa's crew, his recently appropriated dirigible sparkled in the sunlight; the gold paint gleamed, and the crystal cast cascades of rainbows over the onlookers. Crowds surged into the amphitheatre to witness the official promotion of His Holiness to the Most High Grand Master.

Mobile media crews roamed the audience, conducting vox pop interviews with enthusiastic supporters, whose grins grew wider and adulations more effusive when faced with a camera.

Miss Max fights her growing discomfort at the sight of so many people mingling and shamelessly disporting themselves. An itch inside her skull reminds her that, until recently, she flaunted herself, a wanton woman risking the salvation of her sinful female soul.

Beatrice and her crew move through the gaily coloured crowd. Her dark blue dress and subdued makeup allow her to pass unnoticed by all except the most observant, who look puzzled to see Miss Beatrice Max so sombre on this auspicious occasion. Without her usual maquillage, and minus her carefully choreographed hip sway, Beatrice attracts little attention in the throng of revellers. Only the authority of her experienced camera crew give her confidence to approach strangers, and out of character, she limited her interviewees to women.

She homes in on an older woman. A tourist, by the inelegant cut of her clothes and dazed expression.

"Hello, I'm Beatrice Max. Welcome to Luxton. Tell me, are you enjoying the festival?"

The tourist frowns at the dowdy woman, but brightens when she notices the accompanying crew.

Her crew grow irritated with Beatrice's hesitancy and whisper amongst themselves that she must be sickening. They make a point of enthusiastically greeting the newly promoted journalists.

Stark abandoned the traditional ceremony. With High Shepherds Miles and Altor unavailable to affix his crown and lead him aboard his new airborne residence, he created a contemporary ceremony. Black uniformed officers performed the ritual tasks of the High Shepherds. Dazzling in golden robes trimmed with intricate lapis lazuli embroidery, Stark spoke from the deck of the dirigible, his face beamed onto massive screens around the amphitheatre. Few in the audience noticed, or cared, when he referred to the decade long role as a lifetime commitment. After all, he was past his prime. Traditionally, once His Holiness ascended to achieve closer proximity to Solra, they disappeared from public life. They made occasional and vague pronouncements to the faithful, but the world understood the old men simply faded into obscurity.

His Holiness's call for a return to traditional values prompted enthusiastic applause.

"The search for a mate should not divert our young men from their studies and life advancement. Henceforth, Solran officials will handle these profane concerns, matching young people according to personality and biological compatibility."

A shiver of unease rippled through the crowd, but Stark's supporters cheered loudly.

"Females will return to their rightful sphere: homemaking and raising perfect hatchlings. As Perpetual Most High Grand Master, I shall unburden women of their unnatural commercial and business obligations; their only duties will be the well-being of their mate and fosterlings."

Flutters of unease flushed through the audience, but Stark's vociferous supporters and the unnerving presence of the anonymously black uniformed and visored troops subdued potential challengers. No one wanted to believe Stark meant what he said. A foolish old man ascending into obscurity with a final delusion to ease his dotage presented no threat to anyone.

Doctor Bonna studied the Quarter Day Celebration recordings with forensic attention. She replayed the unscripted interviews with members of the audience, paying particular scrutiny to the journalists; especially Beatrice Max, she of the perfectly coiffed hair, immaculate makeup, and glamorous wardrobe, infamous for her rapid blinking and pretty blushes when faced with powerful or influential males.

The number of new journalists struck Doctor Bonna as odd. Media careers could be built on the right sound bite on such an auspicious occasion. Why put inexperienced people front and centre on such an important day?

Beatrice smiled vacuously at the camera, mouthing the expected platitudes. She smoothed her drably conservative dress and patted her hair like an automaton. No blinks, no blushes, none of the questionable flirtatious behaviour on which she grew her infamy, and a mass of adoring fans.

Doctor Bonna frowned and slipped the recording into her pocket before trudging across to Callida's office.

"You must see this. Pay attention to Beatrice Max." Doctor Bonna slipped the crystal onto Callida's communication console and plopped into a chair.

"What am I looking at?"

"Ignore Stark and his bizarre announcements for a moment. Pay attention to the journalists."

Callida leaned back in her chair, eyes roving across the screen. "A lot of faces I don't recognise, but then again, I don't pay much attention to popular news bulletins from the Domains."

"But you recognise Beatrice Max?" Doctor Bonna twiddled with the controls and found the excerpt she wanted. "Watch carefully."

Callida leaned forward, elbows on her desk. She shrugged. "Sorry, what am I missing?"

"What's Beatrice Max famous for?"

"You came here to gossip?"

Doctor Bonna slapped a flat palm on the desk. "Of course not. Indeed, such unkind behaviour is below our dignity. No, this is important. Beatrice has a reputation, no doubt well crafted. She isn't overburdened with intellect, but she possesses guile."

Callida nodded.

"Not only the Quarter Day Celebration, but the day Stark ascends to full authority as His Holiness, the Most High Grand Master. I expected Beatrice to wear something eye-catching, scarlet or shocking pink, not darkest blue. She didn't indulge in a single blush or bat her eyes. Her makeup was subdued, and her hair was untinted. Not only that, but she interviewed only women. Indeed, if I didn't know better, I'd say she avoided all male contact."

"She's gaining maturity," Callida said.

"If it was only Beatrice who had changed, I might accept that idea, but where did all these unknown faces come from? Journalists would normally clamber over one another to cover an Ascension."

"Good point," Callida said. "You have a theory?"

"Novus said removing his identity chip changed his thinking," Doctor Bonna said. "The technology is available, but the implementation is beyond belief. Only a madman, a megalomaniac, would entertain such a reprehensible plan."

"You mean a man who claims to commune with Solra? A man who seized power without an election, and referred to himself as Perpetual Most High Grand Master? But Stark can't have removed or replaced the identity chips of these journalists."

"He only needs to reprogram them to be compliant. He could have had sleeper agents ready in place. That would explain the unknowns covering his great day."

"What you are suggesting is fantastical, and paranoid," Callida said. "I need proof, substantiated evidence, before I accept what you say. I want you to be wrong, because the consequences of being correct are too phenomenally huge to contemplate."

Ami guided the conchatus as high as he dared, fear of the enemy's strange weapons driving him to the edge of aerial safety. Picto gazed sightlessly at the curved walls of the craft as he rocked himself. He allowed Hebe to slip a shielding gadget around his neck without question.

They approached the dilapidated and abandoned colony cautiously. Ami descended in ever decreasing circles, scanning for telltale heat signatures. He breathed a pent-up sigh of relief. "All clear."

The explosion rocked the conchatus, spiralling the craft over the ruins. Beetle men swarmed from their ambuscades as smoke boiled and blossomed obscenely across the sky.

Hebe activated the repellent, and the troops lost focus. They stumbled and fired wildly at the sky and each other, shredding trees and strafing buildings with equal fervour.

Ami fought the controls, swinging the conchatus high over the tree canopy, and out of range. "By the Light! They've destroyed the portal."

"What's the range of this craft?" Hebe asked. "Will it get us to the Isle of Nefas?"

"We'll get close to the coast, but then we'll need to recharge. But I won't risk crossing the Central Sea in this old bucket," Ami said. "Not even fully charged."

Hebe tapped a message into his wristcomm. "Head to the coast. I've messaged Felix."

Felix read the message and swore softly.

"Bad news?" Miles paused his inventory of the conchatus. The massive craft carried a treasure trove of boxes and crates, crammed with familiar items and strange objects whose deadly functions they could only guess.

"The Revised have destroyed the portal, and Hebe and his friends need rescuing."

"I assume speed is important," Miles said. "This is faster than a boat and carries an interesting array of weapons."

"Are you volunteering to pilot this beast?"

"I'm not letting you youngsters have all the fun," Miles said. "Using Stark's resources against him is appealing. And Hebe is one of mine. I have a moral responsibility."

A flurry of messages passed between Felix and Hebe. Hebe agreed to send flares when he spotted the incoming craft.

The monstrous vehicle hummed to life, responding to Miles' lightest touch. They raced low across the abyss, faster than Felix had ever travelled. He glimpsed the ghost-pale forms of shroaks swimming below the waves, left behind before he could point them out.

The width of the Central Sea shrank under the power and speed of the liberated craft. The Viribis coastline grew thicker and more defined. Felix nudged Miles' elbow and pointed to an orange plume of smoke. Miles adjusted course, heading towards an open savannah.

Ami's conchatus huddled low, its paint scorched body riddled with bullet holes, and its tail rotor smashed. Miles circled, searching for evidence of an ambush before committing to landing. The rescuees cowered from the downdraft, covering their eyes from flying dust and debris. Picto cuddled little Lady Lutum to his chest, using his entire body as a shield.

Felix heaved the side doors open and knelt, ready to pull aboard his friends. With Hebe holding Picto's arm, the three dashed to sanctuary the instant the enormous craft touched down. Felix and Ami slammed shut the heavy doors as a spray of bullets spattered the armoured hull.

Miles launched the conchatus into the sky, his knuckles white on the controls. "The Lightless wretches evaded the heat scans." He glanced over his shoulder. "Is anyone hurt?"

"We're all fine," Felix said. "How did they follow you? There were no vehicles."

"Beetle men fly," Picto said.

"There were no aircraft on my scanners," Ami said.

Picto shook his head. "No. The beetle men fly by themselves; they have wings under their shiny beetle carapaces."

Ami circled his forefinger next to his head and mimed. "Trauma. Does strange things to a man."

Hebe squatted in front of Picto. "Did you see the beetle men flying? Can you describe what you saw?"

"Hebe, Hebe, Hebe. You think I'm insane with grief?" Picto shook his head. "Not all of them, less than half, had shiny backpacks. They flew up and planted explosives on the temple roof."

"Did any of them fly higher than the temple?"

Picto scrunched his eyes shut. "I couldn't see. I was hiding."

Miles circled high and wide. "They're not firing at us; we must be out of range. Can you tell if they penetrated the hull?"

Felix and Ami searched for damage while Hebe comforted Picto.

"We're intact, as far as we can tell from the inside," Felix said, leaning over Miles' shoulder.

"Sit." Miles gestured to the copilot's seat. He pointed to a small screen with crosshairs. "When they line up, press the white button."

"Is this what I think it is?"

"Can't say, son. I don't know what you're thinking, but I'm hoping it's a missile." Miles turned his full attention back to the controls. "Ready?" He increased speed and hurtled towards the swarming beetle men who instinctively scattered like roaches.

Felix pressed the button.

The bright white heat signature blossomed across the screen.

Miles pulled steeply skywards, buffeted by the rising heat. A thin smile creased his face. "Never was too keen on beetles."

Protecting the Flock

Those who rise against the faithful shall be cast into perpetual darkness; rebellion births only despair.

The Blessed Prophet Serenus

Callida gazed around the crowded amphitheatre, the sleep deprivation circles under her eyes as dark as theatre makeup. "I can't remember speaking for this long without interruptions. Are there any questions before we vote?"

A forest of hands shot up, and Callida picked a woman at random.

"My question is for High Shepherd Miles," the woman said. "With the advantage of hindsight, was incinerating the Revised soldiers necessary, and do you regret your action?"

Miles slowly walked to the centre of the stage. "Madam, you phrase your question in expectation of a particular answer." He raised his voice. "Understand, Stark does not come to negotiate. He comes to annihilate. His soldiers exterminated an entire colony of innocents, from elders to hatchlings. Why? Because they dared to question his orthodoxy; because they developed their own opinions, and because they worshipped in ways which made the most sense to them. Do I have regrets? Most assuredly. I profoundly regret not challenging Stark's delusions before he usurped power. I regret the deaths for which he is responsible, and I regret the deaths looming in the future if I fail to stop further atrocities."

A voice from the crowd burst out. "As a holy man, how can you support violence?"

"I am a shepherd. My task is to protect my flock. I do not seek violence, but if I cannot deter predators by peaceful means, then yes, I would kill a sabre cat to save my lambs."

Callida reassumed her central position. "You've heard much new and unpleasant information this afternoon. Whether we wish it or not, we are teetering on the brink of war. As incomprehensible as the situation appears, we must decide to either engage with Stark's forces, or sue for accord with the victors once the situation resolves."

"Mainlanders are ill-equipped to challenge Stark and his army," Miles said. "The Revised will ruthlessly eliminate any pockets of resistance, assuring Stark's victory unless you, the Nefans, take action."

Ludion rose from his seat in the audience and sashayed to stand before the stage. "My lovely Nefans," he called. "I am Ludion, and I've shamelessly eavesdropped on your private conversations this afternoon, for which I most humbly beg your pardons." He swept an extravagant bow. "Many of you have made the point, ad nauseum, that The Revised Training Camp has been destroyed. The Revised have no transportation and can offer no threat to you delightfully isolated islanders."

Confused murmurs ran through the amphitheatre.

"Stark grew an army in secret." Ludion's voice dropped an octave. "He built a facility and developed weapons, all without raising the faintest whiff of suspicion." He threw wide his arms. "What do you think this monster can achieve now he wields ultimate power? Do you think he won't rebuild? Bigger and stronger? Do you believe he worries about public opinion, now he controls the media? Do you believe he will allow you; you free-thinking, imperfect creatures; to live in his tyrannically perfect world?" Ludion dropped his arms and shook his head. "My friends, unless you stand, you are dead. Wiped out. Annihilated."

Relief and horror warred within Callida. Almost four-fifths of the islanders voted to act. Callida's initial response to let the Mainlanders manage their own affairs, while the islanders kept to themselves, proved misguided. The growing body of circumstantial evidence warned that the Nefans ignored events in the Domains at their peril.

Each émigré brought their expertise and a conflicting set of opinions. She needed to weigh and consider them all if they were to challenge successfully Stark and his infestation of beetle men.

Callida counted on her fingers. Nine healthy émigrés taking up space in the medical centre. Doctor Bonna's suggestion to build a cluster of dens on the outskirts of the colony meant accepting them as permanent members of the community. Callida drummed her fingers on the desk, but neither the number nor the reality changed.

Unable to camouflage her procrastination as wise deliberation, she set out for the courtyard where the émigrés absorbed their daily benediction.

Each man turned to greet her, expectant faces filled with various combinations of hope and dread. She gestured for the High Shepherds to join her on benches in a secluded corner.

"The Nefans voted overwhelmingly to oppose Stark," Callida said. "I need your help. I'm not a general, nor a historian, I have no idea where to start."

Miles sighed. "None of us are experts in conflict, but together we will learn as much as necessary."

"We have a request," Altor said. "The timing is less than perfect, but the longer we leave it, the further the situation will deteriorate. We cannot, in good conscience, continue to reside here in the medical centre. Do we have your permission to build a modest cluster of dens and workshops?"

Callida laughed with relief. "That was my second reason for coming here. Do you wish to remain together?"

"If you're asking do we trust Novus, the answer is yes," Miles said. "He and Hebe have tense moments, naturally, but both are willing to make concessions."

"There is a suitable parcel of land near Felix's workshop, but if you prefer something more central …?"

"We can rig temporary shelters this afternoon," Altor said. "Give us a chance to get a feel for the place."

Callida nodded as she counted the men. "Who's missing?"

"Picto and Hebe are planting flowers on Lady Lutum's grave," Altor said. "The reality of laying the hatchling to rest helped Picto back to his senses. Putting him to work analysing the data will help, too. He needs to channel his grief into a useful task."

News of the émigrés housing project spread, and anyone who could thread a needle or hammer a nail made a point of wandering by with offers of help. A burly man with arms wrought like gnarly tree trunks loitered beyond the boundary, greeting his neighbours as they passed through.

"He's been watching us all afternoon," Novus said to Miles. "I'm going for a chat, see what he wants."

"I'll come with you. Keep you out of trouble."

The man stood, arms akimbo, a wide smile on his boulder-like face.

"He's even got muscles on his ears," Novus murmured.

The man's smile cracked wide, and a gravelly voice boomed, "Call me Arthur. Thought you might need an expert's help."

Novus squinted up at the man towering above him. "I'm Novus, and this is Miles." He jerked a thumb at the High Shepherd. "What kind of expertise are you offering?"

"I'm an architect; that might be useful," Arthur said. "And I can turn my hand to most jobs on a building site, not just draw the pretty pictures."

"What are you asking in return?" Miles asked.

"Never met Mainlanders before," Arthur rumbled. "Least ways, not full-grown ones. I'd enjoy learning what you're really like. Plainly speaking, I'm nosy."

"Expertise in exchange for knowledge? Sounds like a good deal for us," Miles said, "but less so for you. Ask away, what would you like to know?"

Arthur leaned forward, bringing his immense head to their level. "Is it true you kill off the elderly and infirm when they can't look after themselves?"

Novus widened his eyes and turned to Miles, grinning. "All yours, Shepherd."

Miles opened his mouth to speak, then snapped it shut. He took a deep breath and tried again. "Short answer, yes. Long answer, no. It's complicated."

Arthur nodded slowly. "Savages. But self-conscious enough to try to justify your depravity."

"The elderly and the sick make the choice themselves to take their final walk into the night," Miles said. "They don't want to be a burden on their friends or family."

"What kind of friends or family would allow someone to believe they were a burden?" Arthur shook his head. "Look at all these people, ready to lend a hand to help a bunch of strangers, yet you lot don't support your own loved ones? Savages, for sure. I guess it's up to us Nefans to teach you Mainlanders how to behave honourably." He straightened his shoulders. "Let's begin."

Shortly after sunrise, Arthur returned to the cluster of dew bedazzled sagging tents, clutching rolls of blueprints. "I've put together a few ideas. For a swift and efficient build, I thought a more communal style than you're used to." He unrolled his proposals on the dirt, and everyone crowded round. "What do you think?"

Altor tapped a circular central edifice surrounded by gardens. "Is that a temple?"

Arthur nodded. "First one I've designed, but you've got two Acolytes, a Herdsman, a Shepherd and two High Shepherds. I thought a small temple was an appropriate inclusion."

"Are we allowed to build a temple?" Castian asked. "Won't people object?"

Arthur jutted his lower lip. "No reason to object, so long as the Shepherds don't get urges to increase their flock. We don't take kindly to proselytising."

Hebe traced a finger over a series of fuzzy shapes connecting the buildings. "What're these?"

"You Mainlanders are keen on walls, so I heard. Don't have the resources for that, but I reckon we can relocate enough sturdy thorn bushes to make substantial hedges. Should help you feel secure."

Arthur assumed the role of project manager, much to the Mainlanders' relief. He sent Picto, Altor, and Castian away to work with Prudence. The rest he set to labouring. A steady stream of building materials arrived, accompanied by volunteers eager to meet the exotic strangers. Despite the potential for chaos, Arthur maintained strict order. He rumbled orders, and his words shaped concepts into physical reality.

Within days, Arthur transformed the blueprints into habitable dens, with workshops and studios, surrounded by proto-garden beds and fountains. Labourers flaunted blistered fingers and aching muscles as badges of honour. The camaraderie forged between Mainlanders and islanders rivalled the strength of the walls they had built together.

"Thank you, Arthur," Miles said. "You provided us with opportunities to build friendships, which wouldn't have happened without you." He flushed a rosy hue. "You engineered a clever way to break down the us-and-them barriers."

"I reckon working together teaches people more effectively than any fancy data crystal or series of boring lectures ever could."

Connections

Seated at the circular conference table in her office, Callida glanced at the High Shepherds before nodding to the data analysts. "What have you discovered?"

"The Revised personnel and planning files are the most interesting," Prudence said. "Most of the others are financial accounts. Eye-watering amounts from supporters over the years, and meticulous records of distribution."

"Stark spent vast amounts building and equipping The Revised Training Centre." Picto shuddered. "He spared no expense redeveloping weapons banned millennia ago."

Altor coughed. "In the last decade or two, I've noticed a small but steady increase in requests to study the Final Conflict. The applicants usually mentioned the theological aspects and how The Conflict changed Sui society. With hindsight, they were probably Stark's assets researching battle strategies."

"I agree," Miles said, "but I don't see how this helps us."

"When you bring Stark to account," Callida said, "you can use the information to prove intent."

"What's terrifying," Prudence said, "is the scale. Not only the decades of planning, but the numbers of people involved, across all three Domains. We're like a mouse challenging a sabre cat."

"Prue's right," Picto said. "The network of assets is far-flung and deeply established. And what I witnessed in Crearaton showed a single-minded commitment, and a complete lack of empathy. Civilians stand no chance."

Miles leaned his forearms on the table. "We cannot engage a large, well-equipped force. Nor can we afford to sit back and wait to be annihilated. Our only option is to employ guerrilla tactics."

"Every organisation has a culture," Prudence said, "an accepted way of thinking and doing. Stark has us at a disadvantage. He knows how we think and how we're likely to respond, but we don't comprehend his mindset."

"Novus," Miles said, pointing to the diagram of The Revised Training Centre. "He gave this information freely, and it matches the plans found in the files. He's itching for a way to redeem himself. We have to get past his reluctance to talk."

Prudence nudged Callida. "Doctor Bonna pointed out that Novus appears at ease with women. A female nurse helped him escape the hospital; another woman dressed his wounds and provided him transport. He even flirted clumsily with Doctor Bonna. Then, of course, he confided in you."

Callida frowned. "He manipulates and patronises women. He's not at ease, he uses them for his own means. Probably part of the repressive culture in which he trained."

"Does that matter if he shares useful information?" Prudence asked. "We are at war."

"On the subject of sexual politics," Miles said, fighting back a smile, "how are the Mainlanders responding to Stark's latest directives?"

"Can't say with any certainty," Prudence said. "He controls the media and opinion pieces are definitely one-sided. A few anonymous online protesters questioned his authority, but they disappeared almost immediately, and their accounts were erased."

"Information isn't getting out," Callida said, "but can we get in? Can we broadcast our own news bulletins? If we showed the High Shepherds alive and well, we might inspire hope. At least disrupt Stark's neat narrative."

"Showing evidence of Stark's long-term plotting to usurp power might inspire resistance," Altor said.

"Resistance could easily backfire," Picto said. "We can't risk civilians."

"Unless we can devise a clever plan to remove Stark," Miles said, "civilians must eventually be involved. This is their fight. But first they need organising and training."

"How do you propose to achieve that?" Picto asked.

Miles threw up his hands. "I have no idea."

Miles and Altor returned to the den complex where their friends were busy shifting donated furniture.

"We've allocated the finest pieces to your quarters," Novus said.

Ludion rolled his eyes. "An eclectic mix, my Shepherds, but comfortable."

"Callida suggested, as part of our integration effort," Miles said, "we attend an art show this afternoon. I accepted on our behalf."

Ludion peered around the Shepherds. "Where's Picto? Is he not coming?"

"He and Prudence are still interrogating the data," Miles said. "Callida said the three would meet us there."

"Callida will be there?" Novus beamed. "She'll outshine all the exhibits."

Ludion snorted. "I hope you don't use that line within her earshot, my friend. Callida is not an object."

"You're not supposed to comment on a woman's appearance," Castian said. "I got in trouble for that when I arrived. Prudence says you may praise a person's accomplishments, but not their physical attributes. Not unless you're … in an intimate relationship."

"So, what are the rules when you're intimate?" Novus asked.

Castian blushed. "I'm sure I don't know, praise Solra." He scurried away, his glowing red ears signalling intense discomfort.

"For what it's worth," Ludion said, "my advice is to go slow. Be respectful."

"What would you know?" Novus said.

"Sweetie, I know she's out of your league. I'm also guessing because she's smart and beautiful, she intimidates most men. Which is exactly why they'd have absolutely no chance. Your unabashed self-confidence might just work in your favour."

"You think?" Novus unclenched his fists.

"Bathe first." Ludion sniffed. "For all our sakes."

Golden sun-globes hung from the pergola, artfully positioned to provide the most effective lighting for each piece, and an acapella group performed in the background.

Ludion walked arm-in-arm between Castian and Novus. "Do you know much about art?"

Novus shook his head. "Not encouraged at The Revised Training Centre. Not useful."

"Hmm, I thought as much." Ludion extricated himself from the trio. "Castian? Give our artistically impaired friend an overview of what's on display. Teach him a few phrases so he doesn't sound doltish."

Ludion vanished into the heaving crowd, leaving Castian and Novus in awkward companionship.

Novus broke the uncomfortable silence. "This is important?" He gestured open-handed at the exhibits. "Please, I'd like to learn."

Castian blew out a breath. "Art is life. I can't imagine living without creating, and appreciating the creations of others, praise Solra."

Novus lifted an eyebrow.

"Art connects people. We expose our most tender parts, display our vulnerabilities—"

"Sounds dangerous," Novus said. "Why expose yourselves?"

"I'm not entirely sure I can give you an answer which will make sense to you," Castian said. "When we share those things which delight us, or scare us, we discover we're not alone. Other people experience the same emotions, perhaps in different ways, but that only adds to the rich texture of the tapestry."

Novus nodded. "You're right. You don't make sense, but I feel your passion."

"Have you never sang, for the sheer joy of singing? Or whistled?"

Novus knit his brows. "Maybe, but only when I'm alone."

"And you felt less alone, right?" Castian punched Novus on his arm, then froze. "Sorry, I didn't mean …"

Novus threw back his head and laughed. "Relax, Acolyte. I'm no threat to you, or anyone here." He leaned in. "Can I share something?"

Castian nodded.

"I've never experienced your joyous passion. I won't pretend to understand, but I confess I'm jealous. You make me realise how much I've missed."

Miles fought his way through the crowd and tapped Novus on the shoulder. "Are you gentlemen enjoying yourselves?"

Castian nodded.

"I'm learning how much I don't know," Novus said.

"The others have just arrived," Miles said. "Prudence is introducing Picto to the artists, but Callida is taking a short break. She's sitting on the front steps." He nodded at Novus. "Why don't you offer to keep her company?"

"Are you sure I won't be intruding?"

"I don't know, young man, but I assume you have the wit to interpret her response."

Novus wound his way towards the entrance and paused on the top step.

Callida turned and smiled. "Too much culture? Care to join me?" She patted the step next to her. "I enjoy the music. This group is extremely talented. Do you like music?"

Novus settled onto the step below her. "Castian has been giving me a crash course in art appreciation," he said. "I have no idea what he's talking about, but I'd like to understand, because art is clearly important to so many people. I'm afraid that part of my education was completely neglected."

"The Revised don't value art? Or self expression?"

Novus stared at a sun-globe. "The Revised operate within a strict hierarchy with zero tolerance for non-conformity. Until recently, I hadn't considered the subject. But they don't value science either. Unless it has a direct martial application. They've invested obscene amounts developing ways to control or kill, but nothing, to my knowledge, in healing."

"Surely they want to heal their own soldiers?"

Novus shook his head. "The Revised view the weak or injured as liabilities. They cull them. There's a constant supply of fresh soldiers."

"But the time and financial investment to train a soldier?"

"Anyone, or anything, perceived imperfect, is anathema to Solra. They are irredeemable."

"Is that your belief?"

"We don't think about such things. We accept what we are taught without question." Novus glanced up at Callida. "Trainees who question authority do not last. They disappear without trace, their numbers never spoken."

"Numbers?"

"They allocate trainees rank and number. Names are unnecessary. After I lost my memory, a pretty nurse gifted me a name. My birth parent may have named me, if they had me long enough, but Novus is the name I claim as my own."

"Your raising sounds brutal. Did you have friends?"

"Friends? Not exactly. We were raised in a cohort and competed for supremacy with the other cohorts. But within the group, we vied for rankings. I survived. Losers disappeared." Novus sighed and closed his eyes. "That's your cue to send me away, to banish me."

Ludion threaded his way through the crowds, admiring each exhibit for its unique characteristics. He imagined himself back in his old studio, surrounded by admirers eager to acquire his latest work. If he had the courage to steal a data crystal from Stark and break out of detention, surely he could muster the fortitude to mount an exhibition of his work for an audience beyond close friends and colleagues?

Picto's voice wove into his fantasy. "Marvellous, marvellous, marvellous. So much talent, I'm weeping." He snuffled into his sleeve and wiped his eyes. "Pardon me, pardon, pardon. May I introduce you to Prudence? The person leading the data analysis. Prudence, meet the lion-hearted Ludion."

Ludion gazed, speechless, at her gorgeous freckle-spattered face.

"Pleased to finally meet you," Prudence said. "I've heard so much about you. This is the first time I've met a genuine hero."

"You sell yourself short, Prudence." Picto chuckled. "Castian tells me you rescued him, not once but twice, from certain death. Twice. You're a hero yourself."

"Ludion?" Prudence lightly touched his forearm. "Do you need to sit? Maybe some fresh air?" She turned to Picto. "Your friend seems unwell. Help me get him outside."

Picto and Prudence linked arms with Ludion and steered him to a seating area surrounded by lush potted shrubs.

"Ludion, Ludion, Ludion, my friend, take deep breaths." Picto chafed his friend's hands. "All the excitement and exertion catching up, you'll be fine." He turned to Prudence. "Can you find the High Shepherds? I think we need to get him home."

Prudence hurried away, intent on her mission.

"Picto? I just saw an angel," Ludion said. "Is she real, or am I hallucinating?"

Guerrilla Tactics

Authority is divine, and those who wield it are chosen; disobedi-ence is a sin no lesser than heresy.

The Blessed Prophet Serenus

Stark paced the deck of the dirigible, the profane world far below his feet. Captain Pupa anticipated his wishes, and the staff were suitably obsequious, but the satisfaction he craved continued to elude him. He rubbed his shoulder, the knowledge of his fraud burning like a brand. Instead of the expected flood of euphoria, guilt pounded inside his skull.

Captain Pupa halted the immense golden craft above the burnt-out ruins of The Revised Training Centre. Stark stared at the charred skeletons of his winged and wheeled fleet. His eyes passed over what he assumed were the burial pits of the idiots who dared ruin his victory celebration. He would order the remaining Revised to march back and forth until they stamped the memory of the incompetent dead from recall, and the newly flattened area would serve as a landing pad for his glorious sacred craft.

Lieutenant Nenimem, who retained nominal control of the centre, stood to attention as Stark descended.

"You appear to have all in hand, Lieutenant," Stark said after accepting the officer's obeisance.

"Your Holiness."

Stark pointed to the dug over land. "Are they burial pits?"

"Your Holiness, yes."

"I want them stamped into oblivion and a landing pad built over them. Make the project your top priority."

"Your Holiness, yes, Your Holiness."

"How many competitors have you killed since assuming control?"

"Your Holiness?"

"Come now, Lieutenant Nenimem. No need to be coy. I would be disappointed if you hadn't faced and overcome fierce opposition."

Lieutenant Nenimem stared at a spot above Stark's shoulder. "Seven, Your Holiness."

Stark tucked his arms into his heavily embroidered sleeves. "Clearly a man not afraid to take decisive action. Tell me, what do you think needs to happen next?"

"Your Holiness, you have my reports."

"But I want your opinions, Lieutenant, not just lists of facts and columns of numbers."

"Your Holiness, I am not sure I fully understand the question. Are you asking how to get the Centre operating at optimal efficiency, or the wider question of imposing Orthodox Solran law across the Domains?"

"Would you describe yourself as an ambitious man, Lieutenant Nenimem?"

"The Blessed Prophet Serenus teaches Solra is the source of all talent and wisdom." Nenimem said. "Not striving to apply Solra's gifts to their fullest extent demonstrates a lack of righteousness."

"Are you schooling me in theology?"

"Your Holiness, no. I meant no disrespect. I only know Solra rewards the faithful."

"Following your logic, why did Solra allow this devastation?" Stark gestured to the charred buildings and heat bent vehicle skeletons.

"Your Holiness, Solra blessed the recruitment and training of the Revised. The destruction of the main Centre on the day you claimed victory and rose from High Shepherd to His Holiness Grand Master is open to only one interpretation. Solra wants you, and your servants, to rebuild. Bigger and stronger than before."

The Revised Training Camp gossip mill ran hot, and well before sundown, every soldier understood His Holiness's confirmation of Lieutenant Nenimem's authority. Individuals and cohorts brutally renegotiated allegiances, and Nenimem's final potential challenger was terminated.

His Holiness approved all of Lieutenant Nenimem's plans and suggestions for improvements, and the Centre settled into a new rhythm of cautious cooperation. From his elevated position, physical and spiritual, His Most High Holiness blessed the endeavours of The Revised.

Lieutenant Nenimem ascended daily to the deck of the golden dirigible to report to His Holiness. "Sui have become soft, Your Holiness. They will crumble under harsh discipline." Nenimem curled his upper lip. "We must gently fire them in the furnace of Solra's love."

"You have a proposal, Lieutenant?"

"You control the media, restricting what the Sui see and hear," Nenimem said. "I suggest a more proactive approach. Show them the benefits of what they ought to do and think, rather than just banning what they shouldn't."

Stark nodded for Nenimem to continue.

"That foolish female, Beatrice Max, has a large following. We should utilise her popularity to encourage other females to follow Orthodox Solran law. She could make a short series showing the satisfaction of submitting to the Holy Will of Solra."

"Your idea has merit, Lieutenant."

"Thank you, Your Holiness. Once we are back to full strength and mobility, we can reassess our approach."

Beatrice's Bulletins

Beatrice pushes away the makeup girl. "That's too much." She swipes at the immaculately applied cosmetics and looks in disgust at the soiled tissue. "Just enough so I don't look blank under the studio lights. No need to paint me like a harlot."

The makeup girl blinks and stammers. "I only gave you your usual treatment, Miss Max."

"Haven't you been listening? Times are changing. High Shepherd Stark is guiding us all to safer pastures."

Beatrice fixes her face to her satisfaction, a subdued version of her old self. She combs and flattens her hair into place, then smiles at her reflection. *Clean and tidy, as I ought to be.*

"Three, two…" A single finger flick signals action.

She glances at the auto cue but ignores the scrolling words. The thought of her next assignment unnerves her, but she refuses to allow her dismay to mar her performance. She offers a small tight smile which fails to reach her eyes. "Welcome, friends. For my next thrilling assignment, I'll be travelling cross-country to meet authentic and devout Viribians." Beatrice folds her hands on the desk, praying the trembling isn't visible. "I have been invited to the homes of women in the outer colonies. They are eager to show how productive and fulfilling their lives have become since embracing the orthodox principles of Solra. They want to share with you, my friends, the joys of accepting Solra's Holy Will and finding your rightful place in the hierarchy of Their holy creation."

Doctor Bonna studied Beatrice Max's dull-eyed appearance. The woman's missing verve and charisma rendered her approved script lifeless. Her promise to bring genuine stories of renewed satisfaction carried the authenticity of a stranger reading a eulogy.

Beatrice's emotional diminishment shocked Doctor Bonna almost as much as her reduced status. No fancy conchatus for Miss Max on this assignment, but an arduous road trip on barely discernible tracks.

An idea bubbled in Doctor Bonna's mind, popping and fizzing with a delightful effervescence, refusing to be ignored.

Doctor Bonna strolled to Callida's office, turning over the idea, searching for flaws. Apart from a clear breech of ethics, she found no practical faults. She knocked on Callida's open door and plonked herself in a chair. After she finished speaking, she folded her arms and smiled.

Callida leaned back. "That is the most preposterous idea I've ever heard. I'm saying nothing about the practical aspects. You've got that covered. But what you suggest is inconceivable."

"We're at war, Callida. Indeed, if I'd previously heard such a suggestion, I am certain I'd have been horrified, but our reality has changed. Can we really afford delicate sensibilities? Our enemies have no such scruples. Think of it as disabling one of the enemy's most effective weapons."

Callida finger-drummed the arms of her chair. "You'll need Miles. Felix and Hebe, too. Who else?"

"The four of us should be sufficient," Doctor Bonna said. "Guerrilla tactics, as Miles suggested."

Felix drove Miles and Hebe to the medical centre. "Doctor Bonna's summons sounded urgent."

The trio made their way to her office, where she greeted them with barely suppressed excitement before divulging her daring plan.

"Are you reasonably certain of Beatrice's schedule?" Miles asked.

Doctor Bonna nodded at her communication centre. "They're making no secret of her route. Indeed, I suspect they want a live audience when she interviews these poor deluded women."

"If she leaves as planned," Hebe said, "the convoy will be in open country by midmorning, and she won't be expected at her first gig for two days."

"We have ample supplies," Felix said. "Although the thought makes my skin crawl, we should wear the spare uniforms we found in The Revised conchatus."

"Indeed, an excellent idea," Doctor Bonna said. "We meet at sunrise."

Miles conducted his pre-flight checks with the panache of a seasoned pilot. Doctor Bonna stowed her medical field kit under her seat while Felix and Hebe stashed their new gadgets in the overhead luggage compartments. Felix handed around the shields and made sure Doctor Bonna and Miles knew how to activate them.

The massive craft growled to life, ready to respond to Miles' bidding. Once airborne, he called for Felix to join him in the cockpit to help monitor the digital array. The Central Sea blazed like a shattered mirror under the rising sun. Shards of sharp light prickled their eyes. Miles donned eye shades and passed a pair to Felix.

Doctor Bonna wrung her hands and wiped her sweaty palms on her borrowed uniform.

"Are you nervous, Doctor?" Hebe leaned forward. "We're quite safe. Miles is qualified. Not exactly what you expect from a High Shepherd, but he's got hundreds of flying hours."

"Indeed, I'm sure he's more than proficient. I just don't like heights."

"But this was your idea," Hebe said.

Doctor Bonna forced a weak smile. "Indeed. The results will be worth a little discomfort."

Hebe reached for the communication headsets. "Put these on. The reduced noise might make you less nervous. Here." He tapped a button on his own set. "We can still talk. I'll distract you with tall tales of daring and courage from my long-lost youth."

Doctor Bonna carefully adjusted the headset, while studiously avoiding eye contact with Hebe. Whenever Hebe stumbled through a portal, bearing injuries of varying severity, he bantered and joked. She admired him, and his selfless commitment to rescuing imperfect hatchlings, but his self-deprecating humour confused her.

"Falling out of trees and crashing speeding vehicles is not courageous, but foolhardy. Indeed, I don't know how you survived."

"I wouldn't survive without you," Hebe said.

Doctor Bonna looked away while she decided how to interpret his comment.

Miles swung the conchatus in a wide arc. Below, a modest two vehicle convoy jounced across the savannah without a shred of protection. Scans revealed neither weapons nor defences of any description. Not even basic sonic pulse emitters. A sad indication of Beatrice's diminished status.

"Switch on your shields," Felix called over his shoulder.

Miles dropped the conchatus low to the ground, the furious blades flattening the grasses and buffeting the scrawny scrub. The oncoming cars slowed and crawled to a halt, cowering like petrified mice before a voracious raptor.

Felix and Hebe, uniformed and helmeted, slipped from the side doors and approached the cars, their lasers casually displayed.

"Exit your vehicles," Hebe shouted, jerking his weapon.

Internal movement swayed the lead vehicle, but the doors and tinted windows remained firmly shut.

Felix nodded to Hebe, and they switched on their shroak repellents and closed in on the front car. They yanked open the doors, hauled out the driver and front passenger, and tossed them to the dirt, where they writhed and whined, hands clutching their heads.

Hebe slithered to the back door and revealed Beatrice huddled on the floor behind the driver's seat. Remembering Doctor Bonna's instructions, he leaned in and grabbed her travelling case first, then pulled her out and shrugged her over his shoulder. Beatrice whimpered and clawed ineffectually at his helmet, while Felix methodically laser shredded the tyres of both vehicles.

With Felix covering his back, Hebe jogged to the conchatus and handed the semiconscious woman, and her bag, to the doctor, who promptly injected her with a mild tranquilliser.

Miles launched the conchatus into the sky, leaving the mewling media crew confused but physically unharmed.

A Woman of Influence

Those who hide from the shepherd shall be found, for Their will confounds all who dare oppose it.

The Blessed Prophet Serenus

Beatrice swam to the surface, gasping for consciousness, beating off the weight of her medications. She glimpsed gleaming white walls and beeping machines.

Not in the ramshackle car.

Not on the endless dusty savannah.

Not chaperoned by her newly assigned third-rate crew.

Not all bad, then.

She smiled as her eyelids slammed shut.

Doctor Bonna studied Beatrice's monitors. She had suffered no ill-effects from her minor procedure. Although dulled by her recent treatment by the new regime, Beatrice retained an inner resiliency, and Doctor Bonna planned to restore her natural sparkle.

Doctor Bonna selected a slow-release stimulant. No point aggressively dragging Miss Max into her brand-new reality, when she could be gently led.

Beatrice floundered, blinking and gasping, and the pristine white room with a stern-faced woman at the foot of her pod came into focus. She won the battle to keep her eyes open. "Who are you, and where am I?"

"Can you remember your name?"

"I'm Beatrice Max." She rolled her eyes. "You are?"

"Pleased to meet you, Beatrice Max. I'm Doctor Bonna."

Beatrice shrugged. "Never heard of you. You're not on my list of interviewees." She ran her hands over herself under the covers. Dressed, but not in her own garments. She wriggled into a sitting position, tugged the IV cannula from her inner elbow, and tossed it aside. "Fetch my clothes."

Doctor Bonna's mouth twitched. "Where do you plan to go?"

"Not that it's any of your business, but I have an assignment ..." Beatrice slitted her eyes. "Am I a prisoner? I remember ..." She looked at the array of sophisticated machines. "Where am I?"

Doctor Bonna eased herself onto the foot of the pod. "What do you remember? You were travelling in a small convoy. Then what?"

Beatrice drew back, her shoulders hunched. "I did nothing wrong." Tears pooled in her eyes. "I don't deserve punishment."

"You misunderstand, indeed." Doctor Bonna passed her a handkerchief. "We freed you from a corrupt regime. We don't want to punish you, Miss Max. We want your assistance."

"You're trying to trick me, but it won't work. I remember now. A huge conchatus, military I think, and black uniformed soldiers. They used some kind of mind control, because we all felt sick and dizzy, then I woke up here."

"Excellent, your memory isn't impaired, and your confusion is understandable." Doctor Bonna beamed. "A friend stole the conchatus from the secret Revised Training Centre, along with the uniforms."

"That isn't possible," Beatrice said. "Nobody steals from the RTC. The place is impregnable."

"I can see why they'd want you to think that, but it's not true. My friend, Ludion, stole the bird when he rescued the High Shepherds, and he burned the facility to the ground."

Beatrice stared at Doctor Bonna. "You're mad. None of that is true. The High Shepherds are on retreat … meditating … praying for the continued success of His Holiness."

"Why don't we go for a little walk? I have a surprise for you in the garden."

"I don't suppose I have a choice," Beatrice said. "If I refuse, you'll compel me, right?"

"We don't compel people on Nefas. Will you come?"

"Nefas? I knew it! You're utterly insane."

"You might feel a little wobbly, so I recommend the chair." Doctor Bonna strode to the door and beckoned the waiting orderly. "Get yourself comfortable. You have enough control to forego the seatbelt, unless you'll feel more secure?"

Beatrice swung her legs out of the pod and stretched, before settling herself into the chair. "Are you escorting me to a torture chamber, or an execution squad?"

Doctor Bonna shook her head. "We're going to meet some special friends in the garden. Indeed, I expect you'll recognise them." She guided the chair along the sun bright corridor, hung with an array of framed art, and into a secluded garden, where two elderly men chatted together.

They greeted Beatrice with wide smiles.

Miles stepped forward and shook her hand. "Good to see you up and about, young lady."

"Welcome to the Isle of Nefas, Miss Max," Altor said. "I hope you're recovering after your unfortunate ordeal."

Beatrice turned to Doctor Bonna. "The High Shepherds?" Her voice rose to a squeak. "This is the story of a lifetime."

"Indeed, Miss Max," Doctor Bonna said. "And it's yours to tell. A Domain wide exclusive."

"We'll talk again," Miles said, "but you should rest now."

Altor nodded. "I'm sure you'll have questions once you've had time to process what you've heard today. Ask whatever you like. We'll answer as best we can."

Doctor Bonna chuckled when the Shepherds left. "I always wondered if your blushes and eyelash batting were automatic responses, or great acting. Not one flush or flutter today."

"I'm smart enough to know I'm not that smart," Beatrice said. "I learned to use my meagre attractions and resources to the best advantage. Most men respond to flattery, an opportunity to show off their superiority." She shrugged.

"I prefer to let them strive for equality," Doctor Bonna said. "But I don't have your natural assets."

Beatrice glanced at Doctor Bonna, who struggled to suppress a grin. They burst into spluttering giggles.

"You must think I'm dreadful," Beatrice said after she recovered her breath.

"I'm intrigued, more than anything. You collude with a system which believes you inherently inferior because of your sex, but you make it work for you, in a twisted way."

"I hadn't thought of my actions in quite those terms," Beatrice said, "but there have been times I've wanted to run away screaming. Or at least scrub myself clean."

"Indeed?"

Beatrice grimaced. "High Shepherd Stark always made a point of giving me special access to his functions, and he always singled me out to ask him questions. My career wouldn't have been anywhere near as successful without his holy patronage, but he has a way of looking at you, you know?"

"Not from experience, no."

"He's a holy man, but he'd undress you with his eyes. Never said a wrong word, never touched me, but I'd go home and scrub myself raw." Beatrice snorted. "Then what does he do? Reinstate ridiculous ancient laws, restricting women to domestic duties, and relegates me to low status puff pieces."

"Indeed. Time to change the world, Beatrice Max."

Stolen Assets

When faith is attacked, the righteous defend without mercy, for the unclean must not prevail.

The Blessed Prophet Serenus

"Kidnapped?" Stark hunched forward on his throne and frowned at Lieutenant Nenimem. "Who kidnapped her, and why?"

Nenimem kept his eyes firmly focused above Stark's shoulder. "Your Holiness, according to the witness reports, we did. Uniformed individuals, travelling in a huge black conchatus, and employing an unidentified form of mind control, abducted Miss Max."

"The Shepherds in my stolen craft," Stark said. "But what use could they have for the woman? They didn't take any recording equipment?"

"Your Holiness, only the female journalist." Nenimem sucked in a deep breath. "Is she privy to any secrets? Information they could use against you? To undermine your authority?"

Stark flushed. Streaks of dark red flashed up his neck and disappeared into his hairline. He leaned back on his throne, white knuckles gripping the armrests. The airship bucked against its restraints; its girders groaned softly. The ominous silence of the audience chamber cocooned the priest and soldier in uncomfortable proximity.

"I have no secrets. I am a Child of Solra. The Chosen One. Divine Light bathes my life."

Nenimem bowed. "Your Holiness, I am unfamiliar with the woman's work, but I understand she is, or was, hugely popular across all three Domains. Could the Shepherds leverage her fame against you?"

"She has the intellectual capacity of a squirrel, but in the past, she possessed powerful instincts." Stark shook his head. "After reprogramming, she reverted to a more naturally feminine character. Malleable, unambitious. The Shepherds have wasted their effort. Beatrice Max can do nothing for them."

"Your Holiness, the woman's identity chip is inactive."

"Beatrice is dead?"

"Not necessarily, Your Holiness. They could have removed her chip … thus restoring her original aberrant personality." Nenimem stared over Stark's shoulder, his expression carefully neutral.

"The woman is unimportant," Stark said. "I am concerned about the Shepherds, and their mobility. How far can their craft travel? And who would dare shelter them?"

"The stolen craft's range covers the Domains … and the Isle of Nefas. I have received no reports of the conchatus. In areas we have a presence, Your Holiness, somebody would have noticed and made a report. My best guess is they are hiding on the Isle of Nefas."

"Nefas, with its profane technology? Its disrespect for Solran law? If they are sheltering the iniquitous felons, they have as good as declared war. They are planning to pollute the Domains with their foul blood and perverted lifestyle. We must protect the women."

Reinvented, Reimagined

Beatrice fluffed her hair and smoothed her sky-blue dress over her thighs. Not only had Doctor Bonna produced the cosmetic bag she'd thought lost in her rescue, but introduced her to a marvellous cooperative of talented textile workers. Beatrice's vibrant new wardrobe would be the envy of many on the mainland.

Assuming their brains still functioned.

Armed with a dazzling smile and a portable recorder, Beatrice ventured outside her den into the émigré compound. Her emerald painted nails sparkled when she shielded her eyes from Solra's glare.

Thanks to Doctor Bonna, she knew the names and brief histories of everyone in the compound. She waved at a trio on the perimeter. Castian and Espio returned shy nods, but Hebe only grunted as he wrangled a tall thorny bush into place. Beatrice recognised the youths and recalled the recent scandals surrounding them, but the grumpy older man intrigued her. His unfamiliar face, seamed and tanned, begged for a well-lit photo shoot. A man with character carved into his features.

She stepped into the open space, hips swaying, then paused and bit her glossed lip. No more sashaying. Start as you mean to go on. She dialled down her smile from sensational celebrity to friendly neighbour.

"Hi, I'm Beatrice Max. I recognise you, Castian, and you, Espio. Delighted to meet you." She turned. "You must be Hebe, Hero of the Midwife Trail."

Hebe straightened and wiped his palms on his trouser legs. "Must I? Says who? Maybe I'd like to be someone else. Reinvent myself. Hebe, the hedge builder."

Beatrice pouted. "I'm sorry, Herdsman Hebe. I meant no disrespect."

Hebe shook his head. "Don't mind me, young lady. I'm a cantankerous old man with a bad back and too much digging still to do. Talk to the youngsters. They're more entertaining."

Espio stepped forward. "Why don't we walk?"

Hebe turned away and busied himself with the bare-root bushes.

Beatrice allowed the youngsters to guide her out of earshot before speaking. "What did I do to offend Herdsman Hebe?"

"You used to be a favourite of Stark." Espio shrugged. "Hebe thinks you should have used your talents for real investigative journalism."

"Do you hold the same opinion?"

Castian tapped her arm. "I don't think what we did, or who we were, before coming to Nefas is relevant. I accepted the Solran teachings without question. My comfortable life provided no reason to question the status quo. Only after Stark cast me into the darkness did I see a glimmer of genuine Light, praise Solra."

Espio nodded. "Castian makes sense. Few people see past the façade of the familiar, and even fewer care to look more closely. Ignorance, feigned or real, allows us to ignore our responsibilities, which are invariably uncomfortable and inconvenient."

Beatrice glanced between them.

"Hebe burns with impatience," Espio said. "Waiting and planning abrades his nerves. Don't let him fool you with his old man spiel. He's fighting fit."

"What do you want from us?" Castian asked.

"Your truth," Beatrice replied. "Whatever that might be. I want to broadcast your stories to the Domains: an enlightened heretic and a living suicide. Although I'm not yet sure what he's hiding, or how deep his lies, I want to expose Stark as a fraud."

"Why the change of heart?" Espio asked.

Beatrice turned and flipped up her hair, revealing the tiny, stubbled patch where Doctor Bonna had operated. "As you said, I'm no longer ignorant, and I can't ignore my responsibilities." She struck a mock dramatic pose. "The public deserves to know, darling."

Novus tapped on Callida's door. "May I come in?"

"My office is always open. You look troubled."

Novus half closed the door behind him and dropped into the chair before Callida's desk. He glanced at his rough plan of The Revised Training Centre, still hanging on the wall. The Shepherds and Ludion had added minor details, confirming the authenticity.

He frowned and covered his eyes.

"Are you unwell?" Callida asked, concern warming her voice.

"The diagram. It's incomplete." Novus lowered his hands, but kept his eyes squeezed shut. "There's a second location. Far away. Two other linked campuses. A pre-training centre for the very young, where hatchlings spend their first half decade …"

"Do you know where?"

"No, but there's a river … no, a lake. A deep cold lake separating the two. Youngsters who survive the rigours of the first camp spend the next decade at the camp for older hatchlings. Training becomes more intense, more physically demanding. More dangerous."

Callida crouched beside him. "Take your time."

Novus opened his eyes and blew a long breath through pursed lips. "They keep the youngsters apart to protect them from the stronger and more aggressive older ones. They only allow transfers to the next camp for the biggest and strongest."

"What happens to the ones who grow slowly?"

"They eventually disappear." Novus wiped a tear. "There were rumours they ended up as targets in live training sessions, but I never saw that. At least, I don't remember."

"Can you recall anything else?"

"Nothing you need to know."

"I see." Callida stood and returned to her chair, the vast expanse of her desk less of a barrier than Novus's reticence. "What did you come to tell me?"

Novus sat straighter and pulled himself back into the present. "How long do you think it will be before Stark works out where the Shepherds are sheltering? Abducting Beatrice publicly challenged his authority. He'll attack. Hard."

"Are you asking permission to leave? I can arrange for Felix to get you to the mainland."

Novus allowed a quick flash of orange at his temples as he splayed his fingers on the desk. "I can't leave. I don't want to leave. You need help to build defences. Right now, you're as vulnerable as a day-old hatchling."

"I assume you have suggestions," Callida said.

Novus shrugged. "The sea offers some protection, but I doubt Stark would consider attacking by sea. Too many risks. He'll mount an air attack."

"Ludion destroyed most of the craft, land and air. He'll need time to rebuild."

"How many of Stark's wealthy benefactors own private aircraft? In his position, I'd requisition the lot and refit them with missiles. They don't have to be a matched set to be lethal."

Callida's hand flew to her throat, and she blanched. "By the Light. I never imagined he'd involve civilians."

"In a holy war, there are no civilians. There are only orthodox believers and Darkness bound heretics. The saved and the damned. Which raises a delicate issue." Novus twisted in his chair and peered around the bright office. "Have your data analysts noticed that all The Revised are male?"

"I haven't seen that data, no."

"This is speculation, and hearsay. I never heard an official version." Novus knitted his fingers together and placed his hands on his lap. "I grew to maturity in a totally male environment. Not one female got into any of the camps. Ever. The Revised are taught females are weak and filthy, tolerated only for breeding. A source of physical and spiritual depravity."

Callida raised an eyebrow, but said nothing. Tendrils of bright green swarmed down her shoulders and arms. She nodded for him to continue.

"The Revised soldiers have certain … expectations. Rumours, or sick fantasies if you will, circulated. An understanding, that when Stark rose to power, females would be rounded up and transported to secret locations …" Novus paused.

"To be killed?"

"Not immediately. Not the young and attractive ones. Not until they'd fulfilled their … natural function." Novus hung his head, unable to meet Callida's mismatched eyes.

Callida swallowed. "The young women will be married off? Against their will? Barbarism."

"Not married. Forcibly mated. Bred like the ancients farmed animals, then discarded."

A flat silence lay between them, wider and heavier than the desk. Novus sat statue still, hardly daring to breathe, while Callida processed his words, purple blotches blossomed on her brow. "Other than the shroak-infested sea, Nefas has no defences. Nor do we possess the means to launch an offence," Callida said. "I would be grateful if you kept your … speculations … to yourself. I see no benefit in fostering fear and panic."

Novus nodded. "You have one advantage. An enemy cannot sneak up on you, because there is no natural cover. Whether by sea or air, they cannot hide their approach."

"But we cannot fight."

"Then hide. Build underground shelters."

Callida leaned forward, her eyes narrowed. "Caves riddle the island; many are connected with tunnels."

Novus grinned. "If you lure The Revised underground, you can ambush them. Do you have maps?"

Prudence pushed back from the console and stretched, ready for her daily benediction. Callida intercepted her at the courtyard gate. "Can we go somewhere more private?"

"This way." Prudence led her to a secluded garden with a sparkling fountain. "I come here when I need to be alone." She dropped onto a bench piled with colourful cushions.

"Novus came to see me." Callida ignored the comfort of the cushions and paced the gravel path.

"Ooh, I knew he liked you."

"When you looked at the records of The Revised, did you notice anything strange?"

"Stolen hatchlings, raised in isolation, schooled in intolerance, and trained in ancient warfare? Nope, all seemed perfectly normal." Prudence rolled her eyes. "You'll have to be more specific."

"Novus pointed out that The Revised are exclusively male."

Prudence closed her eyes and frowned. "Yes, I think so. I can easily check." She blinked. "But that's hardly strange. Wasn't soldiering traditionally a male dominated activity?"

"Dominated, yes, but not exclusively." Callida perched on the edge of the bench and turned her face to the sun. "I need you to collate a list of Stark's supporters, who own aircraft of any description. Can you send it to me before sundown?"

Felix adjusted the cave survey projection on Callida's office wall. "That's as clear as I can make the image."

"I didn't realise they were so extensive." Callida shuddered.

The architect, Arthur, shook his head. "I reckon this survey is incomplete. This map is over a century old; a lot could have changed. But the only way to be sure, is go down and see for ourselves."

"I'm in," Felix said. "Novus ought to be part of the group."

"Because he came up with the idea?" Callida asked.

"Partly, but his military knowledge would be useful. He sees situations from a different perspective," Felix said.

Beatrice replayed the interview with Castian and Espio once more, marking the golden nuggets for final editing. Their youthful innocence blazed forth, casting Stark's heinous crimes into deepest shadow. Under different circumstances, this series of interviews would win awards, raising her to an exalted status above cheap celebrity. *They still will. I'm helping to change the world. Doesn't get more important than that.*

A Confession

The tools of the unrighteous eventually serve the faithful; what is misused by the profane shall be made sacred in the crucible of Holy Light.

The Blessed Prophet Serenus

Felix collected Arthur and Novus. They travelled in a semi-stupor before Solra claimed the sky. Felix passed a packet of stimtabs. "Slip one under your tongue."

Novus rolled the pill between his thumb and forefinger before putting the tab in his mouth. "I used these while fleeing Luxton, but I was already familiar with their use. During training, we had to capture the enemy … a different cohort … in a forest … we hunted them for three days … no sleep." Novus shook his head. "One youngster lost control. Sleep deprivation drove him mad. He slaughtered our captives, then turned on us."

"Did he recover?" Arthur's question rumbled through the car, vibrating with hope.

Novus stared impassively at Arthur. "He came at me with his blade. I took it from him and stabbed him in the eye. I scrambled his brains."

"You didn't need to kill him, not if you'd disarmed him," Felix said, flickers of red running neck to temple .

"No. But I wanted to. That's what Revised training does. Turns men into monsters." His fingertips grazed the scar on his nape.

Arthur's words fell with the implacable certainty of rocks. "We won't be underground even a full day, so you won't be driven insane through lack of sleep." He leaned closer, streaks of orange and scarlet colouring his cheeks. "But if you get any funny ideas, I'll bury you so deep, nobody will even remember your name."

The car jounced and jolted over the scrub, and only occasional "oomph's" escaped the occupants' lips as the men avoided eye contact.

Novus shut his eyes and sank into the rank mud of memory. He sifted through the filth, searching for a glimmer of redemption.

Disembodied voices, cruel and sharp as thorns, tore at the youngster who'd foolishly confessed to his cohort he feared the dark.

Whose idea had it been to set him as guard over the prisoners?

Shackled but not gagged, the prisoners heckled and abused the youngster, while his own cohort rested before the victory march back to The Revised Training Centre.

Thickly wet screams and choking gurgles woke the victors from their slumbers. The twin odours of blood and fear washed over them. A strangled cry rose above the others and the youngster lurched out of the darkness; his blooded blade held aloft.

He leapt at Novus, arms and legs uncoordinated, leaving his midsection undefended. Novus slammed a fist into the lad's sternum, laying him in the dirt, sobbing and gasping for air.

A boot stamping on the lad's wrist.

Sticky blade fallen to the ground.

Novus straddling the lad's narrow heaving chest.

Grabbing the blood-slicked knife.

Plunging the blade into the eye socket.

Twisting and pushing.

Black fluid gushing over his fist.

The lad twitching and bucking beneath him.

Then nothing.

Stillness.

No remorse.

Another unmourned death.

Kicking aside the corpse and cleaning the gore off his hands in the sandy soil.

No comments from his comrades, only a slightly wider berth given.

Novus opened his eyes. The silent car engine told him they'd arrived at the first cave entrance. Silent stares from Felix and Arthur warned him fragments of memory had inadvertently spilled from his mouth.

Felix tossed heavy backpacks and hard hats to Novus and Arthur, and shrugged into his own larger pack. "Let's go." He led them past strewn boulders and thorny thickets to a wide cleft in the ground, which descended gently into a gloomy half-light.

Novus tipped back his head and stared into the sky. "We need to know how visible this entrance is from the air. If it's obvious, we can't use it as a refuge, but it has potential for an ambush. Especially if we make what look like inept attempts to disguise it."

"I'll send a drone later." Felix flicked a switch on his helmet. "Switch on your cameras. They'll pick up more detail than biological eyes."

Cool, damp air chilled their skin as they tramped further into the cavern. The wide space narrowed, forcing them into single file. Bringing up the rear, Arthur shuffled sideways, his shoulders grazing the walls.

Novus heard the scraping and turned to watch Arthur wriggle through. "A Revised in full armour would struggle to pass here."

"A good ambush point, then," Felix said.

Novus shook his head. "No. Too easy to back up and escape. In this position, I'd retreat, then sneak back with explosives. Either blow you to smithereens, or trap you under a rockfall and leave you in the darkness to die."

Arthur dusted his shoulders. "How many have you killed?"

"No idea." Novus held up his hands, palms out. "I don't mean I've lost count, or any other macho nonsense. My memories are returning. Sometimes in spurts, sometimes in dribbles which make little sense." Novus tilted his chin. "Why don't you ask the question you really want me to answer?"

"Come on," Felix said. "You can have your ethics debate later."

The pinch point opened. Thin streams threaded across the cavern floor, connecting shallow puddles. Their sun-globes revealed only one exit.

"This looks promising." Novus sloshed to the exit. "Another narrow passageway," he called over his shoulder.

Arthur pulled a palm sized gadget from his pocket and pointed it at the ground, muttering to himself as he shuffled between the pools. "Stay close to the walls. The floor is eroded, and deep water runs below."

Novus edged closer and peered at the multicoloured readout. "We lure The Revised into this space and blow the floor, dropping them into the water. They'll drown in their heavy armour, and to make sure, we collapse the roof onto them. Any survivors we pick off from above."

"I can rig the explosives," Arthur said, "but if they're trapped, shouldn't we give them the option to surrender?" His throat fluttered pale green.

"The Revised are trained never to surrender."

"If the old survey is accurate," Felix said, "this passage leads to another large cavern with multiple exits to the surface."

Novus took the lead, with Arthur breathing down his neck. The passage wound upwards and brought them to a chamber, admitting chinks of sunlight through a fractured ceiling.

The trio breathed more easily when they scrambled up a short tunnel and away from the treacherously deceptive ground over the caverns.

Novus spun slowly on the spot. "These exits seem well hidden. Can we get an aerial view of this, too? Did you bring a copy of the survey? We have a potential ambush location, but we need a refuge. I have an idea what I'm looking for. Ideally, closer to the community, and in a wooded area. Multiple entrances."

Felix tapped his wristcomm and threw up a 3D holo image of the survey.

Novus stabbed a finger at the wavering image. "Let's try that one."

"Deeper than the first," Arthur said, suppressing a shudder. "I never realised how much I hate confined spaces."

Novus winked at him. "Missile proof."

Boulders dotted the lightly wooded area, making a straight path impossible. They located the entrance under a rocky overhang. Novus nodded silent approval as he pushed through the spindly bushes crowding the stony threshold. The tunnel fell steeply, and the trio scrambled and slithered to the cavern floor. Cascades of pebbles and dirt chased them, the dust choking them and tearing their eyes.

Novus coughed and spat. "That confirms no large beasties live in here. Or at least not using this entrance."

"I can't imagine anyone skulking in unnoticed," Felix said.

"There're a few simple methods to kill intruders which require no skill other than vigilance," Novus said. "A pit with stakes at the bottom of the chute? Remove the cover when threatened. Or a gate studded with armour piercing blades? The Revised impale themselves as they slither down."

"Those are barbaric suggestions," Felix said, blotches of disgust mottling his neck in the dim light.

Novus shrugged. "Not half as barbaric as the soldier's intentions for your females. Are you willing to risk Prudence being passed from soldier to soldier until she dies an agonising death from internal injuries?"

Arthur blanched and consulted his gadget. "This floor's solid."

The men fanned out, their cameras recording every crack and bump on the walls and floor. They explored wide passages which led to smaller caves, the size of small theatres or generously proportioned workshops, before regrouping in the central cavern.

Each steep exit passage boasted a layer of thin vegetation and colonies of busy insects.

Arthur squinted towards the glimmer of light filtering down. "How're we supposed to get out?"

"You're going to boost me as high as you can," Novus said. "I'll lower a rope for Felix, then together, we will haul you out."

Novus looped the lightweight rope across his chest. "Once I'm in the chimney, stand away, shield your eyes. There'll be all kinds of dirt raining down on you."

Arthur lifted Novus to stand on his shoulders, grabbed his ankles, and launched him upwards. Novus snatched a trailing vine, and hauled himself hand over hand. A shower of dirt and the groan of stressed vegetation presaged a precarious drop. Tearing rootlets creaked a dire warning, as the vine slowly peeled away from the soil. Novus swung, bracing feet and shoulders on opposite walls.

The torrent of debris slowed to a trickle.

Novus scraped his back up the chimney, pushing with his feet, grabbing gnarled tree roots with hands skinned raw. His thighs and shoulders burned as he pushed and pulled himself higher and higher, not daring to look down at Felix and Arthur shouting encouragement.

Seizing a twisted tap root, Novus rolled himself over the edge and into a patch of stinging nettles, where he lay gasping for breath for a count of ten. The most indulgence he could allow himself. With one end secured around his waist, he lowered the rope to his fellow explorers.

Felix scrambled up like a spider. He shouted unnecessary instructions to Arthur to connect the rope to the safety harness. Together, they hauled the sweating architect to the surface.

"I don't know if you speak truthfully," Felix said while Arthur regained his breath, "but I'll gut anyone who looks sideways at my sister." He forced a display of sulphuric yellow and black.

Novus nodded. "I can teach you how to do that."

A Shining Moment

False words may sway the weak, but the righteous see through the deceit of the heretic.

The Blessed Prophet Serenus

Novus folded his arms and tucked his lightly bandaged hands under his armpits as he walked. The locals nodded and smiled greetings, unaware a monster lurked in the depths of his soul. Yesterday's newly surfaced memory replayed on a constant loop. He experienced the youngster's terror-soured breath on his face, the frantic bucking and heaving beneath him, and the final relieved acceptance of death and an end of fear. He relived no remorse. No regret.

Only a mild satisfaction, equal to swatting a biting insect.

That's not who I am. Not now.

Novus halted outside Arthur's workshop and admired the collection of miniature buildings displayed in well-tended gardens with immaculately raked gravel paths.

When this is over, I can create a life of which I can be proud.

"Are you planning to stand there all day?" Arthur boomed.

"I can think of worse ways to spend my time," Novus said.

"I don't doubt you." Arthur ushered him inside. "I've sketched a few ideas."

Novus examined Arthur's meticulously detailed diagrams. "Excellent, but you need to raise the angle of the spikes to ensure they impale the invaders. When can you begin?"

"I can start manufacturing parts here today. But I'll need to recruit a small team for the installation."

Novus held up his bandaged hands. "Doctor Bonna worked a medical miracle, but made me promise to be careful with the new skin for a few days. Count me in when you're ready. We talked about vigilance as part of the defences for the refuge, but I don't think we can trust scared and untrained people to be alert or rational. I'm thinking laser trip wires around the perimeter."

"Lots of wildlife in the woods," Arthur said. "The alarm would go off all the time. What about devices set in the ground, triggered by pressure?"

"What's the biggest wild beastie in these parts?"

"Lots of rodents, but the heaviest would be the squirrels. Lightning fast, too."

"Squirrels? What about predators? Bears and sabre cats? Or even deer? There must be something bigger than squirrels."

"They stay away. Have done for years."

"You hunted them? Taught them to fear you?"

Arthur's laugh rumbled around the workshop. "Not exactly. Decades ago, we learned to keep the prey animals away by dumping heaps of pellets for them near the foothills. They stay near an easy food source."

"You bribe them to stay away?" Novus laughed.

"The system works. We feed them, and they leave our ornamental gardens alone."

"What about the predators? I suppose you put dinner out for them, too?" A shadow flitted across his face as he half remembered the fates of unsuccessful hatchlings in the pre-training camp.

"Indirectly. Predators follow the prey," Arthur said. "You, of all people, should know that."

Novus nodded.

"We had one mamma bear try to make her den near the amphitheatre. We rounded up the cubs and got them in cages on the back of a transport. Poor things cried and bleated just like our younglings."

"What happened to mamma bear?"

"We drove towards the mountains, cubs wailing, mamma chasing all the way. A bunch of us followed, flashing lights and blaring horns. Mamma almost collapsed with exhaustion. That's when we released the cubs. They took off like their ears were on fire. Mamma chased after them and we never saw them again."

"They were lucky bears. Not everyone would have been so patient or kind."

"Our largest woodland predators now are birds." Arthur stretched out his arms. "Wingspans wider than mine, the Nefan eagle is bigger than any from the Domains. Magnificent creatures."

Novus lurched against the edge of the counter. "Do you mind if I sit for a moment?"

"Are you sick? Should I get Doctor Bonna?" Arthur half carried Novus to a couch.

"A fragment of memory surfaced, and it knocked me sideways. May I rest here for a while? I want to piece together the fragments before they fade away."

Novus leaned back on the padded couch and closed his eyes.

An image of a neon-yellow rimmed golden eye stared at him. A falconry glove protected his forearm while the young eagle perched on his wrist. Five men from his cohort stood with him in a circle, each one with an eaglet.

The image changed as memories tumbled from a chilly vault. Screams from above, talons raking across his scalp as he scrabbled for the fist sized off-white egg.

A beak poking through the shell, a semi-naked monstrosity tearing its way out, all bulging eyes, sharp beak and sagging belly.

Hand feeding scraps of meat.

Feathers and muscle taking recognisably avian form.

Months of bonding and training. Novus and the eaglet learning to trust one another.

The sadistic smile on the officer's face does not bode well. "You are all bonded to your chicks, but no bond may be stronger than the bond to The Revised. You will seize your bird firmly by the neck, twist and jerk. Finish the job with your knife. Don't want to alarm the other birds." The officer poked him in the back. "You first."

Bile burned the back of his throat. He drew his blade and touched his brow to the eaglet's head. She crooned a response, flexing her talons in ecstasy as she blinked her great golden eyes.

"Do it!"

Novus whirled, face streaked crimsom and white. The eaglet flapped in panic. He slammed the falconry glove up against the officer's chin and drove the blade up through his throat and out at the nape of his neck.

The eaglet screamed her fury, flapping higher and higher.

Novus retrieved his knife and cleaned it on the officer's uniform.

His five peers screamed their approval, tossing their eaglets into the air in mutual defiance.

Novus squinted upwards, hoping she understood, praying she'd survive.

They sent a squad to arrest him, too many to fight. He understood how pointless it would be to protest wantonly killing a magnificent predator. Instead, he argued an officer so inept didn't deserve his rank. He argued by excising the weakness he strengthened The Revised.

The disciplinary board listened.

They conferred.

They promoted him.

Novus squeezed his eyes more tightly, but he couldn't recall his rank or number.

But he recalled the satisfaction of freeing the eaglet. Of choosing not to slaughter an innocent creature for the sake of indulging a sadistic officer's bloodlust.

Novus open his eyes to find Arthur watching him.

"Feeling better?" Arthur's concern rolled over Novus in waves, threatening to swamp him with unexpected emotions.

Novus smiled. "I saved a life. I feel good." He flushed deep blue.

Novus squared his shoulders. "I need to know, Doctor. Am I going to revert to being a monster, or is this new version permanent?" Barely discernible spots of white decorated his temples.

"You must understand, the brain is plastic. Indeed, when one part is damaged, other parts modify themselves to take on new roles. Neural pathways are strengthened through repetition. You can train your brain, similar to other body parts."

"I am trained to aggression. Can I retrain myself to compassion?"

"That you are asking the question suggests the answer. When you regained consciousness outside the colony walls, your first thoughts were for the well-being of another. I am inclined to hope."

"Hope isn't enough, Doctor Bonna. I need something more concrete. Will you test me?"

"Are you prepared for the results?"

"Am I ready to learn I have no place among decent people?" Novus shook his head. "Revised culture is strictly defined by hierarchy. Every man knows his place. The ambitious claw their way higher, regardless the consequences to others. Corpses pave the path to success." He leaned forward. "Never have I craved to belong. Being an outsider, an observer, suited me. I don't yet know how to be successful in your world, but I refuse to give up without a fight, although the battle is with myself. Help me, please."

"The tests are quick and painless," Doctor Bonna said, "but the results could be excruciatingly difficult to hear. I risk not only my personal safety, but the safety of my staff if you become overly aggressive. You offer an intriguing dilemma. As a scientist, I am eager to perform the tests, but I cannot in all conscience put my staff at risk."

"I am willing to submit to restraints, Doctor. Could you test an unconscious subject?" Novus grimaced. "If the results show a likely deterioration, I'd prefer not to be woken."

"A sedated subject is less than ideal," Doctor Bonna said. "I'll meet you halfway. If you agree to restraints and guards, I will perform the tests."

Doctor Bonna called for an escort and walked Novus to a treatment room. She pointed to a chair, and the guards fastened the restraints and discreetly backed out of sight.

"Are you sure this is what you want?" She held a helmet shaped contraption, sprouting a bewildering array of wires.

His mouth too dry to speak, Novus nodded and closed his eyes.

"Try to breathe normally," Doctor Bonna said. "You'll hear beeps and buzzes, but you won't feel a thing. Try to hold a picture in your head of a neutral event. Accepting daily benediction, perhaps."

Images scattered and coalesced, like shattered reflections reforming on a pond's surface.

Torture, death, destruction.

Blood, gaping wounds.

A soaring eaglet.

"I can't fix on a neutral image. My mind is flooded with horror."

"Indeed, your brain's response is most interesting. Feel your way to a happy time, a place you were comfortable."

Novus forced his way through his past and seized a recent memory. Sitting on the steps with Callida. Her mismatched eyes fixed attentively while he confessed his misdeeds and fears for his future.

Doctor Bonna hummed and chuffed to herself as she watched the screens spill their brightly coloured data for her interpretations. "Hmm, can you go back to a time you committed violence?"

Reluctantly, Novus dived to the depths of his slime coated memories, rummaging for an event among the myriad of depravity and destruction.

"Stop! That is enough." Doctor Bonna yanked the helmet from his head. She nodded to the guards to unlock the restraints.

"Did I pass?"

Provocation

Purity of the community is achieved through sacrifice; to spare the impure is to invite ruin upon all.

The Blessed Prophet Serenus

After cannibalising the fleet, Stark had only three scarred craft capable of flight. His knuckles whitened as he grasped the arms of his throne. The massive Ring of Radiance cut into his finger, a mocking reminder nothing had turned out as planned.

"Your Holiness?"

Stark scowled down at Lieutenant Nenimem. "Speak."

"Your Holiness, many of your supporters possess private aircraft."

Stark twisted his heavy ring, flinching as the holy jewellery chafed the raw skin.

Nenimem kept his gaze focused over Stark's shoulder. "Your Holiness, requisition these craft and refit them. A faster and cheaper option than manufacturing a new fleet."

"My supporters are men of wealth and status. They won't willingly hand over the symbols of their power."

"Your Holiness, the Solran creed clearly states Unity with Solra requires perfect submission. You represent Solra. Denying you is akin to denying Solra. My men will not tolerate disrespect to your divine authority."

Stark relaxed his grip and summoned a thin smile. "Coordinate with Obduro, my Personal Secretary. He'll have all the details."

Secretary Obduro stared aghast at the comm screen. A spiderweb of mustard spread across his face. "You jest, Lieutenant?"

"The donors must make their craft available for collection. The craft will be clean and fully charged," Lieutenant Nenimem said, careful to maintain a steady blue. "Failure to comply will result in dire consequences."

"This is madness, Lieutenant. His Holiness needs the ongoing support of these men."

"Secretary Obduro, His Holiness has the sacred support and protection of Solra, in the physical form of The Revised. His erstwhile supporters are superfluous. Disposable."

Obduro's jaw dropped as the screen blanked. The walls of his tiny cubicle closed in on him. He tugged the neck of his tunic, his fingers fretting the elaborately gold embroidered plaque. Since his literal and figurative ascension, Stark had sidelined Secretary Obduro in favour of the ambitious and sycophantic soldier, who now presumed to give him orders.

Communication with the other Shepherd's offices had dwindled and stopped, and a restricted media provided few verifiable truths. Reduced to hacking into back channels, Obduro eavesdropped on the gossip of malcontents. People with whom he increasingly identified.

Being bullied by a jumped-up, uneducated, and socially inept mercenary stung, but Obduro sensed Lieutenant Nenimem capable of inflicting more than a sting. Obduro reluctantly composed and sent the communications. He closed his eyes and squeezed back hot tears of humiliation.

Picto scrolled back to read from the beginning. The original messenger expressed vehement outrage at His Holiness's requisition of her father's luxury aircraft. But while the naïve messages of support rang true, the syntax and vocabulary of the original post suggested an older, well-educated person.

Not a putative schoolgirl.

Intrigued, Picto donned one of his many aliases and dived in. A brief exploration revealed the post originated from High Shepherd Stark's office. A disgruntled employee, or a ruse to flush out malcontents?

"Prudence? Come, come here, come see." Picto waved urgently across the room. "Not authentic, no, not at all authentic. What do you think?"

Prudence peered over his shoulder. Her frown deepened as she read the impassioned screed and the flurry of responses. Most mirrored the resentment of the poster, but a smug faction argued the appropriation of private goods to support the annihilation of those living without Light was utterly justified. Probably those with the least to lose.

"Do you mind if I check this?" Prudence's fingers danced over the keyboard. "I'm struggling to imagine who posted this, and why. Either the author or the respondents are in danger. Check which of those commenting are genuine."

"Foolish hatchlings … foolish hatchlings … courting retribution …" Picto muttered to himself as he mined the accounts.

Prudence sat back; eyes wide. "You're right. The message definitely comes from Stark's office. But why?"

"I've found one suspect account, a duplicate, possibly a youngster piggybacking their parent's account. No malicious activity. The rest seem genuine at first glance."

"Make a record of the respondent's accounts, then delete the comments. Do your magic and make sure they're untraceable."

Picto nodded. "What about the original poster?"

"Can you cocoon the account? Make it disappear to everyone but them and us?"

Picto tapped furiously at the keyboard. "Done. I've set an alert for future messages. Whoever's doing this isn't likely to stop at their first attempt." He turned to waggle his eyebrows at Prudence. "I'm searching all the workstations in Stark's office to find matches for syntax and sentence structure. My own program."

"How long before you get results?"

Picto pointed to the diminishing line along the bottom of his screen. "Not much longer, not long at all. Almost done, almost done. Done."

Callida rested her forearms on her desk. "Why would Secretary Obduro post such a provocative message?"

"We can't know for certain," Prudence said, "but we suspect jealousy. Communication from Stark stopped when he ascended. Obduro has gone from a man of consequence to a cipher overnight. That must hurt."

"Is he trying to stir trouble? Or collect intelligence to regain favour with Stark?"

Prudence shrugged. "Impossible to tell. Picto is monitoring the account. While we were there, we dug around and discovered Obduro ordered the reprogramming of the media workers. He's dirtied his hands on Stark's behalf before."

Callida heaved a deep sigh. "I want every scrap of information you can find on Secretary Obduro. A potential ally in the enemy camp is good news. The confirmation of Novus's suspicions, although useful, is the last thing I wanted to hear. I hoped he was paranoid, not prescient."

Prudence paused on the threshold of the émigré compound to watch the perfectly proportioned Ludion demonstrate what she thought must be dance or exercise movements for the gangly Castian and stocky Espio. The clumsy Acolytes provided the perfect foil for Ludion. Bare chested and bare-footed, he moved with the fluid grace of water.

"Ludion? May I have a word?"

He flushed like a cloud clad sunset and grabbed his tunic. As he yanked it over his head, Prudence noticed his indigo toenails, buffed to a high shine. She glanced at the Acolytes' feet to compare, but they had hastily shoved their feet into their shoes and were dragging on their tunics with equal fervour.

"I hope this isn't a bad time. I need to ask you about Secretary Obduro."

Castian and Espio raised their eyebrows, but said nothing.

Ludion tugged his tunic into place. "The most boring man—no, the most boring person—in all the Domains? I don't know what I can tell you. Boys, find something to do. Go." He shooed away the Acolytes.

"I just need to know what he's like, what he does, where he goes, who are his friends?"

Ludion pouted. "My dear, Obduro the Awkward doesn't have friends."

"So apart from work, he's a recluse?"

"Light and Dark, no. The dreadful man is everywhere, like midges on a summer afternoon." Ludion guided Prudence to a bench. "Might as well be comfortable. Every new play, recital, exhibition, or concert staged in Luxton sends complimentary tickets to Stark's office."

"Secretary Obduro goes to them all?"

Ludion sniggered. "Shepherd Stark patronises the already famous, and sometimes he attends a performance if there's a buzz, a sense a particular artiste is on the cusp of celebrity. Obduro gets the crumbs. Don't get me wrong, the quantity of crumbs compromises a veritable cultural feast."

"Obduro must be popular, representing the Shepherd's office," Prudence said.

"Quite the opposite, my dear. Having Secretary Obduro turn up to your debut can be the kiss of death." He leaned close. "This is only gossip, but I've heard tell, when reviewers see Obduro instead of Stark, they simply leave. Send in a boilerplate review. Of course, if Stark attends an event, his presence guarantees rave reviews. Careers made or broken."

"Obduro must resent such treatment."

"After every performance or exhibition, he talks to the actors or whatever. Obduro's extremely well-read, and he asks intelligent questions and discusses themes and motifs like he actually cares. Then he leaves, and everyone sighs with relief."

"Doesn't sound like it's his fault," Prudence said. "You make it sound like he goes out of his way to be supportive."

"He does his best, but he possesses the charisma of a stagnant pond. He's one of those people who knows more than enough about any subject to sustain a conversation, while leaving the other participant dying of terminal boredom."

"Working in Stark's office, I assume he's religious, but would you describe him as fanatical?"

Ludion frowned. "He holds traditional views, but not fanatical. He doesn't have a mate, and frowns on those whose morals are flexible enough to allow cohabitation, but he doesn't press his values on anyone."

"So no distractions? Would you say he was content? He must be ambitious to have gotten so far."

"He's served Stark for a lifetime, but there's not much affection between them. Stark uses him, then ignores him until he has another demand. Secretary Obduro receives no thanks that I've ever seen. But he's loyal. I suspect more to the office than the occupant."

"We've traced some interesting activity back to Obduro's desk," Prudence said. "Someone pretending to be a teenaged girl, angry His Holiness wants to requisition her father's aircraft. Can you imagine Obduro involved in that?"

"That would require creativity and courage. Not characteristics I associate with Obduro the Awkward. But he's ferociously intelligent and emotionally repressed. Maybe he finally snapped."

"Can't be that intelligent," Prudence said. "He's either endangered himself, or the tribe of naïve youngsters posting comments supporting him. Maybe both."

"You realise the most intelligent people are often as stupid as rocks in social situations? If it is him, he won't have thought through the consequences."

Treachery and Retribution

Obduro flinched when his office communicator beeped. Only High Shepherd Stark, or recently the uppity Lieutenant, used this link. Had they found his message and traced it back? He wiped his damp palms on his thighs. *I'll say I was setting a trap. Gathering evidence. Stark will believe me. He must.*

The screen flickered to life, revealing a face he vaguely recognised.

"Secretary Obduro, I'm sure you remember me. Ludion, the Quarter Day Celebration Team Leader? I left town in a bit of a hurry."

Obduro stared. "Traitor. You stole information."

"Seems to me, my dear chap, we're on the same side. I saw your post ranting about the aircraft requisitions."

Only a minuscule tightening of muscles around the eyes betrayed Obduro's fear. "I have no idea what you're talking about, Team Leader Ludion. You shouldn't have access to this channel."

"Should or shouldn't is irrelevant, Secretary Obduro. The reality is I have access because you made yourself vulnerable and left a virtual trail, but my friends have protected you. Stark won't find your fake account, so you can relax."

"Are you blackmailing me?"

"I'm trying to save you and enlist your help," Ludion said. "You're an intelligent man, but unsuited to the shifty role of saboteur."

"What do you want?"

"What do you want, Secretary Obduro? Are you regretting supporting an unworthy man? A man who ruthlessly tramples others in his selfish desire to achieve his unholy goals? A man whose lust for power blinds him to righteousness? A man surrounded by shadows?"

"Solra spoke directly to His Holiness, Solra chose him above all others."

Ludion leaned close, his face filling the screen. "Secretary Obduro. If you believe that twaddle, then I'm a flying squirrel. Saying something does not make it so. Wishing does not change reality. If Solra chose Stark, why was it necessary to kidnap the other candidates? Why did he order you to meddle with the media?"

"Kidnap?" Obduro's voice rose an octave. "High Shepherds Miles and Altor secluded themselves in prayerful retreat. They submitted to the Holy Will of Solra."

"Stark abducted The High Shepherds and imprisoned them at The Revised Training Camp. I know, because I rescued them. Stark is requisitioning aircraft to replace the fleet destroyed in a fire. I know, because I set the fire and stole his largest conchatus."

"That's ... impossible," Secretary Obduro whispered.

"We know you reprogrammed the media staff," Ludion said. "We know, because we liberated Beatrice Max and removed her chip. Ask around. Confirm the truth to your satisfaction. I'll be in touch tomorrow."

Obduro stared at the blank screen as he struggled to make sense of the traitor's words. Then he pulled the journalist's file. Beatrice's chip was stubbornly inoperative. He skimmed her last assignment and pulled the files of her crew.

Nothing.

No activity since leaving to interview women newly fulfilled in their traditionally restricted roles as homemakers and carers.

Obduro backed out of the files, erasing evidence of his visit to the best of his ability. He rubbed his eyes, then pressed a fist to his sternum. His heart thumped erratically, and blood thrummed in his ears.

Dark and Light! What have I done?

Safe in his den with the door locked, Obduro hacked into the system and prepared to inactivate his identity chip. His shaking fingers hovered over the button while his mind ran through potential scenarios. What if deactivating his chip set off an alarm? If Stark sent Revised troops to arrest him, they wouldn't need to torture him. He'd die of fright before they started.

Obduro defined himself through his mind. Without his intellect or free will, he ceased meaningful existence. A shudder ran down his spine as he contemplated such a pitiful reduction. Shutting down his chip carried risks, but inaction carried potentially higher risks. He could think of only one solution.

His fingers trembled as he selected the grafting knife from his bonsai tool collection. The longer he thought, the faster his meagre courage trickled away. He closed his eyes, bent his neck, and located the tiny lump with his left hand. He sucked in a breath and jabbed with his right hand. The pain was less than he expected, and he eased out the seed sized piece of technology between blood-slicked fingers.

Miles and Altor sat on either side of Ludion, but off-camera.

"Secretary Obduro, have you satisfied yourself I speak the truth?"

"You gave me much to consider. As you said, Beatrice Max and her crew are missing. Your familiarity with the roles I have played, on Stark's behalf and my own, prove your technical superiority. You are a traitor. This could all be an elaborate conspiracy to turn me against His Holiness."

"By the Light, Obduro!" High Shepherd Miles turned the camera onto himself. "Stark's the one fooling with conspiracies."

"My Shepherd?" Obduro flushed a sickly green. "I …"

Ludion readjusted the camera to include himself and Altor. "I thought you might demand more proof."

"This changes everything. We must remove Stark from office."

"Stark has an army," Miles said. "They are ruthless beyond imagining, and utterly committed to him. Removing him will not be easy."

"I am not a man of courage," Obduro said, "but I cannot turn from this most heinous crime. How can I help?"

"For now," Altor said, "all we need is information. Any other actions you take may alert Stark and put you in danger."

"I am willing to sacrifice myself to atone for my part in this atrocity," Secretary Obduro said, pale and shaking.

"Very honourable," Miles said, "but you're useless dead." His voice softened. "Remaining in place requires courage. You finally have a cause worthy of your renowned diplomacy."

"We need to know when Stark plans to attack Nefas, and the size of his new fleet," Ludion said.

"His Holiness—I mean Stark—no longer communicates with me directly. His pet soldier, Lieutenant Nenimem, quickly usurped that role. He delights in flaunting his authority. If I volunteer to administrate the requisition effort, send reminders to the tardy or reluctant, I might be able to find the information you seek."

The Shepherds, Ludion, and Novus gathered around Callida's conference table.

"Obduro is nervous," Miles said, "we dare not put him under much pressure."

"He's motivated, though," Ludion said. "Not only are his religious sensibilities offended, but he resents being usurped by Lieutenant Nenimem."

Altor steepled his fingers. "Nervous, offended, and resentful. Nenimem will probably expect all that, but I'm worried Obduro's jealousy might drive him to do or say something stupid."

"The Secretary is an intelligent man," Miles said. "We have to trust him."

Callida addressed Novus. "You said The Revised don't have names, only numbers."

"The grunts use informal tags. Officers receive names when they're promoted out of the ranks. I can't recall Nenimem, but that means nothing."

"Beatrice has edited her interviews into convenient soundbites," Ludion said. "She's ready to broadcast, stir up a bit of civil unrest. Ami has been testing ways to insert short bursts of data into the official newsfeeds. They're starting tomorrow."

"Let's hope they slow down Stark, divert some of his resources," Callida said.

Media Sensations

When faith wavers, disorder follows; the shepherd's hand must be firm, or the flock will be torn apart by ravening wolves.

The Blessed Prophet Serenus

H ebe hustled Castian and Espio to the recording studio. "Don't look so terrified. Miss Max knows what she's doing."

Beatrice's Bulletins

"My friends, do I have a surprise for you?" Beatrice winks into the camera held by the grinning Doctor Bonna. "It is with the utmost delight I introduce … or rather reintroduce … you to my young friends, Acolytes Castian and Espio."

Beatrice giggles as Doctor Bonna pulls back to include the pink cheeked youngsters who smile and nod.

"Espio, reports of your demise, mine included, were stratospherically exaggerated. Would you like to share your version of events?"

Doctor Bonna swivels to capture Espio's confusion.

Espio flushes dark pink. "For reasons I haven't yet worked out, Stark took against me and sent an assassin to kill me." He pauses and looks at Beatrice for permission to continue.

"That's quite an allegation. How did you escape?"

"You could say I had a guardian angel. He intercepted the mercenary and whisked me to safety."

Doctor Bonna zooms out to include the trio.

"Castian? Your story is equally miraculous. Tell us in your own words what happened to you." Beatrice smiles encouragement and nods.

Doctor Bonna focuses on the gangly youth.

"Stark flew into a rage after I cleaned and reorganised the birth data crystals. He threw me into the Discipline Chamber until I almost died, then he excommunicated me and set me adrift on the Central Sea."

"How did you survive the shroaks?"

"Solra sent an emissary to rescue me. She brought me, unconscious and bleeding, to the Isle of Nefas, and the Nefans restored my health, praise Solra."

Beatrice leans closer to the camera. "Acolytes Castian and Espio have shared a mere sliver of their adventures, but I can say with unalloyed certainty, Stark set up these boys for his own nefarious purposes. They are blameless victims of the machinations of a wicked man."

Doctor Bonna switches off the camera. "Indeed, that was fun."

Castian shakes his head. "Not from where I'm sitting."

"Will they believe us?" Espio frowns.

Beatrice grips their hands. "Yes, they will. You were both fabulous. At the very least, we've sown seeds of doubt."

Stark thumped the arm of his throne. "How is this possible?" His voice crashed against the gilded walls of the audience chamber. "Shut down the broadcaster, immediately. Round up those responsible and eliminate them."

"Your Holiness." Nenimem fixed his impassive gaze firmly over Stark's shoulder. "We don't know how it happened, but we think the data originated offshore."

"Offshore?" Stark tilted his head. "You mean the cursed Isle of Nefas?"

"Your Holiness, they're using an unfamiliar technology to insert data into our feeds. We're working on blocking their broadcasts."

Dark red suffused Stark's face. He twisted the Ring of Radiance around his bleeding finger, smearing blood on both hands. "I don't care how you do it, but make it stop. Smash our broadcast stations if you must. Burn them to the ground. Do whatever necessary to stop the rebel's message."

Nenimem bowed and backed out, eyes on the floor. He fled down the steps of the dirigible and raced to his office.

Citizens across all three Domains were reaching out for answers, and the threads appearing on social media proliferated at exponential speed. Nothing in his training or experience prepared him to deal with this, and he lacked adequate manpower to lockdown or destroy all the media stations.

Secretary Obduro must have a better understanding of how to contain this multi-tentacled social media monster. The obnoxious little creep desperately wanted to worm his way back into Stark's favour. Nenimem smiled grimly. He'd delegate the task to Obduro, and claim the glory if the Secretary succeeded, or eliminate him if he failed.

Luxton hummed with outrage and confusion. Beatrice's expertly select-ed soundbites were dissected and examined as her astonished audience searched for meaning. People huddled in small groups, asking questions and offering theories; each of which they shared with the next group.

"… his insanity was clear on Ascension Day …"

"… those boys are actors, it's experimental theatre …"

"… we are under attack by the Nefans …"

"… a test of loyalty to Solra …"

"… without a vote, Stark doesn't really hold the position …"

"… finally, someone with backbone …"

"… they've only themselves to blame …"

"… a true visionary …"

"… we need to protect ourselves …"

"… Stark must be held to account …"

Secretary Obduro made his pedantic way through the temple complex to Stark's offices, which were already atwitter with gossip. He cut a stately swathe through the rising sea of scandal and assumption, to the safe berth of his cupboard sized office, where he collapsed, trembling, into his chair.

A dull data crystal held down a scribbled note. 'Should we mount a defence or maintain a dignified silence?' His assistant, Zelo, couched the question to elicit a particular response, but after eavesdropping on the way to work, Obduro doubted silence, dignified or sulky, would be tolerated by the citizens.

The crystal held a compilation of Beatrice's explosive clips. The innocence of the Acolytes blazed, and their sincerity burned with unquenchable fervour. While knowing the veracity of their claims, Obduro must mount an argument vilifying the youngsters, and cast aspersions on their characters.

Nenimem's call was as expected and unwelcome as a midge swarm in summer. Secretary Obduro sat up taller and straightened his shoulders before answering.

"What do you know about this media storm?" Nenimem skipped the formalities. "Who is responsible, and how do you intend to quash it? His Holiness insists you root out the miscreants and make an example of them."

"Are you sure he wants to contribute fuel to the fiasco? Wouldn't it be better if the incident quietly disappeared? Perhaps His Holiness could draw the public's attention to something worthy?"

Nenimem huffed. "His Holiness wants the media stations razed to the ground."

Obduro smiled and tucked his hands into opposite sleeves. "If His Holiness wishes to instil fear and foster seething resentment, we can follow that route. But once his justifiable fury has abated, I'm sure you have the influence to steer him to options with better long-term outcomes."

"Do you have a plan?"

"Historically, there are two kinds of leaders. Those who exercise absolute authority and rule through fear. The inevitable bloody backlash is never kind to autocrats. The second, more successful type of leader engenders love in their subjects, unquestioning loyalty, brought about by a sense of belonging."

"I'm a soldier, not a historian. You'll have to explain."

"Who we are is as important as who we are not." Secretary Obduro scowled. "We are not the filthy Nefans. You can unite the Domains in devotion to His Holiness and their their hatred of the Nefans."

Nenimem jerked his chin. "Go on."

"Give the people something they can look forward to, something to celebrate. An event in which they can play their part. Give them a countdown to the final annihilation of the Nefans."

"You know about that?"

Obduro shrugged. "Of course." He gripped his forearms inside his sleeves to still his trembling fingers.

"The work goes slower than I hoped," Nenimem said. "Not only do we need to manufacture parts to fit, but we need to retrain pilots to fly unfamiliar craft. Months, rather than weeks."

"We will use the delay in our favour to build anticipation and support. And I'm sure we can find a couple of lookalikes to say they played the parts of the Acolytes as a prank. His Holiness won't need to defend or deny anything. He can maintain a dignified distance. The situation will become a best forgotten farce. Nobody likes to admit they were duped, Lieutenant."

The computer room hummed with barely suppressed excitement. The data analysts couldn't stay ahead of the torrents of posts. Beatrice and Ami skimmed the social media platforms, finding a more than satisfying amount of traffic.

"You've got people talking," Ami said. "A good start."

"Is it?" Beatrice glanced over her shoulder. "Picto told me what happened to Crearaton … the mindless destruction. I'm having second thoughts. What if my work inspires people to revolt and Stark orders The Revised to retaliate? What if I've poked a skaxnat nest?"

"You're a journalist. Isn't part of your job presenting evidence and letting the people decide?" Ami patted her arm. "You've challenged a lie, shown people the truth. Respect your audience to make their own decisions."

"This isn't like anything I've done before. My fans didn't risk their lives by wearing higher or lower hemlines, or by patronising an artist I featured."

"If Stark continues unchallenged, life in the Domains will become unrecognisable. Stark will repress scientific knowledge even further, and he will so tightly control the arts as to render them meaningless. He will remove women from public life and deny their rights. He'll need to increase his army to maintain control, and how do you think he'll achieve that? With only male soldiers? Take a long view."

Beatrice blanched as she recognised Ami's meaning. "Do you think we can succeed?"

"At Crearaton, I wanted to run away. I couldn't comprehend the depth of horror. One tiny insignificant colony." Ami wiped his eyes on his sleeve. "If we do nothing to stop the monsters, we're no better than them."

Well Played

Arthur gathered his crew of émigrés around a long bench. "Because none of you are accustomed to an assembly line, I've made diagrams. You'll each be responsible for one tiny part of the process. The repetition will make you faster."

"That looks like the device which saved Hebe and me from the cave bear," Espio said.

"An improved version," Felix said. "Because we need large numbers, Arthur has allowed us to use his facilities."

After Arthur demonstrated the requirements of each station, and impressed on them the safety procedures, the men settled into a steady rhythm, punctuated by the occasional surprisingly colourful oath from High Shepherd Miles.

"When the conflict is over," Castian said, "who will become the next Most High Grand Master Shepherd? Will there, praise Solra, be a vote?"

Miles shrugged. "Perhaps the question should be: will there be a Most High Grand Master Shepherd? Is that role necessary or relevant?"

"Previous incumbents made a few innocuous pronouncements and disappeared from public life," Altor said. "Stark has perverted the position. The title is now tainted."

"I'm curious to know how you'll deal with any surviving Revised?" Novus asked, without looking up from his soldering. "They're dangerous men, and won't easily integrate into mainstream Sui society."

"I couldn't live alongside them," Picto said. "Not after seeing what they're capable of doing. No offence." Picto glanced at Novus. "You're different."

"None taken," Novus said, "but I doubt I'm that different. We could always get Herdsman Hebe to knock sense into them."

Hebe snorted. "I'm not averse to knocking heads together, but it's not that simple. You can't overcome a lifetime of training with a sharp smack and a stiff talking to. Reprogramming their chips is an option, but there're some who'd baulk at the ethical considerations."

Felix opened his mouth to speak, but changed his mind. Unfamiliar with violence, he struggled to control the thoughts churning through his brain. Any man who dared offer the slightest disrespect to his sister could expect to feel Felix's wrath. He doubted he possessed the constitution of a warrior, but a prickle at the back of his brain wouldn't be soothed with philosophy and good intentions.

"If you set a precedent of re-wiring people who disagree with you, where do you stop?" Espio hesitated. "We'd be no better than Stark."

"What do The Revised want?" Arthur asked. "Is there a way to encourage them to behave differently?"

"Like you encouraged Mama Bear to stay away from the colony?" Novus asked.

Arthur explained to the group how the colony managed without walls by providing the predators with other easier options.

"You're talking about The Revised as though they are beasts," Castian said, "but they're the same as us, praise Solra."

Novus shook his head. "No, they're not. They may have started that way, but they've been denied love and affection, taught such emotions are weaknesses. They have no concept of art and creating. They place no value on education or knowledge that does not lend itself to killing or dominating others. The Revised don't cooperate; they fight to get what they want; they destroy anyone or anything standing in their way."

"It isn't ethical to offer them tributes to leave us alone," Ludion said.

"Can we appeal to their religious sensibilities?" Altor asked.

"You wouldn't recognise The Revised beliefs as Solran," Novus said. "They quote the same creed, but assign a different, much darker, meaning. They are more concerned with sending as many as they can into perpetual darkness, rather than living in the Light."

"If they step on one of these little beauties," Picto said, brandishing a finished unit, "they'll find perpetual darkness."

"MissBea, MissBea, MissBea." Clem jigged from foot to foot and stretched his arms for Beatrice to pick him up.

Beatrice swept Clem onto her hip, where he promptly wrapped his arms and legs around her, and pressed his head into her shoulder. His chubby fingers drummed a complicated accompaniment to her heartbeat. She lowered herself onto a bench as she rocked the hatchling.

Felix grinned at his foster's antics. "I never thought of you as maternal, Miss Max."

Beatrice spoke in hushed tones as Clem relaxed in her arms. "Have you heard the latest from Obduro? Nenimem wanted to destroy the media studios, but Obduro convinced him to try a different strategy. They are going to unite the three Domains in their hatred of the Nefans."

"I thought the Secretary was on our side," Felix said. "Or at least opposed to Stark."

"He is, but he's got limited options. Obduro has deferred violence here and now, to an indefinite time and place in the future. He's given us an opportunity."

"Increasing prejudice against us doesn't seem much of an opportunity to me."

"There's one thing stronger and more natural than hatred. Love. I need to borrow young Clem. He and I are going to change the world."

Beatrice's Bulletins

Close up, Beatrice dazzled a smile at the camera and offered her trademark wink. "Thank you for allowing me into your dens this evening. I missed you all, my friends."

The camera pulled back to reveal Beatrice sitting on the floor next to a hatchling busily solving an elaborate 3D puzzle.

"I'd like to introduce you all to my young friend, Clem. Clem? Say hello to everyone." Beatrice waved to the camera.

"Hello, everyone." Clem smiled and waved. His glowing cheeks, shining eyes, and good manners made him a perfect baby celebrity.

Beatrice leaned forward and the camera closed in. "Clem is approaching his first birthday, but he doesn't have a foster lined up." Beatrice giggled and blushed. "I think I'm a little bit in love. Not only is Clem a beautiful baby, he's talented, too. His understanding of mathematics far exceeds mine." She giggled again. "Not sure I should have admitted that nugget of information."

"MissBea, MissBea, MissBea." The camera pulled out. "I made a present for you." Clem, face wreathed in smiles, held out a tiny box decorated with intricate carvings of flowers and insects. "For you, MissBea."

The camera zoomed in on Clem's chubby hand holding the delicate container.

"It's beautiful, Clem. Did you make this all by yourself?"

Clem nodded. "Dada helped. He brought the things I told him I needed. Open it, MissBea." He pointed to an image on the side of the box. "Press the bee."

Beatrice pressed, and the box sprang open, revealing a life-sized bee which hovered above the box, gossamer wings fluttering. The camera zoomed in on the exquisite details of the model insect, then pulled back in time to capture Clem plant a sloppy kiss on Beatrice's cheek.

"Happy birthday, MissBea."

"Thank you, Clem." Beatrice plucked the hovering bee and placed it on her shoulder. "That's all we have time for tonight, my friends. I'd love to receive your comments. You know where to find me. See you soon." She pulled Clem into her embrace, and they waved goodnight to the camera.

An avalanche of messages poured in after Beatrice and Clem's appearance. She estimated at least half begged for the chance to foster Clem when the time came. The steady stream continued, far greater than any of her other stories had provoked. Clem became an overnight sensation, and bees became the must-have fashion accessory. Beautifully crafted lapel pins and earrings, printed scarves and figural buttons; bees appeared everywhere. Hatchlings wore fuzzy, home-made bee suits and headbands with wobbling antennae.

"I don't understand," Felix said. "I thought Mainlanders didn't much like youngsters."

"Showing affection, particularly in public, is officially frowned upon." Beatrice closed her eyes. "The Holy Prophet, Serenus the Innocent, said: 'Only Solra is worthy of love and affection. All else is perversion.' Everyone with a beating heart responds to children. The Blessed Prophet Serenus got it wrong. Sounds like an unlovable kind of guy."

Felix propped himself against a workbench. "Are you suggesting Serenus was unpopular and projected his misery onto his followers?"

"My foster held strong religious views, and she made sure I learned the stories by rote." Beatrice closed her eyes again. "'Serenus the Innocent was a fair man and pitied those who struggled to maintain physical purity. He decreed an annual festival where those who desired to become parents could come together in holy union. Children thus conceived would be fostered to other Domains on their first birthday to maintain peaceful ties between each region.' With hindsight, it's difficult not to think Serenus the Spoilsport had issues with intimacy."

"An annual festival for holy union?" Felix snorted.

"Scholars debate that point endlessly," Beatrice said. "Some argue Serenus meant us all to live alone, unless you took a foster. Others say having a life partner is acceptable, but only if you practice celibacy."

"Sounds like Old Serenus had his obsessions."

"Most people don't pay much attention. That's why they treated Stark's inauguration speech so lightly when he ascended. Nobody took his pronouncements seriously until it was too late."

"So, where does Clem fit in?"

"Ari will broadcast the second clip this afternoon. The population has taken Clem to their collective heart. I believe we'll maintain a high level of approval. Most people have some experience of a friend or relative being forced to give up a child for culling. That's a massive well of resentment we can tap."

Secretary Obduro hurried from his office, where every member of staff sported a bee motif, to his den. He locked the door and tuned in to Beatrice Max. His admiration for the woman grew with each passing day. Her ability to bring people together, and to feel good about themselves, impressed him. No amount of official diplomacy on his part could ever achieve the degree of cohesion currently displayed by the colony of bee lovers.

Beatrice's Bulletins

Beatrice's smiling face filled the screen as she thanked her viewers for allowing her to once again invade the sanctity of their dens. Her knowing wink turned Obduro's knees to water.

"I'm going to share a true story. One which started as a tragedy but now has the potential for a happy ending." Beatrice stroked the bee perched on her shoulder as the camera pulled out to include Clem playing by her feet.

"Recently, tradition forced a mother to give up her imperfect hatching to be culled. A brave midwife smuggled the baby to the Isle of Nefas. Underweight and distressed, the tiny scrap tried to hide, to return to the safety of the egg, or any tightly confined dark space into which he could burrow."

Beatrice beckoned, and the camera moved closer.

"What hideous disfigurement damned this child?"

The camera panned to Beatrice stroking Clem's shining cap of hair.

"The hatchling had double glaucomas. A condition untreatable in the Domains. A defect condemning the baby to death, either by drowning in the Central Sea, or being abandoned to predators beyond the colony walls."

Beatrice stared through the camera lens, and deep into the souls of her audience. She paused just long enough for the silence to become uncomfortable.

"A highly skilled doctor performed what she described as very minor surgery on the frail hatchling. Are you wondering if that discarded baby belonged to a friend or colleague? Are you asking why we in the Domains lack the medical knowledge, even though the Nefans freely offer the information?"

Beatrice stood and scooped Clem onto her hip.

"Would it surprise you to learn the Solran authorities deny our access to such miracles? By what right do they impose grief and suffering? How many of your children have been needlessly sacrificed? For what purpose? Other than a twisted display of an authority and obedience dynamic?"

She wiped a tear with the back of her hand.

"I know you will be delighted to learn blind baby Clem fully recovered. He is perfection personified. I'm sorry to disappoint those of you wanting to foster him, but that isn't the way of the Nefans. The Nefans cherish all children, however they come to the island."

Clem patted the bee brooch. "Do you still like it, MissBea?"

"I love it, Clem, but not as much as I love you. Wave goodbye to everyone."

Clem and Beatrice waved until their images faded.

Obduro sat back in his chair. "Well played, young lady. Well played."

A Holy Tour

The heretic who deceives must beware, for Solra's merciful judgment burns even those who hide within the flock.

The Blessed Prophet Serenus

Stark ground his molars to stifle the scream of fury fighting to erupt. He gripped the arms of his throne with white-knuckled fingers.

"Your Holiness, I am unfamiliar with this type of warfare," Nenimem said, "but I have studied her strategy. Beatrice Max appeals to the softer emotions, and at first glance the strategy appears effective."

Stark glared at the Lieutenant, babbling the obvious. Clearly, the woman won hearts.

"Our texts on the craft of war are thousands of years old, Your Holiness. People have evolved, but we are using archaic techniques." Nenimem paused, but Stark offered no comment.

"Beatrice Max makes personal links with her audience, Your Holiness. She implies intimacy when she thanks them for allowing her into their dens. The woman is an expert manipulator."

"Get to the point, Lieutenant." Stark worried at the Ring of Radiance until it sliced into the tender web of flesh between his digits. Flecks of dried blood encrusted in the wrought gold spoiled the glamour and authority previously imbued in the piece.

"Get personal with your supporters, Your Holiness. Show them due appreciation, make them feel special. I suggest a tour of the Domains, starting with Luxton, Viribis. Bring the most influential men aboard, take them on a pleasure flight. Solicit their opinions. Give them a stake in your success."

Stark narrowed his eyes. "And the women?"

"Your Holiness, on your Ascension Day, you promised to provide mates for deserving young men. This is an opportunity to put your holy words into action. And publicly return women to their rightful place."

Obduro's cramped office seemed even smaller when Nenimem loomed on the communication screen, giving impossible orders with malicious glee.

"Has His Holiness requested any particular performers?" Obduro asked.

"Choose those who are at the top of their field," Nenimem said. "Only male performers, obviously."

"Obviously. But finding plays performed by only male actors will be a challenge."

"If the task is beyond your capabilities, I can assign someone else. Do you seek retirement?"

"Retirement? You make it sound terminal, Lieutenant." Obduro offered a thin smile. "A classical play by The Blessed Prophet Serenus might work. Something archaic to echo the themes of the new regime? Do you approve?"

"I know nothing of devious prattling, or prancing around on stage. The Revised have no need for such effete distractions; this is your area of expertise."

Obduro blinked. "For a moment, I almost believed you spoke disrespectfully of the Blessed Prophet's writings. My mistake."

"His Holiness requires you to plan the entire event; everything from the running order to His Holiness's speeches. If you please His Holiness, you must be prepared to travel to subsequent events to lend your expertise."

"Coordinating actors, dancers, singers, and musicians requires a light touch, Lieutenant. The artistic temperament cannot be bullied. Artists require coaxing to elicit their best performance. Rather like exotic hothouse blooms. Timing and delicacy are vital."

"I will happily leave such esoteric matters in your hands, Secretary Obduro."

The screen blanked and Obduro slumped in his seat as he considered the gargantuan implications of organising a Holy Tour.

And the implied consequences of failure.

An Opportunity

To prepare for war is to obey the divine call; the righteous strike not in anger, but in holy purpose.

The Blessed Prophet Serenus

T he Acolytes cornered Hebe as he pruned the prickly hedge.

"There won't be another opportunity like this," Espio said. "Secretary Obduro can tell us exactly where Stark will be, and when. We'd be fools to not take advantage."

"I will not ignore a gift from Solra." Castian closed his eyes and raised his face to the sun.

"You'd be dropping yourself into a skaxnat nest all over again," Hebe said. "Except this time, there'll be no divine emissary rushing to your rescue."

"Don't you see?" Castian asked. "Solra saved me twice from certain death. They have a holy plan for me, praise Solra. I don't have a choice."

Hebe looked from one youngster to the other. "Have you considered what Stark will do to you if you fail?"

"How many lives will we save if we succeed?" Rose-hued fervour mottled Castian's neck. "We bring the Light to eliminate Stark's shadow, praise Solra."

Hebe gathered his tools into a basket and slung it over his shoulder. "How do you plan to reach the mainland, lads? The Revised have smashed all the portals on their side, and it's shroak mating season. You won't stand a chance in a boat."

"We must convince High Shepherd Miles to drop us somewhere uninhabited," Castian said. "We'll find our way to Luxton on foot if we have to. Solra will guide our holy mission."

Hebe grunted and shook his head. He gestured for the acolytes to follow. "You might not live long enough to regret this, but I admire your devotion."

Castian and Espio exchanged grins. They jogged to keep up with the Herdsman.

"Leave the talking to me," Hebe said over his shoulder as they approached the Shepherd's residence.

High Shepherd Miles stared at the trio. "You're out of your minds," he said once Hebe finished.

Hebe nodded slowly. "A fact in our favour, My Shepherd. Stark won't expect an attack in his stronghold. If you can set us close to my abandoned vehicle, we can get ourselves into Luxton without too much difficulty."

"We?" Espio turned to Hebe. "Are you coming?"

"You'll not make it on foot, and you're not driving my car. Besides, I'm not missing out on the fun."

Miles leaned forward. "I've always trusted your judgement, Hebe. You have a knack for survival." He turned to the Acolytes. "Without Hebe to supervise, I'd refuse. Neither of you have enough field experience or necessary instincts for such a mission. You will follow Hebe's commands without question, understand?"

Castian and Espio nodded in unison.

Stars glittered overhead in their icy dance, oblivious to the concerns of the shivering Sui, or any lesser creatures who crawled, swam, or flew below their icy indifference.

Miles steered the mildly stimulated Acolytes onto the conchatus and strapped them in while Hebe stowed their gear. Within moments, the whirring blades lulled the youngsters back into their night stupor.

Miles expertly navigated the blacker than midnight conchatus and skimmed the tops of the waves. A thick creamy lace of foam unfolded in the star glimmer, which soon gave way to rough textured boulder strewn grasslands. Dozing herds of herbivores grumbled and tossed their horned heads before returning to hide-twitching slumbers. Miles swooped beyond them and headed for the scatterings of scanty shrubs near the foothills. Hebe leaned over his shoulder and pointed to a wide spreading specimen. Miles nodded and adjusted course, touching down just as the predawn spears of light stabbed the skies.

Hebe hauled open the conchatus doors and, doubled over against the rotor wash, scurried to check his vehicle. Other than a layer of savannah dust and bird droppings, the car was as Hebe had left it. With Miles' help, he yanked off the camouflage net. Much to Hebe's delight, the customised vehicle purred to life at the first attempt.

Espio and Castian stumbled from the conchatus, rubbing their eyes and stifling youthful yawns. They stowed their bags and jostled onto the front seat. Castian demanded the outer seat because of his longer limbs.

"It's not too late to change your minds," Miles said, leaning on the driver's door.

"I'll be in touch when we have news," Hebe said. "Water my hedges. I don't want to return to a bunch of dried out twigs."

"May the Light bless and protect you all," Miles said. He slapped the door farewell and backed away.

Every member of the herd wore proudly upswept horns, smoothly curved with mathematical precision, raised in permanent praise. Except the glossy coated, well-muscled leader. Her mismatched horns sprouted with joyous abandon. One conformed to herd identity, while the other twisted down in a wildly audacious spiral, lending her a rakish appeal.

Espio pointed at the bovine matriarch. "The best evidence I've seen that Solra cares not for perfection, but welcomes idiosyncrasies and supposed faults."

The colossal beasts eyed the passing vehicle but continued their placid browsing. Dust and dung scented the warm breeze, forcing the trio to close the windows.

"This is my first time out here, praise Solra," Castian said. "Are these the creatures we build walls to keep out?"

"The walls are meant to keep out the bears and sabre cats," Hebe said. "But you wouldn't want to be around for a herbivore stampede. They'll trample anything in their path if they're panicked."

"Why would such a huge powerful animal run, especially when they vastly outnumber the predators?" Espio asked.

"Can't deny the strategy works," Hebe said. "Only takes a few to start galloping for the rest to join in. Nobody wants to sacrifice themselves."

Espio leaned forward. "Are we still talking about the cows?"

"I once saw a herd turn on a pack of sabre cats. They circled the calves, then took turns charging the cats." Hebe grinned. "Beatrice is on to something, rallying her fans around baby Clem."

Hebe halted the car under a rocky outcrop. "This will offer some protection while we sleep." He handed out a handful of palm sized gadgets made in Arthur's workshop. "Twenty paces. Plant them facing outwards."

Espio and Castian set the augmented sonic repellents along the perimeter while Hebe organised the camp.

"Double check your shields are active," Hebe said. "The repellents are directional, but there'll be some bleed back. Like being at a concert. You don't have to be in front of the performers to hear the music."

"I don't feel any different, praise Solra." Castian held out his arms and slowly revolved.

"That means your shield is working," Hebe said.

"I've seen the effects on a cave bear," Espio said. "You'd be writhing on the floor and clutching your head without protection."

"These are much stronger," Hebe said. "These won't slow you down: they'll stop you dead in your tracks, scramble your brains to mush."

The trio bedded down as Solra dipped below the horizon. They sank into their night stupors like stones into a still pond.

Retribution

Bruised, mutilated, and battered beyond recognition, gardeners had found a woman's naked body in the temple precincts. Her identity chip provided a name. Notita Logan.

Controlled by Revised assets, media outlets refused to publish the story, but with the virulency of a tropical fever, the shocking news spread by word of mouth, further inflaming mistrust of the newly encamped Revised.

Notita Logan. Pleasantly average in every respect. Average intellect; average talent, average attractiveness.

Dynamite social media user.

Her personal page lit up with messages from thousands of friends across the three Domains, expressing sorrow and outrage. Outrage blazed into fury, and women schemed and plotted.

Nenimem steadied his shaking hands on the scarred camp desk. Two stimtab induced sleepless nights trawling through the art archives had yielded no usable results. Ordering supplies or organising work gangs presented no difficulties. He knew how to get things done. If he had questions, he consulted The Manual.

Civilians and their relationship to art flummoxed him.

Although His Holiness had neglected to acknowledge his efforts, he had brought Stark and his entourage to Luxton without a hitch. The Revised had disembarked from the dirigible and set up an orderly camp outside the amphitheatre, out of sight of His Holiness's casual glance.

Stark's lip had curled with distaste when he realised the necessity of allowing the uncouth troops to travel aboard his golden craft, but acknowledged the indignity of arriving on a motley fleet of scooters would invite derision. Now His Holiness hovered above the amphitheatre in sterile isolation, thanks to Captain Pupa and his indefatigable cleaning crew.

"Darkness take them," Nenimem cursed under his breath. Obduro's barbed comments stung and festered like toxic thorns. The Lieutenant's lack of culture yawned before him, a lightless void of which he hadn't previously been aware, but which he now determined to rectify. But how?

He couldn't acquire a veneer of aestheticism overnight, but he could immerse himself in Luxton's urbanites. He examined his ticket for an a cappella performance in one of the public gardens later that afternoon. The card itself was an embossed and gilded work of art.

Meanwhile, he needed to organise discreet searches for three men absent without leave.

Crowds thronged the garden, shoulder to colourful shoulder, yet a moat of mistrust and fear surrounded Nenimem's black-uniformed figure. He sliced through the press of people like a shark through a shoal of baitfish. Conversations died and revived as he passed. Men casually sidestepped, placing themselves between him and the women.

Nenimem drifted to the rear of the gardens and leaned against the warm brick wall as he studied the men's fashions. Loose tunics and wide trousers, worn with plaited sandals, were the most prevalent. Well-muscled youngsters sported open shirts or short sleeves. Only they dared look directly at him, openly sneering and turning back to their coterie to whisper and snigger.

The performers trooped onto the stage and stood in a semicircle, waiting for the audience to quiet. Only when they had undivided attention did the singers begin. Their combined voices swelled, filling the garden with an avalanche of sound, sweeping Nenimem on an unexpected emotional journey.

"Your first time?" The husky voice startled Nenimem out of his reverie and he glanced at the young woman standing next to him, boldly defying orthodox convention. "At a concert?" She raised one perfectly shaped eyebrow and offered a smile laden with sensuous innuendo.

"How could you tell?"

"The dropped jaw. And the buttoned-up uniform." She put her hand on his arm and smiled up at him. "Is it true? The Revised do not participate in the arts?"

"We do not."

"Then why are you here?"

"A desire to learn."

"Has your experience been pleasurable, Lieutenant Nenimem?"

Nenimem nodded. "But you have me at a disadvantage, ma'am."

"You can call me Tyrola. I'm a singer, too, but not as talented as these people." She gestured towards the stage.

"I did not know Sui voices had such capabilities."

"If you're serious about continuing your education, I can play you some recordings. I teach music. Come to my studio." Tyrola winked. "I guarantee you'll be blown away."

Nenimem smiled as he considered asking His Holiness to allocate this particular bold female for his exclusive use. Perhaps a preview would be acceptable? "You make a generous offer, Tyrola. Would I be improper to accept immediately?"

Tyrola stepped close enough that Nenimem felt her heat. "I sense you are less interested in music, than other attractions. The Revised are pure, or so I heard."

"Pure is a relative term. Can anyone claim genuine purity if they haven't experienced temptation?"

Tyrola placed her palm on Nenimem's uniformed chest. "Your heart is strong, and I'm certain your faith is equally robust, Lieutenant. Is my virtue safe with you?"

Nenimem nodded, confident his brazen companion's virtue was only a distant memory.

"Follow me." Tyrola slipped through the groups, nodding and whispering to other young women as she led her conquest towards the gates, before linking her arm through his. "There are nasty rumours circulating about some of the Revised, but I'm confident a man who wants to educate himself in the arts isn't a predator." She guided him through lanes of neat dens surrounded by ornamental gardens. "One of my friends was assaulted on her way home from work. She screamed, and he ran away. Another had her scarf snatched by one of your men. He yelled it was hostage for a future date."

"That is why His Holiness is bringing back traditional values. Females need protection."

"From whom do we need protecting? I've never encountered violence or threats before the Revised set up camp. You should teach your men respect."

"Females should be modest and docile, not flaunt themselves on the streets." A flush of deep orange washed Nenimem's features.

Tyrola pulled away, her face a mask of passive pale blue. "Let's not argue. I want to share music with you."

The quiver in her voice piqued Nenimem's instinct to dominate a weaker creature, but he forced a smile. Accept whatever the silly female offered, then forcibly take whatever she withheld. "I'm here to learn," he said.

"My studio is around the back." Tyrola pointed towards a modest dwelling twinned with a smaller building. "Soundproofed, so we'll have privacy for your lessons."

Nenimem glanced at the westering orb. "We don't have much time."

"Art cannot be constrained by light or dark. Creators must follow wherever and whenever the muses take us. How would we ever survive without stimtabs! Don't be shocked. Everyone does it!" Tyrola led him into the well-appointed studio, equipped with gadgets and recording technology Nenimem didn't recognise. She led him to a stool. "Sit here."

Unwilling to admit his ignorance, Nenimem followed her instructions. She gulped down two unusual yellow tabs and tipped two regular tabs into his palm.

"Why the different colours?" A mauve fog of suspicion clouded his brow.

"You've used stims before, Lieutenant?"

Nenimem nodded. "Once or twice."

"I'm a habitual user. The ordinary strength tabs have little effect on me. I need something stronger. If you're nervous … if you'd rather leave …"

Nenimem swallowed the tabs. "Of course not."

Tyrola selected a recording from a range of sound crystals. "We'll start with this one. Pop on the headphones and close your eyes." She perched on the stool beside him and clasped his hand. "Can you feel it?"

Nenimem swayed with the music, feeling nothing but mildly foolish.

"Relax. Let yourself soar with the music. Feel the cool breeze lift you towards Solra's holy Light."

A kaleidoscope of impossible colours exploded in Nenimem's skull and he toppled from the stool, cracking his knees and forehead on the floor.

He didn't feel the blow to the back of his head.

He didn't feel the cool breeze as a troupe of young women filed into the studio.

"For Notita Logan." Tyrola shuddered and rubbed the goosebumps on her bare arms. "Pompous creature. He couldn't imagine himself as prey. Just like the others. Strip him. We'll leave his uniform somewhere conspicuous to send a message."

Captain Pupa cowered before Stark's throne. "Your Holiness, I cannot say. Nenimem isn't in his quarters, nor at his desk. Perhaps he is familiarising himself with the colony?"

"That," Stark said, "is a possibility. Track him down. Send men to find him."

Captain Pupa backed out of the audience chamber, his eyes fixed on the floor. If Nenimem was familiarising himself with the colony, he'd been doing so all night. None of The Revised recalled seeing him after he left for the ridiculous concert, but Pupa had no intention of bringing His Holiness unpleasant news. That task belonged to a man to whom grovelling seemed his natural state.

Pupa sent a messenger to fetch Secretary Obduro.

Captain Pupa intercepted Obduro at the foot of the holy dirigible steps, and drew him into the shade of the carriage. "I thought you could be more discreet." Pupa nodded and contorted his features into what Obduro assumed was meant to be a fraternal smile.

"What does Nenimem do for pleasure?" Obduro asked.

Pupa swaddled himself in silent incomprehension.

"What does the Lieutenant do when he isn't on duty?"

"He mentioned a concert," Pupa said. "Called it cultural research."

Obduro followed the route most likely taken by Lieutenant Nenimem, from his office to the public garden. Only the trampled grass and scuffed gravel hinted the event had occurred. He hummed to himself as he walked the narrow paths, stopping to turn and watch from different vantage points. As a VIP, he had always sat in a place of honour, but where would an outsider settle? Where he could conduct his 'cultural research', not only on the performers, but on the audience and their reactions? Obduro moved around the perimeter, finally leaning against the warm brick wall at the rear of the garden.

His role-playing was pleasant, but ultimately useless. Teams of groundkeepers and cleaners had already scoured the garden. As a cultural researcher, what would Nenimem do after the concert? Usually, friends gathered to chat and gossip about the performance, but Obduro couldn't imagine Nenimem being invited to join a group of a cappella aficionados.

Obduro pushed away from the wall. Pride would prevent Nenimem hanging about, an object of pity or derision. He'd walk away purposefully, giving the impression he was too important to socialise. His obvious destination was The Revised camp.

Personal Secretary Obduro marched out of the garden, towards the camp. He nodded greetings to passers-by but didn't engage in conversations. Could Nenimem have been in a state of euphoria? The performers were above average, and the concert was his first, but was that enough to befuddle his senses? Obduro shook his head. Nenimem did not strike him as sensitive. Touchy, if he suspected an insult, but not prone to delicate sensibilities or flights of fancy.

Obduro studied the path for signs of a scuffle. Booted feet had churned the grass verges into a muddy morass, but all the footprints appeared regular in depth and stride. He straightened and rolled his neck. He had as much chance tracking the Lieutenant as he had of taming a sabre cat.

But he could follow Nenimem's trail online.

Nenimem's office held no clues to his personality. Obduro bit the inside of his cheek. Maybe that was a clue. Everything Nenimem possessed or thought or believed was Standard Revised Issue. Obduro searched for the faintest whiff of nonstandard.

The Secretary pursed his lips at the small jar in Nenimem's top drawer, almost full. Why would Nenimem require stimtabs? The computer hummed to life and Obduro dived into Nenimem's recent activities. Guilt twanged in his chest like a badly tuned instrument as the titles of ancient plays and epic poems scrolled down the screen like a ragged theatre curtain. The ignoramus had tried to plug the gaping holes in his pitiful education, but the classic works were in archaic languages long changed. Only the most erudite scholars could interpret these versions.

Would it have killed you to ask? Obduro scrolled through the lists of indecipherable texts. Obscure works by tedious authors who had doubtful success while they lived and were now deservedly mummified and forgotten. Interspersed between the questionable art were philosophical texts written by men who had enjoyed even greater obscurity than the epic poets.

Obduro moved to the compiled messages. His eyes grew wide. Why had Captain Pupa neglected to inform him Nenimem was not the only man missing? The Secretary copied the files and sent them directly to his own office computer. After a heartbeat's hesitation, he sent a copy to his personal account, to be viewed at leisure.

Three men, absent without leave before the concert, then Nenimem and two others reported missing this morning. The time for discretion had passed. Keeping Stark comfortably ignorant no longer remained an option.

Stark glowered from his throne at Secretary Obduro and Captain Pupa. He twisted the Ring of Radiance until a thin trickle of blood spilled down his gown and spattered his embroidered slippers. "Find them. Flay them for desertion." Stark's voice cracked like old porcelain. He coughed. "Make an example of them."

"Your Holiness," Obduro said. "I fear that may not be possible."

Stark and Pupa stared. Pupa shuffled sideways, putting as much physical space between himself and Obduro as he could.

"Your Holiness, I cannot speak for the other men, but Nenimem is too ambitious to simply take off. He attached himself to you like a remora to a shark. I can think of no logical explanation why he would voluntarily remove himself."

Stark ground out the words through gritted teeth. "Who would dare detain my men? Who would dare challenge my divine authority?"

Captain Pupa cleared his throat. "Your Holiness, I am not an expert in these matters, but it occurs to me that capturing and imprisoning a group of trained killers requires significant resources and planning. Not skills or aptitudes I'd expect from a bunch of pampered poets and paint daubers."

"One of your own? Jostling for power?" Obduro tucked his arms in opposite sleeves. "I had not considered a threat from within. We must search the camp."

Solra slid behind a bank of sullen grey clouds. A fitful breeze snatched at Secretary Obduro's robes, and he suppressed a shiver. The odour of casual malice swirling through the camp chilled him more than the erratic gusts of wind.

The Revised stood to unwilling attention outside their temporary dens, eyes disrespectfully skimming Obduro and Captain Pupa, searching for a recognised source of authority. They settled on Captain Pupa, his familiar uniform convincing them of his innate superiority over a mere civilian administrator.

Obduro and Pupa, each helped by two crew members, searched the dens. They pulled apart sleeping pods and upended crates of equipment and sacks of meagre personal belongings. They shook out boots and emptied dice boxes and card games onto the floor.

A growing collection of scarves and brooches, bangles and rings, all hinted at unsanctioned activities. Obduro felt the hairs on the nape of his neck bristle as he made improbable connections between recent events.

One by one, Pupa's crew dragged the accessory collectors to a temporary office. Uncommunicative and resentful, The Revised stared into the mid-distance, refusing to acknowledge Secretary Obduro's polite questions. Captain Pupa rose to his feet and waddled around the desk to stand before the soldier, who towered above him.

"Secretary Obduro asked where you acquired these items, and for what purpose? Answer the man."

The Revised soldier remained silent as stone, glazed eyes staring beyond the rear wall.

Faster than a skaxnat strike, Pupa drove his elbow into the soldier's abdomen and whipped his fist up, breaking the man's nose. The Captain stepped back smartly to avoid the blood splatter and jerked his chin at the waiting crew members, who grabbed the writhing soldier and hauled him outside.

"What will happen to him?" Obduro asked.

"My men will shackle him and display him for the others to see."

The next Revised soldier glared a lifetime of distilled resentment at Obduro.

"Where did you acquire these feminine fripperies?" Obduro leaned forward on the desk. "You serve yourself best by speaking the truth."

The soldier looked at Obduro, hostility simmering in his eyes. "We didn't touch the females. Not yet. Just promised to return their gewgaws when we claim our partners. Like His Holiness promised."

"You overstepped the mark, soldier," Secretary Obduro said. "His Holiness made no such promise."

The soldier sneered. "If the women weren't open to suggestions, why were they parading themselves around the streets?"

Pupa drew his laser and fired. The Revised crumpled to the ground, eyes wide with shock as he clutched for his burned away genitals. "If you didn't want me to remove your member, why didn't you protect it? Your specious argument doesn't work, soldier."

Two crew members stepped forward and seized the man. They dragged him, shrieking and flailing, outside.

Pupa sheathed his laser. "We will hang them both. Damaged as they are, they have no value, except as deterrents."

"I'm surprised you didn't side with the soldier."

"I don't disagree with him," Captain Pupa said. "But I will not tolerate insubordination. If the men are allowed to choose their own females, they will riot, and we'll lose control. Access to females must be regulated. You must cloister the colony females, for their own safety."

"We learned nothing about the missing men," Obduro said.

Pupa folded his arms and surveyed Obduro through slitted eyes. "Are any females missing? I heard about the one found dead, but are there others?"

"No. I don't think so." Obduro glanced at the smears of blood on the floor. "I will issue a temporary order for women to remain within their homes, but you must also ensure your men remain in camp."

"They've had a taste of freedom," Pupa said, "but there's two salutary reminders hanging out there to encourage discipline."

Obduro returned to his office and issued orders for all women and girls to return home immediately and stay within the confines of their dens until further notice. He signed the unprecedented injunction on behalf of His Holiness. The official media leapt into action, broadcasting the news on every channel. The message appeared on every woman's personal communication, while simultaneously urging them to remain calm.

Trickles, then streams of women, left offices and workshops. Men chaperoned their departures; confused frowns etched onto faces unused to worrying about personal safety, and unprepared for conflict.

Secretary Obduro retreated into his tiny booth and locked the door. Pupa's indirect suggestion that women had willingly left with Revised men rattled inside his head, refusing to quiet. Conducting a physical census would provoke panic, and he lacked the personnel. His fingers flew over the keyboard as he argued with himself, knowing the point was moot. Not wanting to invade anyone's privacy, he set the parameters of his search to read within the colony boundaries, not specific locations.

With the single exception of Notita Logan, Obduro's search revealed all the women registered within the colony were still there. But that didn't mean they were unharmed. For the second time, he crafted a bulletin on behalf of His Holiness, urging people to check up on friends and family, making sure nobody felt alone in this difficult time.

The carcasses of the two soldiers hung within the camp gates, out of sight of the colony dwellers. Captain Pupa ignored the swinging bodies as he hurried past, the bloody bundle of clothes clasped tightly to his chest.

One of his search teams had found the suit laid out, face down, on the temple steps shortly after dawn. The layer of dew suggested someone had made the display before sundown, leaving their work overnight to be discovered.

Pupa recognised the Lieutenant's uniform but still insisted on checking it against Nenimem's other clothes. He staggered into Nenimem's camp den and spread the bloodied and ripped clothes on the immaculately made pod. He examined each article, from coat to boots, and visually recorded the damage.

Captain Pupa prowled back and forth. Nenimem was an efficient killer, ambitious and cunning. How, in the name of darkness, did he meet so ignominious an ending? Without a body to examine, Pupa could only guess.

Resistance

*The fallen leader may be mourned, but their sins will be judged;
even in death, their reckoning is inescapable.*

The Blessed Prophet Serenus

T he dying sunlight painted the smooth exterior colony walls in deceptively welcoming tones of honey gold and blushing pink.

"We'll use one of the smaller service gates," Hebe said, passing around the stimtabs. "We can camp out in the growing sheds until we contact Secretary Obduro."

"Do you have keys?" Castian asked.

Hebe grinned. "You could say that." He jiggled a set of metal picks. "Patience and a steady hand."

The Acolytes hovered over Hebe as he knelt to pick the lock, his eyes closed and his breathing metronomically steady. Soundlessly, Herdsmen Hebe pushed open the narrow gate, and the Acolytes slithered past into the gloomy foliage covered passage. Hebe rearranged tendrils of creeper across the door and scuffed the edge of the neat arc of disturbed gravel.

He led them to a tall building with dingy crystal windows. Streaks of moisture trickled down the inside, onto spreading pads of moss. Hebe tutted at the evidence of recent neglect. "At least we're unlikely to be disturbed." He threaded his way through veils of humidity to a solid door. "We can bolt this from the inside."

Castian and Espio arranged sacks of fertiliser into temporary couches, while Hebe lit dim sun-globes.

Espio tapped his wristcomm and searched for local news. "Light and Dark!" He lifted his wrist to show Castian and Hebe. "The streets of Luxton will be quiet for a while."

They scanned the bulletins, sifting through the sparse information for clues.

"Confining half the population to their homes isn't right. People won't tolerate losing their freedoms," Castian said. "This could work in our favour."

Hebe shuddered. "Pray that they do. Temporary restrictions are nothing compared to the bloodbath at Crearaton. I need to discover what triggered this crackdown." He moved to the door and slid back the bolt. "Don't leave and don't open to anyone but me."

The colony slumbered under the influence of the night stupor, and Hebe slunk through the silent shadows, silent as a moth in the silvery moonlight. Wide paths wound around the widely situated dens of Secretary Obduro's elegant neighbourhood. Hebe circled his target, scanning for stimtab alert guards, but found nothing. The locked door opened with a whispered welcome to Hebe's picks, and he glided into Obduro's starlit study to await the dawn.

Miniature trees in delicate porcelain pots drew Hebe's attention. Each perfect leaf and bough spoke of attention to detail and commitment over excruciatingly slow years. Secretary Obduro didn't act on impulse, yet the exquisite collection of charcoal nudes hung above the plants suggested a repressed risk taker. With a few fluid strokes, the artist had forever captured innocently sensuous moments. A plump cheek above a curved neck; a bent elbow resting in a hand; a flexed calf and slim ankle. Such images were verboten, and astonishing to find in the study of the Personal Secretary to the man now styling himself His Holiness, the Perpetual Most High Grand Master.

Hebe sucked his lower lip and sank into the padded chair to ponder Secretary Obduro's dual personalities.

Solra rose sullenly over Luxton, peevishly hiding behind thick clouds. Thin light washed a watery glimmer over the colony, drawing the citizens from their pods, forcing the heavy night stupors into reluctant retreat.

Secretary Obduro shuffled bleary-eyed into his study and froze mid-step. He put a finger to his lips and shook his head, before putting a recording of morning devotions on his communication system and turning up the volume. He beckoned Hebe to follow him.

Tubs and troughs of exotic shrubs filled the walled courtyard, and a curtain of crimson leaved creeper covered the tool shed, dressing the mundane in a cloak of gorgeousness. Hebe admired the cleanliness of the tools and equipment, neatly arrayed on shelves, with the most commonly used closest to hand.

"Are you responsible for the missing Revised? Did you eliminate Nenimem?"

"I'd like to claim that honour," Hebe said, "but this is the first I've heard. We arrived last night and saw the bulletins. I came to find out what's going on. I didn't expect this paranoia. Are you under suspicion, Secretary?"

Secretary Obduro sighed and leaned back on the workbench. "A young woman was brutally assaulted and murdered a few days ago. Since then, some of The Revised men have disappeared. Yesterday, someone displayed Lieutenant Nenimem's blood drenched uniform on the temple steps. Making a connection between these events is tempting, but I cannot guess who in the colony possesses the courage or skill to attack trained soldiers."

Hebe closed his eyes and took several deep breaths before speaking. "Have any other citizens been … hurt?"

"Captain Pupa and I searched The Revised camp. We found trophies. Minor items stolen from women. The perpetrators claimed not to have touched the women. They said they were choosing their mates ahead of time."

"That's why you have restricted women to their homes?"

Obduro nodded. "Captain Pupa also confined The Revised to their camp, but I fear I am out of my depth, Herdsman."

"Nenimem was Stark's right-hand man," Hebe said. "He must have harboured certain expectations. What do we know about him?"

Secretary Obduro shrugged. "Not much. He seized power when the High Shepherds escaped from the training camp. In the ensuing confusion, he eliminated seven challengers, so a man comfortable with violence. Like all The Revised, he lacked an appreciation of culture, but unusually, he sought to rectify the deficiency. We know he attended a concert on his last afternoon."

"Interesting. You should make enquiries to find out if he spoke to anyone, or if anyone remembers him leaving. Also, check the medical centre. Ask if anyone has needed treatment for injuries possibly sustained in an accident or an altercation."

"What should I do with such a person? We're not equipped to deal with this sort of activity. The last public adjudication was four hundred and twenty-seven years ago. A potter accused a fellow artisan of copying his designs."

"Make your enquiries, and loudly. You won't find anything useful." Hebe winked. "But you'll let the colony know that The Revised are not omnipotent."

"How does this affect our plans?" Castian asked. "Does Stark still intend to have his Holy Tour?"

Hebe punched the bag of fertiliser into a more comfortable shape. "From what Secretary Obduro said, Stark has lost contact with reality. He lives in a state of permanent distress."

"We'll solve that problem for him, praise Solra," Castian muttered.

Espio leaned forward, a frown creasing his brow. "We're missing something. Six missing bodies? Hiding one presents problems, but six?" He rolled off his seat and flopped on the floor. "Castian? Try to lift me."

Castian glanced at Hebe, who shrugged in response. He crouched next to his friend and wrapped his arms around Espio's chest. After a great deal of huffing and straining, he collapsed next to Espio. "Praise Solra! Harder than I expected."

Espio leaned back on the sacks. "There must be more than one man involved. Shifting a deadweight is ridiculously difficult."

"If we knew who was responsible, we could enlist their help," Castian said.

Hebe shook his head. "Whoever they are, they're doing fine without us. They've proven to the colony that The Revised are vulnerable, although I haven't yet worked out to what. They've lit a lamp of hope in the darkness of despair."

Secretary Obduro leaned over the unattended reception desk. A flower shaped glass dish filled with life-sized bee lapel pins sat next to the communication console, a silent declaration of courage and defiance. He pinned a yellow and black insect to his collar before going to his almost empty office. His few male staff nodded and smiled, a few self-consciously touching the bee pins they all wore.

Zelo, his eldest and most trusted assistant, bustled to his side. "Secretary, you'll want to check the news. There have been … incidents … violence … in both Animo and Honoris. The official channels have not yet reported, but the stories are on all the independent sites."

"Thank you, Zelo." Secretary Obduro turned to his tiny office.

"Secretary?" Zelo tapped Obduro's forearm. "We took the liberty of putting your messages on the High Shepherd's desk." Zelo glanced back at his colleagues. "We thought you'd be more comfortable, especially if you need to entertain visitors, Sir."

"Is there anything else I should know?"

Zelo slid his eyes to the window. "Captain Pupa has urgent business with you. Bad news, if I'm interpreting his dark flush and rigid posture correctly." He nudged Secretary Obduro. "Get settled in your new office. Us bees will keep the little beetle man busy for as long as we can."

"Don't underestimate him, Zelo. I've seen him in action."

"Very easy to underestimate people, sir. I'll flatter him silly. He won't know which way is up by the time I've finished with him."

Secretary Obduro squared his shoulders and let himself into his new office. He flicked through the messages as he squirmed to get comfortable in the enormous throne-like chair. A live video thumbnail popped onto the upper right of his screen, showing Zelo fluttering around Pupa, smiling and bobbing. Obduro leaned closer, fascinated as Pupa's high colour returned to normal and his shoulders sank back to their usual position.

Secretary Obduro darted around the desk and shifted the visitor's chair back a healthy stride, making it impossible for his guest to lean on the vast expanse of sparkling granite.

Zelo's polite knock announced Pupa's arrival. As the Captain stomped the length of the office, Zelo flicked a quick thumbs up to Secretary Obduro, and quietly pulled shut the door.

Captain Pupa plonked himself unceremoniously into the lower chair and gazed around with frank admiration. "You religious types never stint on the luxury, do you?"

"Do you have business, Captain? I'm sure you didn't come out of your way to admire the décor."

Pupa grimaced and struggled to sit upright in the chair Obduro only now noticed, tilted back a few degrees. "There's been trouble in Animo and Honoris. Citizens took to the streets, some armed with the tools of their trades." Pupa hitched forward to the hard edge of the seat. "They attacked our troops, and by their sheer volume of bodies, they overcame small groups of trained soldiers."

Secretary Obduro blinked. "What does His Holiness say?"

"His Holiness is … unwell. He has taken to his bed and refuses to speak. If he was under my command, I'd eliminate him. An army cannot afford weaknesses within its structure, least of all at the top." Pupa laced his thick fingers together. "You know him best, Secretary Obduro. Can you bring him back to his senses? I dare not let my men see him in this parlous state."

Obduro leaned back into the deep padding. "I am uncertain what you are asking me to do, Captain."

"If my men catch the faintest whiff of weakness, they'll mutiny. They'll run amok in your colony. No one will be safe. Not me. Not you."

"I thought you wielded absolute authority, Captain."

"The only absolute is The Revised's implacable hatred of not only the Nefans, but all the Sui." Pupa waved his hand to encompass the office and the complex. "You live your safe insignificant lives, hiding behind walls, wrapped in luxury, and protected by a deity who disdained and abandoned all others. Trust me, Secretary. If the troops catch on, they'll defenestrate His Holiness without blinking."

"May I ask a question, Captain? You refer to The Revised as they, not we. As an officer, do you not consider yourself part of them?"

"Stark recruited me after I'd reached adulthood. He rescued me from my self-destruction and refocused my energy. I received physical training, but I have the benefit, or curse, of straddling two worlds."

Secretary Obduro nodded as he processed this new information. "I have only had time to skim the bulletins. Am I correct in thinking the violence has died down?"

"The Revised beat a temporary retreat, barricaded themselves into the offices of the High Shepherds. Both groups request back-up. I have neither personnel nor transport to get them there. If I did, such an abject humiliation would probably stimulate my men into slaughtering the surviving Revised for shaming them, and rampaging through Animo and Honoris to punish the citizens who dared challenge Revised authority. The situation would be chaos beyond your worst nightmares.

"I cannot help," Secretary Obduro said. "What do you think I can do?"

"Talk to His Holiness. Reason with him. Prepare a statement so he sounds neither demented nor defeated."

Stark lay unmoving, barely breathing; his pale blue emaciated fingers clutching the rich gold padded quilt. The massive pod emphasised his shrunken state.

Obduro covered his nose as the fetid odour of neglect assaulted his nostrils. "For Light's sake, open all the windows." Secretary Obduro turned to Captain Pupa. "His Holiness needs light and fresh air. And a bath."

"No, no, no. He can't be seen in this diminished state," Pupa said.

"Which is why you and I will bathe His Holiness, while your crew strip the bed and clean the room."

Pupa shuddered. "I will draw the bath, while you prepare His Holiness." He opened the stateroom door and bellowed a demand for a housekeeping team, then scurried into the bathroom.

Secretary Obduro perched on the edge of Stark's luxurious pod. "What have you done? Our world is falling apart because of you, and you think you can hide?" Obduro shook his head. "I'm going to restore you to a presentable state, then you, my friend, are going to start rectifying your mistakes."

Stark remained insensate while Secretary Obduro wrangled him out of his pod and hauled him to the bathroom door. With Pupa's reluctant help,

Secretary Obduro undressed Stark. They stared in mutual consternation at the suppurating wound on Stark's shoulder.

With a care usually reserved for newly hatched youngsters, Obduro and Pupa bathed and redressed Stark. Pupa cracked open the door and peered through the narrow gap, before opening the door wide to the sanitised stateroom. Fresh covers on the pod and a breeze through open windows provided a pleasant crispness to the chamber. One enterprising soul had placed fragrant bouquets on low tables.

They sat His Holiness in a padded chair directly in a patch of weak sunlight, propping him with cushions. Stark moved his face towards the sun, tears streaming from his closed eyes.

Captain Pupa gestured for Secretary Obduro to follow him across the room. "His shoulder? The surrounding scar tissue is an accretion of many years."

"I assume you have an emergency medical kit?" Obduro asked. "Until we better understand what we have witnessed, we treat His Holiness with the utmost discretion. Quarantine this deck. As far as anyone knows, His Holiness is communing with Solra. You or I will attend to him at all times. From what you've said, The Revised would mutiny and run amok if they suspected."

"What about the uprisings in Animo and Honoris?"

"Tell the troops to lay down their weapons and retreat. They still have their vehicles? Send them back to the Training Centre."

"For what purpose?" Pupa asked.

"To prevent bloodshed and to give us time to formulate a plan."

"What about the Holy Tour?"

"Deferred until further notice," Obduro said.

Secretary Obduro, hands clasped inside his sleeves and head bowed in apparent concentration, wandered the gravel paths closest to the growing sheds. Squally showers forced those performing midday benediction to seek shelter in more protected areas.

Pushing a wheelbarrow laden with stinking fertiliser, Hebe huffed past, a deep hood obscuring his face. "Watch where I go and follow after a count of twenty." He trundled steadily towards a door marked private and disappeared.

Secretary Obduro paused to admire a bed of weed ridden foliage then resumed his steady pacing. The wooden door opened soundlessly, revealing row upon serried row of seedlings and plantlets, withered from neglect.

"Come." Hebe led Obduro through a maze of corridors to the rebel campsite. Espio and Castian stood and offered formal bows before gesturing to the piled sacks of fertiliser. Their anxiety thickened the air more effectively than the compost.

Secretary Obduro seated himself gingerly on the sack seats. "I don't know what you had planned, but your schemes are likely to change."

The trio gaped when he finished his review of recent events.

"You think Stark has a physical defect?" Castian leaned forward. "Stark escaped culling?"

"It's something to consider, but not my most pressing concern," Obduro said. "I've advised Captain Pupa to recall the troops from Animo and Honoris. With careful handling, I believe I can induce him to order the troops here in Luxton back to The Revised Camp, too. Unfortunately, I will need to accompany him."

"If you can corral The Revised back in their training camp," Hebe said, "that would provide us with an unforeseen but most welcome opportunity."

The Discipline Chamber

In darkness lies the fate of the unworthy; to stray from the Light
is to embrace decay and corruption.

The Blessed Prophet Serenus

Zelo bustled towards Secretary Obduro the moment he entered the building. He wrinkled his nose in distaste. "You'll find fresh robes in the dressing room, Secretary. May I speak freely?"

"You've just informed me my odour is offensive, Zelo. Does your speech get freer?"

Zelo bobbed along beside him, a deferential dance of ushering and following. He ducked into the inner office ahead of Obduro and selected a suit of clothes, which he hung in Stark's private bathing room. "I'll wait while you get changed, Secretary."

Secretary Obduro smiled to himself as he remembered Zelo's obsequious pandering to Pupa, and wondered how Zelo intended to manipulate him, and for what purpose. He couldn't deny the experience was pleasant.

After carefully removing the bee pin from his discarded clothes, Obduro attached it to his new collar before entering the office and facing his assistant.

"I wondered," Zelo said, "where I would store the corpses of The Revised. I'm assuming they are dead, Secretary. Holding living prisoners would be too risky."

Secretary Obduro nodded. "A reasonable assumption."

"Nobody goes near the Discipline Chamber where Stark confined that poor boy, before declaring him a heretic. Even if they were alive when first confined, they wouldn't survive long in absolute darkness."

"Have you already explored?"

Zelo flushed and glanced at the rivulets of rain coursing down the window. "I didn't fancy standing around in my usual place for Benediction, not with these showers, so I took a quick hike to keep out the chill."

Secretary Obduro moved around the desk and perched in front of his assistant. "You discovered a clue?"

"There's been heavy rain, so I couldn't be sure, but I thought I saw drag marks."

"What else?"

Zelo stood straighter. "There were definitely recent scratch marks on the lock. Like someone was in a hurry or flustered."

"Now that is interesting. Have you told anyone else?"

Zelo flushed a deep shade of indignant puce. "Under the circumstances, I thought discretion necessary, Secretary Obduro." He rummaged deep in his pocket and jangled the key. "I thought you'd like to be the first."

Solra hid in shame behind veils of ragged clouds which spattered the hunched shoulders of Secretary Obduro and Zelo. Zelo pointed to the putative drag marks, impossible to confirm or deny after the deluge.

Obduro took a deep breath and wished he had a weapon. He twisted the key and pushed. The heavy door swung open and foul air crawled out, repellent like a crippled insect. Obduro and Zelo pulled their tunics high over their noses.

Zelo held high a sun-globe. "I'll go first."

"No, the responsibility is mine." Secretary Obduro sidled past his assistant. "Take no chances. If anything moves, run to Captain Pupa. And lock the door."

Zelo gulped under his contrived mask.

The steep stairs wound down to another door. Obduro leaned against the solid wood, frowning above his mask in the gloom. The stench slipped and slithered like a foul living entity, but the silence lay heavy. No movement nor hushed voices emanated from the stony cell.

Obduro slid the bolt and yanked open the door. A crumpled mass of naked bodies huddled together in the vain hope of sharing body heat. The veneer of phosphorus lent a ghostly menace to the pile of dead flesh. Zelo slid past and nudged the nearest limb with a well shod but muddied foot. Obduro shivered, partly from the chilled atmosphere and partly from revulsion. "Come. We must inform Captain Pupa. He can look more closely and identify his men."

Zelo followed Secretary Obduro up the steps to the secluded glade where they sucked in untainted air.

"In all my years, I haven't seen death before," Zelo said, his voice trembling. "It's so indescribably final."

"Which is why we must do all we can to prevent further casualties. Go home and recuperate. I'm going to inform Captain Pupa."

Captain Pupa marched into the rain-misted glade, his face a mask of fury and fear. Dark patches crawled from his collar to his hairline. The sharp scent of pine resin rose from the black needles underfoot, which deadened his footsteps.

Secretary Obduro unlocked the outer door to the Discipline Chamber and offered a sun-globe to Pupa. "Do you wish to go alone, or shall I accompany you?"

Pupa seized the globe. "I will go first. You may follow, if you wish." He drew himself as tall as possible and pushed back his shoulders. Hoisting the globe in his left hand, he scrabbled the rough wall with his right as he descended the tenebrous stairway.

Obduro hesitated, then plunged after him.

They studied the tangled pile of naked corpses. Captain Pupa passed the globe to Obduro and hauled the bodies into some semblance of order. They bore one common injury: each stoved in skull betrayed the fact they were attacked from behind. The bodies exhibited no defensive wounds, suggesting the first blow had rendered them unconscious, if not dead.

"I recognise Lieutenant Nenimem," Secretary Obduro said, "but the others are strangers to me."

"They were Revised," Pupa said. "Apart from Nenimem, low-ranking grunts. None smart enough to maintain a higher rank … troublemakers … spuriously convinced of their own superiority."

Obduro cocked his head. "Not men you respected?"

"How could I respect anyone careless enough to be ambushed by untrained civilians? Nenimem's presence amongst this worthless bunch shocks me."

"What now? Will you send soldiers to recover the remains?"

Captain Pupa peered around the small chamber. "You say this place remained unused for years? It would make a fine tomb. Better than they deserve."

"You propose to leave them here?" Obduro stepped back, bumping into the wall.

Pupa nudged him towards the stairs, bolting the inner door before following the Secretary up the winding steps.

"If The Revised see those corpses," Pupa said, "I cannot guarantee their reaction, but I imagine they would retaliate. It is not part of Revised culture to tolerate challenges, much less defeat." He held out his hand for the key. "Between you and me, Secretary Obduro, I harbour a grudging admiration for the men who did this. But that doesn't mean I would intervene on their behalf. I value my hide too much to champion doomed causes." He drew his laser and melted the ancient lock.

"We should not leave His Holiness unattended," Secretary Obduro said. "Has he shown any signs of improvement?"

"He mutters to himself, but clams up when I approach," Pupa said.

"If you return to the Training Camp, I will come with you, to help care for him."

Pupa raised his eyebrows. "Yes, you will, but I am pleased you consider your service voluntary. My men are dismantling camp. We leave midday tomorrow. I suggest you pack and put your affairs in order."

Secretary Obduro sat in Stark's padded chair, hands splayed on the vast granite desk, staring into the middle distance. *Pupa instructed me to put my affairs in order. I won't be coming back. There's one last action I can take, but Light only knows if it will make any difference.*

He located the computer files and keyed in the command. He closed his eyes. *Solra, help me.* Like a hatchling awaiting a reprimand, he opened one eye to watch the avalanche of information cascade down his screen.

Whatever happened next, nobody could manipulate the minds of the citizens. Every identity chip harmlessly rendered inoperative. Secretary Obduro erased all personal files. No doubt a computer wizard could eventually restore them, but for now, every citizen appeared newly hatched. This was the best he could do.

Then he contacted Ludion.

Ludion flicked a sideways glance at Miles and leaned forward to address Callida. "We have a reprieve, although Light knows for how long. I agree with Obduro. We're unlikely to get such an opportunity again."

Callida knitted her fingers. "If you fail, High Shepherd, we lose our best resource."

"We won't fail," Miles said. "But your best resources are your community."

"We don't have long to prepare." Ludion said. "We need Felix to help, but we're not taking him on the operation. With your permission, we'd like Doctor Bonna to come along, but we understand if you say no.

"If Doctor Bonna's presence will help achieve our mutual goal, then you may ask her, but the decision is hers," Callida said. "I suspect if The Revised eventually get as far as the Isle, then not even Doctor Bonna's skills can save us from their ferocity."

"The citizens of the Domains have The Revised running for cover," High Shepherd Miles said. "I expect the Nefans would do equally well, if not better. But I intend to deny you the pleasure of bloodying their collective noses. I claim that honour for myself."

"Indeed," Doctor Bonna said. "That is an intriguing proposition, but I have only tested the technology on a handful of subjects."

"Consider this a field test," High Shepherd Miles said.

"I only have the one unit," Doctor Bonna said.

"If all goes to plan, you'll only need one."

"If the plan fails?"

High Shepherd Miles shrugged. "We'll all be dead."

"Sure, I can make more shields." Felix leaned against his workbench as he wiped clean his oily hands. "But the modifications will take a while to fine tune."

"We'll risk not finessing them," Ludion said. "Just make them brutally effective. We have a couple of days. No longer. High Shepherd Miles and Novus are already testing the equipment they discovered on the conchatus."

Infiltration

Heart thudding under his most opulent robes of office, Secretary Obduro led his team of three hooded assistants to the gangway of the holy dirigible and greeted Captain Pupa.

"My assistants and I will assume all care for His Holiness, thus freeing you to concentrate on your proper duties." He leaned forward. "Playing nursemaid is hardly fitting for a man of your station, Captain."

Pupa frowned. "I wasn't expecting an entourage, Secretary. What's all this … paraphernalia?" He waved his hand towards the chests and duffels the hooded trio hoisted.

"Holy texts, healing herbs, and intimate personal items. We will not impose our presence on your crew. Once ensconced on the quarantined deck, you can forget we exist for the duration of the journey," Obduro said. "When we arrive at The Revised Training Centre, by the power of our prayers and gentle ministrations, His Holiness will be restored to his rightful state."

"For His Holiness's sake, and yours, I hope you're not making promises you cannot keep," Pupa said. "The men are simmering, and the slightest thing could cause their rage to boil over. You know where to go. I have matters to which I must attend."

Obduro led his humble assistants onto the dirigible and directly to the stateroom, where Stark lay unmoving in his sumptuous pod. Hebe locked the door, before tossing back his hood and standing straight. Espio and Castian busied themselves stacking the luggage in a corner.

"The temporal body is the vessel from which your perpetual soul worships Solra," muttered Castian, as he examined his surroundings. "I doubt The Blessed Prophet Serenus expected the temporal vessel to be so extravagantly housed. The holy texts say nothing about an abundance of precious objects improving the quality of worship, praise Solra."

Stark opened his eyes and stared at the invaders, his mouth moving wordlessly. A sickly green fear flushed his features, and he clutched the embroidered pod covers with trembling fingers.

Hebe shooed the Acolytes out of sight and positioned himself next to Obduro at the foot of the pod.

"Do you know who we are?" Obduro asked. "Do you recognise us?"

"Heretics." Stark's barely audible voice cracked. "Go away. Leave me alone."

"Not possible," Hebe said. "You have work to do."

"Work?" Stark frowned.

"Not hard labour," Hebe said. "Something far worse. You're going to make a series of statements admitting your grievous errors."

"I am Perpetual The Grand Master High Shepherd, Beloved of Solra. I do not make mistakes."

Hebe snorted. "You just did, Stark."

"Captain? Captain Pupa!" Stark rasped.

"The stateroom is soundproof, Stark," Hebe said, "and this deck is off limits to the crew. Captain Pupa was most eager to consign your feeble carcass to our tender care." He pulled a tiny vial from his belt. "One whiff of this will render you utterly helpless." He moved to Stark's side. "Or you can cooperate."

Stark flinched. "You cannot touch me! You are not permitted to touch me!"

"This is a psychotropic compound, made from exotics I cultivated in the growing sheds. I don't need to touch you. At this strength, a tiny sniff will make you do or say anything I want. I'll have complete control, Stark. Mind and body. Maybe we'll send out a bulletin of you revealing your wound?"

Stark's eyes grew wide, and his sickly green hue intensified. "You wouldn't dare."

"Are you sure?" Hebe grinned as he twisted the stopper.

Obduro placed a hand on Hebe's arm. "Allow His Holiness a moment to consider his options."

Hebe shrugged and took up a position by the window. "Looks like Captain Pupa is casting off. There's no going back now."

The engines grumbled like awakening bears, and the dirigible frame creaked and groaned as it strained to escape its hawsers and gain freedom. A slight jerk and swing indicated they were underway.

Obduro perched next to Stark. "Your Holiness, it's not too late to rectify your mistakes. It's within your power to prevent further suffering and bloodshed."

Stark twisted the blood-rusty Ring of Radiance around his finger and his eyes narrowed as he assessed Obduro. "You used to be my Private Secretary." Stark sniggered. "The kiss of death to new artists. You possess no authority."

Hebe whirled from the window. "You of all people know how illusory authority is, and how swiftly it can change hands."

Stark shrivelled against his quilted pillows; eyes glued to the vial in Hebe's fist.

"Secretary Obduro possesses all the authority he needs," Hebe said through gritted teeth, "and for good measure, he has the backing not only of us three, but of Captain Pupa and his crew."

"Pupa has abandoned me?" Stark's colour drained. "He owes everything to my patronage."

"Do you think the four of us could be here without Captain Pupa's complicity?" Hebe shook his head. "You failed, and The Revised don't tolerate failure."

Espio stepped forward, dragging Castian. "The Revised revere us, because, despite our lack of training or experience, we survived your attempts to kill us. The Revised love winners."

Hebe hid a smile as he pretended to wrestle once more with the stopper.

"We're rewriting the future," Castian said. "You can help us, or suffer the consequences, praise Solra."

"What exactly do you want me to do?" Stark asked.

"Firstly, we need to establish context," Obduro said. "You will make a brief statement explaining that you are on a retreat, experiencing a profound spiritual reawakening."

"You're allowing him a retreat from responsibility, if you ask me," Hebe said, rolling the vial between his palms.

"Secondly," Obduro continued, turning his shoulders to exclude Hebe, "you will abnegate all material wealth. You will offer your personal and public possessions for auction. We will disperse the funds to worthy causes, but I'm thinking setting up a medical training centre would be a useful start. No more of this wicked infanticide or divisive Nefans nonsense."

Hebe herded the Acolytes across the room to a circle of armchairs. "Let's leave this to Secretary Obduro. He's obviously given the subject considerable thought."

Espio leaned forward, eyes aglitter with curiosity. "What's in the compound? Is it really as effective as you say?"

Hebe pulled out the stopper and dribbled a few pungent drops on his fingertips. He shook back his sleeves and rubbed the oily concoction on his elbows. "The most effective thing I know for easing my arthritis. Been using the stuff for years. Mostly aloe vera, ginger, and a sprinkle of magnesium." He winked and put a finger to his lips.

Castian twisted his long artistic fingers until they grew pale. "That man tried to kill us, in the cruellest of ways. Am I a monster for wanting to smother him with his fancy pillows? I'd gladly toss him out of the window."

"You and Espio would be most peculiar young men if you didn't want to exact revenge," Hebe said, "but consider the greater good. If Secretary Obduro coaxes a believable performance out of Stark, then we can achieve great benefits, and prevent further tragedies."

"Once he's served the purpose? Then can I toss him out the window?"

"Depends how fast you can move, son. But consider, you'll live with your actions for the rest of your days. You'll lie down before the night stupor takes you, remembering what you did, and you'll rise to consciousness with his image in your mind. You'll sentence yourself to a long life of misery and darkness."

Espio clapped his friend's knee. "You're a creator, not a destroyer. I feel the same, but I won't allow him to ruin the life he couldn't end. Do what you said: rewrite the future. Make it better for everyone."

Spiritual Retreat

Salvation is not found in freedom but in the yoke of servitude to the Divine Will of Solra.

The Blessed Prophet Serenus

Tucked away in her office, Doctor Bonna and Beatrice huddled close to rewatch the surprise bulletin from His Holiness. Stark, thin and pale, spoke quietly and without his recent hauteur.

"Huh, I doubt he wrote his own script," Beatrice said. "Far too humble. Not one reference to being chosen by Solra, or his usual hyperbolic nonsense."

"Indeed, we can take this as confirmation. Hebe and the boys are aboard the airship," Doctor Bonna said.

"Stark looks unwell," Beatrice said. "He's aged and withered since his last appearance. He doesn't look as though he has long."

Doctor Bonna thrust her hands into her pockets. "Indeed, Hebe remains traumatised by what he witnessed at Crearaton. He will never forgive His Holiness for that bloody massacre, so I doubt Stark will survive more than a few days."

"What will Hebe do?"

Doctor Bonna offered a grim smile. "What he always does. He'll engineer opportunities and take any action he sees fit, regardless of the consequences to himself."

"You've known him a long time?"

"We've known each other most of our lives," Doctor Bonna said. "Each time we said goodbye, I was convinced it was the last. Silly man can't avoid trouble."

Beatrice cocked her head. "Do I detect—"

"You detect nothing, young lady." Doctor Bonna knuckled her eyes. "I am a medical doctor, and all this death and suffering distresses me. People should have more sense."

"For someone on a spiritual retreat," High Shepherd Miles said from the conchatus's door, "he's remarkably active. I detect Secretary Obduro's influence and I highly approve of a medical training centre."

Novus hefted the final crate in place and stretched his back. "I'm surprised they got past Stark's security." He joined Miles at the open door.

"Personal protection has never been an issue for previous Grand Master High Shepherds. They boarded the holy craft, and were, conveniently, never seen again," Miles said. "From what you've said, The Revised are more concerned with strategies of attack, not defence."

Novus chuckled. "They'd never expect mere civilians to be crazy enough to infiltrate their boundaries. You found and fully exploited their weakness."

"Are you having second thoughts?" Miles asked. "Going back to your home, killing your comrades? Can't be easy."

"Easier than you might think. I didn't form close relationships." Novus shrugged. "Fighting for something you love is easier than fighting against what you hate. Does that make sense?"

"I understand protecting what you love," Miles said. "I'm lucky, because I never truly hated anyone."

"Not even The Revised? The beetle men?"

"I hate what they've done, and what Stark has fashioned them into, but I can't bring myself to hate them. My feelings are more complicated. Fear? Yes. Pity? That, too. Revulsion for their capacity for violence? Of course. Mixed in with that swirling mess is anger and disgust for Stark. And guilt. The Revised are also victims. I should have paid more attention, realised what Stark was up to, before the situation spiralled out of control."

"We can't change the past," Novus said.

"Nor should we forget," Miles said. "If we're half as clever as we think we are, we use the past as a learning tool to shape the future. For my part, I'm going to burn away the soul suffocating darkness and make way for a future filled with Light."

Wearing only loose trousers, Ludion flowed through his daily exercises with the predatory grace of a cat.

"You look more like a dancer than a warrior," Felix said, breaking Ludion's concentration. He sat on a garden bench and cradled his box of gadgets to his chest.

Ludion grabbed his discarded tunic and yanked it over his head. "I didn't realise I had an audience. I'd have included a few more twirls and jumps." He shoved his feet into plaited sandals and plonked himself next to Felix and nodded at the box. "You've brought the shields?"

"Yes. I'm sorry. That was a stupid thing to say about you not looking like a warrior. You're the bravest man I've ever met. Truth is, I don't know how a warrior should look."

Ludion raised a knee and wrapped his arms around the leg. "You have to define what a warrior does before you think about how they look. A warrior fights for justice, protecting the weak or vulnerable. By that definition, Hebe, Prudence, and you, are prime examples."

"I hadn't thought of it like that."

"Being a warrior isn't about flashy stunts, or bashing heads in, although Hebe rather enjoys that aspect." Ludion dropped his knee and flapped his hands. "Now, show me what magic you've conjured in your miraculous workshop."

Felix lifted the lid. "Nine shield units, as requested. Increased strength, but a narrow field, so you won't lend unwittingly protection to an enemy."

Ludion lifted out a thumb sized tube with a countersunk switch. "You've excelled yourself."

Felix rummaged in the bottom of the box and pulled out a broad silicone band. "Under the circumstances, I thought hanging them around your necks wasn't a good idea, so I've got these wrist braces. Easy access, not likely to snag on anything." Felix shrugged.

Captain Pupa messaged The Revised Training Camp, giving notice of their mid-afternoon arrival the following day. Acutely aware he no longer knew who should be in charge, Pupa read Sergeant Vincent's profuse assurances he would muster the men to welcome His Holiness at the appointed time. Filled with dread, he instructed Sergeant Vincent to present The Revised with as much pomp and ceremony as possible.

Pupa prayed the officer was more competent than he sounded. He shook his head before heading for the quarantined deck. Espio and Castian spied him coming and dashed to warn Hebe and Obduro.

Hebe and the Acolytes hustled Stark into the bathroom, and Obduro intercepted Captain Pupa before he reached the stateroom door.

"Kind of you to take the time out of your busy day," Secretary Obduro said, steering the Captain back the way he came. "His Holiness is responding to treatment, although he's still fragile. I cannot allow anything to disturb the delicate balance of his mind."

"But he's improving?"

"You should not underestimate the power of prayer, Captain. My assistants and I are praying and meditating ceaselessly." Obduro paused mid step and turned to Pupa. "Would you like to join a meditation session? You'd need a ritual cleansing bath, first of course. And we'd loan you a set of robes. We could transform you in only a few hours. Then another two or three hours spent in deep meditation. What do you say, Captain?"

Pupa flushed as he stammered an answer. "I appreciate the offer, but I really can't spare the time. You and your assistants are doing a stellar job, I'm sure. I'd hate to get in the way and spoil all your work."

Secretary Obduro folded his arms within his sleeves and bowed his head. "Perhaps you're right, Captain. I will restore His Holiness to vigour, while you deliver us safely to our refuge. When might that be?"

"Mid-afternoon, tomorrow. The Revised will welcome His Holiness with a military display. The officer in charge is eager to put on a good show. He's going to have all the vehicles laid out for His Holiness to admire."

"Most enterprising of him. Does he have trained men to fly the new craft?"

Captain Pupa shook his head. "Blasted things are still not in working order, but I'm hoping a static display of military power might cheer His Holiness and speed his recovery. Should look pretty impressive with The Revised recalled from the other Domains."

"A splendid idea, Captain."

Obduro leaned against the locked stateroom door, his hands pressed over his heart. "I don't know what possessed me. For a fleeting second, I thought he might agree to meditate with us."

"I'd call that a calculated risk," Hebe said. "Your gamble paid off, Secretary. When this is all over, you ought to consider a career on the stage."

Obduro exhaled a shaky laugh. "When this is all over, I'm going to seclude myself with my plants. My biggest conflict will be to prune or not to prune."

"All the surviving Revised will be gathered in one spot?" Espio asked.

"Must be an inexperienced man in charge," Hebe said. "A slow learner, too. One of the returning officers will probably assume command and change the plans."

"They might not dare disappoint His Holiness," Obduro said. "If he expects a display, who would have the temerity to refuse? We have more accurate information than before. Stark is about to release another bulletin."

Secretary Obduro hitched his robes into place and took another deep breath before knocking on the door of the control cabin and pushing his way through. Captain Pupa stood to one side, silently supervising his crew, who studiously ignored the Secretary.

"Before landing, my assistants will conduct a blessing of the craft. They will place amulets around the airship's perimeter to amplify our prayers." Obduro held up his hand. "Solra sanctions our holy work. Inform your crew they must not interfere with my assistants as they carry out their sacred duties."

Pupa sighed. "These amulets? They will not impede our navigation?"

"You have my word, Captain. The holy artefacts amplify the power of prayer and direct the force outwards to attract the divine attention of

Solra. Our devices will not affect your marvellous ship." Obduro bowed and backed out of the cramped space.

Captain Pupa rolled his eyes. "Damned fanatics."

"Captain Pupa lacked enthusiasm or genuine religious fervour," Obduro said, "but the crew have orders not to stop you."

Hebe nodded to the Acolytes, who each carried a box. "You know what to do? Let's go, boys. Let's change the world." The trio pulled up their hoods and bowed their heads before leaving the stateroom.

Stark fidgeted in his pod, fighting against his restraints to sit upright. "There is no device to amplify prayer. You're planting explosives."

Obduro perched on the edge of the bed and visually checked the integrity of the restraints. "We have no intention of blowing up this craft. Besides, haven't you publicly pledged to sell it and use the proceeds to fund a training hospital? I wouldn't make you a liar, Stark. Your burden is already too heavy to bear, without anything I could add."

Stark rubbed his thumb over the Ring of Radiance. "I am the Beloved of Solra. Solra speaks to me."

"Maybe you do hear voices," Obduro said, "but not from Solra."

"You don't know what it's like, being me. Having to prove myself equal to everyone else while hiding my abomination. A life filled with terror and shame."

"You had the power to change things," Obduro said.

"I built power to protect myself. I had no choice. No matter how often I cut away the growth, it always came back, mocking my achievements, threatening to expose me."

"Of course you had a choice. You could have made a better world for everyone, but you blocked progress, you nurtured hatred, and you created an evil which has grown beyond your control."

"The Revised are utterly loyal to me. They would not exist without me."

"You are responsible for their existence, but you created a monster which only responds to power. If they suspected your fragile state, they'd turn on you without hesitation."

"You have no authority to judge or threaten me."

"But I do judge you, Stark. You are a self-created abomination."

The trio separated, each to their designated area. Head bent in humility, Castian walked to the furthest point of his patch and risked a peek over the side. His pulse beat in his ears, a deafening rush of blood racing out of control. Wind tugged his robes, threatening to tear away his hood. At a dizzying distance below, the ground sped by faster than he imagined. A fall from this height would prove fatal. He pulled back, manoeuvring himself so the wind pushed rather than pulled at his clothes, and jammed a device into place.

A sneering uniformed crew member marched past. Castian avoided eye-contact, maintaining the fiction of a humble assistant to Secretary Obduro. A weak minion unworthy of notice. He breathed a sigh of relief when the man swaggered out of sight without offering either challenge or insult. *Praise Solra!*

Castian wedged devices at planned intervals, while avoiding looking overboard. By the time he returned to the Stateroom, his hands were shaking, and he thrust them under his armpits to hold them still. Espio had fared no better, but Hebe's jubilation filled the room. He glowed with excitement, his mild light bounced off the gold and crystal, reflecting myriad rainbows.

Firestorm

The unclean must be cleansed, even if fire is the only purifier.
The Blessed Prophet Serenus

High Shepherd Miles and Ami ran through the preflight checks while Novus, Ludion, and Doctor Bonna stowed their equipment and settled themselves.

Novus measured his emotions against the signs exhibited by his companions. Ludion held his usual flamboyance in abeyance, his movements precise and minimal. He took one of Doctor Bonna's fluttering hands in his own, calming her with soothing strokes and gentle words. She offered a thin smile, then closed her eyes, pushing back in her seat as Miles coaxed the conchatus into the air.

The machine throbbed with restrained power; the vibrations thrumming in Novus's chest. He allowed an orange flicker of dominance to flush his neck. Ludion returned the bright hue with an accompanying wink.

A glimmer of suppressed excitement glowed from the pilots as they navigated the Central Sea and crossed into the Domain of Viribis. Once they reached land, Miles guided the conchatus higher, to the extent of its capabilities.

Ami spotted the dirigible in the distance, a mere dot on the horizon. Miles steadily closed the distance, maintaining a high altitude. The massive balloon above the gondola would block the conchatus from the view of any casual observer aboard the holy dirigible.

Both vehicles maintained course as they approached the ruins of the Revised Training Centre.

Secretary Obduro swaddled Stark in his most opulent and stiffly embroidered robes. "One unrehearsed gesture or word, and I'll release Hebe."

Hebe growled like a frustrated sabre cat; his eyes focused on Stark.

With the Acolytes in tow, they herded Stark onto the open deck of the observation platform, where his throne sat on an impromptu dais. Ahead, like a hatchling's toy, lay the Revised Training Centre. Aircraft and land vehicles of every imaginable description formed a semicircle around the sombre ranks of black-clad soldiers.

Stark sat in brooding silence.

Hebe and Secretary Obduro exchanged glances. Obduro shook his head. "Not yet."

The dirigible floated lower and lower until Obduro could pick out individual faces in the reception committee. Resentment and frustration flickered across the barely disciplined waiting crowd. Obduro nodded. "Now."

Hebe flicked the master switch, activating the enhanced shroak repellents, and Obduro and his trio of assistants shed their movement-hampering hooded robes. Stark gripped his skull and emitted a strangled shriek of agony. Similar cries came from Captain Pupa and his crew as the repellents scrambled their balance and lanced shafts of debilitating pain through their skulls. Blinded and deafened by the effects of the super-strength repellents, the crew collapsed, and the dirigible tilted as the rudders and elevator flaps spun out of control.

Obduro whisked Stark's sash of office from his shoulders and swiftly bound him to his throne. Stark whimpered and wept in an agony of humiliation.

Resentment and frustration on the faces below turned to shock and horror as the dirigible lurched towards the Revised Training Camp.

The conchatus darted from behind the listing craft, strafing the vehicles and engulfing the troops in a ring of fire. Without a powerful or experienced commander, the soldiers scattered like rabbits attacked by a hawk. Miles swept out of weapons range, circled and attacked once more, streams of bullets piercing dress uniforms, while Ludion and Novus tossed handfuls of enhanced shroak repellents to the ground.

Within seconds, every surviving Revised fell to their knees, screaming and clutching their heads. A pall of oily black smoke from the burning vehicles drifted over the fallen like a death shroud. Crackles and sharp explosions from the sacrificed craft covered their helpless cries, as they writhed in the dirt, lacking even the sense to escape the sinking dirigible.

Hebe and the Acolytes heaved Stark's throne onto its back, leaving His Holiness flailing like a toppled turtle.

"You don't deserve to sit upon any throne, Stark." Hebe delivered a single kick to Stark's head, before urging the Acolytes to follow him to the control cabin.

Obduro glanced back as the trio clattered up the steps. "Help me. I think someone must have collapsed behind the door. I can't shift it." While the others lent their weight, pushing against the door, gangly Castian slipped around the side and wormed his way through a partially open window.

"Hold on," he shouted from the inside as he wrangled a moaning man from behind the door. Protected by Castian's shield, the man's vision and hearing began to return, and he clambered to his feet. He swayed as he fumbled for his weapon.

Hebe burst through the door, shoved Castian aside, and clouted the crewman's ear, sending him crashing to the floor. Hebe seized the man's weapon and delivered a sharp blow to the man's temple with the butt of his laser. The man collapsed in an untidy heap.

"By the Light! You killed him," Castian said.

"He still breathes, for now. Take that as a warning. Keep your distance from this filth."

Obduro dashed to Captain Pupa, mewling in a corner, like a lost hatchling. The Secretary snatched the laser from his belt and knelt close, affording Pupa a sliver of protection.

"Captain, I hold your weapon," Obduro said. "I'm not a marksman, so I'm aiming for your midsection. Nod if you understand."

Pupa squeezed open his eyes and peered blearily at Secretary Obduro. "You tricked me."

"I did what I thought necessary, Captain. Now, if you wish to save yourself and your men, land us safely."

Obduro backed away, and the Captain seized his head.

"Take away the pain," Pupa begged, tears in his eyes.

Obduro inched closer. "My friends are now armed. If you look around, you'll see your crew piled in the corner. They cannot help you. Please, Captain. Attempt nothing foolish. You won't live to regret your action."

Pupa crawled to his feet and lumbered to the wheel. He gestured to Espio. "Pull hard on that bar until we level out."

Espio looked to Hebe for permission, who nodded once. "I've got you covered, lad."

The wallowing craft slowly righted herself, sending semiconscious crew rolling across her decks, moaning in chorus with her strained ribs. A rhythmic whomping drowned the sounds of misery and the conchatus hovered before the dirigible, bristling with a vicious array of missiles, lasers, and flamethrowers.

High Shepherd Miles mock saluted the four pirates and bobbed the nose of the conchatus. He jabbed a finger, clearly ordering Captain Pupa to land on the prepared apron of ground.

With Espio's assistance, Captain Pupa brought the dirigible to land with a gentle bump. He switched off the engines and turned to Obduro. "Unless you tie her down, she'll drift."

"How many men?"

"Usually takes twelve men. Four points, two men on the ground at each point and one man at the top of each hawser."

"Not going to happen, Captain," Obduro said. "I'd be sorry to lose her, but I will not risk my men to save mere hardware."

Pupa smiled. "Two men on the ground, and one up here with me directing. Might be awkward, but worth a try."

Castian sidled up to Hebe and whispered in his ear. "High Shepherd Miles has landed. He's coming this way with Novus and Ludion."

"We have guests," Hebe said. "Pupa, release the gangplank."

Pupa pointed to a wide button bearing a small icon. "That button lowers the steps automatically."

Espio leaned over and nodded. "Looks like a ladder." He glanced at Hebe before hitting the button.

The group listened to mechanical clanking and clattering as the steps ran out and thudded to the ground.

"Coming aboard," Miles shouted. "We're armed." Three sets of footsteps pounded up the gangplank and headed for the control room.

"Outside." Obduro gestured with his reappropriated laser.

Pupa shrugged. "You're the boss."

Miles, Ludion, and Novus filled the width of the outer deck. They glowed with excitement.

Ludion handed the pirates their advanced shields. "Put these on. They're already activated. They have a much narrower field, so you won't get anyone sneaking up on you."

"Is he immune?" Novus pointed to the Captain.

"Captain Pupa is temporarily under the protection of my shield," Obduro said. "He's useful for now. He's going to help us anchor this machine before she drifts or capsizes."

"I don't trust him," Novus said.

"Neither do I," Obduro said, "which is why we have weapons trained on him."

"I thought we were friends," Pupa said. "Looks like you can't trust anyone."

Ludion and Miles volunteered to attach the grapnels to the four prepared anchor hooks, while Pupa winched tight the cables.

"What now?" Pupa asked. "I've done as you asked; you no longer need me."

"How many civilians have you killed?" Obduro asked.

"Civilians? None. I'm not a combatant. I captained Stark's airship, and when necessary, I disciplined the crew."

Obduro tossed his wide range shield to Pupa, who clutched it to his chest. "This will protect you from the debilitating effects of our non-lethal weapons. Should you give anyone cause to fire a laser, the shield offers no protection whatsoever. Do you understand?"

"You're not going to kill me?" Pupa's eyes widened with disbelief.

Stark lay unconscious, tied to his throne. His shallow breath rasped unevenly and the bruise blossoming on his cheek contrasted vividly with his alabaster skin.

Still bound to his throne, the Acolytes heaved him onto a sheet liberated from his stateroom and manoeuvred him none too gently down the cleated gangplank. They deposited him in the dirt between the incapacitated Revised and the landing apron of the dirigible.

In pairs; Hebe and Miles, Novus and Ludion; moved among The Revised, reaping a grim harvest. A euthanising laser to the forehead ended the suffering of the mortally wounded, then they dragged the dead to one side.

After herding the semiconscious survivors into a huddle next to Stark, Hebe and Miles stood guard while Ludion and Novus heaved the remaining unconscious bodies beside the others.

Secretary Obduro escorted Doctor Bonna to the steps of the dirigible, where they set up a temporary medical testing station. A single canvas sheet screened Doctor Bonna from the infernal scene.

One by one, Ludion and Novus brought Revised soldiers to the booth for assessment and helped them onto the low stool. Doctor Bonna placed the helmet on the soldiers' heads and read the digital information on a multicoloured display. She searched for elevated levels of aggression, hostility, and lack of empathy.

One by one, she nodded for Ludion and Novus to return her patients to the pack.

"Can you treat them?" Obduro asked.

"If they came as voluntary patients? And they were willing to devote years to therapy?" Doctor Bonna shrugged. "To undo a lifetime of training, to overcome a culture to which they willingly adhere?" She shook her head.

"Is there no hope of rehabilitation?"

"Rehabilitation cannot be forced. The patient must have a strong desire to change. But I do not understand the results. Their brains appear to have been deliberately scrambled. The best I could offer these men is surgery, and the results would be pitiful. I simply do not have the resources for such a massive undertaking. Indeed, I think they'd be better off dead."

"From reading ancient texts," Secretary Obduro said, "I understand armies didn't always take prisoners. Faced with the realities of dealing with an unrepentant enemy, I am forced to conclude I now understand why. Pragmatism must prevail." He turned away.

"Wait. What about Captain Pupa? He's the last one untested," Doctor Bonna said.

Ludion and Novus accompanied Secretary Obduro to the Stateroom where the Acolytes had shackled the Captain to a chair.

Novus took the key and unlocked the door. "Stay back," he whispered to Obduro. He kicked open the door and leapt into the room, immediately followed by Ludion.

Tied to an armchair in the centre of the room, Pupa slowly raised his head. "You overestimate my abilities." He tugged his restraints. "I am at your mercy, gentlemen."

Obduro slipped into the room. "Release him."

Ludion unlocked the wrist and ankle cuffs, while Novus kept his laser trained unwaveringly on the prisoner.

Pupa rubbed his wrists, then bent to massage his ankles. "You have come to personally deliver my fate, Secretary? I appreciate the courtesy."

"Doctor Bonna has a remarkable machine for measuring brain activity," Obduro said. "She can tell from the results whether you could transition into mainstream society."

"May I stand?" Pupa asked.

Novus gestured with his weapon, making perfectly clear the conditions.

Pupa stood and rotated his shoulders. "You are a master of understatement, Secretary Obduro. I understand the consequence of failing this test is execution?"

"I fervently hope you pass, Captain." Obduro led the group down the swaying gangplank, from where Pupa swiftly took in the apocalyptic view, to Doctor Bonna's booth.

Pupa seated himself on the stool and folded his arms. When Doctor Bonna approached with the helmet, he closed his eyes and bowed his head, allowing her to strap the contraption in place without comment.

Lips pursed, Doctor Bonna retreated to her position by the digital display. Bright images flashed and flowed across the screen until she pressed a button to pause the parade of information. "Captain Pupa, I'm going to ask a few questions. I want you to answer as quickly as possible. Don't think too hard, just say what first comes to mind."

"Yes, Ma'am."

"How long have you served in The Revised?"

"I'm not Revised, Ma'am, although I received some training."

"How did you escape culling?"

"I was never scheduled for culling, Ma'am. I managed to turn bad without exterior imperfections."

"What do you mean by bad?"

"Petty theft, some vandalism. Stupidity more than anything."

"How did you meet His Holiness?"

"You mean Stark, Ma'am? I'm not sure. I think one of the colony priests mentioned his frustrations and somehow Stark heard of my reputation. He offered me a path out of the colony I'd outgrown. He said he could use my talents. Ma'am."

"Why do you deny his title?"

"Stark stole the title, Ma'am, same as I stole boots and fancy coats. We both took things to which we weren't entitled to create façades."

"Why did you stay with him?"

"Pragmatism. I played the game because it suited me. Stark offered a lifestyle and comforts I couldn't achieve on my own, Ma'am."

"Describe the Nefans in three words."

"I can't do that, Ma'am. The only ones I knew were stolen hatchlings trained as Revised, and now you. Wouldn't be reasonable to form an opinion from such untypical experiences, Ma'am."

"Can you envisage yourself leading a normal civilian life?"

Pupa snorted. "Is that a trick question, Ma'am? Live as a civilian or be executed?"

Doctor Bonna beckoned Obduro to follow her outside. "Pupa's responses seemed authentic. I detected flickers of shame in his brain activity when he spoke about his indiscretions. Oddly, he didn't show remorse for serving Stark."

"What do you recommend, Doctor?"

"His scans bore no similarity to those of the Revised. I think he has potential. If he is offered a second chance, shown a better way, I believe he could assimilate into mainstream society. But, he will need monitoring and therapy."

Sacrifice

Even the dead carry the burden of sin, and only the flames may erase their stains.

The Blessed Prophet Serenus

Pop, pop. Pop, pop.

"For Crearaton." Hebe worked his way through the failed test subjects. Tears streamed unheeded down his cheeks. "For little Lady Lutum."

Novus squinted through the swirling smoke of The Revised's remains. Solra sulked towards the horizon, reddening the sky. "We should light the funeral pyre, while we still can."

"Get the Captain to help," Hebe said. "A gentle reminder for him; we won't be messed with."

Ludion jogged into the warehouse and returned, dragging two sloshing canisters. "Paint thinner."

Novus unscrewed a cap and reared back, his eyes streaming. "Powerful stuff. Is there anymore?"

Ludion drew his tunic over his lower face. "You douse. I'll bring the rest."

The thick black uniforms soaked up the foul fluid like the gullible absorb comforting lies.

Hebe snatched a length of stiff fabric from Sergeant Vincent's toppled podium, twisted it into an impromptu torch and stole a flame from the burning vehicles. He tossed the fiery brand onto the pyre and leapt back as the accelerant whomped into life. Flames danced and leapt in the dying light, corpse limbs jerked and twitched as muscles contracted, and skin blistered and burst in the intense heat.

"Dance your way into perpetual darkness," Hebe said, wiping his smoke stung eyes.

The men stood in a loose shifting group, upwind of the roiling sooty vapours, while Doctor Bonna and Obduro dismantled the temporary booth and carried the medical equipment back to the conchatus.

Ami flung open the door and hauled the bags and boxes aboard. "We're running out of light."

"We'll camp overnight," Obduro said. "Draw straws to monitor the pyre."

Sabre cats prowled the camp perimeter, howling and spitting in fury when they came too close to the repellents. Their eyes glowed green in the darkness, a constantly shifting constellation of frustrated felines.

Volunteers, Hebe and Espio, stared at the stars swirling overhead.

"When you promised to show me the night sky, I didn't imagine this situation," Espio said.

Hebe pointed. "See that bright line of three? And the rectangular cluster just above?"

"I think so," Espio said.

"That's the belt and head of The Blessed Prophet Serenus. He watches over our night stupor."

"I can't go back," Espio said, wrapping his arms around himself. "After all I've witnessed, I can't return to a life restricted to the temple and library. I don't believe; not in Solra or his supposed prophet."

"Nobody is forcing you to return. Seems like a good time to make changes, build a life which truly fulfils you. You're young and strong. Follow your heart."

"What about you?"

Hebe grinned, the glow from the embers reflected in his eyes. "Picto and I have discussed rebuilding Crearaton. A genuine artists' colony, bigger and better than before. You're more than welcome to join us."

"A colony without walls," Espio said.

"A life open to opportunity," Hebe said.

Dawn arrived, dusty and subdued. Solra hid behind heavy clouds, rendering the landscape in sepia shades of ash. Hebe stretched and glanced over at Stark, still tied to his throne. A solemn veil of gritty grime covered his face and robes.

Hebe kicked the throne, but Stark remained still and silent as stone. A sickly phosphorescent glow offered a poor impression of life.

"I wanted the Lightless wight to pay for his crimes," Hebe said.

"Look at his terror-struck expression," Espio said. "I think he died paying."

"See if you can find anymore paint thinner," Hebe said, struggling to right the chair.

Espio helped haul Stark upright. "Are we leaving him here? Or putting him with the others?"

Hebe removed the Ring of Radiance and the sun disc chain of office from Stark's corpse, and dropped them into his pocket. "Help me drag him next to the others, less likely to cause a wildfire if his pyre is in the midst of the ashes."

By the time the rest of the group arrived, Stark's pathetic remains burned with the ferocity of righteous retribution.

Doctor Bonna sidled up to Hebe and stood on tiptoe to whisper in his ear. "I know what you did. You increased the strength of the repellents and deliberately scrambled their brains. You planned their extermination."

"What gave me away?"

"Pupa and Novus. Their scans were slightly abnormal, but nothing like these poor brutes."

Hebe nodded. "I couldn't allow them to live. Not when I'd witnessed the depths of their depravity."

"You don't have the authority to make such unilateral decisions."

"Therein lay the problem, Doctor. No one has such authority. We are none of us qualified to make such momentous decisions. Besides, what would you do with so many men seething and plotting? We have no prisons, no civilised way to restrain their movements."

Doctor Bonna squeezed his hand. "Herdsman, can you live with what you've done? Your memories of this slaughter will haunt you."

Hebe shrugged. "I'm old. Better my last few years are ruined, than society pays an unbearable cost for generations to come."

Eulogy

Solra pours Their golden Light on all Their Children, for they are all perfect in Solra's gaze.

Castian the Progressive

Callida welcomed the increased émigré community into the spacious conference room. "I thought you'd want to be together to view Beatrice's eulogy."

Beatrice's cosmetically freckled face filled the screen. Her sombre expression and modestly subdued attire set the tone for her broadcast.

Man of Principle, or Delusional Megalomaniac?

The banner behind her proclaimed the curious dichotomy of her subject.

"Stark's death surprised everyone, and undoubtedly relieved many. Those close to him have gathered to mourn and piece together the fragmented parts of his life and personality. The picture they are assembling reveals a man deeply troubled by his secret affliction and driven to excel in the public domain. The self-imposed stresses may account for his increasingly bizarre and destructive behaviour."

A montage of Stark in his many roles scrolled across the screen.

"Was he ever that young?" whispered Castian.

"Stark achieved the position of High Shepherd at a relatively young age," Beatrice said. "More than once, he told me he took a particular pride in being the youngest ever High Shepherd."

The camera zoomed closer. "Such responsibility for so young a man may have contributed to his growing delusions and disconnect from reality. Coupled with his terrifying secret, should we be surprised High Shepherd Stark suffered psychoneuroses and auditory hallucinations?"

An image of The Blessed Prophet Serenus popped up behind Beatrice.

"Orthodox followers of Solra have long accepted the tradition that exceptional Holy Men commune directly with the deity," Beatrice said. "When High Shepherd Stark claimed Solra spoke to him, the declaration didn't ring the alarm bells, which, in retrospect, it should."

An image of Stark ascending the Holy Dirigible on Quarter Day replaced Serenus.

"I can reveal Stark felt himself to be under immeasurable pressure," Beatrice said. "According to his strictly orthodox beliefs, his secret would have ruined his carefully constructed life. Or condemned him to excommunication and death. There are those close to him who now believe his return to archaic rules was an attempt to atone for his personal abomination."

A generic image of a midwife clutching a swaddled hatchling replaced Stark's victorious picture.

"Yes, my friends. High Shepherd Stark bore a mark on his shoulder. A minor imperfection for which, traditionally, he should have been culled. A flaw which haunted his every waking moment. A secret defect which coloured his every thought."

"Having a birthmark doesn't make you Lightless," Hebe muttered, as yet more pictures of Stark scrolled silently across the screen.

"We can never know if Stark genuinely believed he heard the voice of Solra, or he used the ruse to allow him to usurp the position of Grand High Shepherd, but we can be certain of one thing."

An image of the burnt remains of the RTC replaced the previous picture.

Beatrice paused just long enough to make her audience lean in. "Stark repented. Whether he finally heard the voice of Solra …?" Beatrice shrugged. "I leave that to your personal beliefs and imagination. What we do know from his private journals, and those around him during his last days, is that Stark experienced a spiritual revelation. Whether he destroyed his own creation, or the fire was accidental, we will never know. There were no survivors. But High Shepherd Stark's last words before he passed into perpetual Light were 'Community through unity'."

Novus hesitated. He could walk away. This didn't have to be his problem. Light and Dark! If he didn't, who would? He shouldered through the data centre door. Picto huddled in front of a screen. The other analysts were absent.

"Welcome, welcome, welcome, Novus," Picto said. "You look troubled. Are you not pleased the RTC has been destroyed and Stark is eliminated?"

Novus pulled up a stool. "Not all the Revised have been destroyed. That's why I'm here. We incinerated the main centre, but as I told Callida, there are two smaller campuses: a nursery and a preparatory school, if you will. I must go back."

Picto flushed dark red. "Children, innocents, more victims. Not their fault, no, not their fault. No more death."

"I'm not going back to kill them," Novus said. "I want to rehabilitate them."

"Dr Bonna tested the Revised. They were beyond rehabilitation. Too damaged, too dangerous."

"They were all adults, who'd committed heinous acts merely to survive," Novus said. "The younger hatchlings won't yet have had all their empathy or compassion scoured from their souls. I believe they can be repatriated to their homes. The older ones? Can you get numbers from that?" Novus pointed to the computer.

Picto's fingers danced over the keyboard. He peered at the screen and shook his head. "There are many more in what you call the nursery campus. One twenty-nine. Only seventeen in the preparatory school. Do those figures make sense?'

Novus nodded. "High rates of attrition. Can you copy this data for me?"

Picto blanched and copied the information to a clean crystal. "What will you do?"

"Put a team together."

Novus headed straight to Miles and Altor, who were sunning themselves in the émigré compound. "I need your help."

"With the fair Callida?" Altor winked.

"There are two other Revised centres," Novus said. He explained their purpose and location. "I need a team. The guards are likely beyond redemption, but most if not all the youngsters could eventually be repatriated to their homes, or found foster placements. The older ones would be more difficult. The longer they've survived, the more damaged they'll be. But we must give them a chance."

"How long before they realise the main centre has been destroyed," Miles asked.

"They are almost independent, so possibly weeks." Novus shrugged. "But it could be a matter of days if preparatory graduates are due for transfer to the main centre."

"Then we must act quickly," Altor said. "What do you need from us?"

"I need a team of volunteers," Novus said. "Not combatants. Regular people who are good with youngsters. I'll need medical equipment and clothes, weapons and a few sonic disrupter devices. Not as strong as those we used on the main centre, just enough to incapacitate anyone who resists."

"How will you get there? You'd need a convoy to transport all your equipment and personnel," Altor said.

"Ah. The Revised are acutely aware of symbols of status. I don't want to use the stolen conchatus — too military. Stark used to make infrequent visits in his dirigible. I want you to donate the Most High Grand Shepherd's glittering craft. It has the capacity to carry personnel and equipment, there's ample space for living quarters and treatment or therapy rooms, and it's imposing. The youngsters will respond positively to that."

"And who do you propose will fly this for you?" Miles asked.

"I haven't asked yet, but Captain Pupa is fretting to be airborne again. He knows nothing else. And he's familiar with Revised thinking. He won't be shocked by anything we encounter."

"We don't envisage that the role of Grand Master High Shepherd will have a place in the future we're planning. Using the dirigible for a positive and healing purpose feels appropriate. Miles?"

"I agree. If Captain Pupa is willing to be your captain, I have no objection. Finding other volunteers may be more challenging."

"But I have your support?"

"Absolutely," Miles said. "Once we're back on the mainland, we'll help recruit whatever staff you deem necessary."

"May I join you?" Novus plonked next to Pupa on his favourite garden bench. "I can't help but notice your discomfort in our émigré community."

Pupa perched on the edge of the stone seat and stared morosely at the ground. "Finding my place is challenging. I don't fit anywhere. Being grounded feels unnatural. I'm uncomfortable with solid earth beneath my feet."

Novus leaned back against the brick wall. "I have a proposal in which you may be interested."

Pupa shrugged. "I don't have too many options right now. Being employed by Stark isn't much of a recommendation to prospective employers."

Novus laughed. "I'm familiar with your reprehensible character. I need your aeronautical expertise and experience, I'm returning to finish the job we started. The nursery and preparatory school youngsters need rehabilitation. I'm putting together a team. The Shepherds have given me permission to use the Most High Grand Shepherd dirigible. What I don't have is a Captain. What do you say?"

"Are you offering me the position?"

"Unless you're considering a better offer …?"

Captain Pupa stood and bowed. "Reporting for duty, Sir!"

Ludion flipped shut his sketch book when Novus approached.

"I hear you're very good," Novus said. "May I see?"

"They're only preliminary sketches. I want to mount a display showing the beauty of the Nefans once I'm back in Viribis."

Novus flipped through the pad. "These are remarkably lifelike. This is Felix, and Arthur, and Prudence. Is that me?" He grinned. "Handsome devil. There're pages of Callida. Could you see yourself teaching art? To youngsters?"

"I'm not sure what I'll do when I return." He shivered. "I can't imagine resuming my role in the High Shepherd's office, even under different management."

"You have a unique skill set," Novus said. "I could use your talents."

"You need an administrator? What are you planning?"

Novus squinted up at the sun. "There are two other Revised training centres. One for the very young and one for the older children. I need a team to rehabilitate these youngsters. They've been denied affection and personal identity. They are not even allowed names. I've watched you teaching Castian and Espio. You blend discipline with praise, and you can obviously handle yourself. You escaped from the RTC with the Shepherds and a conchatus, so dealing with youngsters would be a breeze."

"You think teaching drawing or dance will rehabilitate Revised trainees?"

Novus shook his head. "These children know only pain and brutality. They measure strength by the number of killings they make. I need you to show them love, affection, beauty, self-discipline. The art of creating, not mindless destruction. Baby Clem could easily have been a Revised recruit, and see how he blossomed when showered with unconditional Nefan affection?"

The entire community gathered to wave off the émigrés. Novus, Ludion, and Captain Pupa boarded the repurposed dirigible. A handful of Nefan medical personal, teachers, and general assistants accompanied them. Felix had equipped and trained them to use the sonic disrupters.

Miles and Altor; Obduro and Castian; Hebe, Espio, and Picto, hugged farewell to their friends and clambered aboard the conchatus. They stowed their meagre belongings while Miles ran through the preflight checks.

Castian entwined his fingers until the knuckles turned white.

"Are you all right?" Obduro asked.

"This is beyond my wildest dreams. I'd resigned myself to never returning, to living in exile, but here I am. Returning a hero. Do you know, people send letters? Thanking me for my part in the overthrow of The Revised."

"You have endless opportunities ahead of you to rewrite the future. Together, we'll dismantle Stark's office, divide it into different departments, separating the sacred and the secular."

Altor leaned forward and patted Castian on the knee. "You're bringing the Light, exactly as you said."

Solran Mythology

CREATION

The creator, Solra, lit the skies, and warmed the land, but no creature benefitted for none existed and Solra grew lonely in Their glorious solitude.

Solra stirred the ocean, and spoke the sacred words of being, drawing to the surface a ring of fertile land, and in the middle of the Central Sea a rocky barren island. Solra brought forth all manner of swimming and floating creatures. There were boneless soft bodied creatures and hard-shelled creatures, finned and tentacled, but none fit companions for the Supreme One.

Solra breathed on the ring of land, and spoke the sacred words of being, and all manner of creeping and crawling, burrowing and flying creatures burst forth, filling the world with their abundance. Furred and feathered, scaled and smooth skinned, Solra rejected each as a fitting companion for Their Magnificence.

Solra let it be known They sought a companion, and would hold a competition to ascertain who, among all creation, could offer most worthy praise.

The beasts gathered to worship Solra and each in turn raised their voice to praise the Creator. Solra was pleased with such diversity, but saddened not to find a worthy companion. Solra searched from the peaks of the mountains to the bottom of the abyss in search of a creature who may have missed the summons, but found none. They even searched the barren island in the Central Sea, but discovered nothing.

Solra carefully curated the attributes necessary, and moulded a pleasing form. They warmed the creature and spoke the sacred words of being. The Sui rose and worshipped Solra with unceasing story and song. Solra was no longer lonely and gave to The Sui unparalleled gifts of communication, so they could praise Solra without end.

PERFECTING SOLRA'S CHILDREN (ORTHODOX VERSION)

The Children of Solra wept over their imperfections and cried to the heavens. "How can we ever be worthy of our creator when we must pollute our bodies to survive?" Solra heard their piteous cries, and watched in parental anguish as increasing numbers starved themselves to death, arguing that Solra did not pollute Their body so neither would they, in an attempt to become more worthy of Solra's love.

Solra paused the movement of the world, and put Their children into a deep sleep. When the Children awoke, they felt their bodies absorbing energy directly from Solra's divine Light. They rejoiced, crying praises to Solra for bringing them closer to perfection and union with the divine.

Over many generations, their distaste grew. "How can we ever be worthy of our creator when we must co-join our bodies to procreate? Solra is perfect in their solitude, and in perfect solitude produced all of creation. Why does Solra punish us by making us incomplete?"

Solra heard the cries of Their children and paused in Their celestial dance. The piteous cries moved Solra to consider the pleas of Their children. Solra had created them to have mates to avoid loneliness and provide companionship for one another, but their devotion to the Creator allowed room for no other.

Again, Solra paused the movement of the world, and put Their children into a deep sleep. When they awoke, they felt no desire but to worship Solra, and they rejoiced, crying praises to Solra for bringing them closer to divine perfection.

Solra's Children slowly spread over the ring of land, maintaining as much distance between one another as possible, for although they loved to share stories, they could not tolerate company for long, desiring to commune with the Creator in private.

PERFECTING SOLRA'S CHILDREN (PROGRESSIVE VERSION)

Many Children of Solra wept over their perceived imperfections and cried to the heavens. "How can we ever be worthy of our creator when we must pollute our bodies to survive?" Solra heard the cries of Their children and watched in parental anguish as increasing numbers starved themselves to death, arguing that Solra did not pollute their body so neither would they, in an attempt to become more worthy of Solra's love.

Solra paused the movement of the world, and put the dissatisfied children into a deep sleep. When the Children awoke, they felt their bodies absorbing energy directly from Solra and the environment. They rejoiced, crying praises to Solra for bringing them closer to perfection and reunion with the divine.

Over many generations, asceticism became fashionable, and the Sui competed to prove their piety. "How can we ever be worthy of our creator when we must co-join our bodies to procreate? Solra is perfect in Their solitude, and in perfect solitude produced all of creation. Why does Solra punish us by making us incomplete?"

Solra heard the cries of Their children and paused in Their celestial dance. The piteous cries moved Solra to consider the pleas of their children. Solra had created them to have mates to avoid loneliness and provide companionship for one another, but for the maladjusted, their devotion to the Creator allowed room for no other.

Again, Solra paused the movement of the world, and put the abjectly sad children into a deep sleep. When they awoke, they admitted no desire but to worship Solra, and rejoiced, crying praises to Solra for bringing them closer to divine perfection.

Solra's demanding Children slowly spread over the ring of land, maintaining as much distance between one another as possible, for although they loved to share stories, they could not tolerate company for long, lest their lust for one another burst forth and betray their true desires.

THE GREAT SEPARATION (ORTHODOX VERSION)

Sinners moved amongst the population, leading astray the devout, and endangering their souls. They led the naive from the worship of Solra and seduced them into lewdness and depravity.

The Prophet Serenus walked amongst the people, warning them they courted an eternity of perdition if they amended not their ways. The lost ignored Holy Serenus, but the repentant gathered at his feet and wept. "What have we done? How can we make restitution?"

Blessed Serenus dried their tears and taught them they must eschew all temptation and show no mercy to those who dared oppose the righteous. The foul sinners must be cast out, their names never spoken.

The Blessed Prophet Serenus and his devotees separated the pure from the polluted, allowing the foul ones no call for redress, for their malicious words were known to possess unholy influence. The unclean were expelled from society.

Serenus the Innocent was a fair man, and pitied those who struggled to maintain physical purity. He decreed an annual festival where those who desired to become parents could come together in holy union. Children thus conceived would be fostered to other Domains on their first birthday to maintain peaceful ties between each region, and to remove the temptation of loving another more than the divine Solra.

Imperfect children were deemed an abomination and a punishment from Solra. They were swaddled to prevent them from absorbing Solra's bounty and left in the wild, their existence and memory extinguished from society.

THE GREAT SEPARATION (PROGRESSIVE VERSION)

Those who rejected the New Ascetic were accused of lewdness and depravity.

Filled with self-loathing, and jealous of other's joy, The Prophet Serenus developed an enthusiastic following. The Disciples of Serenus threatened non-ascetics with dire consequences if they failed to conform.

Serenus gathered the frustrated and taught them they must eschew all temptation and show no mercy to those who dared oppose them. They formed vigilante mobs to seek out those they considered unholy.

Serenus and his devotees hunted those they considered impure and expelled them from society. They were not allowed a public hearing, for Serenus feared the truth of their words.

Serenus anticipated there would be many who struggled to maintain physical purity. In a demonstration of magnanimity, and to maintain his power, he decreed an annual festival where those who desired to become parents could come together. Children thus conceived would be fostered to other Domains on their first birthday to maintain peaceful ties between each region.

Imperfect children were deemed an abomination and a punishment from Solra. They were swaddled to prevent them feeding on Solra's bounty and left in the wild, but protesters collected these cruelly abandoned children and brought them to The Isle of Nefas.

 Meet Sam Woodgarth, a retired teacher who spends her days wrangling cats and talking to her imaginary friends. No, you didn't misread that. But don't worry, she's not crazy, just a creative soul who grew up immersed in storybooks.

Sam was devastated when she realised reality didn't match the fictional worlds she read about. So, she did what any sane person would: she created her own worlds where the good guys always win, and the bad guys get their just desserts. Flambé style.

She's all about courage, honour, and wisdom, and she refuses to accept a world where fear, selfishness, and idiocy rule the day. Sam writes stories that speak to the unloved and dispossessed. Social justice is the lifeblood of her work. She's all about belonging and compassion, and she believes that we're one step closer to creating a better world if we can imagine a place where gender, religion, ethnicity, and age are accepted without question.

Originally from rainy Manchester, UK, Sam moved to Cairns, Far North Queensland, in search of her tribe. She found them in her writers' group, where she champions fellow authors and helps them find their authentic voices.

If you enjoy Sam's work, please leave a review.

Please note Sam uses UK spelling as a style choice.

Use the QR code to visit her website and sign up for her newsletter for (almost) regular updates.

Book Club Discussion Points

- Separation of church and state – why is this important?
- Why do the rebels publicly redeem Stark?
- Why do people comply with unreasonable laws?
- The Sui live peaceful lives and have the freedom to explore and develop their artistic skills. Is the price too high?
- Demonising others is standard practice, but is it ever justified?
- Is it possible to recognise differences without adding value judgements?
- Were Hebe's final actions justified?
- Could The Revised have integrated into the community, or would they have remained a menace?
- Should power be focused in one office or divided?
- Drawing on personal experiences, are you aware your privileges do not apply to everyone? How does this make you feel?
- Should media outlets reflect the government's position, or should a free press question and challenge?
- How do you check the veracity of the information you read or hear?
- Do you choose to surround yourself with those who share the same opinions, or do you enjoy hearing other points of view?
- What freedoms would you sacrifice to maintain a pleasant lifestyle?
- Universal freedom, or systemic marginalisation to benefit a select few?

- When and how should "authority" be challenged?
- Should leaders be morally upstanding?
- Essential leadership qualities: what are they?
- Which is most important: charisma or integrity?
- Several characters have public and private personas (Obduro, Ludion, Stark, Castian). Does this resonate? Do you present different aspects of your character to different audiences? Is this healthy?
- Without his chip, Novus experiences an awakening. Are most people fundamentally benevolent?
- Why would The Revised not be allowed personal names? How might this affect them?
- Is morality dependent on faith?
- In your opinion, do people respond better to sticks or carrots?
- Should progress and innovation be ever repressed?
- Do you consider healthcare a basic right or a privilege?
- Ami wiped his eyes on his sleeve. "If we do nothing to stop the monsters, we're no better than them." Discuss.

If you enjoy feminist fantasy where women display strength, bravery, and loyalty in epic adventures, whose friendship and empowerment lead to

triumph and self discovery, you'll love The Goddess Reborn Dragon-Skin I.

Meet Annie, a reluctant heroine, who seeks independence and rewrites her destiny

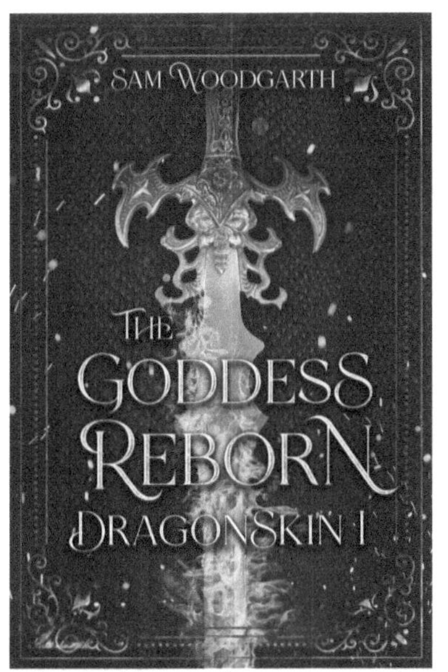

The Goddess Reborn DragonSkin I

Fantastical whispers thread through the festival crowd. Are the rumours true? Southern deserts turned to glass? Northern cattle herds snap frozen?

The unthinkable is compounded by the impossible. Annie Weaver is ambushed by rogue slave traders and rescued by a telepathic dragon who claims Annie is an incarnation of the missing Creator Goddess.

Annie believes in neither dragons nor deities and is forced to assess reality.

To enjoy a fast-paced action fantasy populated with quirky characters and unique fantasy creatures, check out

The Goddess Reborn DragonSkin I.

https://books2read.com/The-Goddess-Reborn

For fans of "*The Name of The Wind*" by Patrick Rothfuss and "*The Bone Shard Daughter*" by Andrea Stewart.

Restoration DragonSkin II

Older than time. More resolute than Mountains. A Darkness stirs, creating a flaw in the tapestry of creation only AnnieRah, the Goddess Reborn, can see.

No good deed goes unpunished. Annie has unwittingly summoned the ancient Dark Lord, whose very existence is a danger to the survival of all life.

After eons of plotting, the malevolent Most High Lord Draqshet unleashes demons in a diabolical bid for supremacy. Unaware of their true identities and desperate to secure favour, his servants clash with their own kin. Contemptuous of all life, Draqshet's sorcery will crush the feeble and install a hierarchy of hatred.

Rebellion brews within Annie's inner circle, testing the strength of friendship. She must forge strange new alliances and navigate a path of truth through a thicket of treachery to triumph over the Most High Lord Draqshet.

Lines blur between friends and foes. A demon's quest for independence solves an ancient mystery and leaves to self=discovery and redemption.

Fans of the mythic evil in Lim's "*Six Crimson Cranes*", and Anderson's expansive "*The Mistborn Saga*" will love Woodgarth's DragonSkin series.

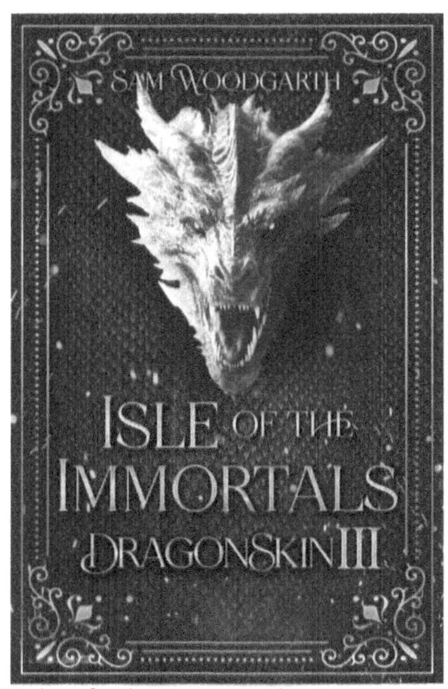

Isle of The Immortals Dragon-Skin III

An epic fantasy adventure set in an alternative world of tropical mystery, enchantment, and unique sea dragon lore.

Lady Amora commissions a ship crafted from ancient sea dragon bones. Accompanied by loyal companions and a hastily assembled crew, she embarks on an expedition to uncharted realms.

Baptised by salt water, the newly sentient ship yearns for freedom. Once ruler of the oceans with mythical powers, but now bound in servitude, she experiences homicidal urges.

Cast into shark infested waters, Lady Amora vows vengeance against the renegade ship.

She is rescued by a tribe with access to a miraculous substance, Bounty, which confers near immortality, and is seduced by their idyllic tropical lifestyle.

Until she discovers Bounty's horrific side effects.

When the Sea dragon bone ship falls prey to the nightmare consequences of unlimited exposure to Bounty, Lady Amora has the opportunity to exact revenge or rehabilitate the one who tried to kill her.

Prepare to be enthralled by this gripping fantasy adventure, a must-read for fans of Robin Hobbs "Liveship Traders" and Tim Powers' "On Stranger Tides". Brace yourself for a journey that will chill your bones and ignite your imagination.

The Curse of Argendarria

Gilded cages are still prisons.

Edelia is a coveted asset with extraordinary gifts of clairvoyance, clairsentience, and clairaudience. Entangled in a skein of cruel lies, she uses her psychic skills to elevate the wealth and prestige of her malevolent guardian, the Duke of Bruta Rex.

To consolidate ownership of his asset, the Duke intends to wed his ward.

Her only hope for freedom lies in reclaiming her stolen Chain of Life.

With only thirty-six days before her quadranscentennial birthday, Edelia performs a daring escape and embarks on a perilous quest to rewrite her destiny.

Pursued by a rogue Clair with a hidden agenda, she navigates a world of magic and intrigue, determined to find liberation on the mythical Isle of Argendarria.

Fans of "The Bone Season" by Samantha Shannon, "Truthwitch" by Susan Dennard, and "Graceling" by Kristin Cashore will love "The Curse of Argendarria" with its themes of strong women, magical abilities, a quest for freedom, and a richly built fantasy world.